OTHER PEOPLE'S CHILDREN

READERS GUIDE ONLINE
www.penguin.com/guides

Praise for Joanna Trollope

"The Roman poet Horace once said that the exceptional writer was one who could wield ordinary words so skillfully that, in his hands, the ordinary was made new. But for the fact that Horace said it more than two thousand years ago, he might have been speaking of Joanna Trollope. Here is a writer who marshals simple prose and constructs stories around everyday people, but in her hands the humdrum is made strikingly fresh."

—*The Washington Post Book World*

"A masterful storyteller."

—*San Francisco Sunday Examiner & Chronicle*

"[Trollope] writes fluently, her plot flows, and the conversations are wonderfully real."

—*The Christian Science Monitor*

"Trollope is adept at creating believable characters—and at making her readers care about what happens to them."

—*Richmond Times-Dispatch*

"Some books are simply delicious, every word meant to be tasted, savored, then remembered with pleasure. The novels of Joanna Trollope . . . are just such delightful treasures . . . Imagine, if you can, what it must have been like for the first woman to read the work of Jane Austen—the shock and pleasure of self-recognition—and you have some idea of the treat that lies in store . . . If you love the fiction of Iris Murdoch, Mary Wesley, or Laurie Colwin, you will love the work of Joanna Trollope."

—*The New Orleans Times-Picayune*

"[An author who] makes her readers want to drop everything in order to keep on reading."

—*Publishers Weekly*

"Trollope is one of those rare writers who creates fully human characters living in recognizable worlds doing regular jobs and suffering all the bitter disappointments that flesh is heir to . . . a writer who seldom strikes a wrong note."

—*Kirkus Reviews*

"Her astute observations cast her as modern-day Austen."

—*Library Journal* (starred review)

JOANNA TROLLOPE

Other People's Children

BERKLEY BOOKS, NEW YORK

𝐵

A Berkley Book
Published by The Berkley Publishing Group
A division of Penguin Group (USA) Inc.
375 Hudson Street
New York, New York 10014

PRINTING HISTORY
Viking edition / April 1999
Berkley trade paperback edition / June 2000

Berkley trade paperback ISBN: 0-425-17437-9

The Library of Congress has catalogued the Viking hardcover edition as follows:

Trollope, Joanna
Other people's children / Joanna Trollope.
p   cm.
ISBN 0-670-88513-4
I.   Title.
PR6070.R57085   1999
823'.914—dc21   98-40004

For Di-Di,
with my love

Other People's Children

BEHIND HIM, SOMEONE said, "They shouldn't be called weddings."

Rufus felt his ears glow. He leaned forward and stared at the tips of the new shoes his mother had persuaded him to wear instead of sneakers. The person who had spoken behind him had been a woman. She sounded vaguely familiar.

"Not second time round," she said. Her voice was calm, as if she had no personal ax to grind but was simply stating a fact. "There should be another word for second time round."

Rufus raised his head very slowly and transferred his stare from his shoes to the wall twenty feet ahead of him. The wall was covered with white satiny paper, flowered and ribboned in more white, and on it hung a picture of the queen in a white dress and a tiara and a broad blue ribbon running across her bosom with a brooch thing on it. Just below the queen was the neat brown head of the lady in the gray suit and gold stud earrings who was, Rufus's mother said, the registrar. Being a registrar meant you could marry people to each other. This registrar—who had smiled at Rufus and said, "Hello, dear"—was going to marry Rufus's mother in a minute. To Matthew. Rufus did not let his stare slide sideways from the registrar to include his mother and Matthew. Matthew had a gray suit on, too, and a yellow flower in his buttonhole, and he was half a head taller than Rufus's mother. He was, also and above all things, not Rufus's father.

He was, however—and this fact lent added alarm to an already disconcerting day—several other people's father. He had been married before, to someone else whose name Rufus couldn't remember, and he had three children. *Three.* All older than Rufus. And *all*—Rufus swallowed hard—people he didn't know. Actually standing beside him was Matthew's younger daughter, Clare. She was repeatedly doing up and undoing the bottom button of her black cardigan. Below the cardigan she wore a crumpled orange skirt almost to the floor, and black boots. She was ten. Rufus was eight. Rufus's mother had said that he and Clare would get on because they could play computer games together, but to Rufus, Clare was as foreign as if she came from another planet. She was like someone you see on a bus and know you won't ever see again. So was her brother, Rory, standing on her far side, in a black leather jacket and black jeans. Rufus's mother had made him wear a tie, but Rory was wearing a T-shirt. He was twelve, and his hair had been shaved up the sides and back of his head, leaving him vulnerable and gawky—soft-looking, like a baby bird. He had played football with Rufus earlier that day with a Coca-Cola can, kicking it around the patio of the house that Rufus was now going to share with his mother and Matthew. And, some weekends and during school holidays, with Clare and Rory and Becky, who was fifteen and who had—well, she didn't go straight down in front, under her sweater. Becky was chewing gum, Rufus thought. She wore the denim bomber jacket she wore all the time except in bed, and every so often, she gave the left breast pocket of the jacket a little tap. Rufus knew why. She kept a pack of Marlboro Lights in there, and she wasn't supposed to. When she tapped her pocket, she looked pleased and defiant.

Rufus's grandmother, on his left side, stooped toward him a little. She was going to say, "All right, darling?" He waited.

"All right, darling?"

He nodded. She tried to take his hand. Rufus liked his grandmother, but he did not wish to hold her hand, especially not in public, with Clare and Rory and Becky in their enviable solidarity of being three, not one, on his right-hand side. He put his hand in his trouser pocket. There was an acorn in there, and a screw of foil from a Kit-Kat, and the rubber stopper from a water pistol. He held the acorn. It was warm, from being in his pocket, as if it had a little kind life of its own. He had picked it up on a walk months ago, a school walk to the playing fields, in Bath, where he used to live, where his father lived now and would be, at this minute, at this very minute, instead of being here in this white room with the glass lights and Rufus's mother. Where Matthew was, instead.

Matthew took Josie's hand under the restaurant tablecloth.

"Mine."

She smiled, entranced, but not daring to look at him because of all the other people sitting round that table, and mostly looking at her.

"Oh, Matt—"

"Mine," he said again, squeezing her hand. "Can't believe it."

"Now, now," Matthew's father shouted jovially from the far side of the table. "Now, now, you two."

"It's perfectly legal," Matthew said, "as of an hour ago." He sounded quite at ease. He raised Josie's hand from under the cloth and, in view of everyone, kissed her wedding finger. "Legally Mrs. Mitchell."

"Good luck to you!" his father shouted. He seized a nearby champagne bottle and sploshed wine approximately into all the glasses he could reach. "Drink up! Drink to them!"

"Good luck, dears," Josie's mother said. She lifted her glass. "Long life together, health and happiness." She nudged Clare, who was next to her. "Raise your glass, dear."

"I don't like it," Clare said. "I don't like champagne."

"You can pick up your glass," Josie's mother said, "can't you? You don't have to drink out of it." She looked across at Rufus. He was sandwiched between Rory and Matthew's younger sister, Karen, who was a nurse. Rory had drunk two glasses of champagne already, very quickly, and was looking dazed. Rufus looked, his grandmother thought, as he used to look just before he sang a solo in his school nativity play and was certain something would go wrong. She indicated to him to raise his glass.

"Toast to Mummy and Matthew, darling. Come on."

She glanced toward her daughter. Josie looked so happy, so pretty, in a cream silk suit with her red hair done up somehow behind her head, that it seemed downright unkind to have misgivings. But how could she not? As a divorced woman herself of thirty years' standing, with Josie her only child, how could she not have terrible apprehensions about Josie's leaving Tom Carver and all the settled, acceptable comfortableness of that life in Bath for a secondary-school deputy headmaster with three uncouth children and an eccentric-sounding ex-wife apparently spitting tacks with rage from the hovel in Herefordshire she'd taken herself off to? It wasn't that Matthew wasn't a nice man, because he was nice, and quite attractive if you liked men who needed to shave twice a day, but he—well, his position, to be fair, seemed so perilous beside Tom's. And he knew it. He'd said, when they'd had their first awkward prospective mother-in-law, son-in-law meeting, shifting glasses of indifferent white wine about on beer mats in a local pub, "I suppose, Elaine, I should apologize."

She'd looked at him, startled.

"What for? For taking Josie? Nobody's ever taken Josie in her life. Josie's never done anything Josie didn't want to do. You needn't apologize for that."

"I don't. But I'm not the catch Tom Carver was."

Elaine had looked at her wineglass. She thought of the house in Bath, of the long windows on the first floor, of the immaculate basement from which Tom ran his architectural practice, of the little walled garden behind with its statues and stone urns. Josie had told her that Matthew Mitchell earned thirty-three thousand a year. She had also now seen the house they would live in, always two of them, mostly three, and sometimes six. It had three bedrooms. She took a swallow of wine.

"No good pretending," she'd said to Matthew. "But no. You're not."

She looked round the restaurant now. It was Italian, with rough white walls and rush-seated chairs and a menu that featured, among other things, fifteen kinds of specialty pizza. That's why it had been chosen. For the children. Pizza for the children.

"Are you strong enough for this?" Elaine had said to Josie. "Are you sure? Can you really take these children on? It's harder than climbing Everest."

"Mum," Josie said, "I've been there and done it. I've been a stepmother."

"But that was different. These children are younger and—well, not very amenable—"

"We'll do it together," Josie said. She'd been brushing her hair, that astonishing coppery river that gave her a glamour disproportionate to the rest of her. "I love him. He loves me. We'll cope with the kids together."

Now, beside Elaine, Clare, Matthew's youngest child, said, "What's this?"

"What, dear?"

"This," Clare said. She jabbed her fork at her pizza.

"It's an olive," Elaine said.

Clare dropped her fork.

"Yuck. I'm not eating it. Looks like a beetle."

"Leave the olive, then," Elaine said. "And eat the rest."

"I can't," Clare said. "I can't. Not if the olive's been there."

Across the table, Rufus and Rory ate ravenously side by side. Rory was tearing at his pizza with his fingers, Rufus was just eating steadily, mechanically, looking at nothing but his plate. On Elaine's own plate lay a little mound of pasta shaped like bows in a sauce of salmon and dill. She didn't feel like eating it. She had never felt less like eating anything. She turned to Matthew's daughter Becky, on her other side. She had a nose stud shaped like a tiny crescent moon, and alternate fingernails on both hands were painted black. The pizza in front of her was completely untouched.

"Aren't you eating?" Elaine said. She had meant to say "dear," but the word had not somehow emerged.

"No," Becky said. Her right hand strayed to the left breast pocket of her denim jacket.

"Aren't you hungry?"

Becky turned briefly to look at her. Her eyes were a startling, pure, pale delphinium blue.

"I'm dieting," she said.

Karen, Matthew's sister, tried to avoid her father's eye. He was overdoing it, drinking too much, shouting false jolly things across the table to try and cover up the fact that Matthew's mother should have been there, and was not because she had refused to come to the wedding. She'd not only refused to come but had made a continued and noisy fuss about refusing, culminating in shutting herself in her bedroom on the wedding morning.

"I'm not getting her out," Karen's father said. "I'm not even trying. There's disapproval coming from under that door like black smoke, and she can just choke on it."

Karen had a headache. She'd just finished eight days of night duty on the geriatric ward, and a large part of her was so tired she didn't really care who married whom. She thought wearily of all the seventeen years that Matthew had been married to Nadine, and the steady stream of abuse of Nadine that her mother had kept up, of Nadine's appearance and lack of housekeeping skills and wrong-headed (in her view) political commitment and endless student zeal to embrace new skills, new languages, new causes.

"When will she stop playing about and damn well earn some *money?*"

But when Matthew had fallen in love with Josie, Karen's mother's tune had changed overnight. Nadine became "Matthew's wife," "the mother of my grandchildren," "my daughter-in-law," as if she'd suddenly sprouted a halo. Nadine, to her credit, took no more notice of the change of opinion than she had of the original one, but Matthew was up in arms. He'd had blazing, bellowing, roaring rows with his mother, pursuing her round the house bawling and yelling and telling her, over and over again, that her real trouble was that she was jealous, plain, bald, ugly old jealous, because he had had the guts to leave a bad marriage for a prospect of happiness, and that she'd never had the nerve to do the same, but preferred to grind on as she was, taking her disappointment out on everyone around her in revenge. Which was true. Karen sighed and picked up her champagne glass, which she had managed to make so smeary it had lost all its brief look of festivity. Of course it was true. What else, she sometimes wondered, but the spectacle of her parents' palpable unsuitability to spend a weekend together, let alone a lifetime, had ensured that she was still unmarried at thirty-six and had never even lived with anyone for more than a month? She took a swallow of champagne. It was flat and warm and tasted sour. Beside her, Josie's little boy, Rufus, had put down his knife and fork and was sitting back in his chair, far back, as if he felt he didn't belong.

"You okay?" Karen said.

He was a sweet-looking kid. He said, "I got tomato on my tie."

"Shouldn't worry. Look at my dad. I should think he's got half his lunch down his. D'you want some ice cream?"

Rufus shook his head. He looked, Karen thought, like those kittens and puppies you saw in pet shop windows all begging you to take them home with you. He looked so lost. He probably felt it. Karen had seen plenty of kids in his position in the hospital, trailing down wards to see parents who weren't their parents, who never would be or could be, except in the mere name society gave them, for its own convenience. A lot of those kids looked stunned,

as Rufus did, as if the process of mourning for the loss of a previous family—not even, in many cases, the tidy acceptable birth family—had been so painful at first, terrified glance that they simply
hadn't done it. They'd gone, instead, into a dazed, accepting stu-
por, as if they knew at some deep level of their heavy hearts how
powerless in all this they were. Karen touched Rufus's arm.

"You'll like him, you know. Matthew. When you know him
better."

Rufus blushed slowly.

"He's good with kids. He likes them."

Rufus bowed his head a little but didn't speak. Karen looked
past him to her nephew, Rory. He had eaten all his pizza except for
the very rim and was drinking Coca-Cola rapidly out of a can.

"You should put that in a glass, Rory. This is a wedding."

He paused in his breathless drinking to say, "They gave it me
like this."

"That's no reason," Karen said. Rory was a bright kid, all
Matthew's children were, but he had, as did his sisters, Nadine's
defiance. Nadine thrived on defiance: defiance of the orthodox, the
traditional, the accepted way of thinking and behaving. It was this
defiance that had attracted Matthew to her in the first place, Karen
was sure, because it appeared so fresh and vital and questioning,
after the rigidly respectable limitations of his and Karen's own
upbringing. Nadine had seemed like someone flinging open a window to let great gales of wild, salty air into the confined stuffiness
of Matthew's life, and he had adored her rebelliousness. But then
in time it drove him mad, so mad that, just before he met Josie,
he'd gone to live in a rented room for a month, a bed-and-break-
fast place, and they'd all had to cover up for him in case the parents
at his school found out and thought he was going round the bend.
He nearly had. It started when Nadine had gone off to join a

women's camp at the gates of a military base in Suffolk almost eight years ago, and even though she came home again, she couldn't stop. She fell in love with being anti things—antimotherhood, antimarriage, anti the educational endeavors of Matthew's school, anti any kind of order. She hunted stereotypes down as if they were sewer rats and stuck radical slogans to the fridge door. She was, Karen knew, impossible to live with, but she had something, all the same. All that crackling energy, and the jokes, and the mad meals cooked in the middle of the night, and the sudden displays of affection that won you over, time after time, even though you'd vowed to tell her she was a selfish cow, and you *meant* it.

Karen stretched across and put a hand on Rory's arm.

"You should look after Rufus."

Rory didn't glance at her.

"Why?"

"Because he's your stepbrother now, and there's three of you lot."

Rory belched.

"Don't show off," Karen said.

Rory said, staring across the table, "Nothing's changed."

"What?"

"Mum said. About this wedding. It doesn't change anything. She said."

Karen took a breath.

"Excuse me, but it has. A lot's changed. You've got a stepmother and a stepbrother now, and you'll have to get on with it."

There was a small sound between them. A tear, quite unbidden, was sliding down Rufus's cheek, and he had flung up a horrified arm to stop it.

"Oh, my God," Karen said.

Rory took a last swallow of Coke and shoved his chair back.

He said, without looking at Rufus, "Want to play Kick the Can?"

"Okay?" Matthew whispered.

Josie nodded. Despite her elation at the day, at being truly Matthew's, she hadn't been able to keep her gaze from straying permanently to Rufus. He looked to her incredibly small, much smaller than eight, as small as the first day she had taken him to primary school and he had said, looking at the playground he had visited so often the previous summer term in order to accustom him to it, "No."

"Rufus," she'd said, "this is school. This is what you've been longing for. You'll love it."

He had taken his hand out of hers and put it out of her reach behind his back.

"No," he'd said again.

He couldn't say no now, in the same certain, careless-of-opinion, five-year-old way, but he could look it. Everything about him looked it—the way he sat hunched over his plate, the way he wouldn't look at anyone, the way he only spoke in whispered monosyllables. Josie had seen Karen trying to talk to him and had then sensed rather than seen, because her view was blocked by Karen's half-turned back, some kind of little incident that resulted in Rory slouching away from the table followed by Rufus, with his head down. Neither had asked permission to go.

Matthew leaned closer. She could feel his breath warm on her ear.

"Can't wait till later."

"Matt—"

"Yes."

"The boys have gone—"

"They'll be scuffling about in the car park. They'll be fine."

"I don't think any of the children are fine."

"No," he said. He took her hand again. "No, they aren't. But they will be. This is just the beginning."

"Perhaps we shouldn't be going away—"

"Honey," Matthew said, "we are going away for three whole nights. That's all. And that's for us. Like today is." He glanced round the table. "Look. Your mother, my father, our children, your best mate, my sister, my best mate, all here for us, because of us, because of what we're going to make of the future, what we're going to repair of the past." He shook the hand he held. "I love you."

"Same," she said. "*Same.* I tell you though, my best mate thinks we haven't done it quietly enough. She thinks we should have just sloped off at dead of night with a couple of witnesses."

"Let her," Matthew said. "Let her. We're not marrying her. We're not marrying anybody but us."

"I don't like being disapproved of," Josie said. "Not even by someone I know as well as I know Beth."

"How lovely," Matthew said. "How just lovely that you *mind.*" He gazed at her, his eyes on her mouth in a way that always made her feel faint. "Nadine would have relished every moment."

On the other side of the table, Beth Saddler, Josie's oldest school-friend from long-ago schooldays in Wimbledon, asked Matthew's father if it would be all right if she smoked.

"Don't see why not," he said. "Ashtrays everywhere, aren't

there? I'd join you except it's the one thing I've given up that I'm sticking to."

Beth took out a packet of cigarettes and a lighter from her handbag and put them beside her plate.

"I've been dying for one for hours."

"It's times like these," Matthew's father said. "They give you the fidgets."

"I was at Josie's first wedding. It was the full white works, in church. Even though she was pregnant. Was Matthew's?"

"Nope," Matthew's father said. He emptied the last of the nearest bottle into his glass. "It was registry office and a curry lunch." He made a face. "I can taste it still."

"I can't quite take this talk of *weddings*, somehow. A second marriage isn't a *wedding*, it's just a second marriage. It ought to be so quiet you can hardly hear it. Is that how your wife feels?"

Matthew's father drained his glass.

"I haven't had the foggiest, for forty-five years, what my wife feels."

Beth said, almost as if he hadn't spoken, "I mean, it's this step thing. I know it's frightfully common and all that, but a stepparent must be a very unsatisfactory parent for a child to have. I know it's nobody's fault. I know it's just a *fact*. But all today we've kind of assumed that it's all going to be all right, this wedding, this marriage, these children, that it's *natural*."

Matthew's father looked at her.

"You married?"

"No," Beth said, "but I've been living with someone for seven years."

Matthew's father grunted.

"Children?"

"No."

He scratched his ear.

"Seems to me," he said, "that there's good parents and there's bad parents and there's good stepparents and there's bad stepparents and the whole thing nowadays is such a bloody muddle that if you get a good one of anything you're pretty bloody lucky."

Beth picked up her cigarettes and her lighter, and then put them down again, neatly and sharply, one on top of the other.

"Oh," she said.

"She's smoking," Becky said.

Ted Holmes, who had met Matthew on a climbing holiday in France twenty years before and had remained a friend ever since, said so what.

"So I'm going to," Becky said.

Ted eyed her. She was tall for her age, with a pronounced bosom already and her mother's astonishing blue eyes, as light and blank as the eyes of beautiful, dangerous aliens in a John Wyndham novel.

"Who are you aiming to upset, then?"

Becky shrugged.

"No one."

"Or everyone."

"Who'd notice?"

"Your father. Your grandfather."

Becky said, "Mum doesn't care."

"She isn't here," Ted said, "to care or not to care."

Ted had always found Nadine a complete nightmare. Matthew had met Nadine soon after that first climbing holiday, and Ted had been horrified.

"Boy," he said to Matthew. "Boy, don't do it. Don't. She's chaos. She's crazy."

Matthew had punched him. They'd had an awkward, clumsy unpracticed fight in a pub car park that the publican had easily broken up by simply telling them to stop. Matthew had gone ahead and married Nadine, and then Ted had met a girl at his local squash club and had embarked on a courtship so long and uneventful that he sometimes thought it would still be going on if she hadn't said she'd leave him if he didn't marry her. He liked being married, once he was. Penny was an even better wife than she'd been a girlfriend, and after five years, without much fuss, she gave birth to twin boys who were now at home, with measles, and Penny was at home, too, nursing them, instead of being here with Ted in an Italian restaurant in Sedgebury supporting old Matthew.

"I think," Ted said to Becky, "that you want to leave that cigarette until you're on the train. You're going back to Hereford tonight, aren't you?"

Becky nodded.

"Mum meeting you?"

"If her old banger makes it. It's a complete wreck. It's all Dad'll give her."

"Now, now."

"It's got a hole in the floor in the back. You can see the road."

"Your mother," Ted said, eyeing Becky's piebald fingernails, "she got a job?"

"No."

"If she had a job, she could buy a better car."

"Why should she?"

"We've all got to try," Ted said. "We've all got to do our bit."

Becky pulled a strand of hair out in front of her face to inspect it.

"Not when it's all unfair."

"Unfair?"

Becky said, not looking at Josie, "*She's* got a new house, hasn't she? And their car is pretty nearly new."

"And who's that unfair to?"

"Mum."

"Becky," Ted said, suddenly not caring, "your mother wouldn't know something fair if she met it in her porridge."

She dropped her strand of hair and glared at him.

"Pig," she said.

He shrugged. "Okay," he said. "If it makes you feel better."

She took a breath.

"Nothing does!" she shrieked. "Nothing does! And nothing ever will!" and then she burst into tears and banged her head down into her cold and untouched pizza.

"Ted said sorry," Matthew said.

Josie, lying back with her eyes closed against the headrest of the passenger seat of the car, said, "Why did he feel he had to?"

"For upsetting Becky."

"What did he say?"

"He wouldn't tell me, but it was something to do with Nadine. Some home truth, no doubt. He couldn't stand Nadine."

Josie felt a small glow of affection for Ted Holmes. It warmed her, creeping across the chill that had settled on her, despite all her earlier happy excitement, at the moment of saying good-bye to Rufus. He was going to stay with Elaine, her mother, for three days. He held up his face for a kiss, and his face was quite empty of expression, as if he were being kissed by someone he hardly knew because he'd been told to allow it.

"Bye, darling."

"Bye," he said.

"Have a lovely time," Elaine said. "Don't worry. Don't think about him."

Josie looked at her gratefully. None of this was what Elaine would have chosen, but she was trying, she was really trying to accept it, to make something of it.

"Mum was good," she said to Matthew now.

He reached out for her nearest hand.

"She was," he said. "And Dad was fine and Karen was fine and my mother was a disaster."

Josie rolled her head so that she could see his profile and the jawline she so much admired, which was such a surprising turn-on when she was never conscious of even noticing men's jawlines before.

"And the children—"

"Josie," Matthew said. He took his hand away from hers and put it on the steering wheel again. "Josie, we've got three nights together and two days, and during those three nights and two days, we are not even going to mention the children." He paused, and then he said in a voice that was far less positive, "We've got the rest of our lives for that."

ELIZABETH BROWN STOOD at the first-floor windows of the house she had just bought and looked down at the garden. *Down* was the operative word. The garden fell away so steeply to the little street below that some previous owner had terraced it, in giant steps, and put in a gradual zigzag path so that you could at least get to the front door without mountaineering. If Elizabeth left this bedroom, and went into the little one behind it that she intended to turn into a bathroom, she would see that the land, as if it were taking absolutely no notice of this terrace of houses that had been imposed upon it, rose just as sharply behind as it fell away in front, culminating in a second street at the top, and a back gate and a garage. The whole thing, her father had said when he came to see it, was like living halfway up a staircase.

"I know," she said. She loved her father and relied upon his opinion. "Am I mad?"

"Not if you want it."

She did. It was unsettling to want it because it was so entirely not what she had intended to buy. She had meant to buy a cottage, a cottage that would be a complete contrast to the efficient but featureless London mansion-block flat in which she spent her working week. When Elizabeth's mother died, and her father decided to sell his antiquarian book business in Bath and move to a flat there big enough to accommodate the books and whisky bottles and cans of soup that were all he required for sustenance, he gave Elizabeth some money. Serious money, enough—if she chose to—to change the shape of her hardworking, comfortable, but uneventful professional life. Enough to buy a cottage. A cottage in the hills around Bath, with a garden.

"You ought to garden," her father said. "Seems to suit women. Something to do with nurturing and producing. Look for a garden."

She'd seen dozens of gardens, dozens, and the cottages that went with them. She'd even made an offer on a couple and found herself oddly undisappointed when someone else made a higher bid and won. She looked at cottages and gardens for a whole summer, traveling down on Friday nights to Bath, staying with her father in considerable discomfort among the book piles, viewing all Saturday and sometimes on Sunday mornings, and then returning to London on Sunday afternoons to order herself for the week ahead.

"There isn't an idyll," her father said. "You have to make those." He'd looked at her. "You're getting set in your ways, Eliza. You've got to take a leap. Take a punt."

"You never have—"

"No. But that doesn't mean I think I'm right. Buy a tower. Buy a windmill. Just *buy* something."

So she did. On a warm Sunday morning in September, she

canceled the viewing of a cottage in Freshford and went for a walk instead, up the steep streets and lanes above her father's flat. It was all very curious and charming, and the hilly terraces were full of gentle Sunday-morning life: families, and couples with the radio on, audible through open windows, and desultory gardening and dogs and a pram or two, and washing. Here and there were For Sale notices thrust haphazardly into front hedges, but Elizabeth didn't want a town house, so she didn't look at them except to think, with the wistfulness that was now so much part of her daily thinking that she hardly noticed it, how nice it must be to need to buy a house in a town near schools, to put a family in. How nice to *have* to do something, instead of wondering, with a slight sense of lostness that her friends loudly, enviously, called freedom, what to choose to do.

She stopped by a gate. It was a low iron gate, and on it was a badly hand-painted notice that read, "Beware of the Agapanthus." Beside it, a For Sale notice leaned tiredly against a young lime tree, as if it had been there for some time. She looked up. The garden, tousled and tangled, but with the air of having once been planned by someone with some care, rose up sharply to the facade of a small, two-story, flat-fronted stone house in a terrace of ten. It had a black iron Regency porch and a brick chimney, and in an adjoining garden a small girl dressed only in pink knickers and a witch's hat was singing to something in a shoebox. Elizabeth opened the gate and went up the zigzag path.

Now, three months later, it was hers. There were no leaves on the lime tree, and the garden had subsided into tawny nothingness, but the lime tree was hers and so were these strange semicultivated terraces that were, Tom Carver said, full of possibility. Tom Carver was an architect. Her father knew him because architecture had been one of the specialty subjects of her father's bookshop, and he had suggested to Elizabeth that she get him in to help her.

"Nice man. Good architect."

"Well, I'm good at *this* sort of thing," Tom had said, standing in the tiny sitting room. "I'm good at making space."

She nodded gratefully. It disconcerted her that she, who spent all her working life either subtly directing people toward decisions or briskly making them herself, should feel so helpless in this house, as if it represented all kinds of possibilities that she doubted she was up to.

"I'm not sure I want a house at all, you know," she said to Tom Carver.

"But you want this one."

"I seem to—"

He was perhaps in his mid- or early fifties, a burly man with a thick head of slightly graying hair and a surprising ease and lightness of movement. He wore his clothes, she noticed, with equal ease, as if they were exactly what he had intended to wear. Elizabeth seldom felt like that. Work was fine, work was no problem because all it demanded sartorially was an authoritative but sober neatness. It was play that was the problem. She never, all her life, could quite get the hang of clothes for play.

"I think we should knock this right through," Tom Carver said. "And give you one really good space for living in. Then you'll have north and south light as well as room to swing an armful of cats." He ran his knuckles over the wall to the room behind. "What do you do?"

"I'm a civil servant."

"Treasury?"

She blushed, shaking her head.

"Heritage. Mostly—libraries."

"Why are you blushing? Libraries are admirable."

"That's the trouble."

He smiled.

"Shall we make this house very bohemian?"

She was laughing. She said, "I'd be appalled."

"I'm not serious," he said, "but it doesn't do any harm to undo a few buttons. If we put the kitchen on the north side of this room, you'll have the south side for sitting."

"I mustn't sit," Elizabeth said. "I mustn't. I must garden."

I must learn how, she thought now, looking down at it. In the efficient flat off Draycott Avenue, there wasn't so much as a window box, and the houseplants friends brought her—she was the kind of woman, she had noticed, to whom friends did bring plants, and not bunches of flowers, armfuls of lilies or lilac—always died, mostly, she thought, because of her anxiety over them. But this garden was different. Gardens had Nature in them, not just instructions on plastic tags. Nature plainly, and however arbitrary it was, went on providing its miraculous energies and respites, so that there was some other element to gardening than just following the recipe. I suppose I'm the age for gardening, she thought. Isn't rising forty when people start, when they realize it's the only chance they'll have to make living things grow and happen?

A car stopped below at the little gate, and Tom Carver got out. He had a long roll of paper under his arm, the drawings he had promised to bring of her new living space, her new bathroom, her new ingenious guest bedroom made out of the old bathroom, her new patio at the back to be gouged out of the hillside and decorated with a table and chairs at which, Tom Carver promised her, she would eat breakfast in the brief morning sun. She banged on the window as he climbed the path, and he looked up and waved.

She went down into the narrow hall that was soon to be absorbed into the living space, and let him in.

"Bloody cold," he said.

"Is it?"

"Much colder up here than down where I live. How are you?"

"Fine," she said.

"When I was going through my divorce," Tom said, "and people asked me how I was, I used to say, 'Rock bottom, thank you,' and they'd look really offended. It's a social obligation to be fine, isn't it, otherwise you're a nuisance."

"But I *am* fine," Elizabeth said.

He gave her a brief look.

"If you say so."

He went past her into the sitting room and unrolled the drawings on the floor.

"This house isn't in the least regular. We always think of the Georgians as so symmetrical, but most houses in Bath are just approximate. I like it. It makes them more human somehow, those eighteenth-century builders saying to each other, 'Just wallop that bit in there, Will, they'll never notice.' "

Elizabeth knelt on the floor. The drawings were very appealing, all those orderly lines and shaded areas in faded indigo, lettered with a quiet architectural flourish.

"Did you always want to be an architect?"

"No. I wanted to be a doctor. My father was, and so was my grandfather, and I refused to consider it, out of pique, after my elder brother won a medical scholarship to Cambridge."

Elizabeth ran her finger over the shaded rectangle that would be her south window seat.

"Do you regret it?"

"Yes."

"Do you think that regretting it makes you a better architect?"

He squatted on the floor beside her.

"What a very nice question, Miss Brown."

"Elizabeth."

"Thank you. The truthful answer is that it's made me quite a successful architect."

"And I," said Elizabeth, "am quite a successful civil servant."

"Is that a reprimand?"

Elizabeth stood up.

"Just a little warning. Why haven't you put the sink under the north window?"

"Because I've put a door to the garden there."

"But I don't want two outside doors in this room."

Tom stood, too.

"Then we shall think again."

"I'll need space for gumboots, won't I, and coats, and somewhere to be out of the rain when I take them off."

Tom stooped and laid his finger on the plans.

"There."

"Oh," she said. "Sorry."

"And there's an outside door for all that there. This door was for the summer. To carry trays through. That sort of thing. A summer Saturday. Friends coming for a drink." He stopped. He straightened up and looked at her. He said, in a different voice, "You can't really imagine living here, can you?"

"No," she said. She put her hands in her coat pockets. "At least—I thought I could, when I first saw it. But perhaps that was partly seeing all the life that was going on around it. But I'm sure it will happen. Imagination has never been my strong suit."

Tom gave the drawings on the floor a small, deft kick so that they obediently rolled themselves up again.

"Tell you what. I'm going to take you down to my house, which at least is warm, and give you some coffee, and we'll talk—"

"I'm not having second thoughts—"

"I'd like to be certain of that before I tell you how much I've already cost you."

Elizabeth said, with some force, "I want this house."

Tom bent and picked the roll of drawings up. He glanced at her. He was smiling.

"I believe the first two words of that sentence," he said, "at least."

Elizabeth sat at Tom Carver's kitchen table. It was a long table, of old, cider-colored wood, and it had a lot of disparate things on it—a pile of newspapers, a bowl of apples with several keys and opened letters in it as well as fruit, a clump of candlesticks, a stoppered wine bottle, a coffee mug, a flashlight—but they looked somehow easily intentional, as Tom's clothes did. The kitchen was a light room, running right through the depth of the house, with French windows at one end through which Elizabeth could see the painted iron railings that presumably belonged to a staircase going down to the garden. It was the kind of kitchen you saw in showrooms or magazines, where no amount of supremely tasteful clutter could obscure the fact that every inch had been thought out, where every cupboard handle and spotlight had been considered, solemnly, before it was chosen.

Tom Carver put a mug of coffee down in front of her.

"Your expression isn't very admiring."

"I'm not used," Elizabeth said, "to being in houses where so much care has been taken."

"That's my profession, however."

"Yes, of course. I didn't mean to be rude."

"I didn't think you were." He sat down opposite her. "The original occupants of this house would have taken a fantastic amount of care. Wouldn't they? Especially in the public rooms. Think how fashionable Bath was." He paused, and pushed a bowl of brown sugar toward her. "Why do you want to live in Bath, anyway?"

"My father lives here. I know it. It's easy from London."

"Why didn't you buy a house in London, with a garden, and just come to see your father the odd weekend?"

Elizabeth put a spoonful of sugar into her mug and stirred it slowly.

"I don't know. I didn't think of it. My mind got taken up with this cottage and garden idea."

"The Anglo-Saxon rural idyll."

"Perhaps."

"It's a very romantic idyll," Tom said, "very persuasive. Saxons dancing round maypoles—"

"But they didn't," Elizabeth said. "Did they? They crept about in the mud dressed in rags and were dead before they were thirty."

"Idylls don't like that kind of fact. Idylls depend upon an absence of mud and the presence of all your own teeth. Do you have an idyll?"

Elizabeth took a swallow of coffee.

"No."

"Sensible girl," Tom said.

"I'm not sure I am," Elizabeth said, "but after my mother died, I was very conscious of wanting to change something, do something new, add something. I didn't want to change jobs because I'm only a year or two away from something quite senior, but I felt—

well, I felt that I might be turning into one of those women who taught us at school, and who we used to pity, in our superior and probably quite inaccurate fourteen-year-old way, for having nothing in their lives but us."

Tom cupped both his hands round his mug.

"Have you ever been married?"

There was a tiny beat.

"No," Elizabeth said.

"Have you ever wanted to be?"

Elizabeth looked down into her coffee. Half of her wanted to tell him primly that he didn't know her anything like well enough to ask such a thing and the other half wished to confide, in a rush of relief at being able to, that she only ever seemed to want to marry men who were already firmly married and that it troubled her that she only felt able to release herself into loving if there was no real danger she might have to commit to it. And yet—and this was an increasing pain—the loneliness caused by this inhibition was getting daily harder to bear. It was beginning to color everything. It was making her think, as her father had pointed out, that every half-full glass of whisky was in fact merely half empty. When she had stood in the little house in Lansbury Crescent that morning, she had been able to visualize her solitude there, but not the scene that Tom had suggested, of a summer evening, with the garden door open and a tray of drinks on a table on the patio, and a group of friends. She had friends, of course she did, friends she went to the cinema and theater with, friends who asked her round for Sunday lunch and failed to fool her, for a moment, despite their loud comical wails of complaint, about the deep proud satisfaction they felt in having children. You could—and she had other single friends who did this—make friends into a kind of family, but in the end your separateness awaited you, not so much in your empty flat as in your heart. This fact had struck her very forcibly only the week before, when she was filling in a kidney-donor card at her local surgery. Who should be notified in the event of her death? My father, she wrote. And then she paused. When her father was dead, who would it be then?

"I thought," she said to Tom Carver, "that we were going to talk about my house."

"We are."

"But—"

"I'm luring you into telling me if you really want to spend maybe fifteen thousand pounds on something your heart might not quite be in."

"Why should it matter to you?" Elizabeth said rudely. "Why should you care? You'll get your fee in any case, whether I like the house or I don't."

Tom Carver got up and went across to the kitchen counter where he had left the coffeepot. He said equably, "You're quite right. With most clients, I don't really care. They're the ones who are making the choices after all, and the consequence of those choices is their responsibility. But—" He paused.

"But what?"

"You're a nice woman," he said simply. He held the coffeepot above her mug. "More coffee?"

She shook her head. He filled his own mug. He said, "Can I show you something?"

"Of course."

He put the coffeepot down and went to the other end of the kitchen, which was arranged as a kind of sitting room, with a sofa and armchairs and a television set. He came back carrying a framed photograph, and set it down in front of Elizabeth.

"There."

It was a photograph of a little boy, a boy of perhaps—Elizabeth was never very certain of children's ages—about seven. He was extremely attractive, with thick hair and clear eyes and a scattering of freckles. He wore a checked shirt and jeans, and he was sitting astride a gate or a fence, staring at the camera as if he had nothing to hide.

"My boy," Tom said. "He's called Rufus. He's eight."

"He looks angelic," Elizabeth said.

"I rather think he is," Tom said. "At least, in his absence, I do."

Elizabeth moved the photograph a few inches away from her.

"Is he away at school then?"

"No. He lives with his mother."

"Oh dear," Elizabeth said.

"His mother left me," Tom said. "Almost a year ago. She left me for the deputy headmaster of a secondary school at a place called Sedgebury, in the Midlands."

Elizabeth looked at the photograph again.

"I'm so sorry."

"She's a teacher, too," Tom said. "They met at a conference on pastoral care in state education. He has three children. They were married last week."

"I'm so sorry," Elizabeth said again.

"Perhaps I should have expected it. Plenty of people told me so. She's fifteen years younger than I am."

Privately, Elizabeth thought that this vanished wife might be about the same age as she was, herself.

She said, cautiously, "Mightn't it be a matter of temperament, not age? My parents were twelve years apart, and they were very happy—"

He smiled at her.

"In our case, it was both."

The telephone rang.

"Excuse me," he said.

He went across the kitchen to where the telephone hung on the wall and stood with his back to Elizabeth.

"Hello? Hello, darling. No. No, I've got someone here. No, a client. Yes, of course you can. Sunday morning. All well with you? Good week? I wish they'd get you a carphone with all that traveling. Okay, darling, fine. Lovely. See you tomorrow."

He put the telephone down.

"My daughter."

Elizabeth looked up.

"Your daughter!"

He came back to the table, smiling.

"My daughter, Dale. This is turning into rather a confessional. It must be something to do with your face. I have a daughter of twenty-five and another son of twenty-eight."

"How?" Elizabeth demanded.

"By the conventional method. My first wife died twenty years ago, from some virus contracted on holiday in the Greek Islands. She was dead in ten days."

Elizabeth stood up.

"Saying what bad luck seems rather inadequate."

He looked at her.

"But that's all it was. I thought, at one point, I would simply die of grief, but even at the lowest ebb, I knew there was no one to blame. It was chance, a hazard, that random blow the ancient world was so respectful of."

"Did you bring the children up on your own?"

"Yes. Until nine years ago, when Rufus was on the way and I married Josie."

"But your first children were nearly grown up then——"

"Nearly. It wasn't easy. In fact, it was largely awful. Dale and Lucas—Dale particularly—were used to having me to themselves."

Elizabeth turned to look for her coat.

"I've never had any competition for my father. Maybe I'm lucky—"

Tom said, "Look, I'm sorry. I really am very sorry. I never meant to burden you with all this, I never intended to do anything except, in the kindest way, discover what you really want to do about the house."

She lifted her coat off a nearby chairback. He rose and took the coat from her and held it out for her to put on.

"I don't know now."

"Now?"

"You've made me think. Or at least, this morning has."

He left his hands on her shoulders for a second after the coat was on.

"Have you enjoyed it?"

"Yes," she said.

"Even though I've dumped on you?"

"I didn't mind that. Sometimes—" She paused. "Sometimes, people don't, because they don't think I'll understand."

He came round to look at her.

"I would so like to give you lunch."

"Now?"

"Right now," he said.

"Well!" Elizabeth's father said. "All settled?"

"No," Elizabeth said. She looked round the room. "At least,

not about the house. Did you say you'd found somebody to clean this?"

"Yes," Duncan Brown said. "Two mornings a week."

"Has she been yet?"

"It's a he. Part-time bartender at the Fox and Grapes. No, he hasn't."

"It's awful, Daddy. It's really dirty."

"Is it?"

"Yes."

"I don't seem to notice."

"Or mind."

"Not in the least."

"I think," Elizabeth said, "I must do something about the bathroom, at least."

"Why don't you tell me about the day instead?"

"I feel a bit shy about it——"

"Why?"

"Because I've learned a lot about Tom Carver in a short space of time."

"Why," Duncan said, taking his reading glasses off, "should that make you feel shy?"

Elizabeth leaned in the doorway to the tiny hall.

"Because he told me so much. I'm not used to it. I'm not used to people telling me things about themselves unless they want to show off to me. And he didn't. He seemed to—well, to want me to know."

"Ah," Duncan said.

"Don't sound so knowing."

"It wasn't so much knowing, as light dawning."

"There isn't any to dawn. We had lunch in a wine bar, and he talked much more than me."

"That doesn't surprise me. You never were much of a talker."

"Daddy," Elizabeth said, "I'm beginning to wonder if I should have bought that house."

Duncan put his reading glasses back on and looked at her over the top of them.

She said, "Tom asked me if I could imagine living there, and I'm not sure I can."

"Dearest," Duncan said, "when you were five and we were going camping in Brittany, you said very politely to your mother and me that you didn't think you'd come because you couldn't think what it would be like."

"What did I think when I got there?"

"You seemed to like it. I taught you how to ask for bread, and you went trotting off every morning to the baker's, looking extremely serious, and came back with the right loaf every time."

"But this is different."

"Is it?"

"It's bigger."

"Only proportionately. You're bigger, too."

"I don't want," Elizabeth said suddenly, "to buy another chunk of solitude. I don't want to delude myself that I'm making a change when I'm actually only doing more of the same in a different place."

Duncan stood up. Crumbs from the pale dry water biscuits he ate with his mugs of soup showered like dandruff from the creases of his cardigan. He looked, as he had always consolingly looked, like an elderly heron, his head thrust forward on a long thin neck, on a long thin body.

"You're an old bag lady, really," Elizabeth said fondly.

He smiled at her. He said, "And you're a nice woman."

"Tom Carver said that."

"Well," Duncan said, "at least he's old enough to know."

When he got home, Tom Carver opened a tin of rabbit in jelly for the cat. He didn't much like cats, but this cat had been Josie's, and she had left it behind when she departed, so that it became for Tom a kind of ally, a partner in abandonment. It was, in any case, an amiable cat, a huge, square, neutered tom called Basil who lay like a hassock in patches of sunlight, moving ponderously round the house all day as the sun moved. He had developed an infected ear recently, and when Tom took him to the vet, the vet had said he was grossly overweight and his heart was under strain. He prescribed a diet, which included these tiny gourmet tins of prime lean meat in savory jelly. Basil thought they were delicious, if pitiably small, and had taken to supplementing them with anything Tom left lying about—butter or bacon or packets of digestive biscuits. He was probably, Tom thought, rubbing the broad cushiony space between his ears, now fatter than ever.

When he had fed Basil, Tom went down to the basement. If Elizabeth Brown had found his kitchen contrived, he reflected, she would think even less of the basement. It was a kind of artistic engine room, except that it was silent. It was pale and calm and furnished with immense drawing boards and long low cupboards, like map cases, into which Tom slid his plans and drawings. The lighting was immaculate. The only ugly thing in the room was the giant photocopier, and it lived behind a Japanese screen of cherry wood and translucent paper. The room was austere and serene, and to Tom's eyes, that Saturday afternoon after the lunch in the wine bar with Elizabeth, it looked very faintly precious.

He moved to the nearest drawing board and switched on the carefully angled lights above it. On it lay plans for a barn conversion. It was a handsome barn, a big strong nineteenth-century barn, and Tom was having trouble persuading the owners not to fill the huge east and west gables, through which the wains had once driven, with glass. He slipped onto the stool in front of the board and looked at his drawings. They were good, but not wonderful. They lacked originality. He thought of Elizabeth kneeling on the floor of the sitting room at Lansbury Crescent, looking at other drawings. He thought of her sitting across the table from him in the wine bar, listening to him, eating a salad Niçoise very neatly. He thought how nice it would be if they were going to eat together again that evening, after a concert perhaps, or the cinema. He thought that perhaps he would ring her at her father's flat and suggest lunch tomorrow, on Sunday, before she caught her train back to London. Then he remembered that he couldn't. He got off his stool and began to wander down the basement. Dale was coming tomorrow. Dale had had a bad time recently, being ditched by that boy and everything. Tom reached the windows at the end of the basement and looked out into the dusky garden. He would not, he thought, tell Dale about Elizabeth.

BECKY WONDERED IF, at fifteen, the cold could kill you. She
knew if you were old it did, because you couldn't move about
much and you got scared about turning the heating on because you
couldn't pay the subsequent bills. Becky could hardly imagine feeling like that. In her view you did, insofar as you could get away
with it quite easily, what you wanted or needed to do, and left the
problem of paying for it to someone else. At least, mostly she felt
like that. But now, oddly enough, lying rigid with cold as she now
was, with all her clothes on in a bed in her mother's house that was
so cold itself, it felt damp. If there'd been a heater in the room—
which there wasn't—even Becky would have hesitated to turn it
on. Not because she'd been told not to—after all, doing things
she'd been told not to was one of her lifelong specialties—but
because of that awful scene downstairs two hours ago when Rory
had said he was still hungry and Nadine, who'd been laughing her
head off at something ridiculous she'd found in the local paper,

suddenly switched to screaming rage and had scrabbled about the disheveled kitchen until she'd found her bag and had then emptied what was in her purse over Rory's head and shoulders, shrieking all the time that he could eat that if he bloody well wanted to because it was all there was until his fucking father got round to remembering his responsibilities.

Rory had sat there, ashen, with pennies and twenty-pence pieces sliding down his leather jacket and off his jeaned legs to the floor. There was one pound coin. It had lain on the matting by his feet, looking somehow obscenely wealthy and golden among the lesser coins. He hadn't tried to pick the money up. None of them had. They'd simply stayed where they were, frozen, not looking at each other, not looking at Nadine.

"Two hundred quid a week!" Nadine yelled. "Two hundred crappy quid! How'm I supposed to live on that? How'm I supposed to look after you?"

The children said nothing. Very slowly, Clare drew her booted feet up under the flimsy folds of her orange skirt and held her knees hard against her. Dad had told her—and Becky and Rory—that there was enough money to pay the rent on Mum's cottage, and that he would buy their clothes and stuff for school. But Mum said that wasn't true, nothing Dad said was true, *nothing*. She said Dad was a liar. She also said Dad was a number of other things, not all of which Clare had entirely understood. But shivering in this cold, cluttered kitchen with Nadine yelling and Rory looking as if he might throw up at any minute all over the money on the floor, Clare understood very well that, whether her father was a liar or not, his absence meant suffering. Real suffering, for all of them.

Once Nadine had started yelling, she didn't seem able to stop. She'd yelled about Josie and about Matthew, and then about Josie and Matthew together, and about how they—her children—

should never have been so disloyal as to go to their wedding, and about the state of her car and the state of the cottage and how her life was over. Then she'd started on Rufus.

She'd only met Rufus once, but she called him names and accused him of taking things—comforts, money, love—that were her children's really, by right. When she began on Rufus, Becky had raised her head and caught Rory's eye, and his eye had warned her not to speak, not to utter, not to *move*. It had seemed to go on for hours, the yelling and the accusations, and then, as suddenly as it began, it stopped, and Nadine was hugging them and kissing them and telling them they were all the world to her, and digging in the cupboard to produce, triumphantly, a box of sachets of hot-chocolate powder that only needed boiling water and not milk, which had run out anyway.

When they'd drunk the chocolate, Nadine said they should go to bed. Becky had protested, pointing out that it was only nine-thirty, and Nadine had asked—with that alarming edge to her voice again—what Becky proposed to do at nine-thirty at night in a dump in the middle of nowhere where even the television had given up the ghost, and who could bloody blame it? Becky had clumped upstairs, wordlessly, behind Clare. She thought of asking Clare to get into bed with her for warmth, but she could tell, from the way Clare's shoulders were hunched under her cardigan, that Clare would say no, to punish her, because after an episode like that downstairs, you just had to punish someone for everything being so awful.

They'd gone into their bedrooms, equally silently, Clare and Becky into the one they shared, and Rory into the crooked space under the cottage's eaves that he had chosen in preference to sleeping in the third bedroom, which Nadine had made into a kind of studio, full of paintbrushes in jars, and a small weaving frame, and bursting plastic bags of hanks of wool and cotton, and half-made sculptures of wire netting and papier-mâché. Rory had made himself a sort of tent under the eaves there, and in it a nest of old duvets and sleeping bags. You could only get in by crawling. Becky watched him crawl in and knew that he would, as she would, sleep just as he was, in all his clothes, even his boots.

She lay in the raw dark, wondering if even her internal organs were warm. She didn't think she'd ever been so cold, ever felt so paralyzed by it, helpless. Across the room, Clare was a darker shape against a dark wall. She was still now. Before, she'd been crying, but when Becky said, "Clare?" she'd said, "Shut up!" Her orange skirt and black cardigan were lying in a jumble on the floor because Clare had undressed and put on an old tracksuit instead. It was a tracksuit Dad had given her long ago with characters from the Disney film of *The Jungle Book* stamped on the front in soft, flexible plastic. Clare wore it in bed all the time now, and sometimes— Becky was saving this knowledge to jeer about next time they had a major row—she sucked her thumb.

The house was very quiet. Becky hadn't heard Nadine come upstairs yet. There'd been some banging about half an hour ago or so, as if Nadine was performing her version of putting the house to bed, but since then, there'd been silence. It wasn't a serene silence, but then, Becky supposed, a scene like the one they'd witnessed left the air a bit shaken up, like thunder. She rolled over onto her other side, shoving her hands down between her thighs and feeling the hard seams of her denim jacket press uncomfortably into her side and arms. Perhaps she should get up and find some gloves, some of those mitten things Nadine wore knitted from brilliantly colored wools by people in Peru. Nadine had had a thing, last year, about Peru, about the corruption of the government and the extent of poverty and child prostitution in the capital, Lima. It was one of the last things Becky remembered Nadine and Matthew having one of their really big fights about, when he'd discovered she'd given a hundred pounds to a charity appealing for funds to help the slum dwellers of Lima. Nadine had flown at him, all nails and teeth, and for a moment Becky had thought he would really land her one. But he didn't. He had gone from shouting to silence, utter silence, and had walked out of the house. Clare had tried to follow him. She always tried to follow him. All those rows, all those horrible, howling quarrels with Matthew telling Nadine she was mad and Nadine telling Matthew he was worthless, always ended with Matthew walking out and Clare trying to go with him.

Until now. Becky pulled her cold hands up again and began to blow on them. Until now, when Matthew had finally married Josie and they had all known that there would be no more rows, for the simple reason that Matthew and Nadine would never live together ever again. Becky couldn't bear that. It gave her a pain to think of, a pain so acute that she tried not to think of it at all, but to tell herself instead that nothing was final, nothing. There was nothing you couldn't change, if you wanted change enough. *Nothing.*

She sat up. It was hopeless. She was colder than she'd been when she came upstairs.

"Clare?"

There was no answer. She might be asleep, or just faking being asleep, but in either case, Becky wasn't going to get an answer. She pushed the duvet back and put her feet on the floor. They were so cold, even inside her boots, that the soles felt lumpy. She stood up. She'd go downstairs and see if she could find something, somewhere, to make a fire with. Nadine hadn't let them light the fire in the sitting room because she said the chimney smoked, but Becky didn't care about smoke. Smoke didn't matter at all beside the prospect of a hot flame or two.

She opened the door. The landing and narrow staircase were in darkness, but peering down, she saw a line of light still under the kitchen door. She went down the stairs, stiffly, and paused at the bottom. The thing with Nadine—always true, but never more so than in this last year—was that you never quite knew what to expect. Becky put her hand on the kitchen door handle and turned it cautiously.

"Mum?"

Nadine was sitting at the kitchen table, wrapped in an old rug. She hadn't cleared away their supper things, nor their chocolate mugs. In fact, she didn't seem to have moved except to get up and find the rug. She was sitting with her head in her hands and her long dark hair falling unevenly over them and over her shoulders, and she was crying. She was crying in a way that made Becky think she had probably been crying for a very long time.

"Mum?"

Slowly, Nadine looked up. Her face was wretched, drowned.

"I thought you'd be asleep."

"I couldn't. I'm so cold—"

Nadine said, "It's awful, isn't it, the cold. I've never been so cold either."

She pulled up a corner of the rug and blotted her eyes with it.

Becky came farther into the room.

"D'you want some tea?"

Nadine said, "There isn't any milk." She found a tissue in her sleeve and blew her nose.

"You could have it black."

"Thank you," Nadine said. She was shivering, from crying so much.

Becky went past her and ran water into the kettle. It was a grotty kettle, choked with lime on the inside and all its shine gone on the outside. Heaven knows where it had come from. It wasn't in the least familiar to Becky.

"I'm sorry," Nadine said.

Becky said nothing. She leaned into the sink and stared hard at the water running into the kettle.

"It's just—"

Becky waited.

"It's just that it's so awful and I get so angry because I'm so powerless. This horrible cottage—"

Becky turned off the tap.

"You chose it," she said.

"I did not!" Nadine shrieked. "I did *not!* It was the only one we could afford!"

Becky closed her eyes for a moment, and swallowed. Then she opened them again, fitted the plug into the kettle, and switched it on, staying by it, while it spluttered into life, her back to Nadine. She shouldn't have said that, she shouldn't have answered back. It would just start everything off again. No matter that she was right, no matter that she and Nadine and Rory and Clare had driven round and round Herefordshire for what seemed like weeks, looking at cottages for rent, with Nadine saying, "No, no, no," to every one, even the decent ones with proper bathrooms and bus stops nearby, and then at last, when they'd pulled up in dismay in front of this utterly doomed place that looked like the witches' house in a fairy tale—there were even mushrooms growing on the roof— miles from anywhere, she'd said, "Yes." They'd all groaned, wailing with incomprehension and horror. "Yes," Nadine had said again, *"Yes."*

"Did you hear me?" Nadine said. Her voice was calmer.

"Yes," Becky said.

"It's true. This is the cheapest, and the cheapest is what we had to have. You know why."

Becky said nothing. She thought of the car, which Nadine had also spent a long time finding, with its rust patches and holey floor, parked outside in a moldering lean-to of planks and corrugated iron. It was frightening to think that something so fragile was her only link back to the outside world, a world in which, at this precise moment, even school seemed attractive. She thought, briefly, of her father's car and then switched the thought off again, abruptly, bang.

"I know it's awful for you here," Nadine said. "I feel really badly about it. It's awful for me, too. I've never lived like this, not even as a student."

Becky put a tea bag in a mug, poured boiling water onto it, squeezed the bag against the side of the mug with a spoon, and fished it out. She turned and put the mug down in front of Nadine.

"Could you get a job?"

"How?" Nadine said. "How? With no one to get all of you to school and back but me?"

Becky tried not to remember all the cottages they'd seen on bus routes.

"Could you get a part-time job, in Ross or somewhere, while we're at school?"

"Shop girl?" Nadine inquired sweetly.

"Maybe. I dunno. I wouldn't mind a Saturday job in a shop."

"You're too young. Anyway, how would you get there?"

Becky shrugged.

"Bike, maybe."

"And where will you get a bike?"

Becky opened her mouth to say, "I'll ask Dad," and closed it again, too late.

"From your father, no doubt," Nadine said. "Your honey-mooning father with his nice new house to come home to."

"It's not very new," Becky said.

"But rather," Nadine said dangerously, "newer than this."

Becky was suddenly very tired. She put her hands on the table among the dirty plates and let her head hang, feeling her hair swinging down, heavy and dark, like Nadine's.

"I wish—"

"What do you wish?"

"I wish—you didn't hate him like this."

Nadine took a swallow of tea and made a face at it.

"What would you do, in my place?"

Becky said nothing. She observed that her black nail varnish had chipped, and resolved that she would just let it chip until it all came off of its own accord, bit by bit. Then she'd paint them green.

"If the person you loved and had been married to for seventeen years—*seventeen*—suddenly told you he was marrying someone else, and that you would have to go and live somewhere else on almost no money, how would you feel?"

Inside Becky's head, a little sentence formed itself and hung there. It read: It wasn't like that. She said, "But *we've* got to see him. We've got to go on seeing him."

Nadine looked at her. Her light blue eyes were wide with fervor.

"Exactly. *Exactly.* And can't you just use one ounce of imagination and see how agonizing that is for me to bear?"

In the morning Nadine drove them all to school, Clare to the nearest junior school and Rory and Becky to the comprehensive where Clare would join them, when she was eleven. They had been at their new schools for two terms, ever since it became plain that Matthew really did mean to marry Josie and Nadine had decided that it was intolerable for her, and the children, to stay in Sedgebury. Matthew had wanted her to stay, so that the children at least had the continuity of school and friends and grandparents, but she had refused. She had been in such violent pain that she had believed, passionately, that the only way she could possibly assuage it was by getting out, getting away from everything that was familiar and was now denied to her. The children had complained bitterly—they complained a lot more then, she had noticed, than they did now—but she had told them it had to be. Nobody wanted this new life, but they had to live it.

"You must reconcile yourselves to it," she'd said. "You must learn."

They didn't, she thought, much like their new schools, but they bore them. They were inevitably more rural than the schools in Sedgebury, and though no rougher, the roughness took a different form, and Nadine worried that her children didn't quite understand the unspoken rules of this more reticent, countrified community with its own kind of unarticulated toughness. She thought they'd got quieter. When she was talking to them, or angry, she blamed this new quietness on Matthew and Josie, but when she was alone in the cottage in the middle of the day, she sometimes, and despite all the frightening turbulence of her feelings, admitted that it was not as simple as that. When she dropped them at school, she always said, "Three-thirty!" to them, as if encouraging them to think she was only seven hours away. Becky had suggested that she didn't drive them all the way to school but dropped them at a collecting point, halfway, where they could join the school bus. But she'd said no.

"You need me," she said to Becky. "For the moment, anyway. You need me to be there."

"And I," she thought to herself, reversing the car badly in the gateway to Becky and Rory's school, "need them to be there. I'd just drown without them."

When she got home, she resolved, she would clean the cottage and do some washing and put at least clean pillowcases on the beds—if there were any—and find something to make a fire with. She might even ring the chimney sweep. She would also, with the screwed-up fiver she had found in her jacket pocket—a heavy knitted jacket she hadn't worn since last winter—buy something for supper. Macaroni and cheese maybe, or potatoes and eggs. When she was a student, she'd lived on potatoes and eggs. For half a crown, you could buy enough of both to last you as egg and chips for three days. Her skin had got terrible. She remembered it clearly, because she'd always had good skin, the kind of skin you didn't have to bother with because it seemed to take care of itself, and it developed spots and rough, dry patches and went dead-looking, in protest at all the egg and chips. So she'd switched, with the kind of exaggerated enthusiasm that she'd always been at the mercy of, to a macrobiotic diet and ate bean curd and brown rice. Her skin took a pretty poor view of that, too. Nadine put her hand up now, in its rough bright mitten, and touched her face. Her skin had never recovered really. Matthew had told her, when she complained to him about it, that she'd gone too far, pushed it beyond its limits. He was always accusing her of that, always telling her that she pushed everything too far, people, causes, opinions, him. Matthew . . .

At the thought of his name, Nadine gave a little scream out loud and beat impotently on the steering wheel.

She drove the car slowly up the lane to the cottage—they'd first seen it when the hedges were bright with blackberries and rose hips, but now they were only dark and wet with winter—and parked it in the lean-to. There were so many holes in the corrugated-iron roof of the lean-to that the car might as well have lived outside for all the protection it was afforded. But it suited something in Nadine to park it there, religiously and pointlessly, every time she returned to the cottage, forcing everyone to struggle across the neglected garden carrying school bags and shopping and the things she bought, all the time, because she had had a brief, fierce conviction when she first saw them that they would change her life for the better—a birdcage, a secondhand machine for making pasta, a Mexican painting on bark.

The kitchen in the cottage offended her by looking exactly as they had all left it over an hour before. She'd offered the children a breakfast of cereal softened with long-life orange juice out of a carton, because there was no bread or butter or milk, and they'd all refused. Clare had drunk another mug of powdered hot chocolate and Becky had found, somewhere, a can of diet Coca-Cola over which she and Rory squabbled like scrapping dogs, but they would none of them eat anything. Nadine had remembered children in the younger classes at Matthew's school, whom he'd found scavenging in Sedgebury dustbins in their dinner hour, having had no breakfast and possessing no money for lunch.

"At least I tried," Nadine said to the kitchen. "At least I *offered.*"

She went across the room and filled the kettle. It would be more economical to wash up and wash the kitchen floor with water

boiled in the kettle than to use water heated by the electric immersion heater. It *ate* money. There was a meter in the dank hall, and it
ticked away loudly all day, whether the lights or the cooker or the
immersion heater were on or not, menacingly reminding Nadine
that it was devouring money, all the time. She looked out of the
window above the sink and saw the despondent winter garden and
felt a wave of new despair rise chokingly up her throat at the
prospect of being stuck here, for the next four or five hours, alone
with her thoughts, until the blessed necessity of going to get the
children would release her briefly from her cage. She had never
minded solitude before, indeed had sought it, insisted on it, told
Matthew she would, quite literally, go mad for lack of it, but now
she feared it; feared it as she had never feared anything before.
Tears of fright and misery (self-pity, Matthew would have called
it) rose to her eyes, and she lifted her mittened hands and pressed
them into her eye sockets.

"Oh God," Nadine said. "Oh God, oh help, help, oh help."

The telephone rang. Nadine took her hands away from her
eyes and sniffed hard. Then she moved sideways and lifted the
receiver.

"Hello?"

"Nadine?"

"Yes—"

"It's Peggy," Matthew's mother said. "Didn't you recognize
my voice?"

"No," Nadine said. She leaned against the kitchen counter.
Throughout her marriage to Matthew, Peggy had never telephoned
Nadine until Josie had come on the scene. Then she had begun to
ring in a way that suggested to Nadine they were in some kind of
conspiracy together. Nadine had put the phone down on her. She

might have welcomed some kind of conspiracy against Josie, but not with Peggy.

"How are the children, dear?"

"Fine."

"Sure? Have you got enough money?"

Nadine said nothing.

"Look," Peggy said. "Look. I've rung with a little suggestion. Derek and I'll help you. We can't spare much, but of course we'll help you. For the children."

"No, thank you," Nadine said.

"You don't sound well, dear."

"I'm tired," Nadine said. "I didn't sleep very well last night—"

"Shame," Peggy said. "So much on your mind."

Nadine held the receiver a little way from her ear.

"Peggy, I've got to go—"

"Yes. Yes, of course you have. You must be so busy, doing it all single-handed. I just wanted you to know we're always here, Derek and me. Money, whatever. You only have to ask."

"Okay."

"Give my love to the children. And from Grandpa."

"Bye," Nadine said. She put the receiver down and bowed her head over it. Why was it, why should it be, that when she was longing for company, for some communication, for some tiny sign that she wasn't really as abandoned as she felt herself to be, that a telephone call should come from one of the few people she had always truly detested, a person who had steadily conspired against any chance of success that her marriage to Matthew might have had?

The kettle began to boil, its ill-fitting lid jerking under the pressure of the steam inside. Nadine leaned over and switched it off. She went across to the table and stacked the bowls and plates and mugs scattered about it into haphazard piles, and carried them over to the sink and dumped them in a plastic washing-up bowl. Then she picked up the washing-up liquid bottle. It was called "Ecoclear" and had cost almost twice as much as the less environmentally friendly brand on the supermarket shelf next to it. It also, as Rory had pointed out, didn't work, dissolving into a pale scum on the water's surface and having little effect on the dirty plates left over from the night before. Nadine squeezed the plastic bottle. It gave a wheezy sigh. It was almost empty.

Nadine went over to the dresser on the far side of the kitchen and unhooked the last clean mug. She spooned coffee powder into it and filled it up with water from the kettle. Then she found a hardened cellophane packet of dark brown sugar and chipped off a piece with the handle of the teaspoon, stirring it round and round in the coffee with fierce concentration until it finally melted. She took a sip. It tasted strange, sweet but faintly moldy, as almost everything had tasted during those uncomfortable but exhilarating months in the women's protest camp in Suffolk.

Holding the mug, Nadine went back to the kettle and with her left hand poured the contents awkwardly over the dishes piled in the sink. Then, cradling the mug in both hands, she went out of the kitchen, down the hall past the ticking meter, and up the stairs to the landing. All the doors were open on the landing, revealing piles of clothes on the floors, and rumpled beds and the plastic carrier bags of nameless things that the children carried about with them. In the bathroom, the lavatory seat was up, and there were lumps of damp towel by the bath, and the rickety shower curtain had come down, halfway along, drooping in stiff, stained, plastic folds.

Nadine went around the landing and closed all the doors. What she couldn't see, she might not think about. Then she stooped down and, holding her mug of coffee carefully so as not to spill it, crawled into Rory's tunnel of duvets under the eaves and buried herself there.

"We've been waiting nearly an hour," Becky said. She climbed into the front seat beside Nadine. In the driving mirror, Nadine saw Rory slide in next to Clare, his face shuttered as it always was when he didn't want anyone to interfere with him, ask him things.

"I'm sorry," Nadine said. "I went to sleep. I didn't sleep much last night, and I went to sleep this morning, by mistake. For too long."

She glanced in the driving mirror. Clare was yawning. Her hair, which she had wanted cut in a bob, needed washing, and fronds of it stuck out here and there, giving her a neglected look.

"I'm sorry," Nadine said again. "Really. I was just so tired." She put the car into reverse. "Had a good day?"

The children said nothing. Nadine gave them, as she turned the car, a quick glance. They weren't sulking, she could see that. They just didn't know how to reply to her in a way that was both truthful and wouldn't upset her. The car was moving forward again. Nadine gave Becky's nearest thigh a quick squeeze.

"Hungry?"

"You bet," Becky said.

"We'll stop at the village shop," Nadine said. "I found a fiver. We'll buy potatoes and eggs and have a bit of a fry-up. Egg and chips. What about that? Egg and chips."

There was a pause. Rory was gazing out of the window and Becky was staring at her chipped nail polish. Then Clare said, "We had egg and chips for lunch. At school."

DALE CARVER PARKED her car with great competence in a space hardly bigger than its length, almost underneath the first-floor windows of her brother's flat. She fixed the steering-wheel lock, got out, pulled the back window screen over the car stock she carried all the time as a publisher's traveling rep, and locked the car. She glanced up. The curtains were pulled across the windows of Lucas's sitting room, and there were lights on inside. At least he was home. He'd said he'd try and be home by seven, but that so many people at the local radio station where he worked had flu, he might have to stay late and cover for someone. Or maybe the lights meant that Amy was there. Amy was Lucas's fiancée. She was the head makeup girl for the nearest television station, and they had met in the course of their work. Dale knew that her father, Tom, while liking Amy—"Sweet," he'd say. "Very nice. Sweet"—felt that Lucas's choice of future wife was, to put it mildly, unadventurous.

Holding a bottle of New Zealand sauvignon blanc and the

proof copy of a new American novel for Lucas—Dale found she couldn't help giving him these slightly intellectual presents in front of Amy—Dale climbed the front steps of the house and rang the middle bell. There was a crackle, and then Lucas's voice said, "Dale?"

"Hi."

"Come right up."

"Ten seconds," Dale said.

It was a game between them, to see how fast she could race along the hall—it depended upon what she was carrying—and up the stairs, lined with old prints of Bath and Bristol (there was a penalty if she knocked one off), to Lucas's front door, where he'd be standing, counting.

"Eleven," he said.

"It never was!"

"Nearly twelve."

"Liar," Dale said.

He kissed her. He was wearing a black shirt and black trousers and an open, faintly ethnic-looking waistcoat, roughly striped in gray and black. Dale indicated it.

"Cool."

He winked.

"Present from a fan."

"Hey. Does Amy know?"

"Yes, I do," Amy said. She appeared behind Lucas, her blond hair in the curly froth round her face that Dale sometimes privately wondered how Lucas could bear to touch. It had a faintly woolly look to it, like a poodle.

Lucas winked at Amy.

"It's better than knickers. Or condoms."

Amy pulled a face.

"Shut up."

"I've brought these," Dale said to Lucas, holding out the book and the bottle. He took them, peering at the book's title.

"Wow. Great."

"It's brilliant," Dale said. "You think you never want to read another word about Vietnam, but this is different."

"Thanks," Lucas said, still looking at the book. "Thanks."

Amy took the wine bottle out of his hand.

"I'll chill this."

She was wearing leggings and ankle boots and a big T-shirt.

"He's an amazing guy," Dale said to Lucas of the author of the book. "He had an awful childhood with almost no education, but he's just a brilliant natural writer."

Lucas smiled at her.

"I'll look forward to it."

From the kitchen off the sitting room, Amy called, "Want a coffee?"

"I'd rather have a drink," Dale said. She moved into the center of the sitting room, between the twin sofas covered in rough pale linen. "A drink drink. I've been down to Plymouth today. The traffic was vile."

Lucas picked a vodka bottle off the tray inserted into a bookcase and held it up, inquiringly.

"Lovely," Dale said. "The very thing."

"Why," Lucas said, pouring vodka, "don't you get another job? Why don't you do something that doesn't mean all this traveling? If you want to stay in publishing, why don't you go on to the editorial side or something?"

"It would mean going to London," Dale said. "I don't want to go to London."

Amy came out of the kitchen holding a mug.

"I thought you liked London."

"I do. To visit. Not to live there."

"It's funny," Amy said, "the way you two always want to stick around your dad."

Lucas handed Dale a tumbler of vodka and tonic and ice.

"We don't," he said, "not deliberately. It's just happened, because of the areas we got jobs in."

"I couldn't wait to get away from Hartlepool," Amy said. She sat down on the nearest sofa, holding her mug and looking at Dale, taking in her trouser suit and her small jewelry and her smooth hair, tied back behind her head with a black velvet knot. "Or my father. Nothing on earth would make me live within miles of my father."

"We're not going to," Lucas said. He looked at his sister. "You're too skinny."

Dale made a face. She sat down on the sofa opposite Amy and took a big gulp of her drink.

"Things haven't been brilliant lately. First Neil walking out—" She paused, took another gulp of her drink and then said, "And now Dad."

Lucas sat down next to Amy, leaning back with his arm across the sofa behind her.

"What about Dad?"

"He's got a woman," Dale said.

Amy looked amazed.

"He hasn't!"

"He hasn't," Lucas said. "I've seen him often lately, and he's never said a word."

"He hasn't said a word to me, either," Dale said. "But I know."

"Come on," Lucas said. He was half-laughing. "Come on. Josie hasn't been gone a year—"

"Men do that," Amy said. "Don't they? They can't stand being alone, so when their wives die or push off, they just grab the first next one. My dad did that. Mum hadn't been gone to Canada a month, and he'd got that tart in there."

"Dale," Lucas said, ignoring her, "you're making this up. You're understandably upset about Neil, and you're seeing shadows. There isn't any evidence. Anyway, we wouldn't need any. Dad would tell us. Dad would say."

Dale pushed an ice cube in her drink under the surface.

"He wouldn't say, if he didn't want us to know."

"But why wouldn't he want us to know?"

"Because he'd know," Dale said, "that we wouldn't like it."

Lucas grinned. He gave Amy's shoulders a squeeze.

"Speak for yourself. I wouldn't mind."

"Wouldn't you?"

"No."

"I don't believe you," Dale said.

Amy leaned forward and put her mug on the black coffee table.

"She's right, you know. She really is. You don't want other women moving in and taking what's yours. You've had Josie already."

"She didn't take much," Lucas said.

Dale said, still looking at her drink, "Rufus did."

"Hey!" Lucas said. "Cool it! Poor old Rufus. He's your half-brother, remember!"

"He wouldn't be," Dale said, "if it wasn't for Josie."

"Look," Lucas said. He took his arm away from Amy and leaned forward, his elbows on his knees. "Look. Josie's gone. Josie's over. Dad doesn't have to pay another penny to Josie. He gave her some money to help buy a house, but he isn't supporting her, because she's married this Matthew guy. He just has to support and educate Rufus as he did us, and then Rufus'll find a job and be independent, like we did."

"Okay," Dale said. "Okay, okay. Forget Rufus. It's this new woman I'm bothered about."

"What new woman——"

"She's called Elizabeth Brown. She's a client of Dad's. Her father used to run that antiquarian bookshop off Queen's Square. The drawings of her house are all over Dad's office. It's a minute house. It's a tiny commission."

"So what are you so fussed about? Dad has an unimportant client who happens to be a woman——"

"I heard him on the phone," Dale said, "asking her to have lunch with him. Or dinner or something."

"Can't he?" Lucas said. "Can't he have a meal with someone sometimes?"

"Of course. There was just something about his voice. You know. You can't hide it, in your voice, if you're talking to someone special."

Amy looked at Lucas.

"*He* can."

Lucas ignored her again. He said to his sister, "You're jumping to conclusions."

"I'm not. He looks happy."

"He's that sort of bloke. He usually looks happy——"

"No," Dale said. "No. Not just things-are-okay happy, but things-are-exciting-and-wonderful happy."

"So?"

Dale banged her glass down on the coffee table.

"Stop pretending you don't bloody *mind!*"

Lucas got up from the sofa. He went over to the drinks tray

and poured a bottle of diet tonic water into a glass, and then a
splash of vodka, and then a neat wedge of lemon and two ice cubes.
He had started trying to go to the gym regularly just recently, and
going to the gym had suddenly begun to seem incompatible with
the amount he used to drink. Dale still drank, if you offered it to
her. He picked the tumbler up and tasted the drink. The vodka
was hardly noticeable. He might as well have left it out altogether.

From behind him Dale said accusingly, "Next thing you'll be
saying is you didn't mind Josie!"

Lucas didn't turn. He looked at his bookshelves, at his collec-
tion of contemporary male novelists, of modern poets, of travel
books. He hadn't minded Josie, in the end. In fact, once he had got
over his eighteen-year-old shock that his father could give his love
to anyone in the world but himself and Dale, he had begun, quite
early on in his relationship with Josie, to feel that the house was
better for having her in it. It felt more balanced, it had more vitality. And he had, from the first, liked Rufus. It was disconcerting to
imagine Rufus's conception, because Lucas, deeply preoccupied
with his own turbulent teenage sexual drive at the time, was thrown
to think of his father being driven—even temporarily—by the
same urges. But once Rufus was there, he seemed to make no special claims, and to their credit, neither Tom nor Josie made any
special claims for him. He was the baby, like Basil was the cat, and
in his father's attitude to Rufus—almost diffident at first—Lucas
sensed an element that had never occurred to him before. He began
to see, or thought he could see, that his father felt guilty; guilty for
impregnating Josie in the first place, guilty about the carelessness
that that implied over the one thing you should never, ever be careless about—human life. Maybe he'd married Josie out of guilt, and
that guilt had compounded another guilt about introducing as radical an element as a stepmother into the stable Carver household.

All these thoughts had knocked about together for some years in Lucas's head, quite gently because he couldn't honestly say that his own life—increasingly independent—was much disrupted by Tom's remarriage or Rufus's birth. Once or twice, he'd tried to talk to Dale about it, to suggest to her the complex humanity that might exist in a father you thought you knew inside out. But there was something in Dale that couldn't hear him. She was deafened by what she felt for her father, by her need for him.

Lucas turned slowly from the bookcase. Amy had swung her legs up onto the sofa and was lying along it, her eyes half-closed. Dale was sitting back, her arms tightly crossed, as if she was containing something dangerous or painful. They might have been in separate rooms for all the consciousness they showed of one another. Lucas wished, and not for the first time, that his fiancée and his sister would realize that there was plenty of him to go round.

"Dale," Lucas said.

She didn't look at him.

"Dale, Dad's not going to marry again."

Amy opened her eyes.

"Think about it," Lucas said. "Just think. He lost Mum tragically, and he was on his own for over ten years. He didn't try and marry anyone all that time, did he? We know he didn't. We were there, and we know he didn't. I think he had his reasons for marrying Josie, and they weren't, on the whole, just because he was mad about her. He was fond of her, and she was pregnant. You *know* that, Dale. You saw it. And then she left him, and he was shattered. He couldn't believe that anyone he'd done so much for could treat him like that. He was in pieces, wasn't he? He felt all that trust had just been chucked in his face. We were really worried about him during the divorce. Remember? You wanted him to go to a doctor, didn't you? Now—" Lucas paused and took a breath. Dale was very still.

"Now," Lucas said with emphasis, moving across the room to stand over his sister. "Now, is a man like Dad, a man with a personality like Dad's, with two—in different ways—such bitter experiences of the end of marriage, ever going to risk it again?"

Dale unfolded her arms and reached for her drink.

"But he's lonely. Now we're living away from home and— Josie's gone, he's lonely."

"Sure. But the solution isn't marriage, for God's sake. The solution, for Dad, is enough work, which he has, and the companionship of a few Elizabeth Browns. All the advantages and no strings."

Amy said, from the sofa, "Would you like that, Luke?"

He took no notice.

"Dale," he said. "Dale. Dad is not going to remarry. Do you hear me? Dad is not *going to remarry.*"

Dale looked at her drink for a long moment, and then she looked up at her brother.

"Promise?" she said.

After Dale had gone—she was plainly hoping to be offered supper, but Lucas seemed to forget to suggest it, and Amy, though she remembered, certainly wasn't going to—Amy boiled some pasta and tipped into it a tub of pesto sauce from the supermarket and laid the island counter of their tiny kitchen with two mats and two forks and a candle, to try and prevent Lucas from eating in front of the television. Amy liked television, but she didn't like coming second best to it, as company for Lucas. She didn't drink alcohol herself—didn't like the taste—but she put out a wineglass for Lucas in a small attempt to compensate him for the absence of television.

Then the telephone rang. It was the producer of the late-night phone-in chat and music show at the radio station to say that the presenter's three-year-old had been rushed to hospital with suspected meningitis, and could Lucas stand in?

"Don't," Amy said.

It was a creepy show, the late-night one. It attracted all the weirdos and the saddies, people who couldn't make relationships in real life so they relied on phone-ins and the Internet as substitutes. They were the kind of people who liked the nighttime, too, and the fact that you couldn't see who you were speaking to. Amy thought it wasn't good for Lucas to involve himself with people who were a bit off this way, twisted.

"Got to," Lucas said. He looked at her. "Sorry. Really. Think of the extra money."

"I'd rather have you here—"

"Can't do it. Think of that poor little kid, then, and how her parents feel."

Amy thought how nice it would be if she believed Lucas ever considered how she was feeling. When they first met, his thoughtfulness was one of the first things she'd found attractive, but after he'd asked her to marry him and she had moved in with him, he didn't seem to feel that considering her feelings mattered so much. It was as if he knew them now, and that his early concern for them was really only a process of discovery, which he had enjoyed for its own sake. But there were some things he had discovered, like Amy's very difficult feelings about Dale, which he then seemed to wish he had not unearthed. If she said to him, now, "I don't want you to go back to work, partly because I don't like that show, but mostly because I want us to have supper together so I can tell you what bothers me about Dale, and Dale and you," he'd look at her as if he hadn't heard her, and change the subject.

"Okay," Amy said. "You go."

He leaned forward and kissed her.

"We'll go out, tomorrow, promise. Or Friday."

She nodded. He picked up his leather jacket and a bunch of keys and the photographer's camera case he carried his tapes and discs in.

"Sleep well," Lucas said. He smiled at her. "Make the most of the next five snore-free hours."

Amy went back into the kitchen and scraped the pasta off their two plates into the bin. Then she put two slices of toast into the toaster and plugged the kettle in. On the draining board sat the mug she had been drinking from earlier, and Lucas's and Dale's vodka tumblers. Dale's had a red-lipstick mark on it, very precise, as if she'd put her mouth in exactly the same place at every swallow. Amy turned the glass round, so she couldn't see the lipstick mark.

Lucas had told Amy that Dale had been absolutely devastated by their mother's death. She'd only been five, and a very dependent, mummy-clinging five at that, who had just, reluctantly, started school from which she emerged, every day, bowed down with the burden of separation she'd had to endure. When Tom told his children that their mother was dead, in the hospital, and would never be able to come home anymore, Dale had rushed upstairs and burrowed into her mother's side of the double bed and refused to come out. Then she'd had hysterics. Lucas told Amy he would never forget it; the darkened bedroom with only one lamp on and his distraught father bending over the screaming, twisting child on the bed and he, Lucas, standing in the shadows full of a weight so heavy he thought he might just break into pieces because of it.

Then Dale transferred her fierce affections to her father. She screamed when he wouldn't let her sleep with him. She would creep down in the night and try and defy him by getting into his bed when he was asleep and wouldn't notice her. Amy had wondered, aloud, why Tom didn't get some help with her.

"He did. There was someone called Doris who was there after school, if he wasn't."

"I mean shrink help," Amy said.

Lucas flinched a little.

"He knew what was wrong," Lucas said. "It was Mum dying that was wrong. He felt—"

"What?"

"Well, I guess he felt it was up to him to put it right. As far as he could."

But he hasn't, Amy thought. Fathers can't. Fathers don't know how to deal with daughters because they're men and men never grow up really, whereas most women—most daughters—are born grown-up. Except Dale. You could look at Dale now, all got up with her suits and briefcase, without a hair out of place, and still see that kid on the bed, kicking and screaming and scaring the hell out of her father and brother.

Amy took the two pieces of toast out of the toaster and flipped them quickly onto the breadboard. She liked Tom Carver; she thought he was a nice bloke, and he spoke to her as if he could really see her, but it didn't get to her when Dale threw a scene at him. But with Lucas it was different. When Amy saw something in Dale affecting Lucas, affecting him in a way that distracted him from everything—*everything*—but his work, then that got to Amy exactly where it hurt the most.

Dale lay in the bath. The water was scented with lavender oil—they'd recommended it to her, at the alternative health center in Bath, for stress—and there was no light except a candle, and no sound except for some vaguely New Age music coming from the CD player in the next room. Dale had her eyes closed and was trying, with a steady, rippling movement of her hands that washed the warm water across her breasts and stomach, to emulate that soothing, repetitive movement in her mind.

After she had left Lucas's flat, Dale had driven home via the house of a friend she'd made on one of her bookshop visits. The friend was an accommodating person, a single mother of two, who kept a kind of open house in which she expected visitors to help themselves to the bread bin and the coffee jar. Dale had been there a good deal after Neil, the actor and singer with whom she believed she was building her first deep, interesting, loyal adult relationship, had announced, quite abruptly, that he was leaving the area for London, and that, while he was at it, he was leaving Dale, too. Dale had cried buckets over her friend Ruth's hospitable kitchen table about that, and even though she could now think about Neil without instantly dissolving into helpless tears, she kept up the habit of going to Ruth's house several times a week.

That night, however, Ruth's house was busy. Ruth's children had four friends staying the night, and there was also a couple from the single parents' day center where Ruth worked part-time, who had come round to have a discussion—or a whinge, Dale thought—about the way the place was being managed. The result was that Dale could not talk to Ruth about Tom and Elizabeth Brown. Ruth had given her some supper—a baked potato and salad—and had told her she was too skinny and had rings under her eyes.

"Bed," she'd said. "Early bed for you. How many miles did you say you did today?"

So Dale had driven on home to her flat on the edge of Bristol, with her mind still burdened. She had bought the flat with Neil, because he said his career chances were better in Bristol, with the theater and a big broadcasting presence, and she had agreed, partly because she liked agreeing with him and partly because she was delighted to find that, because of him, she could contemplate leaving Bath. Even for somewhere only a dozen miles away. But when Neil left, he seemed to take the charm of the flat in Bristol with him. He took very few things, but he managed to take a great deal of atmosphere. A flat that had seemed to offer stimulus, satisfaction, retreat, and self-sufficiency dwindled overnight into just somewhere to live.

Dale thought about Lucas. She appreciated how patient Lucas was with her and how much he had genuinely, all her life, sought to reassure her. Even choosing Amy was a kind of reassurance in itself, because Amy could never be considered as a threat or a challenge to Dale, or to the relationship between Dale and Lucas. Even when she was jealous—"And I," she had told Neil once, laughing at her own ability to admit such a thing, "*invented* jealousy"—she acknowledged it wasn't because of anything Amy did or even because of Amy's presence. It was because she, Dale, was in a jealous mood, like the phases of the moon. Her jealousy, she sometimes thought, grew out of fear, the fear she had had all her life, that everyone she loved and needed would, in the end, leave her. There were times when she wondered if her need for them was, in itself, alienating. Nobody, except Neil, had ever deliberately left her in fact—you could hardly blame poor Mum for dying by mistake, even though, in your loneliness, you wanted to—but that reality didn't seem to affect how she felt. She lived with an appre-

hension of people leaving that had a reality, or force, quite independent of what had actually happened.

There had even been a small lurch of panic when Josie left. She
had wanted her to go, had connived at it, but when she saw the
devastation Josie's departure wreaked upon her father, she didn't
feel so much triumph as an alarming brief rerun of those first
childhood years without her mother. And then her reawakened
fears about that gave rise to a new—and, she now recognized,
groundless—fear that Tom would leave her and Lucas and go off
after Josie. Neil had grown very exasperated with her about that.
Looking back, it was probably the beginning of the end of their
relationship. He said it was impossible to live with someone who
was so deliberately, intentionally irrational.

"It feels real to me!" Dale cried.

The bathwater was getting cold. Dale stopped swishing her
hands about and fumbled in the dimness for the soap. Ruth had
said to her once, in those black weeks after Neil had gone, that
she'd got to realize that love wasn't owning people, having them
right by you in case you needed them; it was, instead, setting them
free, letting them go.

"And another thing. There isn't a finite amount of love to go
round, so there's a danger someone else might nick your share.
Some people can only love one person, some can love hundreds,
but it doesn't mean it's the same amount of love in each case. I
might fall in love again, mightn't I? So will you. But when I do, I
won't love my kids any less, any more than you'll stop loving your
brother and father."

Dale stood up in the bath and reached for a towel. She
wrapped it round herself, like a sarong, under her arms, and
stepped out of the water. Then she padded in her bare, wet feet
across the scratchy sisal flooring of the sitting room that she and

Neil had chosen with such care, to where the telephone lay, with its integral answering and fax machines, on a low table. She picked up the receiver and dialed Tom's number. It rang out, once, twice, three times, and then the message on his answering machine clicked in.

"You have reached Tom Carver Associates. I am afraid there is no one—"

Dale put the receiver down and stood looking at it. Tom was out. She clenched her teeth slightly. With whom?

5

"WON'T YOU COME in?" Matthew said gently to Rufus.

Rufus sat on the low garden wall with his back to the house, and kicked his sneakered heels against it in a steady rhythm. Elaine had just brought him back. She had parked her car outside the house, and Rufus had got out of it slowly and submitted to Josie's hug, and then mutely declined to go indoors. He had, instead, moved out of her embrace to sit on the wall and kick his heels.

"I should leave him," Elaine said. She raised her voice just a little so that Rufus could hear her. "He can come in if he gets cold."

Josie had looked anxiously down the street. It was an unremarkable residential street, lined with pairs of semidetached houses, all built in the late seventies, all just like their own. Some of the gardens were neat and empty, some were densely, busily planted, but most just indicated, with scatterings of toys and washing lines and dustbins and cars on blocks waiting to be mended, the random preoccupied nature of family life. Josie didn't know anyone in the street yet, didn't know what kind of street it was, whether it was a safe street for an eight-year-old to sit out in, and whether the traffic that raced down it periodically, using it as a rat run to and fro from the center of Sedgebury and work, was about to race again.

"Come in," she said coaxingly to Rufus. "Come in. We've brought you a present."

He didn't look at her. He looked, instead, across the street at the house opposite, which had an ornamental wishing well in the garden with a plastic cat creeping down its roof.

"No, thank you," Rufus said.

After a while, Josie and Elaine went into the house. Rufus didn't turn, but he sensed, rather than saw, that they were by the sitting-room window watching him. He thought of getting up and walking off, but he couldn't quite summon up the rebelliousness for that. Nor did he want to frighten Josie. He just wanted her to know, in a way she could make no mistake about, that 17 Barratt Road might be the place she had taken him to live, but it was not his home. A home was somewhere different. A home had emotional associations that you were absolutely familiar with, that you had known for a large part of your life, that made it a natural place for you to be. Seventeen Barratt Road had no such associations— at least, not for Rufus—and was in no way a natural place for him to be. It was, instead, a very hard place for him to be, and he wanted to make this extremely plain. To Josie, to his grandmother, to—Matthew.

It seemed a long time until someone came out to him, so long that he was really quite cold and was beginning to notice that it was getting dark. Some of the houses down the street already had their Christmas trees up, and Rufus could see the lights. They were mostly colored lights, which Rufus knew were in some way inferior to plain white ones. He supposed they'd have a tree at No. 17. He didn't much want one, but you sort of had to, at Christmas. Despite the sparkling trees in the street, Rufus couldn't believe that Christmas was coming. It didn't feel Christmassy at all, away from Bath and with the prospect of Matthew's children coming. Rufus kicked harder. Matthew's children were a problem to him that Josie didn't even seem to begin to understand. He heard footsteps on the concrete strips of the drive—not Josie's footsteps—and then he observed, out of the corner of his eye, that Matthew was sitting on the low wall about eight feet away. Matthew didn't speak. He sat facing the opposite way to Rufus, and he had his hands in his pockets. Rufus hunched his shoulders.

"Won't you come in?" Matthew said after a while.

Rufus said nothing. He didn't want to go in, but he was beginning not to want to stay outside, either.

"I won't come in with you," Matthew said. "I've got something to do in the garage. If you go in, it'll only be Mum and Granny."

Rufus ducked his head. He muttered something.

"What?"

"It's not that—"

"No," Matthew said, "I don't expect it is. But it's all I can think of, at the moment, to help you."

He looked at the house. They'd bought it two months ago, after eight months in a cramped flat where they assured each other, repeatedly, of how different things would be when they had a proper home. The lights were on in the sitting room, and Josie and Elaine were seated on the sofa and an armchair, with mugs of tea. The armchair came from the house Matthew had shared with Nadine, and Josie had found the sofa on a skip in the next street.

Half their furniture had been obtained that way, the half that wasn't Matthew's, or didn't belong to Josie from her years in Bath. The other side of Sedgebury, stacked in a locked garage belonging to a friend of Matthew's who wasn't using it, was Nadine's share of their joint furniture. She had refused to take it to Herefordshire with the same vehemence that she had refused to use her share of the proceeds from the sale of the previous family home to buy a flat in Sedgebury. Matthew knew she had bought a car, but he didn't know what else she had done with the money. There hadn't been much of it, heaven knows, after they'd paid off the mortgage, but there was enough for Nadine to make a mess of, or even just to lose. She lost money like other people lost socks in the wash. It used to drive him insane.

He glanced at Rufus. It was quite dark now, but he could still see his face faintly, staring down at his relentlessly kicking feet. Rufus had come into Matthew's life with his own money, Tom Carver's money, which would feed him and clothe him and transport him and send him on school trips. It was, of course, right that it should be so, right that Tom Carver should support his own son, but there was something about Tom Carver's money being in Matthew's household that was difficult to bear. Matthew was worried about money—without Josie's help, he'd never have been able to put down the deposit on this house—but that didn't stop him preferring the independence of anxiety to the need to acknowledge that another man's money was helping him to scrape by. Josie had said that almost all the money she had put into the house was her own, money she had saved from her teaching job in Bath, but, looking at some of her clothes and her possessions, Matthew sometimes wondered if she was being tactful. Too tactful, perhaps, almost patronizing, as if she thought that the truth about her money was something he couldn't be expected to handle. And he felt that, felt it keenly. Josie was so openly admiring of so much

Matthew did, notably of his teaching skills, his capacity to like the young, work with them, send them on their way with higher hearts. "You do *good*," she'd said to him several times. "You do the good that matters." But when it came to the handling of money, or attitudes to it, she didn't seem to have that confidence, and he noticed.

Cars were beginning to come down Barratt Road, their headlights swooping up and down as they negotiated the ridges in the road that the council had put there to slow them up. Some of them caught Rufus and Matthew in a brief yellow glare and showed Matthew that Rufus was shivering.

"You have to come in—"

Rufus didn't look at him.

"Why didn't Mummy come?"

"To get you in? Because I offered. You looked a bit lonely."

"I like it," Rufus said.

"Yes," Matthew said. He stood up and came to put a hand on Rufus's shoulder. "Come on."

Rufus sprang away from him onto the pavement, then he ducked sideways through the drive gate and tore up the concrete strips to the house. Matthew heard the door open and then slam. He remembered, when he was about Rufus's age, indulging in a fantasy that sustained him for months about being an orphan, about being an object of pity and admiration in a world that did not, most definitely, include his mother or his father, or his baby sister, Karen. He could recall, even at a distance of thirty-five years, the glamour of that imagined loneliness, that solitary courage. And then he looked up and saw, in the lit sitting room ahead of him, Josie rising to greet Rufus, who was coming into the room very slowly, the picture of deep reluctance. My Josie, Matthew thought, stirred at the sight of her, mine. He saw her try to put her arms around Rufus, and Rufus gracefully elude her to sit on the sofa by his grandmother. Matthew turned away and began to walk toward the garage. Mine—and also someone else's, long before me.

Clare stood in the bedroom doorway.

"Is this where I'm sleeping?"

"Yes," Josie said. She was smiling. It had taken her several days to get the girls' room ready, including extracting, from the locked garage, duvet covers and pillowcases that belonged to Matthew's children. She had laundered these and made up the beds with them, and bought bedside lamps and a pinboard and put down a white wool Greek rug that used to lie on the floor of Rufus's nursery in Bath, when he was a baby. The results were very pleasing. Matthew, who had painted the walls and hung up dark blue curtains patterned with stars that Josie had found in a charity shop, said the girls would be thrilled. They'd never, he said, had a room half so pretty. He had taken Josie in his arms and kissed her, and told her she was generous.

"Our first Christmas, all together. And you're putting so much into it."

"I like doing it," she said. It was true. She did like it, did relish the feeling that she was doing something to stabilize the lives of Matthew's children, who, it was plain, had always lived in a very uncertain and irregular way. Josie had only had one encounter with Nadine, which had been brief and disconcerting, but which had left her with the hope—a very real hope—that Nadine would not be a hard act to follow.

"They're afraid of her," Josie said to Matthew.

He had looked doubtful.

"Yes, they are," she'd said, and then she'd said it again, insisting, "They're afraid of her moods."

"I think," Matthew said unhappily, "that they love her."

Even if they did, Josie told herself, brushing out the fringe on the Greek rug, it wouldn't prevent them from seeing how good it was, how reassuring, to have meals at regular intervals and a clean, cheerful house and no rows. There would certainly be no rows. Rows, Matthew said, had punctuated his life with Nadine with relentless regularity, sending china and children flying. Josie had been shocked, listening to him. She and Tom had argued, certainly—mostly about Dale—but neither of them had ever thrown anything. It wouldn't have occurred to them, and if she had her way, it would soon not occur to Matthew's children either, as a means of communication. She would be very patient with them, she told herself, *very*, and not ask or expect anything in return for months. She felt, being in charge of the house and the family, that she would have endless patience with the members of it in return for that power, a power she had never really had in the house in Bath because she had walked into it already complete with the Carver family and all their habits and traditions, including—and this had been abidingly hard—the ghost of Tom's dead wife, Pauline. Pauline, canonized by dying so young and so unjustly, pervaded the house with a subtle strength that Josie would have respected if she hadn't felt so threatened by it. It was years before Dale would even allow Josie inside her bedroom, let alone permit her to help choose its decor and bed linen, and when she finally did, Josie was much taken aback by the number of photographs of Pauline. Nadine, by comparison with Pauline, was a most manageable opponent; she was clearly a rotten mother, a lousy housekeeper, she'd never earned a contributory penny, and she was alive.

Clare dropped three or four bulging carrier bags on the floor by the nearest bed. They keeled sideways, and various discouraging and grubby garments flopped out.

"Do you like it?" Josie said.

Clare said nothing.

"Those are your duvet covers and pillowcases—"

Clare gave the beds a cursory, indifferent glance.

"Are they?"

"Yes. Aren't you pleased to see them again?"

Clare began to fiddle with her bottom cardigan button.

"I don't remember them."

"I hope," Josie said, persisting, "that I've put them on the right beds. I've put yours there, and Becky's on the bed by the window."

"Becky won't sleep by the window," Clare said. "She only uses the window to chuck her fag ends out of."

Josie smiled.

"Sorry, but I don't want her smoking in here."

Clare sighed. She trailed across the room, stumbling over the Greek rug and rucking it up, and looked at the pinboard.

"What's that for?"

"Posters. Your posters and postcards and maybe paintings you do at school."

"In my year," Clare said, "we do pottery."

"Well, surely you've got some posters, haven't you? Pop groups and models and things?"

Clare stared at her.

"*Models?*"

Josie stooped to flick the rug straight.

"It was only a suggestion."

"Becky likes Oasis," Clare said. "They won't fit up there."

"Clare," Josie said, "I'll leave you to kind of look about. Open cupboards and things. You know where the bathroom is."

Clare shot her a quick glance.

"I'm not using the bathroom," Becky had said that morning, at Hereford station. "I'm not. I'm not sitting where *she's* sat."

"What you gonna do then?" Rory said.

Becky blew out a cloud of smoke.

"Crap in the garden."

Rory and Clare had taken no notice of this. Becky had long ago lost the power to shock them. But Nadine, waiting with them until the train came, had cackled with laughter. Something in Clare had wished Nadine wouldn't, and wished that she didn't always make something much harder that was hard enough anyway. Like standing in this room with someone she didn't want in her life and who plainly wanted something from her, some sign that the room was nice, that she'd been kind. Clare turned her head and stared out of the window. If she put toilet paper on the seat, maybe it would be okay to sit where Josie sat. As long as Becky didn't see her doing it.

"We haven't decorated the tree," Josie said, "have we, Rufus? We left it for you and Rory to do, didn't we?"

Her voice sounded false to her, bright and silly like a parody of a nursery-school teacher in a class of recalcitrant four-year-olds.

She said to Rory, "Did you do a tree for your mother in Herefordshire?"

"No," he said. He wore, as all the children did, the same clothes he had worn for the wedding. He stood beside the boxes of Christmas-tree ornaments and bags of silver tinsel, gnawing at a cuticle on one thumb. He had a spot, Josie noticed, one side of his nose and a generally stale air, as if neither he nor his clothes had been washed for weeks.

"Come on," Josie said to Rufus.

Rufus bent and picked up the box of Christmas-tree lights.

"These are new ones—"

"I know."

He looked at her. He gave her a long, steady glance of reproach for having Christmas-tree lights that were different from the tremendously long string of little white lights, bought by Tom, that adorned the tree each year in Bath.

"I couldn't get plain," Josie said. She should have said, truthfully, that the colored ones, bought from a Sikh trader in Sedgebury market, had been the cheapest she could find, but she was not yet ready, she found, to admit economic exigency to Rufus.

"These are common," Rufus said disdainfully.

Rory stopped chewing for a moment and looked at him.

"They should be white," Rufus said.

Josie put her hands up to her hair and adjusted the band that held it back from her face.

"They're all we've got."

"Where's the telly?" Rory said.

Josie pointed.

"There."

Rory made as if to move toward it.

"When you've done the tree," Josie said. "Come on, it's lovely doing the tree." It was too, once, with Tom in charge and tiny Rufus laboriously hanging things on the lowest branches and even Dale, in the end, joining in. It was one of the few moments, increasingly, in the year when Josie could feel that she had been right to marry Tom, that they had a good life together, that it didn't matter that she couldn't love him as she had always hoped she would love a husband, with that excited, triumphant love that she had tried to *make* happen, defiantly, marching up the aisle, nearly five months pregnant, in an ivory corded silk dress cut high under the bust, like a medieval dress, to disguise her growing bump. Now, of course, that kind of love was easy. She only had to think of Matthew, let alone see him, to feel a leap inside her, like a flame or a jet of water. She had wondered, at the beginning, if this exhilaration was just sex, but it was still here, almost eighteen months after that first meeting at the conference in Cheltenham, and not only here, but stronger. She loved Matthew, she *loved* him. He made her happy and proud and pleased and, in the best sense, provocative. And it was Matthew's child, standing in her sitting room, who was being so obdurate about a task that had always, during long years of emotional disappointment, managed to lift Josie's heart.

"Okay," she said to the boys. "Okay. I'll challenge you. I'll challenge you to take these inferior lights and all the other tacky things that you so plainly despise and *make* something of this tree. I'm going to get lunch. What about spaghetti bolognese?"

Neither boy indicated that he had even heard her.

"I'll be twenty minutes," Josie said. "And then I'll come back in here and expect to be amazed. Okay?"

She looked at them. Rufus, sighing, took the lid off the box of lights, and Rory, still chewing his thumb, bent to flick out of the nearest bag with his free hand a skein of silver tinsel. Josie went out of the sitting room and closed the door. Rufus looked at Rory. Rory didn't look back. Instead, he dropped the skein of tinsel and ambled over to the television.

"Where's the remote control?" he said.

Becky had been smoking. When she finally dawdled into the kitchen for lunch, she brought a strong waft of cigarette smoke with her. She was wearing her denim jacket and a long black skirt with a rip in it, and her hands were almost obscured in thick mittens knitted of black and fuchsia pink and emerald green wool. She was also carrying something screwed up in an old white plastic bag, and when she sat down, she dumped the thing in the bag on the straw table mat in front of her.

Josie, standing by the stove with the ladle for helping out the pasta, decided to wait and say nothing. This wasn't easy. Nothing that morning had been easy, and tears and temper were knotting themselves up inside her chest and throat in a way she couldn't remember them doing since the early days as Tom's wife, when sixteen-year-old Dale talked incessantly, and directly, to her father about her dead mother. This morning's troubles had been different in kind, but no less upsetting in intensity. There had been no attempt by Matthew's children to unpack or to evince the slightest interest in the house or the possibilities of the life they might live there, even when it was pointed out to them that they would be back among their old Sedgebury school friends. Becky had even left her bags outside the back door, refusing to look at her bedroom at all, and had then vanished. When Josie went upstairs to see if Clare was all right, she found her bedroom just as they had both left it and the bathroom floor mysteriously strewn with pieces of unused but crumpled lavatory paper. There was no sign that either soap or a towel had been touched. In Rufus's room, which Rory was to share, Rory's rucksack, black and white and covered

with badly applied stickers citing the names of football players for
Newcastle United, sat directly in the doorway, as if poised for
flight straight back out again.

It was at that moment that Josie thought she heard the television. She went downstairs and opened the sitting-room door. On
the floor, lolling on cushions dragged off the sofa and chairs, lay
Rory and Clare. Rory was holding the television remote control
and was flicking rapidly through the channels. Clare was sucking
her thumb. Rufus, looking miserable, was looping tinsel and glass
balls onto the tree, all on one side and as far away from the others
as possible. He shot Josie a glance as she came in. Rory and Clare
didn't look up.

Josie had taken a deep breath. She then arranged her voice to
be as friendly as possible.

"Please turn that off."

Rory took no notice. Clare took her thumb out and wrapped
it in her skirt. Josie stepped forward and took the remote control
out of Rory's hand.

"Jesus—"

"What did you say?"

"Jesus," Rory said tiredly. He rolled over on the cushions away
from her.

Josie turned the television off and put the remote control in
the back pocket of her jeans. She said to Clare, "Won't you help
Rufus?"

Clare looked at the tree.

"He's done it."

"No, he hasn't. He's only done one side."

Clare got, very slowly, to her feet. Rufus moved round the tree
so that she was completely hidden from his view. Clare picked up

a red glass ball and hung it in the only part of the tree that was already densely decorated.

"There."

"That's no good," Josie said. She tried to keep her voice light. "Is it? Three-quarters of the tree is absolutely bare still."

From the floor Rory said, his voice muffled by the cushion his face was pressed into, "Who's gonna look at it anyhow?"

"We are," Josie said. "You four children, and your father, and me. It's a Christmas tree for—for the family."

The moment the word was out of her mouth, she wished she hadn't said it. Each child became suddenly and perfectly still, and the room filled with a palpable air of cold offendedness. She bit her lip. Should she say sorry? Should she say oops, sorry, my mistake, shouldn't have said that word so soon? She looked at them. She thought of those rooms upstairs and the pasta and salad almost ready in the kitchen with the table laid, and a red candle, because it was the week before Christmas. Then something rose in her, something that elbowed out of the way her first feelings of apology, of needing to acknowledge her first failure at being angelically, superhumanly patient.

"It's a *word*," Josie said to the still children. "Family is a word. So is stepfamily. Stepfamily is a word in the dictionary too, whether you like it or not. And it's not just a word, it's a fact, and it's a fact that we all are now, whether you like that or not, either." She paused, then she said to Rory, "Get up."

He didn't move.

"Get up," Josie said. "Get up and put those cushions back."

With infinite slowness, he dragged himself to his feet and began to dump the cushions back on the sofa and chairs, not putting them where they belonged.

"Properly," Josie said. Out of the corner of her eye, she could see Rufus silently imploring her not to antagonize Rory. "Go on."

Rory sighed.

"You heard me."

Clare moved from her position by the tree and began to sort the cushions out. She kept her head bent so that Josie couldn't see her face. Rory watched her, his hands in his pockets.

"If your father was here," Josie said, "is this how you'd go on? Or are you just saving up the hard time for me?"

Clare put the last sofa seat cushion back, the wrong way round so that the zip showed.

"Where is Dad?"

Her voice sounded uncertain, as if she were on the verge of tears.

"At school," Josie said. "Doing all the end-of-term correspondence."

"I want him," Clare said. Her eyes were brimming.

Me, too, Josie thought. Oh God, and how. Me, too.

She tried to touch Clare, and Clare twisted away and hid herself behind her brother.

"He'll be back soon. He'll be back after lunch." She fought down the urge to scream and said instead, in a voice rigid with control, "Shall we have lunch?"

"I don't want any," Becky said now.

"Won't you take your mittens off?" Josie said.

Becky put her hands on the table.

"I'm cold."

"But you can't eat in mittens—"

"I'm not eating," Becky said, glancing over at Josie and the steaming pans on the cooker, *"that."*

Rufus looked blanched with tension. Rory and Clare looked as if they were quite accustomed to hearing Becky going on like this.

Josie said, "Everyone likes pasta. Everyone likes spag bol."

Becky gave her a brief, pale blue glance.

"I don't."

Josie took a breath.

"Did you have breakfast?"

"No," Becky said.

"Have you had anything to eat all day?"

Becky said nothing.

"Look," Josie said, "if you left Hereford at eight something and it's now half past one and you haven't had anything to eat, you must be starving." She ladled out pasta and sauce onto a plate and put it down in front of Rufus. "There. Doesn't that look good?"

Becky began to fumble with the knot she had tied to secure the plastic bag.

She said to Clare, "Where's a plate?"

"I don't know—"

Clare looked across at Rufus.

"Where's a plate?"

Rufus turned toward his mother. Josie held out a plate to him from the pile in front of her.

She said to Becky, "Do you just want salad?"

"No," Becky said.

Rufus passed the plate to Clare, and Clare, without looking at him, gave it to her sister. Becky put it on her table mat and put the plastic bag on top. Then she went back to fumbling with the knot. Josie helped out two more plates of pasta and put them in front of Clare and Rory. Neither acknowledged by even the merest movement of the head that she had done so. They were watching Becky.

So was Rufus. They were all concentrating on what would finally be revealed when Becky got the knot undone.

"Stop staring," Becky said.

Josie gave herself a small portion of pasta and went round the table to the place she had deliberately laid for herself between Becky and Rory. She sat down.

"Could you pass me the pepper, please?"

No one seemed to hear her. All eyes were on Becky's mittened fingers, unraveling the last of the knot. Then, very slowly, she peeled back the sides of the carrier bag and tipped onto her plate, with enormous care, a lump of grayish rice studded with smaller lumps of orangey red and soft-looking black.

Josie stared at it.

"What's that?"

"Risotto," Becky said. Her voice was proud. "Mum made it."

She glanced at Rory and Clare, daring them to object, daring them to say that, when Nadine had cooked the risotto the previous night, they had all flatly refused to eat it and there'd been a row about that, and then another row a bit later when Nadine had found Clare and Rory under the eaves with a plastic bag of sliced white bread, cramming it wordlessly into their mouths in great hungry unchewed bites.

"I thought you weren't hungry," Josie said, looking at the mess on Becky's plate.

"I said I didn't like spaghetti."

"I see. So while we eat this hot, newly cooked food, you are going to eat cold risotto?"

"Yes," Becky said. She looked across the table at Rufus. "I've got more," she said to him. Her voice was conversational, almost pleasant. "I've got enough to last me till I go home again. I don't need to eat anything here."

SHANE, THE PART-TIME bartender, said that cleaning Duncan Brown's flat was like being in a lady's boudoir after dealing with the jakes at the Fox and Grapes.

"I would like," Duncan said, "my daughter, Elizabeth, to hear you say that."

Shane winked.

"Women have terrible trouble with their standards. They never understand priorities. Now, in my view, dust is not a priority. I'll get the kitchen and bathroom clean enough to lay a newborn baby in, but I'll not be troubling with the dust. Nobody ever died of a bit of dust."

Duncan looked at the carpet. Even he could see that the pattern on it, a pleasingly asymmetrical Afghan pattern, was largely obscured by crumbs and bits of fluff and ends of thread. Where, he wondered, had the threads come from? He had never had a needle in his hand in his life.

"She did say something about vacuuming—"

Shane looked at the carpet, too.

"Did she now?"

"I don't seem to remember about a plate, when I eat water biscuits—"

"Tell you what," Shane said. "Because we're not wanting to waste my time or your money, now are we? I'll run the vacuum through this little path here and skim it along over there and spray a bit of that remarkable stuff that settles the dust about, and hey presto."

"She said something about mice—"

"Now, I like a mouse," Shane said. "A home isn't a home to me without a mouse or two."

Duncan was growing tired of the conversation. Domesticity had never seemed to him a subject on which much could be said, being, by its very nature, something that required action, not words. He didn't mind talking to Shane, but he would have preferred to talk to him on topics that were equally familiar to Shane, like horse racing or the effects of alcohol on the human frame, but also more interesting to Duncan.

"Look," he said. "Just do what you can. It's just that she'll be down for Christmas in a couple of days, and I don't want to be ticked off."

"I'll do the windows," Shane said. "There's nothing like a clean window to distract the eye from the dust."

Duncan looked at him. He was an odd-looking, small man, somewhere in his late thirties, with the eyes and skin of someone who lived in an atmosphere steeped in beer and tobacco.

"What have you got against dust?"

Shane grinned. He picked up the two-liter bottle of bleach he had brought with him.

"It's not the dust I object to. It's the dusting," he said. "Now, that is woman's work."

"Dad," Dale said, "we've got to have a tree."

Tom Carver took his reading glasses off.

"I'd rather not."

"Why?"

"We don't need a tree. Four adults on Christmas Day don't need a tree."

"Yes, we do," Dale said. "Adult or not, we're still a family. At least, we are except Amy."

"And she soon will be. Dale—"

"Yes?"

Tom put his glasses back on.

"You may not like me saying this, but I don't want a tree, because of Rufus."

"But Rufus isn't here."

"Precisely. But last year, he was. Rufus and I went out to a place near Freshford and chose a tree and brought it back and set it up down there by the garden door and decorated it together. That was only, and almost exactly, a year ago."

Dale stopped fiddling about with the blender. She was making a great performance out of blending soup, insisting that her father needed it, as if she were a nanny making him take medicine. She came to sit at the table opposite Tom.

"Dad."

"Yes."

"May I point out that you've still got us? Lucas and me? Your firstborn children?"

"I know. And nothing and nobody will ever replace you. But Rufus is my child also, and since he was born, I have never had a Christmas without him, and—" He stopped.

"What?"

"I'm not looking forward to it."

"Thanks a million," Dale said.

Tom reached across the table for her hand. She removed it just far enough away for him not to be able to touch her.

"He's eight," Tom said. "He's still a little boy. Little boys—and girls for that matter—give Christmas another dimension. You know they do. And another thing. It's just too soon for me to feel that Christmas is as Christmas was."

"Was?"

"When Rufus was here."

"Well," Dale said. She could feel her voice hardening and was not, somehow, able to stop it. "Well, it may be too soon to play at Christmases again, but it doesn't seem to be too soon to play at having a girlfriend."

Tom lifted both hands to his face, took his spectacles off again, and folded them on the table in front of him.

"Elizabeth Brown, I suppose you mean."

"Yes."

"Friend, not girlfriend."

Dale said nothing. She got up and ladled a scoop of chopped leeks and vegetable stock into the blender.

"How do you know about her?"

"I looked at the plans in your studio. I heard you on the telephone. And you haven't been here on three nights when I've rung. You're always here, always. I always know it'll be you and Basil listening to opera or snoozing in front of the telly."

"Dale," Tom said, "did I ever question your right to your relationship with Neil?"

Dale gave the blender switch a flick on. Above the roar of its motor, she shouted, "No. In fact, I sometimes wondered how much you cared."

Tom said, steadily and loudly, "I cared very much. Switch that thing off."

She obeyed him.

"I have had two meals with Elizabeth Brown," Tom said. "And she has come down from London on three weekday evenings, once for a concert, once for the cinema, and once for a private view of a painter friend of her father's, which was very indifferent indeed."

Dale rocked the blender a little, and the thick greenish liquid swelled against the sides.

"But you've never even done that before."

"No. Because I was married. I went to concerts and the cinema with Josie, and you didn't like that much either."

"Josie was OK," Dale said.

"You can say that now, because she's safely gone. But I need a life, Dale, I need to do something that isn't just work and feeding old Bas. I'm a human being, as well as being your father."

She looked directly at him, smiling.

"But you're my father first."

He smiled back.

"Of course. Always will be."

She came round the table and leaned against him. He put his arm around her.

"D'you remember that song you made up for me? The Christmas one? After Mummy died?"

"Remind me—"

"It began, 'Crackers are for Christmas, but fathers are for keeps, like dustbins are for dustmen and chimneys are for sweeps.' Remember?"

"Yes," Tom said. "You made me sing it until I nearly expired with boredom."

Dale bent down and put her cheek against his. Her cheek was smooth and cool and faintly resilient, as Pauline's had always been.

"Dad."

"Yes?"

"We can have a Christmas tree, can't we?"

"I'm so sorry," Tom had said to Elizabeth, "that I can't see you over Christmas."

"That's fine," she said. She meant it. It was fine, of course it was. She had known him after all for only a month or two, and only the last few weeks of those months had signified anything even faintly more than mere friendship. They had had half a dozen very pleasant times together, and on the last two occasions, seeing her off from Bath station on a late train back to London, he had kissed her cheek and made her promise to take a taxi. But he hadn't done anything else. He hadn't given her flowers, or held her hand in the cinema, or left meaningful messages on her answerphone. He'd simply seemed very pleased to see her each time they met, and had not said good-bye without arranging for another meeting. If he had suddenly said that he wanted to see her at Christmas, Elizabeth would have been surprised, even a little disconcerted. He had children, didn't he? And he knew she had her father. Christmas was such an accepted family time that she would have felt there was almost too much significance in an invitation from Tom Carver.

"Will you stay down for the New Year?"

"Yes," she said. "Probably. Sometimes I go and stay with friends in Scotland, but not this year."

"What," he said, "do you and your father do at Christmas?"

"Oh, we go to a service in the Abbey, often midnight mass, and we go for a walk and I cook something for him that isn't tinned soup and we have rather too much to drink with it and after it and go to bed quite early."

"Very decorous."

"Very. And you?"

Tom had paused. Then he said, "I'm afraid we rather relive the Christmas we've always had. Crackers, tree, everything. Dale— Dale wants us to have stockings again. It was all perfectly seemly when Rufus was around, but without him I feel a bit of a fool, a bit as if we're insisting that nothing has changed when it has."

"But Dale is still your child—"

"Of twenty-five."

Looking back on that conversation, Elizabeth had a small but certain feeling that Tom was in some way asking for her sympathy. He had suggested, with infinite lightness, that Dale was somehow too much for him, too strong, too decided in what she wanted, and also about the implications of those desires. Elizabeth had seen photographs of Dale in Tom's house, and photographs of her older brother, Lucas. They were very good-looking. Not pretty, or handsome, but plain good-looking, with strong features and even teeth and shining hair, like prime examples of admirable, attainable human-being-ship. Tom had told Elizabeth about Dale and how violently her mother's death had affected her. Elizabeth had listened politely. When her own mother had died, she had felt a decent sorrow appropriate to the small affection and vast requirement for mutual tolerance that had existed between them, but certainly no depth of grief. When her father died, she knew it would be different, and she would experience all the intensity of losing an extraordinary ally while having, for the first time in her life, no one to stand between her and the stars. She had looked at Dale Carver's photographs very intently and wondered at the raw need behind the outward poise that drove her to try and exert some kind of control through insisting on a stocking, still, on Christmas morning. She wondered, too, if behind Tom's "Very decorous" comment on hers and Duncan's Christmas lay just a hint of envy. There was no glamour to the Browns' Christmas, that was quite certain, but there was an adult freedom to it, and a lack of pretension—and pretense. The thought that a man like Tom Carver could look at anything she, Elizabeth, possessed or did with envy or admiration gave her, to her surprise, a sudden thrill, a thrill of tiny but significant power. And that thrill made her determine to pause on her way home from the last working day before Christmas, at Harrods Food Hall, and buy a hen pheasant and a jar of Stilton and a box of candied apricots, to take down to her father in Bath.

"I can't help it," Lucas said. He was struggling into his clothes. Amy, in a T-shirt with teddy bears printed on the front, was sitting up in bed watching him.

"You didn't have to say yes."

"I did," he said. "I did. There's so many down with flu, and Mike's little girl's still in hospital. There's no one else."

"What about Chris?"

"He did last Christmas."

"Or Mandy," Amy said with venom. Mandy fancied Lucas and left messages for him on sticky memos on his studio tape deck, and sometimes these inadvertently found their way into Lucas's camera case, to be discovered later by Amy.

"She's got to go back to Sheffield. Her mother's ill."

"Poor her," Amy said sarcastically.

Lucas laced up his left boot.

"Poor me, actually."

"Poor *you?*"

"Yes," Lucas said. He got up and limped round the bed, holding his right boot, and sat down next to Amy. "I don't *want* to work on Christmas Day. I don't *want* to spend four hours playing Bing Crosby and the Spice Girls to bed-sit land. I want to be in Dad's house with you and him and Dale."

Amy pleated the duvet cover up between her fingers.

"You always say yes. Whenever they ask you to do anything, you say yes."

"I say yes if it's important. Christmas is important. If Joan Collins came to the TV station on an inconvenient day, wouldn't you drop everything to do her makeup?"

"She has her own makeup people," Amy said. "She takes them everywhere."

Lucas bent over to put on his right boot.

"I'll be there by teatime. Five at the latest."

Amy said in a small voice, "I can't go without you."

"What d'you mean?"

"I can't go round to your father's house till you come."

Lucas stopped lacing and looked at her.

"But you've been there dozens of times——"

"Not by myself."

"You're being stupid," Lucas said.

Amy leaned out of the duvet and clasped her hands round Lucas's nearest arm.

"I'm not. It's different now. Last year Josie was still there, and Rufus, and Josie was a kind of outsider, too, so it was OK for me. But this year, it's just your dad and Dale."

Lucas looked at her.

"You like my dad."

"Yes," Amy said, "but he's your family, and so is Dale. It's just me that isn't."

Lucas pulled his arm away and stood up.

"I give up."

Amy lay back on the pillows and yanked the duvet right up to her chin.

"I'm going to wait here. On Christmas Day, I'm going to wait here until you've finished, and then you can come and pick me up on your way to your dad's house."

Lucas stood looking down at her.

"Amy, you're my fiancée. We're going to get married. You are legally going to be part of my family. I think of you as part of it now, and so does my father. You belong."

Amy gripped the duvet.

"Try telling that to Dale," she said, and shut her eyes.

On Christmas Eve, Tom Carver said he would like to go to midnight mass in the Abbey.

"Why?" Dale said.

"I feel that I'd like to."

"But you never go to church. You don't believe in all that stuff. I bet the last time you went to church was when you married Josie, and you only did that to please her because she was so insistent."

Tom picked Basil up from where he lay on the kitchen table waiting for someone to forget to put the lid on the butter dish, and carried him over to the garden window at the end of the kitchen. He hadn't been in the garden for weeks, and it had a wet, dark, flattened look, a winter sulkiness about it. Even the sweet stone statue of a girl holding a dove that he so loved looked as if she'd had enough. He and Josie had found her in an architectural reclamation yard just before their marriage and had pounced on her with relief, as if she was a symbol for them both, a symbol of hope and harmony. It was something of the same hope that had carried Tom into church on his second wedding day, an anticipation that by marrying Josie in such a place—whatever it did or didn't mean to him—would somehow open up the possibility of making his relationship with Josie as profound as his relationship with Pauline had been. Or, at least, as he earnestly believed it had been. Josie had challenged him about that. She told him he had romanticized his first marriage, that he'd made it—by idealizing it so much—impossible for any real woman even to begin to replace a dead saint. He bent and rubbed his chin slowly across Basil's obliging broad head. He hadn't thought Pauline was perfect, but he had preferred being married to her to being married to Josie. Except for Rufus. Whatever the lost perfections of Pauline, it was Josie who had given him Rufus. And it was something, however obscure, to do with Rufus that made the idea of an hour in Bath Abbey at midnight suddenly strongly alluring. He turned round.

"Dale."

"Yes?"

"You've got your Christmas tree?"

"Yes."

"And Christmas stocking?"

"Yes."

"And a turkey, even though Lucas and I would have liked to experiment with a goose?"

"Yes."

"So I am going to midnight mass. You needn't come with me. I shall be quite happy to go alone. But I'm going."

Dale came down the kitchen toward him. She was wearing black jeans and a tight pale gray polo-necked jersey, and she was holding a mixing bowl of brandy butter. She held out a wooden spoon.

"Taste that."

Tom took a small lick. Basil craned interestedly upward, purring like a traction engine.

"Excellent."

"More sugar?"

"No. Definitely not. I think you should stop playing the perfect housewife and go out and see a friend or go for a walk or something."

Dale looked at him, her head slightly on one side.

"I'll probably come to the Abbey. I don't want to make a thing—"

"Good."

"I just do wonder why you've suddenly got the urge to go."

Tom shrugged. He bent down and let Basil roll heavily out of his arms onto the floor. He waited, with resignation and a degree of dread, for Dale to continue, "I suppose it's because you hope you'll see *her* at the Abbey," but she didn't. He heard the click of her boot heels go sharply back up the length of the kitchen, and then he straightened up.

"I'm going down to the basement."

"Lunch?" Dale said. "Soup? A filled croissant?"

He shook his head.

"No, thank you. Sweet of you, but no."

She smiled at him.

"No trouble," she said. She began to scrape the brandy butter briskly out of the mixing bowl into a green glass dish. "It's just when I'm here, I like to look after you. That's all."

Elizabeth couldn't see Tom in the Abbey. It was packed, of course, hundreds of people, and he had never indicated that he would be there, but something in his faint unspoken envy of her own projected Christmas had made her feel there was the slightest possibility she might see him. She had a new haircut—much shorter—and a new overcoat, with a fake-fur collar and cuffs, and she had achieved both these startling changes on an impulse, just a few days before Christmas, amazing herself. Her father had admired both.

"Very becoming," he'd said of her hair. "Very. You look much younger and far less responsible. And a red coat. Red! I thought you were color-blind to every color on earth but navy blue."

He stood beside her now in the voluminous old tweed coat he'd had all her life, with, on the pew beside him, a tweed hat in which a few fishing flies of long ago still clung, peering at his hymn book through reading glasses she had mended that afternoon with fuse wire. He'd been very proud of the flat.

"I hope you notice the diamondlike glitter of the windows."

"I do."

"And the brilliant purity of the lavatory."

"Dazzling."

"He wanted four pounds an hour. That's twenty pence more an hour than they pay him at the Fox and Grapes."

"You must have felt like Lady Bountiful."

"I've never employed anyone for their hands before, rather than their wits."

"Then you have lived in a very secluded world."

"I know," he said. His voice had an edge of regret to it. "I know I have."

Elizabeth felt very fond of him, standing there beside him in the Abbey. She felt, if she thought about it, oddly fond of everyone round her, too, and of this church with its profusion of eighteenth-century monuments, and of her new haircut, and the glossy black cuffs of her new coat, and of Christmas and of England, and life. She felt she wanted to sing lustily and in a heartfelt way, pleased to be part of such a congregation, such an occasion, with Christmas about to break upon them all, intimate and immense all at once. She turned to Duncan and smiled at him. He winked. Then he leaned sideways until the corner of his spectacles brushed her hair.

"What vandals the Victorians were. Even with carols."

"If," she whispered back, "you'd been yonder peasant, what would you have said to Good King Wenceslas?"

Duncan winked again and returned to his singing. From some distance away, Tom Carver, with Dale beside him, realized that it was indeed Elizabeth Brown over there, in a red coat with much shorter hair. He glanced at Dale. She had her hymn book held up, almost ostentatiously, in front of her face and was singing with apparently solemn concentration. Tom pushed his reading glasses down his nose so that he could see comfortably long-distance over the top of them and, singing still, fixed his gaze upon Elizabeth.

"Hello," Elizabeth said.

Rufus regarded her. He had Basil in his arms, and the possession of this huge fur pillow seemed excuse enough not to say anything.

Elizabeth smiled.

"I'm a friend of your father's. He's helping me with my new house."

Rufus rubbed his face against Basil. This friend of his father's looked nice, normal and nice, unalarming. She had on the kind of skirt that the teachers in his old school in Bath used to wear, with pleats, very tidy-looking. The teachers in Sedgebury didn't have pleats, and they didn't have cozy voices either. They sounded tired, mostly, and when there was too much noise in the classroom, which was often, they sent a child out to find another teacher to help them make everyone shut up.

"Did you just get here?" Elizabeth said. She sat down on the arm of one of the chairs by the television so that she was more or less the same height as Rufus.

He nodded.

"Daddy met me."

He closed his eyes for a moment. It had been such a relief to see his father and his father's car in that lay-by, where they had all agreed to meet, that he had wanted, to his shame, to cry. But he didn't, because he felt guilty about Josie. He knew Josie was looking awful, her face pinched and pale by contrast with her exaggerated hair, and he knew his father must have noticed this, and also how hard Josie had hugged him, at the handover. They hadn't said much to each other, his mother and father, but concentrated on getting his bag and his gumboots and stuff from one car to another, and when Rufus was in his father's car, he had bent his head for ages over the fastening of the seat-belt buckle in case his mother saw his face and saw what he was feeling, to be back in his father's car at last, with the same rubber mats on the floor and the same maps and pencils and extra-strong peppermints in the glove pocket.

Elizabeth put out a hand and touched one of Basil's nonchalantly dangling paws.

"Did you have a good Christmas?"

Basil was getting heavy. Rufus tried to adjust his weight in his arms and failed and had to let him slither out of his grasp onto the sofa.

"I don't know——"

"I know what you mean," Elizabeth said. "When you look forward to something so much, you can't really believe it when it happens. And then you can't decide if it's as good as you hoped it would be."

Rufus began to kick gently at the leg of the sofa.

He said uncertainly, "It was weird when they went away."

Elizabeth let a pause fall. She felt it had been unnecessarily meaningful of Tom to leave her alone with Rufus, but for all that, she was going to talk to him if she could.

She said gently, "Who went away?"

"The others," Rufus said. He stopped kicking and put his hands on the back of the sofa and began to spring up and down, his coppery brown hair jumping with him. "Their mother rang. So they went."

"Oh," Elizabeth said. "You mean your stepfather's children."

Rufus nodded. The telephone call had come quite late on Christmas Eve, after he was in bed and waiting rather tensely for

Rory to be sent to join him. He'd heard his mother shout, "Becky, it's for you," in the voice she used when she was in a temper and trying to hide it, and then there'd been mutterings for a while, and then he'd heard the phone banged down and there was pandemonium. Becky had screamed and Josie had screamed and Clare had cried and Matthew had shouted and Rory had turned the television up so loud that the people next door began to bang on the party wall and yell at them all to shut up. After a bit, Rory came tearing into their room and started to ram all his stuff into his rucksack. Rufus reared up in bed.

"Where're you going?"

"Back to Mum's—"

"But it's Christmas—"

"Does it matter?" Rory said. He kept his face averted from Rufus. "Does it bloody matter *what* it is?"

Rufus watched him. He heard Becky and Clare thumping about in the room next door. Clare was still crying, and he heard Becky say, "Fuck," several times, very clearly. Then he heard the car being reversed down the drive to the gate and all the children thundered down the stairs and slammed the house doors and then the car doors and the car went roaring off like a car racing at Brand's Hatch. Then there was silence. The silence was worse than the noise had been. After a bit, Rufus got out of bed and went out onto the landing. His mother was sitting on the stairs, with her head in her hands.

"Are you crying?" Rufus said.

She looked up at him. Her eyes were dry.

"No."

"Why've they gone?"

"Nadine told them to."

"Oh."

Josie held out an arm.

"I'd rather like a hug—"

Rufus had gone down the stairs and sat next to her, leaning on her.

"Are you pleased they've gone?"

He said slowly, "I don't know—"

"I know," she said. "Nor do I. I want to kill Nadine. Why did Matthew give in?"

Rufus didn't know. He didn't know now. Matthew had been very quiet all Christmas Day, and he had dark rings under his eyes. Josie and Rufus had been pretty quiet, too. Josie said Matthew was disappointed. The odd thing was that there was something disappointed in how Rufus felt, too, and that was troubling in itself.

"It's hard for you," Elizabeth said now. "It must be."

Rufus stopped jumping. He was slightly out of breath. He hung over the sofa back so that his face almost touched Basil, who lay peacefully exactly where he'd been dumped. "It's hard for you," she'd said. She'd said it quite ordinarily, not in a soppy, sorry-for-you voice, but as if it were true, a fact, something that no one should pretend was otherwise. A feeling arose in Rufus that some kind of thank-you was called for, some kind of acknowledgment of this unaffected sympathy.

He said, not looking at her but still looking at Basil, "Would you like to see my bedroom?"

NADINE LOOKED AT the piece of cold pork in the larder. She wasn't sure how long you could go on eating meat after it had been first cooked, and she'd cooked this almost a week before, on Christmas Day. She couldn't remember cooking pork before—it had been one of the many things on the hit list of foods she would never touch—but she couldn't avoid cooking this bit. It had been a present, on Christmas morning, from the farmer half a mile away, along with a paper sack of potatoes and a bag of brussels sprouts. If he hadn't come, she didn't know what they would have eaten. Food—quite naturally, she thought—had hardly been uppermost in her mind when she'd telephoned Matthew's house and begged Becky not to leave her alone, all alone, for Christmas.

She'd agreed to meet Matthew halfway and retrieve the children. She hadn't wanted to, she'd wanted Matthew to come all the way to the cottage so that he could see how she lived, what she was reduced to. But he had refused. He'd said if he had to go more than halfway, he wouldn't bring them at all, and in the background Nadine could hear Becky pleading with him and Clare crying. She couldn't believe that Matthew could hold out like this, against his own children. She imagined Josie and her son smirking with satisfaction in the background, with the central heating on and a bulging refrigerator. Then Matthew put the phone down on her, and when she tried to ring again, the answering machine was on and she was so afraid she might miss meeting the children that she had leaped straight into the car and driven off into the night, crouched over the steering wheel as if that would somehow help it to go faster.

The children looked exhausted. She had determined she would neither look at Matthew nor speak to him, but she saw enough to reassure herself that he looked exhausted, too. And he was thinner. He'd always been inclined to thinness, but now he looked scrawny, and much older. He'd hardly said good-bye, even to the children, but just let them get silently from one car to the other, only helping Clare with her bags. Clare's skirt had got caught in the door of his car as she scrambled out, and it had torn, and Clare had begun to cry again. She looked as if she had been crying for weeks.

And then, a mile from home, Nadine's car had stopped. Just stopped, dead, in the middle of the road and would give nothing but a faint groan when Nadine turned the key. It was very dark, and they had no flashlights. Nadine said, as cheerfully as she could, that they'd have to walk.

"No," Becky said.

"But—"

"I'm not carrying all my stuff, and I'm not leaving it in the car either. It doesn't lock."

Nadine said, with an edge of sarcasm, "So what are you going to do instead, may I ask?"

"Go to the farm."

"What farm?"

"The one up there. The one the cows belong to."

"But we don't know them—"

"Not yet," Becky said.

She had made Rory go with her, and they had gone off in the dark together and returned, in a surprisingly short time, in a Land Rover with a farmer called Tim Huntley. He was youngish and grinning, with heavy shoulders and hands. He winked at Nadine and told her she'd run out of petrol.

"I haven't—"

"You have—"

"You have!" Becky shouted.

Tim Huntley had filled the tank from a can in the back of his Land Rover.

"You all right in that cottage?" he said to Nadine.

"No. How could anyone be?"

He grinned.

"We never thought they'd let it again."

"It was all we could afford," Nadine said. She saw the children shrink back as she spoke. In the light of the Land Rover head-lights, Tim Huntley looked at them all, consideringly.

"Start her up now," he said.

Nadine tried.

"Plenty of choke."

Nadine tried again.

He put his hand on the driver's door.

"Hop out," he said. "I'll do it."

He got into the driver's seat and pumped the accelerator. Then he turned the key. The engine coughed once or twice, and turned.

"There."

He got out of the car and held the door open for Nadine.

"I'll be down in the morning," he said, "to see if she'll still fire."

"Thank you—"

"No problem. Up at five for the cows anyhow."

He'd come at nine in the morning, on Christmas Day, dumping the meat and vegetables on the kitchen table. He patted the pork.

"One of ours. Should crackle well."

Nadine had been in her dressing gown, with her hair down her back, making tea and apprehensively counting bread slices, to see if there were enough. She smiled at him.

"You are really, really kind."

"It's nothing."

"I mean it. Thank you."

He had blushed very slightly and slapped the pork again.

"Thirty-five minutes to the pound. Hot oven. Don't salt the crackle."

She had suddenly felt extremely happy, standing there in her kitchen with such a reassuring bulk of food on the table. She gave him a deliberate, quick glance.

"I wouldn't dream of it—"

Later, she heard her car being started up in the lean-to, and later still, she found a pile of logs outside the door. She'd said to the children, "See? See? You were *meant* to be home for Christmas, weren't you?"

Clare had muttered something.

"What?" Nadine said. "What? What did you say?"

But Clare, who had said, with some desperation, "I don't know *where* we're meant to be," wouldn't repeat herself.

They'd eaten the pork on Christmas Day and Boxing Day and

on the day after, and then the children wouldn't eat it anymore. Nadine put the rest of the meat—it was a huge, real farmer's joint—in the damp larder, where blue and green molds lived under the shelves, and baked potatoes instead for every meal. In between baked potatoes, the children did things she asked them to— washed up or brought wood in or emptied the kitchen bin—but listlessly, and at every opportunity escaped upstairs to do things with Christmas presents they tried to pretend they hadn't got. Nadine told herself she was too proud to ask what these furtive presents were, but she could hear the whine and tattoolike beat of battery-operated games, and Becky, under her mitten, was wearing a silver ring shaped like a fish curled round on itself. It came from the Indian craft shop in Sedgebury, Nadine was sure. It was prob- ably the one Becky had wanted for her birthday but which Matthew, in one of his suburban frenzies about money, had said she couldn't have. But plainly she could have it now, couldn't she? Now that Becky had to be bribed to love him, to stay with him and the Randy Redhead in their dinky little house.

"Mum," Becky said, from behind her.

"Do you think we could curry that?" Nadine said. She pointed to the pork. A pinkish liquid had seeped from it and congealed into a thin layer of jelly.

"No," Becky said. "Can we go into Ross?"

Nadine looked at her.

"No. Why?"

Becky twisted her hidden ring under her mitten.

"Just—wanted to—wanted to go somewhere. We've been stuck here for days—"

"What will you do if we go to Ross?"

Becky shrugged.

"Go round the shops—"

"With what?"

Becky muttered something. She ducked her head so that her hair fell forward. Josie had given her a black nylon wallet for Christmas with a ten-pound note in it. The wallet was gross, of course, but the ten pounds were okay.

"Did she give you money?" Nadine asked.

"A bit—"

"Don't you know," Nadine demanded, "when you're being bought, when someone is trying to *bribe* you?"

Becky thought of all those meals she had refused to eat, the beds she had declined to make, the washing-up she had just left, defying her father to push her toward the sink, to dare to touch her. Nadine's unfairness in the face of this steady opposition to her father's new marriage made her eyes water.

"How can you be so disloyal," Nadine shouted suddenly, "as to take anything from her?"

Becky moved away from the larder door and slumped in a chair by the kitchen table.

She said, into her hair, "It's all the money I've got."

"Hah!" Nadine said. She marched past Becky with a handful of potatoes and dropped them thudding into the sink. "Welcome to the club."

Becky leaned her elbows on the table and put the heels of her hands into her eye sockets. If she pressed, colored flashes and stars and rings exploded against the blackness, and briefly, blessedly, cleared her mind of thoughts. Such as the thoughts that had pursued her all morning, which she had sought to escape by suggesting an expedition to Ross, thoughts of her father, and how she wanted him to be there and how she kept remembering times when he was there, bringing with him a sense that not only were some things in life to be relied upon but that there were other things to be aimed for, striven for, which would bring mysterious and potent reward. Without her father there, Becky had lost a sense of the future, a sense that round the next corner might be something other than just more of the same. She raised her head and looked at Nadine's narrow back, bent over the sink.

"Mum—"

"What?"

"When you and Dad sold our house—" She paused.

"Well?"

"Where did the money go?"

"Into the bank," Nadine said shortly.

"Couldn't—couldn't we use just some of it?"

Nadine turned round. She was holding a potato and an old nailbrush.

"No."

"Why not?"

"Because," Nadine said, "it's all the money *I've* got. All I'll *ever* have."

Becky didn't look at her. She spread her hands out flat on the table and said in a rush, before her courage fled, "Why don't you get a job?"

There was an ominous silence. Becky heard the potato and nailbrush fall into the sink.

"Sorry?" Nadine said. Her voice was cold.

Becky mumbled, "You heard me—"

"Yes, I did," Nadine said. She came away from the sink and leaned on the opposite side of the table, staring at Becky. "I heard you. I heard you the other night, too, when you said the same thing. Do you remember what I said to you?"

"Yes—"

"Well. The same reason is true now. I can't work because of you children and where we are forced to live. And you have no right to ask me to, no right at all." She leaned forward. "*Why* are you asking me?"

Becky said, to the tabletop, "Other mothers work—"

"Hah!" Nadine shouted again. She slammed her fist down on the table. "So *that's* it, is it? *That's* what you're getting at! *She's* got a job, has she? She's got everything that should be mine and a bloody job, too?"

"No, she hasn't. Not yet. But she's going to—"

"Becky—"

Becky closed her eyes.

"Becky, how *dare* you speak to me about her? How *dare* you even begin to make comparisons when you think what I've done for you and she's destroyed? How *dare* you?"

"I wasn't comparing—"

"Weren't you? *Weren't* you?"

"I was just telling you. You asked if she'd got a job, and I was just telling you—"

"You should be ashamed of even *mentioning* her in my presence."

"I didn't. I never do mention—"

"Shut up!" Nadine yelled.

Becky pushed her chair back from the table, tilting it to get away from Nadine's furious face.

She said, persisting, "I'm thinking of you—"

"What?"

"You ought to get away from here. You ought to see other people than us. You ought—" She stopped.

"What ought I?"

Becky cried wildly, "You ought to use your energies for something else than just hating Dad!"

"Right," Nadine said. "Right. That does it."

She marched round the table and gave Becky's tilting chair a swift kick. It lurched and toppled, sending Becky onto her knees on the kitchen floor. She put her hands down to steady herself and waited, on all fours, for the next thing to happen.

"You have no idea about pain," Nadine said. Her voice was odd, as if she was restraining a scream. "No idea about suffering, about being rejected, about the end of love. You have all your life before you, and what have I got? Nothing. Seventeen years' investment in a relationship, and what do I have at the end? Nothing. *Nothing.*"

Very slowly, Becky sat up on her heels. She looked up at Nadine. She had no idea why she wasn't giving in, why she wasn't retreating into the silence that had always been, in the end, her only defense. But she wasn't. She was sick with fright, but she was going to say it, she was *going* to.

"You *could* have something," she said. Her voice shook. "You could have something, even now, if you wanted to. You could have had something, all along. But you wouldn't."

There was a small, stunned silence, and then Nadine leaned down and slapped her hard, across her cheek. Becky gave a little cry. Nadine had never struck her before. She'd screamed and shouted and ranted and slammed her own hands or herself against walls and furniture, but she'd never hit Becky before. Or the others. Hugs, yes, violent cuddles and kisses, and when she was in a good mood, tickles and squeezes, but not blows. Never blows. Becky put a hand to her cheek. It was stinging.

"Oh my God," Nadine said. She yanked the chair upright and collapsed onto it, putting her face in her hands. "Oh my God. Sorry. Oh, sorry—"

Very slowly, Becky stood up. She leaned on the table. She felt slightly sick.

"That's OK—"

"No," Nadine said. She stretched out one hand to Becky. "No, it isn't. Come here. Let me hold you—"

"Can't," Becky said. Her voice was hoarse.

"Please—"

Becky shook her head. Nadine raised hers from her remaining hand and looked full at Becky.

"I'm sorry. I'm really sorry. Can't you see? I should never have done it, I should never have hit you. It's just that I get so wound up, so angry—"

"I know."

"Can't you understand?" Nadine said. "Can't you see what it's like to have made such a mess of everything and then to find that you're stuck?"

Becky sighed. Her face was beginning to glow now, and to throb faintly as if a bruise was gathering itself up ready to form.

"Whatever—" She stopped.

"Go on."

"Whatever it's like," Becky said, looking down the leaning length of her body to her boot toes, "you shouldn't take it out on us."

The kitchen door opened. Clare, wearing her Disney tracksuit and an old Aran jersey of Matthew's, came in holding the headphones of her new personal tape player.

"Rory's gone."

Nadine swiveled on her chair.

"What d'you mean?"

"He's not upstairs, and he's not downstairs."

"He'll be outside—"

"It's raining," Clare said.

"Perhaps he's in the car, seeing if it'll start—"

"I've looked," Clare said. She had been impelled to go and find him because of the sudden silence from his burrow under the eaves. He was in one of his refusing-to-speak moods, but Clare had seen him, a couple of hours ago, tunneling into his bedding with his new Swiss army knife and a small log from the pile Tim Huntley had brought. For some time Clare could hear chippings and whit-tlings, and then she put her headphones on and could hear nothing but the soundtrack from *The Sound of Music*, which she only played when alone for fear of being mocked for listening to anything so creepy, so sentimental, so pathetic. But she loved it, she loved its sentimentality and its portrayal of a family as a safe haven, a happy unit, loving, unthreatened in their togetherness. When she had heard to the end, she took the headphones off and noticed that the wood-carving noises had stopped. She put her head out onto the landing and saw that Rory's leather jacket—it was only a cheap one from Sedgebury Market, and the seams were beginning to split—had gone from where he'd dumped it on the floor. She went across to his burrow.

"Rory?" she said.

There was no answer. She crawled in. The bedclothes were scattered with little chips of wood, and they were cold. On his pil-low lay the log. He hadn't been carving it, he'd just hacked at it. It was full of gashes and slashes, as if he'd just tried to kill it with his knife. She reversed out onto the landing and did a tour of the upstairs and then the downstairs. Then she went out into the driz-zle and looked in the lean-to and the awful shed where a stained

old lavatory crouched in the corner like a toad. Then she went
back into the cottage and sought her mother in the kitchen.

Nadine looked as if she was about to cry.

"I can't face it—"

"It's OK, Mum," Becky said. "Don't panic. He can't be far."

"I must go and look for him—"

"If he isn't back for lunch—"

"What?"

"We'll go and look for him if he isn't back for lunch."

"But—"

"He's twelve," Becky said. "He's nearly a teenager. Anyway,
what could happen to him round here with nothing for miles
except cows?"

Nadine glanced at her. Then she looked at Clare. Then she
took a deep breath and pushed her hair off her face.

"I hope you know," she said, and her voice shook a little. "I
hope you both know how much I love you? All of you?"

"Hey," Tim Huntley said. He'd come round the corner of the
Dutch barn with the tractor to cut more maize for feeding, and a
movement had caught his eye. It was a quick movement, someone
on top of the great maize stack, someone not very big. And then
the someone had moved again, and revealed itself to be the kid
from what Tim and his mother called No-Hope Cottage. The boy
kid. He was crouched up there looking down at Tim as if he
expected to be shouted at.

"Hey," Tim said. "What you doing up there?"

"Nothing," Rory said. He was wearing jeans and a leather
jacket that had seen better days and a T-shirt, and he looked blue

with cold. Tim opened the tractor-cab door and swung himself down. He looked up at Rory, twenty feet above him.

"How long have you been up there?"

"Dunno—"

"You better come down."

Rory hesitated. He'd climbed up on impulse, rather to see if he could, making toe- and fingerholds in the maize wall as he went. But getting down was another matter. Tim went close to the maize.

"I'll catch you."

Rory shrank back.

"I'm not going to lam you," Tim said. "I just want you down." He moved to stand directly below Rory. "Lie on your stomach and move yourself over the edge feet first. There'll be a drop, and then I'll catch you."

Rory's head disappeared from view, and then his sneakered feet appeared over the edge above.

"Slowly," Tim said.

Rory maneuvered himself until he was holding on only with his arms.

"Let go!"

Rory fell. Tim caught him clumsily around the waist as he dropped, and they both tumbled to the floor.

"Bloody hell—"

"Sorry," Rory said. He scrambled sideways away from Tim's bulk and got to his feet. "Sorry."

Tim got up slowly, brushing down his boiler suit.

"So you should be. Why are you here in any case?"

Rory said nothing. He didn't know, except that he'd been driven from the cottage by a sudden desperation to be out of it, and the farm had seemed a simple destination.

"You know what trespass is?"

Rory shook his head.

"It's being on someone else's land or property unlawfully. It's interfering with what belongs to someone else."

"I didn't interfere—"

"Suppose you'd knocked some of that maize down?"

"I didn't."

"You could have." Tim looked at him. He was shivering. He hadn't enough flesh on him to keep a sparrow warm. Tim jingled the keys in his pocket. "I'll take you home."

"No," Rory said.

"Why not?"

Rory said nothing, just kicked at the soft dust on the floor of the barn.

"You in trouble?"

"No," Rory said.

"Then—"

"I'll go," Rory said. "I'll go. You don't need to take me. Thanks."

"Where'll you go?"

"On a bit," Rory said.

"You're not dressed for it."

"I'm OK."

Tim let a pause fall, and then he said, "Where's your dad?"

"He's not here—"

"Working?"

"No," Rory said. His head was bent as if he were intent on watching the scuffing patterns his feet made. "He lives in Sedge-bury."

"So your mum's on her own there, with you lot?"

Rory nodded.

"You better ring her," Tim said. "Tell her where you are."

"No—"

"Why not?"

Rory couldn't explain. He couldn't tell this man he hardly knew that if he rang Nadine there'd be a scene and a drama and she'd insist on coming to get him and on thanking Tim Huntley as if he'd rescued Rory from drowning. He said, instead, hurriedly, "I got bored. I'll—I'll go now—"

"Home?"

"Yes—"

"Mind you do," Tim said. He remembered Nadine distraught in the dark lane on Christmas Eve and then in her kitchen the next morning, cool as a cucumber in her dressing gown, as if she'd known him all her life. She must be over forty, to have these kids, must be. But she didn't look it. She looked younger than Tim's sister, who was only thirty-two but had had three children and let herself go in the process and now looked fifty. Fat, frumpy, and fifty. This boy's mother, chaotic though she was, still took a bit of trouble. Tim had discussed her and the children, at length, with his mother.

"You keep an eye," Mrs. Huntley had said. "Remember those kids in the caravan? We don't want that happening again, we don't want to be accused of turning a blind eye. You look out for this lot, see things don't slip too far."

Tim put a hand in his pocket and found a packet of chewing gum. He held it out to Rory.

"Hop it."

"Thanks—"

"I'm going to ring your place, dinnertime. And if you're not home, you'll cop it."

———⟨◦⟩———

"Why did you go?" Nadine said.

Rory shrugged.

"Why didn't you tell anyone?"

"Didn't think—"

There were baked beans on the plate in front of him, and he was pushing them about with the blade of his knife, making a mess, not eating. It occurred to him to say that he was bored here, fed up, stuck in the cottage with his sisters and a television so old that, even when mended, it couldn't get a proper signal, but he knew it wasn't worth risking it. He'd only have to start talking like that and everything would blow up again and he was too tired for that. He was tired all the time, it seemed to him, tired of having nothing to do, nowhere to go, tired of tension, tired of having to watch what he said, tired of baked potatoes. He used to feel tired this way in the past, when Matthew and Nadine quarreled or Nadine went off somewhere and left Matthew to cope. Rory swallowed. He mustn't think of Matthew. If he was tired, he certainly mustn't, because it would make him start wanting him to be there, wanting him to be as he used to be, just Dad, and not as he was now, only partly Dad because of what had happened, because of Josie and Rufus. Rory didn't hate Josie and Rufus the way Nadine wanted him to, but he hated what their arrival had done to his life. It had been a rough old life before, in a lot of ways, but at least Dad had been in it, at the center, a necessary presence making tea, yawning in the kitchen in the early mornings, wearing an old plaid dressing gown that Rory knew was as impregnated with his smell as his skin was. Tears pricked behind Rory's eyelids. He put the knife down and rubbed the back of his hand across his nose.

"Aren't you hungry?"

"Sort of—"

Nadine looked round the table. Clare had eaten half her beans, but Becky's and her own were virtually untouched. We're a sorry lot, she thought, a sad little crew of human rubbish, the bits and pieces chucked out when other people's lives change and they want to throw out what they don't need anymore. Poor children, poor scruffy, weary children with their disrupted lives and their dependency and their genuine desire not to cause me pain. I shouldn't have slapped Becky, I shouldn't have. And I shouldn't shout at them for things they can't help, like having expressions or gestures that remind me of their father, of what happened, of what got us here. They're good children, they are, they're good, loving children, and they're all I've got, all the future I've got anyhow. She smiled at them.

"Eat up."

Becky slowly shook her head.

"No thanks."

"Look," Nadine said.

They waited. She leaned forward, her forearms either side of her plate, and spread her hands flat on the table.

"We've got to make a go of this." She paused and then she said, "Haven't we?"

They didn't look at her.

"We've got to make a go of living here and going to school here and of each other's company. We're not going to give in. Are we? We're not going to let our lives be ruined by other people's choices. Tell you what—"

Clare and Becky raised their heads.

"Shall we go into Ross this afternoon?"

Becky said, "You said there wasn't any money—"

Nadine smiled.

"I might get some out of the bank. Just a little. We could go to the cinema maybe. What about that?" She stretched one hand out and squeezed Rory's nearest one. "Okay?"

He nodded.

"Okay, Clare?"

Clare nodded, too. Nadine turned full face toward Becky.

"Well, Becky. Okay?"

Becky glanced at her. She smiled wanly.

"Okay."

THE LETTER HAD come in the post, along with three bills, some junk mail, and a children's clothes catalogue. Matthew had taken the bills very quickly, snatching them up as if he didn't want Josie to see how the very sight of a brown envelope alarmed him, and he had then handed her the letter.

"That's his writing, isn't it?"

Josie looked at the letter. It was indeed Tom's writing, his elegant, architect's handwriting, which she used to tell him was too feminine for so solid a man.

"Yes."

"You'd better take it then."

She put her hands behind her back.

"I don't want to hear from him, Matthew."

He gave her a glance and then a quick, relieved grin.

"You ought to open it. It might be about Rufus."

"He rings me about Rufus. Letters—" She stopped.

"What?"

"Letters are significant somehow. Letters always mean that someone is ducking saying something to your face."

"Shall I open it?"

"No," Josie said. "I'll leave it. I'll leave it till later, after the interview."

He leaned over and kissed her, on her mouth. She liked that, the way he always kissed her on the mouth, even the briefest hello and good-bye kisses. It made her feel that he meant them.

"Good luck, sweetheart. Good luck with the interview."

"I'm nervous. I haven't interviewed for a job since Rufus was two."

"You'll be great. *I'd* employ you."

"You're biased—"

"Yes," he said. "Hopelessly."

Josie looked at the letter.

"Tom didn't really want me to work."

"I want you to. If you want to."

"I do."

He glanced at the bills in his hand, almost shamefacedly.

"It'll help—"

"I know."

"I'm sorry," Matthew said suddenly. "I'm sorry so much has to go on—"

"Don't mention her."

"I don't want you to think it's what I want."

"Surely," she said, the unavoidable sharpness entering her voice that seemed inseparable from any mention of Nadine or the children, "you want to support your children?"

His shoulders slumped a little.

"Of course I do."

He leaned forward and laid Tom's letter on the kitchen table, weighting it with a nearby jar of peanut butter.

"I'd better go."

"Yes."

He looked at her.

"Good luck. I mean it."

She made an effort to smile.

"Thanks. I'll ring you."

The interview had turned out to be very unalarming. The larger of the two primary schools in Sedgebury needed a supply teacher for English and general studies, for two terms while the permanent teacher took maternity leave. It was twins, the head teacher said, so the extended leave was something of a special case. She was a plump woman in a knitted suit whose chief concern, she told Josie, was pastoral care. That was why she had liked Josie's résumé, with its mention of the conference in Cheltenham.

"We can't teach these children anything," she said, "until we've taught them a little self-respect."

Josie nodded. In the school where she had taught in Bath—and where she had never intended that Rufus should go—the children, though not inadequately clothed or fed, came from an area of the city where communication appeared almost exclusively to be through acts of casual violence. They had all grown up with it, they were all used to quarrels and frustrations being expressed in yelling and blows, they all accepted physical rage as the common currency. Sedgebury would be no different. All that would be different in Sedgebury was that she, Josie, married to Matthew and not to Tom, would be closer in every way to the children she was trying to help, and there was a small unmistakable pride in the thought.

Escorting her out of the school's main door, the head teacher said, "Of course, your stepdaughter was here. Clare Mitchell."

Josie was startled.

"Yes—"

"And her older sister was here earlier. The boy was at Wickhams, as far as I remember. How are they doing?"

Josie found herself coloring.

"I'm afraid we don't know each other very well yet. I think—they've all settled, in their new schools."

"Nice children," the head teacher said. "Clever." She looked at Josie slightly sideways. "You'll find a lot of people knew the Mitchell family, in Sedgebury."

Josie looked straight ahead.

"I'm becoming aware of that."

"It's good that you'll be working—"

"Is it?"

The head teacher put her hands into the pockets of her knitted jacket.

"It will mean you won't have to apologize too much, that you'll have your own status."

"Apologize?"

"People don't like change."

"You mean apologize for being Matthew's second wife?"

"It's more being a stepmother, Mrs. Mitchell."

Josie spun round.

She said sharply, "I didn't have any *choice* in taking them on, you know. It was him I chose!"

The head teacher took one hand out of her pocket and laid it briefly on Josie's arm.

"I know. I'm just warning you that not everyone will see it that way. I'll report to my governors, Mrs. Mitchell, and we'll let you know as soon as possible."

Josie looked at her.

"I really want the job."

Later, cycling home—Matthew had the car—she knew she shouldn't have made herself appear vulnerable, needy, just as she shouldn't have reacted in any way to the suggestion, however kindly meant, that she was on some kind of local trial as Matthew's new wife. At Rufus's school, it was fine, she was his mother, his real, birth mother, but elsewhere in the town it was beginning to dawn on her that her role was not so comfortably accepted. She had come in, from the outside, to take the place of someone else, who had been dispossessed by her coming. It didn't seem to matter what people thought of Nadine because, with maddening and arbitrary human adaptability, they had got used to their opinion of her, however disapproving, and her going had made a change that they resented.

"It isn't you," Matthew had said, after Josie had had a mild confrontation with the garage that had always serviced Matthew's cars. "It isn't you, the person, Josie. It's that you're different, so they've got to make an effort and they don't like that."

"So have I," Josie had said. Her voice had been higher than she intended. "So have I! The only difference is that I have to make a hundred times more effort because I'm the newcomer!"

It had never struck her that being a newcomer could be so difficult. She told herself that changing a renowned and lovely city like Bath for a profoundly unremarkable town like Sedgebury would only be hard superficially because the roots of her life with Matthew would be nourished as they had failed to be nourished in her marriage with Tom. She saw herself not just building a new life but being in charge of it in a way she had never been able to be before, because so much of her previous life had been mapped out by Tom's past. She had visualized the energy she would put into her life with Matthew, the compensations she would make to him for the deprivations of his years with Nadine, the slow, tactful progress she would make with all these new relationships swirling round her—herself and his children, her son and him, her son and his children, herself and his sister, herself and his parents, herself and the people he had known here for years, those years of life— so painful, often, to think about when they had as yet so little shared history between them—before he met her.

But it didn't seem to be being like that. She didn't seem to be being given a chance to effect things for good as she wanted to. There were all kinds of elements she hadn't taken into account out of sheer ignorance, inexperience, elements that appeared to con- spire against her making that headway she had so earnestly planned. Sedgebury was proving not only an unremarkable town but also rather a sullen one; Rufus missed his father plainly and perpetually, and seemed bewildered into passivity at any suggestion that he should make friends with either Matthew or Matthew's children; Matthew's children declined to give an inch in her direc- tion, and Matthew seemed helpless in the face of their obduracy; and there was Nadine. Josie gripped the handlebars of her bicycle and took a sharp, self-controlling breath. What had ever, ever pos- sessed her into thinking that Nadine could be kept out of her life, their lives, in fact *any* life? Because of her, Karen was apprehensive about seeing Josie, and Matthew's mother simply refused to. Because of her, Matthew's children were, for the moment, hardly coming to Sedgebury at all, and Matthew minded about this a good deal and was unable to talk about it to Josie. Because of her, a large proportion of the bills that came to the house seemed to require Matthew's embarrassed and furtive attention, and it had occurred to Josie more than once that when—if—she got a job, she would be paying for their lives so that Matthew could pay for Nadine's.

She turned her bicycle up the right-hand concrete strip of the drive of 17 Barratt Road and rode it into the garage. She would not think about Nadine. It was becoming a refrain, like the line of a song stuck in her head, "Don't think about Nadine." She got off her bicycle and padlocked it to Matthew's workbench. The night before, Matthew had asked Rufus if he would like to learn how to screw two pieces of wood together, properly.

"No, thank you," Rufus had said.

Josie had opened her mouth to remonstrate with him, but Matthew had shaken his head to silence her.

"OK," he said to Rufus. "Go without."

Rufus had colored. Josie had bitten her lip.

"Sorry," he said to her, later.

"There was no need."

"I know."

"He's a good little boy."

"I *know*," Matthew said. "I know. I'm sorry. I said so. I meant it."

Josie put her key into the back door and turned it. The kitchen was quiet and empty, just as she had left it, with breakfast cleared away and the table bare except for a jug of forced early daffodils Matthew had brought her from the market, and the letter under the peanut-butter jar. She must get a cat or a budgerigar, or even a goldfish. There had to be some animate thing to welcome her when she got back to this house that was not a home yet, but just the place they all lived, while they tested each other out, tried to get used to things. A dog would be lovely, a dog would be ideal, a focus, something they could all practice their painful new family feelings on, but who would look after the dog if they were all out all day?

Josie took her coat off, and her gloves and scarf, and put them down in a heap on the kitchen chair. Then she ran water into the kettle and plugged it in. The letter was watching her. Even with her back to it, she knew it was. She put her hand on the lid of the kettle. When it boiled, and she had made herself some coffee, she would open it.

Outside Rufus's school—Wickham Junior—several other mothers waited. A few had prams and baby buggies, and one or two wore their babies in slings across their chests and adopted above these expressions of elaborate detachment as if defying mockery, or even comment. Josie knew quite a lot of the mothers by sight now. "Hi," they said to each other. "Bitter cold, isn't it?" Their children came roaring out across the playground at three-fifteen, and at the sight of them, a faint despairing collective moan arose, as if they were all being reminded, simultaneously and forcibly, of the reality of their responsibilities.

Rufus was almost always nearly last. For the first term, he had also always been alone, walking very carefully and steadily toward Josie with his head bent. But this term, he seemed to have found a friend, another redhead, an awkward-looking boy with spectacles and huge ears. Rufus appeared relieved to have a friend, if not exactly proud of this one, and it was unquestionably better to see him walking with someone, than alone. The friend's name was Colin, and that was all Rufus seemed to know about him and all he thought he needed to know.

"Good day?" Josie said. She stopped and kissed him. He hadn't told her not to, yet, so she thought she would go on until he did. He nodded. He nodded most days, having discovered that it averted questions.

"Good," Josie said. "I'm so pleased. I went for an interview. It was a nice school, so was the head teacher. I feel quite hopeful."

Rufus remembered Josie's working days in Bath.

"Will you use the same bag?"

"I should think so. It hasn't fallen to bits yet. Are you hungry?"

"Yes."

"What was lunch?"

Rufus thought.

"Shepherd's pie and spaghetti."

"No vegetables—"

"Carrots, but I didn't eat them."

"Nothing green?"

Rufus shook his head. That had been a relief. In his view there were peas, which were fine, and then there were vegetables, all of them, which were not fine at all.

"Would you like it," Josie said, "if we went and had a burger?"

He looked up. He was beaming.

"*Yes.*"

In the burger bar he chose a cheeseburger with chips and a banana milkshake. Josie had a cup of coffee. She watched him carefully extracting the lettuce and tomato from his bun. It was amazing to her that someone who, from babyhood, had had to be bribed and cajoled and bullied into eating anything acceptably healthy could possess such luminous skin, such clear eyes and shining hair.

"Rufus—"

He looked at her over his bun, his mouth full.

"I've got something to tell you. Maybe—maybe it's easier to tell you here than at home."

He stopped chewing.

"I had a letter from Daddy this morning—"

He was watching her, waiting, only his eyes and nose visible above the burger bun.

"Darling, I think Daddy is going to get married again."

It was her turn to wait. He regarded her for a moment and then seemed abruptly to relax. He took another bite.

"I know," he said, through his mouthful.

"*Do* you?"

He nodded. He swallowed and reached for his milkshake.

"Did he tell you?"

"No," Rufus said, sucking through his milkshake straw. "But she was in the house."

"After Christmas?"

"Yes."

"And you—sort of guessed?"

Rufus took another long suck.

"They were laughing."

Josie looked down into her coffee. A pang she could give no name to clutched her briefly, and let go.

"Did—did you like her?"

Rufus nodded.

"She didn't make a fuss."

"What do you mean? Of you? Of Daddy?"

Rufus picked up a chip in his fingers.

"She was just there. She's called Elizabeth."

Elizabeth, Josie thought to herself. Elizabeth Carver.

"What did she look like?"

Rufus considered. He ate another chip. Elizabeth wasn't pretty, but she was OK as well. Sort of peaceful. A bit like Granny.

"A bit like Granny," he said.

"*Granny!*"

"Not so old," Rufus said, "but kind of not showing off." He thought of Becky and Clare. "Not boots and nose rings and stuff."

Josie looked at him carefully. He looked completely calm, really calm, almost, to her dismay, as if this new development in his life was actually rather welcome.

"Don't you mind?" Josie said.

"What?"

"Don't you mind if Daddy marries someone else?"

"I wouldn't like him to marry anyone really fat," Rufus said, licking melted cheese off his forefinger. "Or an old tart."

"But you don't mind Elizabeth—"

"No," Rufus said. He gave Josie a sudden, sharp look. "Do you?"

Josie said confusedly, "It just seems a bit quick—"

"I expect he was lonely," Rufus said. "Just him and Bas."

"Yes."

Rufus picked up his bun again.

"I showed her my bedroom."

"Oh—"

"Daddy's going to put a desk in there, with a proper lamp."

Josie picked up her coffee and took a long swallow.

"They want to get married quite soon. They want you to go."

Rufus nodded. Josie found a tissue in her pocket and blew her nose hard.

"I'll write back then, shall I, and say you'd—like to?"

"Yes," Rufus said. He took another enormous bite of his burger and said through it, "Elizabeth can ice skate. She said she'd teach me."

"You can't mind," Matthew said.

"What can't I mind?"

"Tom getting married again."

Josie was stacking plates in the sink.

"It's not his getting married—"

"Oh?"

"It's this Elizabeth woman."

"You don't know anything about her except what Rufus told you, which was good. She sounds fine."

Josie turned slowly round and leaned her back against the sink, pushing her hair off her face.

"But I'll have to share Rufus."

"Only occasionally."

"He's been mine and only mine all my life."

Matthew pushed his coffee mug away from him.

"You don't know that Elizabeth wants to change that. You don't even know if she wants him—" He stopped abruptly. Danger zones loomed. "Why," Josie had said, in tears after their disastrous Christmas, "am I supposed to love your children when nobody expects them to even *try* and love me?"

"She said she'd teach him to skate—"

"That could just be manners," Matthew said. "He's a nice little boy, and she's in love with his father."

"Yes," Josie said. It was unsettling to think of another woman being in love with Tom. She might not want Tom herself, but the thought of Tom and his house being taken over by someone else was not conducive to a quiet mind, either. There had been a moment in the burger bar when she thought Rufus was going to remind her, with inescapable logic, that as she had Matthew, and had chosen to have Matthew, how could she possibly object to Tom having Elizabeth? But he had said nothing, only allowed an eloquent pause to fall, and had then finished everything on his plate except the salad items and asked, suspecting quite accurately that nothing this afternoon would be denied him, for another milkshake and a chocolate brownie. On the way home he had even held her hand.

"It's better for everyone," Matthew said. He stood up, rattling the change in his trouser pockets. "Rufus doesn't have to worry about Tom being lonely, and you don't have to feel guilty about leaving him." He came round the table and kissed her. "It's *good* news."

She looked up at him.

"It's—just that mother love is such a killer."

"Father love isn't a picnic, either."

"Sorry—"

"At least Rufus lives with you."

"Matt, I'm sorry, I shouldn't have said it—"

"Just think," Matthew said. He put the back of his hand briefly against her cheek. "Sometimes, just think before you speak."

She nodded. She wanted to say to him that, however bad things were for him, being without his children, he didn't labor all the time under everyone else's impossible expectations of him. If he got things right, everyone applauded; if he failed, they shrugged and said, "Oh well, poor bugger, at least he tried." Whereas for her, for women . . .

"I've got to go and do some work," Matthew said gently. "Sorry."

"Of course—"

"Just an hour or so. We've got one of these government assessment inspections coming up—"

"I know."

He kissed her again.

"Thanks for supper."

He went out of the kitchen, collecting the canvas briefcase in which he kept his papers, and up the stairs to the first floor. The landing light was on, and Rufus's bedroom door was slightly ajar. Cautiously Matthew put his head in. The room was in darkness, and by the light coming in from the landing, Matthew could only see Rufus's outline, humped under his duvet with his pillow, as usual, on the floor. Across the room, the other bed—Rory's bed, in Matthew's mind—lay empty.

He turned away and, with the use of a hooked pole, pulled down the extending ladder that gave access to the roof space. Up there, Matthew had made himself a study. It was small, and inevitably makeshift, but it was the only space and the only privacy that 17 Barratt Road afforded for his box files and folders. Josie had wanted to adorn it for him, soften it with paint and fabric, but he had declined. It was a working space, a thinking space, and its lack of domestic comfort and natural light gave it a seclusion he valued. It was also becoming—and he had the odd twinge of guilt about this, having promised himself openness in all things with Josie—the place where he could think freely about his children.

Of course, he told himself, he could think about them anywhere. His thoughts were his own, after all. But there was something constrained in his thinking about them because—and it was no good attempting to delude himself about this—she couldn't see anything likable, let alone lovable, in any of them. To be sure, they had given her a relentlessly hard time ever since she had come into their father's life, but Matthew doubted that Josie, even though she paid lip service to the idea, really had any notion at all of the degree of loyalty that Nadine demanded of them. Christmas had been appalling, he knew that. His children's behavior toward Josie, particularly Becky's, had been equally appalling. And he had been so torn between the two that he had ended up passive, helpless and despising himself for his own weakness.

"Stand up to her!" Josie had cried on Christmas night. "Why don't you stand up to her!"

He had been so heartsick and weary, he remembered, that he had briefly wondered why he'd started all this, why he'd ever hoped he could be free of the past.

"Because," he'd said, not looking at her, "she'd only take it out on the children. Whatever I do, I have to think of whether it'll make it worse for the children."

He sat down at his desk now and switched on both lamps. The plywood walls he had put up served as pinboards, too, and in front of him was a patchwork of photographs of his children, taken at all ages, in the bath, on bicycles, by the sea, in the garden, at the Tower of London, asleep, in fancy dress, in solemn school groups. He put his elbows on his desk and propped his chin in his hands. In the midst of the pictures was one he liked particularly of Rory, in pajamas and a cowboy hat, holding a kitten that had succumbed soon after to cat flu. Rory must have been about six. His expression was stern, full of protective responsibility. Nadine had rung Matthew several times recently—and always at school—to say that Rory was playing truant. Not often and not with other boys, but the local farmer had found him in his yard a couple of times, and his school had noticed that, while he was there for morning and afternoon registration, he was often absent for subsequent lessons. She had been, inevitably, loud with reasons for Rory's behavior but had refused, as yet, to allow Matthew to do anything about it.

"Then why ring?"

"Because you're his father."

"When you'll let me be."

He'd had to put the telephone down after that, hurriedly, fearful that the school secretary would hear Nadine's abuse through the thin wall that divided her office from his own. Rory was preoccupying, of course he was, but at the moment Nadine was refusing to let him, or his sisters, come to Sedgebury. They were settling, she said. They were all at last settling as a new little family, and she didn't want them disturbed by contact with a stepmother they detested. Matthew's solicitor had said he must be patient.

"Give it a month or two. Don't give her the fun of a fight. If you haven't seen the kids by Easter, then we'll start some action."

Matthew closed his eyes. Was he, he wondered, romanticizing his own children because he missed them? Did he excuse them all the glowering and sulking and whining he knew they possessed in full measure, because their absence was a permanent pain? Was it missing them that made him sometimes brusque with Rufus, who seldom merited any brusqueness? Rufus was so young. Sometimes, looking at the back of Rufus's neck when his head was bent over a bowl of cereal or his homework, Matthew could see the baby in him still, and when he saw that, he would think of Rufus as a baby and then of the inevitable manner of his conception, and a wave of sexual jealousy—deep, wild, hopelessly irrational—of Tom Carver would almost knock the breath out of him.

"Matt?"

He turned. Josie's head and shoulders were through the opening in the landing ceiling.

"Hey, I didn't hear you—"

"I took my shoes off. Are you OK?"

"So-so."

"I shouldn't have said that about mother love. I shouldn't have implied—"

"It's all right."

"I was thinking—"

"What?"

"If they won't come here, do you want to go and see them at— at her place?"

He smiled at her.

"I don't think so. The lion's den—"

"Or somewhere neutral. I mean, I don't have to come."

"You wouldn't want to—"

"I'd like to want to," Josie said. "But it's difficult to want to when you're so plainly not wanted in return."

"I know."

"Matt—"

"Yes?"

"It's hard, isn't it?"

"Yes. But not impossible."

"What happens," Josie said, "when it does get impossible?"

"I don't know," he said. He leaned out of his chair and touched her nearest hand, holding onto the wooden frame of the opening. "We'll have to wait and see."

"I'LL SELL IT," Elizabeth said. She stood with her arm through Tom's, looking up at the house she had bought only months before.

"You've only just bought it."

"I know."

"You could keep it and do it up and sell it at a profit."

"I can't be bothered," Elizabeth said. "And I'm not interested anymore. I'm grateful to it, but it's not going to be my life now."

He pressed her arm against him.

"Good."

"I asked my father if he would like it, and he said he had vertigo just thinking about it."

"What did he say," Tom said, "about you marrying me?"

"I think he thinks you're a safe bet."

"In what sense?"

"Past the male menopause and old enough to know your own mind."

"I know *that*, all right."

Elizabeth scuffed at some dead leaves round her feet.

"In fact, I think he's less surprised than I am. That I'm getting married, I mean. I'm amazed."

"That anyone should take pity on your single state?"

She looked at him, without smiling.

"Yes," she said. Then she looked back up at the house. "I suppose Dale wouldn't like it?"

"Dale—"

Dale had been very effusive, to Elizabeth. They had met several times, always in Tom's company, and Dale had been extremely hostessy, fussing round Elizabeth with cups of tea and extra cushions and conversation. She told Elizabeth how much she loved her family home.

"I've known it all my life, you see. I came home from being born in the hospital to it and never really went away, except to school. I hated school. Did you? And I hate this flat I'm in now. It's so impersonal."

"Why do you mention Dale?" Tom said now.

"Because she said she hated her flat. And she doesn't like Bristol—this is home. So maybe—"

"I don't think so."

"Too big?"

"Too close," Tom said.

"To us?"

"Yes."

"Come *on*," Elizabeth said. "We're all grown up and Dale has her own life and in any case she's shown absolutely no resentment toward me at all."

Tom smiled. He turned Elizabeth and began to walk her slowly back down the hill.

"Too close for me, then."

"But you love her."

"Dearly."

"What then?"

"She has an overwhelming quality, as you will discover. She can't help needing to know, needing to be involved—"

"Well, she's just been jilted."

"No doubt," Tom said, "for that very reason."

"I think I'll ask her anyway."

"About the house?"

"Yes."

"Don't."

Elizabeth stopped walking.

"What are you really trying to say to me?"

He paused, and then he said, "That I want to be married to you without a permanent extra around."

"Would she be?"

"Yes."

Elizabeth shrugged. "If you say so. But I think it's a bit hard."

He put his arm around her.

"Dearest, I'm thinking of you."

"Are you?"

"I remember Josie saying once—or screaming, to be truthful—that no woman in her right mind ever *wanted* to be a stepmother. I don't expect you want to be one, either."

"I don't mind—"

"Because you don't know. You don't yet know. But I know, because I've seen it. We must start as we mean to go on, which is without Dale fifteen minutes' walk away. Rufus is different."

"He's sweet," Elizabeth said warmly.

"And he's also a child. Not a complicated adult. Lucas, being a man, is a bit of both, but he is also independent."

"My father said——" She stopped.

"What?"

"That there ought to be training courses for stepmothers. Motherhood comes after nine months' preparation with a whole package of helpful emotions, but stepmotherhood is more like an unexploded bomb in the briefcase of the man you marry."

"How," Tom said, "would he know so much about it?"

Elizabeth pulled up her coat collar.

"He's been reading fairy stories, on my behalf. He says they've made him think."

Tom was laughing.

"He's wonderful——"

"I know."

Tom tightened the arm he had around her.

"But are you worried?"

She looked at him. His face was very close.

"About being a stepmother?"

"Yes."

She smiled. "Not in the least. We're hardly in Snow White country, are we?"

He kissed her.

"Do you know why I love you?"

"No, of course not."

"Well, for about a hundred reasons, but the hundred and first is because you are so *sane*."

Later that day he said, apologetically, that he had a client to see.

"I'll only be a couple of hours. But they're weekenders, so site visits with them are difficult."

"Of course."

"Why don't you," he said, "have a good look at the house. Without me."

"Heavens—"

"Well, you should. It's going to be your house, after all."

She pulled a face.

"You've had so many wives in here already—"

"Time to change it round then," he said. He was smiling at her. "Time to change it for you and me."

"Oh," she said, startled and pleased. "Oh—"

He kissed her.

"Think about it. Walk round the house, and think about what you'd like to change. It could be anything. Anything you want."

When he had gone, she sat where she was for a while, at the kitchen table, nursing the last half of a mug of tea. A sweet contentment lapped round her, filling the room, flowing peacefully over the sofa and chairs at the far end, over the table and worktops, over the bottles and jars and cups and jugs, over Basil, stretched along the window seat with his immense spotted belly exposed to the winter sun. It was hard to believe the last few months, hard to credit that the purchase of a house she didn't really want had turned out to be the manifestation of a submerged desire for change she wanted very much indeed, and which had come in a form she had given up hoping for, given up believing in. The house had drawn in Tom Carver, and with Tom's appearance a whole new extraordinary world was wheeling slowly into view, revealing itself as not just alluring but something she had, at some level, been longing for, for years.

Sitting here in Tom's kitchen—soon to be her kitchen—Elizabeth could acknowledge to herself at last, and with almost confessional relief, that it wasn't just wanting Tom that had overtaken her so powerfully. There was something else, another wanting, the desire, from the position of being a single, professional woman, for the peculiar domestic power of the married female: the presiding, the organizing, the quiet, subliminal dictatorship of laundry and Christmas turkeys and frequency of guests, the knowledge that one's own decision-making—based, very largely, on what one did and didn't like—lay at the heart of things. Elizabeth looked round the kitchen, her eye lighting upon this and that, a copper colander, a bottle of olive oil, a jug of wooden spoons, a stack of newspapers, a pair of reading glasses, a bunch of keys, a candlestick, and thought, with a sudden glow of happiness, "I'd like an open fire in here."

She got up, poured away the last inch of now cold tea, and put her mug in the dishwasher. Basil, hearing movement and hoping it indicated either the fridge or a promising cupboard being opened, rolled over onto his back, his huge paws doubled up, his deceptively sleepy gaze turned on the kitchen rather than the view. Elizabeth stooped to lay a hand on his tummy. He purred, not moving a whisker.

"You'll be my stepcat—"

She straightened up.

"Walk round the house," Tom had said. "Think about change."

She opened the kitchen door and went out into the narrow hall, elegantly floored in black and white. From it, the staircase rose to the first floor, where the drawing room was, looking into the street, and behind it, the bedroom where Tom had taken her, just after Christmas for the first time, and then many times since.

On a half-landing, there was a bathroom for that bedroom, projecting out from the back of the house above the ground-floor utility room, and then the stairs climbed on up to what Tom referred to as the children's rooms—Rufus's room, Dale's room, the room that had been Lucas's but that was now full of suitcases and metal racks holding Tom's architectural archives and Rufus's discarded toddler toys.

Elizabeth began to climb the stairs. It was Josie, Tom said, who had painted the walls yellow, a Chinese yellow, a much bolder color than Elizabeth would naturally have chosen, but she rather liked it. Josie, in any case, had left no threatening presence behind—she had gone because she had chosen to, because she had preferred something else, and in her absence her yellow walls looked impersonal and cheerful to Elizabeth. She put a hand out and patted the nearest space of wall.

"You can stay."

The drawing room was rather different. Pauline had liked it, Tom said, had used it, had chosen the elaborate, urban, feminine curtains and the fragile furniture. Josie had disliked it, had almost never even entered it and had made the far end of the kitchen into an alternative sitting room instead. There seemed to be no sign of Josie in the room but, instead, a feeling that she had never come in willingly to confront all those photographs of Pauline, on her own, with Tom, with her children, staring down from a portrait over the fireplace in a seventies gypsy dress with her hair in a fringe. Good-looking, Elizabeth thought, gazing up at her, good-looking as Dale was, with the same kind of finish and polish, the same physical assurance. Maybe I can't move the portrait, but perhaps just one or two of the photographs could go, and the curtains, and the frilly cushions? Maybe it would be tactfully possible to suggest to Tom that the room was a bit of a shrine, a little fossilized, a little overtaken, now, by change? She glanced down at the nearest photograph of Pauline. She was wearing a dress or a shirt with long, theatrical, drooping cuffs, and her hands were clasped round Dale, who was on her knee in a sundress. Dale looked very small, not much more than a baby with fat bare baby feet. Above her head, Pauline gazed out at the camera with composure, her dark hair smooth, her dark brows winged. Stealthily, Elizabeth put out a hand and turned the photograph until it was facing the wall behind it. Then she let out a little involuntary breath of relief.

Tom's bedroom, she could bypass. It was comfortable and undistinguished. Josie had put up curtains of rust-colored linen and then lost interest in going any further. In his year alone, Tom had allowed a comfortable masculine encroachment of his own possessions to spread across the room, clothes and shoes and compact discs and books. On the chest of drawers stood photographs of his children—there were three of Rufus—and behind them, half obliterated by a postcard reproduction of a Raphael Madonna propped against it, one of Pauline. There were none of Josie. Elizabeth had sometimes been on the point of asking to see a photograph of Josie but had never actually gathered up the courage to do so. Tom found it hard to speak of Josie with any charity, but Elizabeth felt obscurely that she was, in an odd way, some kind of ally, a silent supporter in the subtle war of independence against the impregnable perfection of the ghost of Pauline.

Elizabeth had only been on the top floor once, at Rufus's invitation, to see his bedroom. He had been very proud of it. He had shown her the airplane mobile he had made himself, a model destroyer he had decided not to start until his ninth birthday, the particular bedside lamp clipped to the headboard of his bed, his bean bag, the cupboard where he kept his collections—shells and stickers and pictures of watches cut out of magazines. Without him there, she could also open his hanging cupboard and his drawers and see his clothes hung and folded there, and his socks balled up in pairs and a striped elastic belt and a short made-up tie, on a loop of elastic. They were very poignant, these drawers, redolent of an innocent expectation that they would always go on being used, day in, day out, during the weeks and years of an uninterrupted childhood. Nothing, Elizabeth vowed, would be changed here, nothing would happen that wasn't instigated by Rufus, in case whatever frail sense of continuity that still remained was inadvertently damaged further. She reached into a drawer and patted the folded sweatshirts and pairs of jeans and then closed the drawer, almost with reverence.

Lucas had not occupied his room for six or seven years. He had moved out when he went to university, only using it as a parking space for the detritus of his life—cushions, music equipment, ski boots, lamps, a tennis racket, posters in cardboard tubes—between academic terms and the long wandering foreign trips he took each summer. With his first job had come his first flat, and he had removed almost all his possessions except for the cushions and posters, since his taste had by then progressed from primary colors and politics to monochrome and culture. The room felt raw and unused, and there was a patch of damp above the window that looked down into the charming little courtyard garden below and, either side of it, neighboring gardens of equal charm. But it was a pleasant room, a benevolent room. It was a room that might, in time, become—a nursery.

Elizabeth went out onto the landing. A faint sound from below caught her ear. She leaned over the banister rail and peered down.

"Tom?"

Silence. A motorbike in the street outside was kicked into

angry life, and the windows, as they always did in response to sudden and uncouth sound, shuddered elegantly. Elizabeth moved across the landing and turned the handle of Dale's closed door. It was locked.

"Nonsense," Elizabeth said aloud.

She turned the handle again, and shook it. She turned it the other way. It was locked, most decidedly. Elizabeth looked at it. Rufus's door had stickers on it, Lucas's, for some reason, a small brass knocker shaped like a ram's head. But Dale's had nothing. The smooth white paint stared back at Elizabeth as if defying her to guess what was beyond it. She crouched and put her eye to the keyhole. It was quite black, as if taped up from inside. Nothing could be more plain than that Dale regarded this room as her territory, as the place she had always had, as hers, all her life, and the place she intended to keep as hers, whatever.

Elizabeth stood up. Tom had told her about Dale, about the effect of her mother's death on a personality already volatile and needy, about the scene in the shadowy bedroom with Dale hysterical on the bed and Lucas, white-faced with fear and grief, looking on in stunned silence. Elizabeth had felt sorry for Dale, sorry for Tom, sorry for Lucas, all of them plunged into an abyss by the abrupt removal of the linchpin of their family life. She had listened with respectful sympathy. Her own life had never had any such drama in it: there had been silences—especially between herself and her mother—but never scenes. She had never felt, as she was now beginning to feel, entering the world of Tom's past and Tom's present, much rawness of emotion, much violence, the kind of atavistic human passion she had previously associated only with Greek tragedy, with Shakespeare. She looked at Dale's locked door and felt, for the first time, a tiny twinge of apprehension that some things—emotional things—might not be capable of being dealt with just by calm and reasonableness. She gave herself a little shake. Don't, she told herself in the voice her mother used to use to her, be melodramatic. That door is locked because Dale did not get on at all with her first stepmother. She has, on the contrary, been nothing but nice to you.

She turned away from the landing and began to go slowly down the stairs. You can't be too careful, a colleague at work had said to her the previous week; you can't go too slowly, you can't be too patient. But I must, Elizabeth thought now, be myself, too, I must be allowed to be Tom's wife in my way, to live in this house as my house. She paused outside the drawing room. I must make that room mine, not Pauline's. Even if one remembers the dead, and with love, one shouldn't live with them as if, somehow, they weren't really dead at all.

She straightened her shoulders. She would go down to the kitchen and start making plans for her fireplace, for, perhaps, rather less aggressively modern chairs than the ones Josie had chosen, and she would also go down into the garden and poke about among the unswept leaves from the previous autumn, to see what was lurking there and beginning to stir to life. She descended the last flight of stairs to the hall and went into the kitchen. Dale, in a navy blue blazer and sharply pressed jeans, was standing by the table, reading Tom's post.

"Dale!"

Dale looked up, smiling. She didn't put the letter in her hand down. She looked absolutely at ease.

"Hi!"

"How did you get in? I didn't hear the bell. Perhaps Tom didn't latch the door—"

"Key, of course," Dale said. She dipped a hand in her blazer pocket and produced a couple of keys on a red ribbon. "My keys."

Elizabeth swallowed.

"Do—I mean, do you often do that?"

Dale was still smiling, still holding a letter of Tom's in her other hand.

"What?"

"Let yourself in—"

Dale said, laughing, "When I need to. This is my home, after all."

Elizabeth went over to the kettle, so that her back was toward Dale.

"Would you like some tea?"

"There isn't any. I've looked."

Elizabeth said quietly, "I bought some Lapsang this morning."

Dale looked surprised.

"Where is it?"

"Here."

"Oh, but tea doesn't live there. It lives in that cupboard, by the coffee."

"That seems a long way from the kettle—"

"It's always lived there," Dale said. She put the letter down. "I see Dad's got across the planning boys again."

Elizabeth opened her mouth to say, "*Should* you be reading your father's correspondence?" and closed it again. She ran water into the kettle.

"Is Dad out?"

"A site meeting—"

"Damn. My car's playing up."

"Do you want him to have a look at it?"

"No," Dale said. She was grinning. "I want him to pay for it."

"But—" Elizabeth said, and stopped. She plugged the kettle in and picked up the packet of tea.

"He started when I was a student and he's just sort of gone on. Look, I'll make tea. You sit down."

"I'm fine—"

"You shouldn't be doing the work," Dale said. She came past Elizabeth, opened the cupboard, took out a teapot Elizabeth had never seen before, and went back, past Elizabeth again, taking the tea packet out of her hand. "Were you looking at the house?"

"Yes—"

"The drawing room's lovely, isn't it? It was the only room Mummy had really finished when she died. The portrait was painted by a friend of hers who was just getting famous, a Royal Academician and all that, and just after he'd finished it, he was killed mountaineering in Switzerland. I've always thought it was kind of prophetic, especially as he was in love with her."

"Was he?"

"Oh yes," Dale said airily. "Everybody was."

Elizabeth went over to the window seat and nudged Basil to make room for her.

"Did you have a good week?"

Dale sighed. She began to bang mugs and cupboard doors about and to clatter noisily in the fridge, looking for milk.

"So-so. I was just a bit tense about the car, all those miles. I had to go to Jersey and Guernsey on Wednesday—that's always rather a lark. But the rest was South Wales. I don't know what they read in South Wales, but it certainly isn't what I'm trying to sell."

Elizabeth began to stroke Basil's warm plushy side.

"Surely your company will mend your car for you?"

Dale pulled a face.

"I've exceeded my repair allowance already, and I've used it a bit more privately than I'm supposed to. I don't think it's serious but there's something knocking and you can get a bit wound up about that sort of thing on motorways. Dad gave me a carphone, thank goodness, only last week, and that's made a huge difference." She spooned tea into the teapot—too much, Elizabeth noticed, and said nothing. "Do you know how long Dad will be?"

"About another hour, I should think."

"The thing is," Dale said in a confidential tone, "I rather want to ask him about something other than the car—"

"Oh?"

"I want to move," Dale said. "I want another flat." She poured boiling water into the teapot, and then pulled a chair away from the table so that she was close to Elizabeth. "In fact, I've seen one."

Elizabeth glanced at her.

"Have you?"

"Yes. It needs everything done to it. I mean *everything*."

"But your father's an architect—"

"So handy, isn't it? But it's money again, really."

Elizabeth thought of her house, which, although she no longer wanted it, she felt an absurd responsibility for, because of what it had brought her. She steeled herself.

"There's my house—"

Dale smiled. She leaned over and patted Elizabeth's arm, then she got up to pour the tea.

"Thank you. That's really sweet of you. In fact, I'll confess I went and had a bit of a snoop. But it's a bit *permanent* for me, a house. A bit committed. Do you know what I mean?"

"Don't you want to feel permanent?"

"Not till I've got somebody to be permanent with me. I thought, you see—"

"I know. I'm so sorry."

Dale carried the two mugs over to the window seat and held one out to Elizabeth.

"Dad's been so supportive. And Lucas. Have you met Lucas?"

"Not yet. We are having lunch with him and Amy tomorrow."

Dale's face changed.

"Oh. Are you? I didn't know—"

Elizabeth took a sip of tea. Time for another small display of conscious generosity. Without looking up she said, "Why don't you come?"

"Why didn't Dad say?"

"I don't know."

"I spoke to him yesterday. Why didn't he say?"

Elizabeth looked up at her. The smiling composure was gone.

"My dear, I don't know. But come along, come along and join us."

Dale stared at her tea, her face dark. Then she retrieved a smile.

"Yes. Yes, of course I will. And now, if you'll excuse me, I'll just go and rummage about upstairs for some things I need."

"Of course."

Dale moved over to the door. By it she paused, looking back over her shoulder. Her voice was very kind.

"Make yourself comfortable," she said.

Upstairs, it didn't look to her as if anything had changed. Tom and Elizabeth were presumably sleeping together—that was something, Dale decided, simply to avert one's mind from—but Elizabeth appeared to have left not so much as a toothbrush. When Josie had started sleeping with Tom, Dale remembered, she'd arrived wholesale as it were; her clothes in his cupboard, her pots and bottles in his bathroom, her shoes kicked off on the floor in front of the television. Dale had once found a long red hair stuck to the side of the kitchen sink. She had wanted to be sick.

But Elizabeth was different. Climbing the stairs to the top floor and taking her keys out of her pocket, Dale told herself firmly that she must remember—and make the *effort* to remember—how different Elizabeth was. She had even made herself say so, as proof of her good intentions, to Lucas and Amy.

"I may not want her," Dale had said. "I may not want Dad to marry again, ever, but if he's going to, she's OK. She's different."

"What kind of different?" Amy said. Amy had liked Josie, who had been kind to her and allowed her to practice new makeup techniques on her. They'd had a lot of laughs together, up in that bathroom. Josie had been fun.

"A quiet professional," Dale said. "Very decent. And not clinging. She isn't all over Dad all the time."

Lucas said, teasing, "There wouldn't be room for two of you." Dale ignored him.

"I feel better, now I've met her. I really do."

"She sounds pretty boring," Amy said.

"She is. But that's fine. Fine by me."

Lucas had looked at her, a long, hard look.

"She'll still be his wife, Dale."

"What do you mean?"

"Wives come first."

"No—"

"They do."

"Not always. Not necessarily. Only if they insist on it."

She put the key into the lock on her bedroom door, and turned it. She could never see her bedroom without emotion, never enter it without a rush of remembering enveloping her, all those years of remembering, intense years in which she had battled with so much, with grief, with longing, with the knowledge that she must one day leave home, and the terror of doing it. When she had met Neil, she had packed up half the room in an extraordinary spirit of release, only taking one photograph of her mother and nothing from her teenage years. She had been exhilarated, proud of herself, congratulating herself on taking only things that would contribute to the future, not detain her damagingly in the past. But even then, even when she left to live with Neil, she had taped up the keyhole and locked the door behind her. Josie wasn't a snoop, but she wasn't on Dale's side, either. In any case, Pauline had to be protected from Josie, who was openly jealous, Dale told Neil, if you can believe that it's possible—or seemly—to be jealous of a woman dead at thirty-two when you're alive yourself. And Dale's bedroom was full of Pauline.

She went over to her dressing table, her teenage dressing table flounced, at her thirteen-year-old request, in pink and white, and laid the key on the glass-covered top. She looked round her. Composedly, from many angles, her mother looked back at her. Elizabeth Brown was nice, Dale was certain of that; she was nice and decent and a bit boring, but for all that, she was marrying Dale's father, and in consequence, Dale's bedroom would have to stay locked. Not just for present privacy, but to safeguard the past, Dale's past: Dale's childhood.

10

"BUT THIS IS the third time," Clare's form teacher said. "The third time this week you've said you couldn't do your homework."

"I can't," Clare said. She was wearing the approximation of school uniform that most of the kids wore, and the hem of her skirt had come down at one side. She didn't seem to have noticed.

"Is there somewhere at home you can do your homework?" the teacher said.

Clare thought of the kitchen.

"There's a table."

"Is it quiet?"

It was quiet, Clare reflected, if her mother wasn't in the kitchen but was upstairs in her studio making clay coil pots, which were her new passion. There was clay everywhere. The bottom of the bath was gritty with it.

"Yes."

"Then really you have no excuse. Your brother and sister have homework, don't they?"

"Yes."

"Where do they do theirs?"

Clare considered. Becky spent angry half-hours on the floor of their bedroom with music on so loudly it made Nadine scream, and emerged announcing the shitty stuff was done. Rory never seemed to do any homework at all. He took his school bag into his burrow, but Clare didn't think he even opened it. They both gave Clare the strong impression that not only was it not cool to do homework, but it was utterly pointless to do it. Homework was for nothing, it was just some meaningless discipline devised by teachers for their own obscure ends. Clare was not sure she believed this. Something in her didn't mind homework, no doubt part of the same thing that didn't mind school, either. It was nice belonging, it was nice going somewhere every day that stayed the same, that treated you the same as everyone else. It wasn't rebelliousness that prevented Clare from doing her homework, but hopelessness. Every night, she got her books out and put them in the space she'd cleared in the remains of the last meal that was almost always still there, and sat down in front of them. And sat there. She sat and stared and could do nothing. She couldn't look at words, she couldn't pick up a pencil.

"Where," the teacher said patiently, "do your brother and sister do their homework?"

Clare looked at her. She was young, with a round face and brown curly hair. Clare would have hated to have had curly hair.

"Around somewhere—"

"Clare," the teacher said. "You *must do* your homework. Do you understand? You must do it, not because I say so, but so I can see if you understand what you've been taught in class."

Clare nodded. She felt, in the face of such a reasonable explanation, that she must be truthful in reply.

"But I can't."

"What d'you mean?"

"I can't do it."

"Do you mean, you don't understand it?"

"No," Clare said. "But when I get home I can't do anything."

The teacher regarded her. She looked tired, but then so many of the kids looked tired, with unsupervised television sets in their bedrooms and parents too weary for repetitive discipline.

"Is your mother at home? When you get home?"

Clare nodded.

"Maybe I should talk to her—"

"No," Clare said.

"Why not?"

Clare said, quoting Nadine, "We've got to make a go of it."

"Because," the teacher said delicately, "you're on your own?"

Clare nodded again. Her eyes were filling. She hadn't seen Matthew for six weeks and three days, and there'd been a battle that morning when Nadine had wanted to wash the Disneyland tracksuit.

"You'll shrink it!"

"I won't—"

"You will, you will, don't touch it, I don't want it washed—"

Nadine had snatched it from her, and when she was in the lavatory, Clare had retrieved it from the pile of dirty laundry and hidden it inside Rory's duvet cover. There'd be trouble, when Nadine arrived to collect her and confronted her about the tracksuit.

"Can you have one more try tonight?" the teacher said.

Clare sighed. It wouldn't be any good. She said miserably, "I can't think."

"I see," the teacher said. She stood up. "Are you sure I can't talk to your mother?"

"Yes."

"Well, then I'd better talk to someone else."

Clare looked up at her, with a gleam of hope.

"My dad?" she said.

In the sitting room of the cottage, Becky sprawled on the sofa. It was broken-springed, inevitably, and she had padded the places where there were no springs at all, or they stuck up through the worn cretonne cover like spears, with a cushion and an old blanket. The television was on some kids' program with one of those pitiful over-zany presenters in big specs with scrubbing-brush hair, but Becky could hardly see it because of the snowstorm effect on the screen, as the reception was so bad. She didn't care. She didn't want to watch the program anyway; she just wanted the company of having the television on, the illusion of having people around, things happening.

It was cold in the sitting room. Becky had become quite adept at lighting fires, but there was something wrong with the way the wind was blowing, and the fire wouldn't burn up properly. She had rolled herself in the duvet off her bed, but even all wadded up like that, she felt cold inside, like you do when you're scared about something. She moved slightly, so that the cigarette packet in her jacket pocket wasn't pressing uncomfortably into her breast, and thought of what else was in that pocket. A white tablet, wrapped in foil, with a bird stamped on one side and smiley face on the other. A boy at school had given it to her. He'd said he could get a fiver for it, but he'd give it to her if she'd go out with him at the weekend. Clubbing, he said. He was a big, loose-limbed, heavy-looking boy from the year above Becky, and most of the time that he was talking to her and nonchalantly tossing the little foil packet from hand to hand, he was looking at her breasts.

Becky wasn't sure why she had accepted the foil packet. It was flattering, in a way, to be asked out, to be offered, as a bribe for going out, membership of a particular group, and the boy who'd asked her was definitely one of half a dozen or so in the school regarded as a catch. He had a reputation, of course, a name for wanting to go all the way, for refusing to wear a condom, for knowing the scene, but that made him dangerous, which in turn made him desirable. If she went out with him at the weekend, she couldn't pretend she didn't know what she was in for, and in any case, part of her wanted to be in for it very much, wanted to feel high and wild and sexy. And free. But there was another part. It was a part that had only grown up in her recently and whose constraining effect she resented very much. But she couldn't pretend it wasn't there. She couldn't tell herself, any longer, that as someone of not yet sixteen she had no responsibilities or obligations and shouldn't be asked to have any. Burdens had arrived, whether she wanted them or not, with her parents' divorce, and the most complicated of those burdens was Nadine. Nadine was a mother, a mother three times over, but she wasn't what you thought of when you said the word *mother* to yourself. She was more, Becky was coming to realize, like someone who needed a mother herself, a higher authority who'd help her get her act together. Becky could see—she thought the others could see, too, by the way they were behaving—that things were slipping out of control. It wasn't just the household things, it was more a feeling that Nadine didn't know where she was going or what the next days or weeks were for, and her fear of not knowing hung around her, almost like a smell.

If Becky went clubbing with Stu Bailey on Saturday night and took her Ecstasy tablet and ended up having sex—for the first time—in a multistory car park at four in the morning, she might feel she'd made it. she might feel she'd broken out of some cage and was at last flying free, but she'd still have to come home sometime afterward, sometime later, and find Nadine. It might be worth it, it might be worth anything Nadine could say or do, to get right out of their tangle of troubles for a single night and blow her mind. But then, on the other hand, it might not. You couldn't separate things, Becky was unhappily coming to realize, you couldn't do a thing and then not expect the consequences to come trolling back sometime later and smack you in the face. It was a risk she was facing, if she went out with Stu Bailey, and even if she wanted the risk, she wasn't sure she could face the consequence.

She sat up and took her cigarettes out of her pocket and lit up. Then she took out the Ecstasy tablet and unwrapped it. It looked as innocent as glucose. She sniffed it and then, with a small leap of excitement, licked it. It tasted of nothing. It smelled of nothing. It lay on her palm smiling up at her. It would cost her, it occurred to her, five pounds—her last five pounds—to own it, and at the same time to be free of Stu Bailey and his stare fixed on her breasts. If she wanted to be free, that is. If she wanted not to be wanted anymore, never mind what he wanted her for. And he'd want her more if she turned him down, anyway.

She folded the foil back carefully round the tablet and put it in her pocket. Her cigarette tasted sour and tired. She closed her eyes for a moment. She ought to go for it, she knew that, she ought to take the brief power to decide that had been handed to her and use it any way she bloody well wanted. But . . . She opened her eyes and chucked her cigarette into the sulking fire. Suppose Nadine found out? Suppose Stu Bailey really hurt her? Suppose . . . Becky leaned forward and turned the volume up on the television until the room seemed to judder and then she flung herself back down on the sofa and pulled the duvet over her head.

"That's the fifth time," Tim Huntley said. He stood, legs astride, hands on hips, in Nadine's kitchen, looking down at her. She was sitting at the table. Beyond her, with a rip in his black school blazer, stood Rory, leaning against the refrigerator and fiddling with the plastic magnets on the door.

"I'm sorry," Nadine said. Her voice was low.

"A farm isn't a play place," Tim said. He looked from Nadine to Rory. "A farm's lethal. It's not just the machines, it's the poisons. I've got enough weedkiller there to finish off half Hereford. And a gun. You're lucky I didn't turn the gun on you."

Rory mumbled.

"What?" Nadine said.

"I wasn't doing nothing—"

"You were *there*," Tim said. "You were there, without my knowledge or permission. If you're there, a stranger, you might do yourself harm and you might cause harm, too. A cow might miscarry, you might spread an infection—"

Rory bent low over the refrigerator door.

"Sorry—"

"I should think so. Why weren't you at school, anyway?" He looked at Nadine. "Why wasn't he at school?"

She was trembling slightly.

"I thought he was."

"I don't like it," Rory said, and then, muttering, "It's boring."

Tim moved forward and leaned on the table.

"That's no excuse. It's the law you have to go to school, and it's the law you have to stay there."

Nadine glanced at Rory.

"Are you being bullied?"

He shook his head.

"What's wrong, then?"

He hesitated. Then, with a sweep of his hand, he detached all the magnets from the door and sent them scattering across the floor.

"I can't stay there," he said. "I can't stay here, I can't—" His voice shook a little.

"You got homework?" Tim asked.

Rory nodded.

"Why don't you go and do it, then? While I have a word with your mum?"

Rory kicked the refrigerator.

"I'm hungry—"

"I expect you know where the bread bin is."

Nadine stood up.

"I'll get it—"

Tim watched her. He noticed, as she sliced the bread and spread it clumsily with peanut butter, that her hands were shaking. Rory didn't offer to help her. Tim opened his mouth to tell him to get off his idle backside, and closed it again. He'd shouted at Rory enough for one day, hauling him out physically from the shed where the tractors lived and ripping his blazer in the process. Rory had accepted the shouting mutely. He hadn't seemed frightened, and he hadn't seemed sullen. He just appeared to accept what Tim was bellowing as more of the same, more of what he was already tiredly used to. Tim had flung him into the Land Rover bodily, like a sack or an animal carcass, and had then relented and given him half a chocolate bar that was lurking in the mess in the glove compartment. Rory had pretty well swallowed it whole.

"There," Nadine said. She gave Rory the sandwiches on a plate and then leaned forward and kissed him. "Don't worry."

He didn't look at her. He took the plate and began to shamble toward the door.

"Thank you," Tim Huntley said loudly, commandingly.

Rory paused briefly.

"Thanks."

"That's OK," Nadine said.

Rory went out of the room, letting the door bang behind him. They heard him cross the tiles of the hall and then begin to climb the stairs, his tread slow and unsteady, like the tread of someone very much older than twelve.

"I expect he'll eat it in bed," Nadine said.

"In bed—"

"He's made himself a sort of bedroom under the eaves. It's very private. He won't let any of us in there." She looked at Tim. "Coffee?"

"Please," he said. He pulled out a chair from the table and sat down on it, resting his forearms on the table top. He looked at Nadine. "We've been discussing you, Mum and me."

"Oh."

"You're not coping, are you?"

Nadine filled the kettle, plugged it in, and put two mugs, very precisely, beside each other on the countertop.

"If it's any business of yours."

"We're neighbors," Tim said. "This is the country, not some bloody town where you could drop dead and nobody'd notice." He paused, and then he said, "There were kids here, four or five years back. Living with their dad in a caravan. If you can call it living. He was useless, the dirty devil. Stoned or smashed half the time. The littlest kid got killed on the Ross road, hit by a truck, wandering about on her own, famished. The other kids got taken into care, and their dad vanished. We knew they were there, Mum and me. But we didn't know how bad it was. We didn't know the half until the little girl got killed."

Nadine said nothing. She spooned coffee into the two mugs and screwed the lid back on the jar, very carefully.

"You know what's going on, don't you?" Tim said.

Nadine put her hand on the kettle handle.

"About what—"

"Your kids."

She bowed her head.

"It's not just the boy pitching off half the time," Tim said. "Is it? It's the girls, too. The little 'un looks half-starved, and the big one's playing around with one of the Bailey boys."

"Who," Nadine said tightly, "are the Baileys?"

Tim grunted.

"You wouldn't want to know. They're a load of trouble. Four boys as bad as their dad. You don't want your girl mixed up with the Baileys."

The kettle blew a noisy stream of steam into the air and switched itself off. Nadine, holding her wrist with the other hand to steady it, poured water into both mugs.

"Milk?"

"Please."

"Sugar?"

"Two," Tim Huntley said. "Cheers." He watched her set a mug down in front of him. Then she sat down herself, opposite.

"Becky is in the sitting room," Nadine said, "doing her homework. I take her to school every day and I collect her every day and I know where she is, all the time."

Tim eyed her.

"You don't know what she's doing at school. And you can't keep her shut in forever." He thought, briefly, of Becky's overdeveloped, ungirlish figure. "She'll break loose soon. One trip to Hereford or Gloucester, and you'll have lost her."

Nadine bent her head over her coffee.

"Go away."

"Look—"

"Go away!"

Tim Huntley leaned forward.

"Don't shout, because I'm not going. I haven't come to interfere, I've come to help you stop something before it starts, before your kids really lose it."

Nadine lifted both hands and put them in front of her face.

"We're getting there, we are—"

"No, lady," Tim said. "You aren't. And if I find your boy in my yard again, without my permission, I'm calling the rozzers."

Nadine took her hands away and stared at him, aghast.

"You wouldn't!"

"I would. For his sake, for yours. It's no help to anyone to be allowed to run wild."

"I don't *allow* it."

"But you can't stop it. And soon there'll be more you can't stop."

Nadine said, unsteadily, "We've had a bad time. We—well, we got thrown out, or at least, that's what it amounted to."

"Sorry," Tim said. "Why you got here's nothing to me. It's what happens now that counts."

Nadine swallowed.

"I—don't know what happens now."

"You shouldn't live alone," Tim said. "You look to me like you've had a bit of a breakdown. You should live with other people. Maybe that commune place over toward Hay." He looked at the clay around Nadine's fingernails. "Art and stuff. Gardening."

Nadine closed her eyes. She said, in the most decided voice she had yet used in this conversation, "I love my children."

Tim hesitated a moment, and then he said, "There's something else."

"What?"

"Their dad's a headmaster, isn't he? The lad said—"

"Deputy," Nadine said with contempt.

"Maybe—"

She fixed him suddenly with her penetrating blue stare.

"What?"

"Maybe," Tim said, cradling his coffee mug. "Maybe you should let their dad take his turn for a while?"

Matthew sat by the telephone in the sitting room. He sat very quietly, as if his quietness might suggest to Josie, next door in the kitchen, that he was still speaking. He needed her to think that because he needed time to think, himself.

It had been Nadine on the telephone. She seldom rang him at home—had hardly rung him anywhere, except twice about Rory, for over a month—and Josie had answered the telephone.

"Hello," she said, and then her expression blanked. Matthew took a breath.

"I'll get him," Josie said. She held the receiver out to him. "For you."

He took it. Josie was looking at him, as if she wanted something badly and he was supposed to guess what it was. Slowly, he turned his back, putting the receiver to his ear.

"Hello."

Josie rushed past him into the kitchen and slammed the door, shudderingly. Nadine was crying. She was crying and crying the other end of the telephone, and through the crying she was trying to accuse him of all the things she had always accused him of.

"There's no point to this," Matthew said, disgusted.

"There is! There is!"

"Then tell me," he said. "Cut the abuse and *tell* me."

He heard her blowing her nose violently.

"They're in bed," she said. "They can't hear me."

Matthew waited. She blew her nose again. Then she said, "They're coming to you."

"What?"

"They're in trouble," Nadine said. Her voice was now a fierce, hoarse whisper. "They're playing truant and not doing their homework and getting into bad company. That's what you've done to them, that's what's happened because you—"

"Shut up," Matthew said. He was gripping the telephone receiver.

"You made the problem," Nadine said. "You got them into this. Now you get them out."

"What's brought this on—"

"You know, you two-timing bastard, what brought this on!"

Matthew took a deep breath.

"You want the children to come here—"

"I don't *want* it!"

"Okay, okay, the children are to come here. Permanently? School and everything?"

Nadine said faintly, "Yes."

"Have you asked them?"

"No."

"Before you start shipping them wholesale about the place, hadn't you better ask them?"

Nadine said, spitting the words out separately, "There isn't any point."

"Because you don't intend them to have any choice?"

She shouted, "Because there isn't one! If you don't help, if they go on like this, if something happens, then we'll *neither* of us have them!"

"What?"

"There's someone watching me," Nadine said unsteadily, "someone who saw some other children go wrong, someone who—" She stopped.

"Might report you?" Matthew said.

Nadine said nothing. He could hear her breathing, quick and ragged. Something close to pity stirred in him for a second, and then stilled.

"I see," he said. He glanced toward the closed kitchen door. His heart was rising in him, with a sudden, luminous happiness. He said, trying to keep his voice empty of all potentially provocative emotion, "Do you want to discuss arrangements now?"

"No."

"Tomorrow? I'll call you from school—"

"Okay," she said. She was beginning to cry again.

He opened his mouth to say, "Give them my love," and closed

it again, in case his rejoicing betrayed itself. Instead he said, "Till tomorrow then. Bye," and put the phone down.

Then he sat there. He sat beside the quiet telephone, with his eyes closed, and said thank you, fervently, to somebody. His children back, his children home again, his children where he could encourage them, protect them, supervise them, see them as he hadn't seen them for almost eighteen months in the precious, trivial course of ordinary daily dull family life. He felt almost dizzy, almost tearful. He had been gearing himself up for the last few weeks for a protracted, ugly, exhausting wrangle with Nadine about the children, about reasonable access to them, about even being able to telephone them in some kind of freedom—and he had never dreamed that this might be the alternative, that he might simply be handed the children with a suddenness that almost knocked him over. He said their names to himself. He visualized them.

"Thank you," he said silently. "Thank you, thank you."

He opened his eyes. Across the room, the kitchen door stood firmly shut. Behind it, he could hear Josie clattering things in the kitchen and the sound of the classical music radio station she played all day, carrying the portable set around with her from room to room. He stood up. The first radiance of relief and happiness was dimming slightly. It was no good hoping Josie would share it. It was no good expecting Josie to greet the news of his children's coming to live with them with anything other than alarm. She might be horrified. She might be angry. She might, even, refuse. Matthew went across the sitting room and opened the kitchen door.

"Hi."

Josie was washing the saucepans left over from cooking their supper. She didn't turn round.

She said, "Why does she have to be so bloody dramatic?"

"She is dramatic," Matthew said. "She just is. Always has been." He came farther into the room and stood behind Josie. "And she was in a state tonight."

"So what's new?"

"Josie," Matthew said.

She turned round, holding a pan and a coiled wire scourer. Her hands were dripping with suds.

"What's happened?"

"Some kind of crisis. I don't know exactly what because I didn't ask because if I ask I get another earful about how it's all my fault—"

"The children?"

"Yes."

Josie put down the pan and scourer and wiped her hands on a tea towel.

"In trouble?"

"Yes."

"Serious trouble?"

"I don't know."

She looked at him. His eyes were alight. A small, cold dread settled heavily and suddenly in the pit of her stomach.

"Does she want you to go there?"

"No—"

Josie bit her lip. He put his arms round her, but she wouldn't let him pull her to him.

"Honey, she can't cope. She's sending them here."

"Here!" Josie said. "To live?"

"Yes." He leaned forward and kissed her unresponsive neck. "Yes, to live here, go to school here. With us."

Josie said nothing. He put his nose tip to tip with hers. He couldn't help smiling. "Is that okay?"

She closed her eyes for a moment, and then she said, in a hard, bright voice that neither of them recognized as hers, "Of course."

RUFUS LAY IN bed and looked at the curtains he had chosen
when he was four. They had flowers on them. Blue flowers on a
pale yellow background. For a year or two, he'd been so used to
them, he'd stopped seeing them, but now he'd noticed them again,
and they really embarrassed him. Surely, even if flowers were what
he thought he wanted when he was four, Josie should have had the
sense to deflect him onto something else? He looked at his desk. It
was new. It was sitting there waiting for him when he got to Bath,
and it had two drawers and an angled lamp on a hinge, like the
ones Tom had in his office. So far, Rufus hadn't done anything
with his desk except sit in the chair that went with it and slide the
drawers open and shut. They ran very well. Rufus admired that.
Elizabeth had given him a box of colored pencils, a huge box with
seventy-two pencils in it, all their colors shading gently from one
to another like a rainbow. They were artist's pencils, Elizabeth

said, and when she was about Rufus's age she had had a box exactly like that. Rufus thought he would not take the box of colored pencils back to Sedgebury but would keep them here, in one of his new desk drawers. Now that Rory was in the same bedroom with him all the time, there was very little privacy, and Rory's reaction to a box of colored artist's pencils was not something Rufus cared to think about.

He sat up in bed. It was very, very nice to be in that bed, in that room, to be alone and quiet. Dale was next door, of course, having suddenly decided to stay the night, but the walls of this house were thicker than the walls of what Rufus thought of as Matthew's house, so it was like being alone. When he got out of bed and pulled the curtains—which he would do quite soon because you couldn't see the flowers so well with the fabric scrunched up—he would see the view he knew he'd see, the back of the house opposite across two gardens with a tree between that grew pale green bracts in summer and dropped them all over the place like tiny primitive airplanes. In the winter, you could see the house opposite and watch the people in it brushing their teeth and reading the paper and vacuuming the carpet, but in summer the tree hid them from view. Once, a man saw Rufus watching him, and waved, and Rufus was appalled and pitched himself onto the carpet under the window, out of sight.

He got out of bed and padded over to the window, yanking the curtains as far sideways as they would go to squash the flowers up. The tree looked bare still, but a bit fuzzy, because of the new buds on its branches, some of which had minute little leaves beginning to come out of them. All the curtains and blinds in the house opposite were still drawn—it was Saturday after all—and down in the garden below, Rufus could see Basil, sitting by the stone girl

with the dove on her hand, washing one paw very slowly and carefully, over and over again. Washing—and only ever washing very
small sections of himself—seemed to be the only exercise he took.

Rufus went into the bathroom beside Dale's bedroom and had
a pee. Josie always said to pull the plug, but as she wasn't here to
say it, he didn't. He had a quick look in Dale's sponge bag. It was
very neat inside and smelled of scented soap, and beside it was one
of the elasticated velvet loop things she tied her hair back with.
Rufus picked it up and twanged it experimentally. Then he went
downstairs, jumping the last three steps of each flight, which he
had always done since he discovered, about two years ago, that if
you jumped at an angle you could also get a bit farther across each
half-landing at every jump. His father's bedroom door was open,
but the bed wasn't made, and there was the sound of an electric
razor whining away behind the bathroom door. Rufus gave the
door a friendly thump and sauntered on down to the kitchen.

"Hello," Elizabeth said. She was already dressed and was laying bowls and plates round the table.

He smiled, not looking at her, feeling suddenly shy.

"Sleep well?"

He nodded.

"Are you pleased with your new desk?"

He nodded again. "Brilliant."

She was opening cupboards. She said, with her back to him,
"Do you like eggs?"

"Yes," he said.

"How do you like them?"

He thought a moment.

"Cooked—"

"Yes," she said. She was laughing. "But scrambled, fried—"

He hitched himself onto a chair.

"Scrambled," he said.

"Won't you be cold, just in your pajamas?"

He shook his head. He looked at the cereal packets. They were all the muesli stuff Tom ate, nothing decent.

"I don't like muesli either," Elizabeth said, watching his expression. "It gets stuck in my teeth."

Rufus thought of the row of cereal packets at Sedgebury, six or seven of them, all different, all bought by Josie in an attempt to buy the right thing, to buy something Matthew's children would eat. They did eat them, too, but not at meals. They wouldn't even come to meals, sometimes, but there were cereal bowls all over the house and dropped bits on the stairs and floors. Rufus felt he was being a right little prig, coming to table when Josie called him, but he felt, even more strongly, that he didn't have a choice. He only had to look at her face—not angry so much, though she was, but kind of desperate, with big eyes—to believe he wanted to do something to make her feel better, and if sitting at the kitchen table made her feel better, then he'd do it. Even if he had to suffer for it, and sometimes he did.

Clare had said to Rory, last week, "Shouldn't we go? Shouldn't we go with Rufus?"

And Rory had snorted.

"Rufus?" he said. "Rufie Poofy? Who wants to do anything with a frigging baby like that?"

Elizabeth said now, "We could go out a bit later and get the sort of cereal you like. I just didn't know which one it was."

Rufus jerked his chair closer to the table.

"I like the really sugary ones but I'm not supposed to have them."

"Well, we won't buy one of those then," Elizabeth said.

Rufus eyed her. She gave him a quick smile and said, in the

firm, kind sort of voice the teachers in his Bath school used to use, "No cheating on your mother."

He thought a moment. He said, "I could tell her about the curtains—"

"What curtains?"

"In my room. They've got flowers on. I hate them."

"That's different," Elizabeth said. "Your room here is yours, for you to choose."

His face lit up.

"Is it?"

"Of course. Your room is quite different from your upbringing. I'm not going to break any of your mother's rules about you, but I'm sure you can have new curtains."

Rufus picked up a spoon and looked at his distorted reflected face in it.

"Wow."

"What would you like? What would you like instead?"

"Black, probably—"

"*Black*—"

"Or green. A nice green. Not that sad kind of green."

"Or blue?"

"No," Rufus said. "Everything's always blue."

Elizabeth broke eggs into a pan.

"Scrambled eggs then?"

"Yes," Rufus said and then, with emphasis because of having momentarily forgotten, "please."

"I wondered," Elizabeth said, stirring the pan, "if you'd like to come out with me this morning."

Rufus hesitated. The shy feeling, which had abated, crept back into his throat and made him look down at the table.

"To see my father. My father lives in Bath. I always go and see him at weekends. I suppose he will be your stepgrandfather."

Rufus breathed into the spoon he still held and then drew a worm in the mist, with his forefinger. He hadn't got a grandfather, of any kind. Josie's father had pushed off, and Tom's father was dead. So was his mother. They'd both died the year Rufus was born, which, Tom had said, trying to make a joke of it, was very careless of them. So Rufus only had Granny. Some people he knew had grandfathers who had fought in the war, real soldiers who'd fought the Germans and the Japanese.

"Was he in the war?" Rufus said.

Elizabeth lifted the pan off the cooker.

"He was a prisoner in Italy, for a lot of the war. He was only nineteen when the war started, a schoolboy really. He was wounded, so he couldn't run away, and then he was captured. Would you like your egg on some toast or by itself?"

Rufus looked at her. It occurred to him unexpectedly that he felt safe, there in the kitchen, with Elizabeth holding the egg pan and talking about her father being a prisoner in a very ordinary voice and the sun beginning to come in through the windows and show up all the little freckles on the glass, which were dried-up dirty raindrops. Rufus smiled, very quickly, and curled his bare toes round the stretcher of the chair he was sitting on.

"Toast, please," he said.

"So she's bringing the boy round, then?" Shane said. He had made Duncan buy a sponge mop on a pole so that he could wash the kitchen ceiling. The dust still lay soft and undisturbed on books and furniture, but the kitchen and bathroom were scoured to the bone and reeked of bleach.

"Yes," Duncan said. "Most odd. A sort of ready-made grandson."

"Is he a nice child, by all accounts?"

Duncan stirred the coffee he had just made for them both. Shane took four spoonfuls of sugar in his.

"Yes, he is. They're all nice. Tom's nice, his son's nice, his daughter's nice, his future daughter-in-law is perfectly all right—" He paused.

Shane stopped mopping and squeezed murky water from his sponge into a bucket.

"Well?"

"I probably shouldn't talk to you like this," Duncan said. "I probably shouldn't say it to anyone, but I'm very struck by something, very struck indeed."

Shane began again on the ceiling, making broad whitish tracks in the grime.

"Better out than in—"

"The thing is," Duncan said. He took a swallow of coffee. "The thing is, and I've no idea whether it's bad or good, that, most of my life, I've played in a nice, manageable little three-hander— me, my late wife, and my daughter. And now, with Elizabeth proposing to get married, I seem suddenly to be part of some mad musical with a very poor director and a cast of thousands. This child coming this morning has a mother somewhere who's married someone else with three children, and *they* all have a mother and an aunt and grandparents. It's bewildering, really it is. And I keep thinking—where will it stop?"

Shane clicked his tongue.

"I blame it on the pope."

"Do you?"

"Stands to reason. If man won't curb his own appetites, they'll have to be curbed for him."

"Are you talking about contraception?"

"What else?" Shane demanded.

"Ah," Duncan said. He picked up his mug and held it in both hands. "But I think the little boy I am to meet this morning was wanted. And is much beloved. Even my daughter, who has no reason to love him except the instincts of her own good nature, seems fond of him already."

Shane ran the sponge into a corner. He said piously, "My mother, God rest her soul, said each one of us was wanted, even my brother with no roof to his mouth and the eyes that wouldn't look the same way together. There were nine of us."

"Ah," Duncan said again. Shane's family background always sounded suspect to him, and he was beginning to have doubts about County Kerry and to think more in terms of Liverpool. He went slowly out of the kitchen and into his sitting room. On the low table by the electric wall fire, among the piles of books and papers, lay two cans of Coca-Cola and a packet of crisps, purchased at Elizabeth's suggestion, also his boyhood stamp album and a small microscope he had bought on impulse, in a junk shop, in case it should appeal to this child Elizabeth was taking on because of marrying Tom Carver.

He crossed over to the window and looked down into the street. He was surprised at how much he did this now, stand at the window and watch the small comings and goings, the old lady in the top flat opposite who spent all winter in an overcoat and headscarf, even indoors; the Chinese family who ran a laundry two streets away and worked all hours, all week; the group of lounging students who lived in the basement below and never drew their curtains back, hardly ever emerging in daylight. The boys, Duncan had observed, had longer hair than the girls, and wore as much jewelry, the kind of runic jewelry Duncan associated with midsummer rituals on ancient tombs and tors. He glanced down the length of the street now, his eye caught by some movement. Elizabeth was coming along the street, wearing the navy blue coat she had had for as long as he could remember and holding the carrier bag she always brought, full of things she thought he should be eating, rather than things he chose to eat. Beside her walked a boy, not a particularly little boy, but just a boy, in jeans and a duffel coat with a neat thick head of reddish brown hair. He was walking quite close to Elizabeth, but not touching her, and he was talking. Even from this distance Duncan could see, from his gestures, that Rufus was talking, animatedly, and Elizabeth was listening. He thought of everything that he had read just recently, of all those fairy stories of stepmotherly malevolence and cruelty, of the betrayal of childish trust, of the relentless perversion of all accepted notions of maternity. He put his glasses on and took them off again. The stories had shocked him, shocked him deeply with their remorseless insistence on the inevitable wickedness of any woman when faced with the care of children not her own, with their powerful suggestion of a second wife's witchlike sexual dominance over her husband, a dominance that drove all thoughts of fatherhood from a man's helpless heart. Duncan looked down the street. Rufus gave a little skip and glanced up at Elizabeth. They seemed, Duncan thought, with a small rush of emotion, perfectly normal together, perfectly comfortable, as far removed from the black world of spells and curses and unnatural enchantments as they could possibly be. He had read too many fairy stories, perhaps; he had allowed his vision to become distorted. Elizabeth had said so, and she had been, as she was in so many instances, quietly right. Duncan leaned forward and banged on the window glass to attract their attention.

"She's nice," Lucas said.

He was sitting with Dale in a wine bar, got up to look like a Spanish bodega, with rough low white arches and dark rustic beams. There were several plates of tapas on the table between them, and Dale had a large glass of red wine. Lucas had ordered beer, and then remembered, and changed his mind to mineral water.

"I know."

Lucas gave her a long look. She had been very in charge when they all had lunch together in that restaurant, very much Tom's daughter playing the hostess. Amy hadn't liked it. Lucas had noticed that Amy, who used to endure things she didn't like mutely, was now beginning to articulate her objections. She'd said, on the way home from that lunch, that anybody'd think Dale was Tom's wife, the way she was going on.

"Dad doesn't take any notice," Lucas said.

"Well, he doesn't protest, if that's what you mean. He just lets it happen. It's what men always do when they don't know what to do, they just roll over and play dead."

Playing dead or not, Lucas had thought his father looked really happy. Not ecstatic, exhilarated, mad happy, but deep and strong and rich happy. He'd looked at Elizabeth a lot, with a kind of profound contentment, and sometimes he hadn't seemed to hear what people were saying because he was looking at Elizabeth and thinking about her. It had unsettled Lucas a bit. Not, he realized, because he minded his father's happiness, but because it wasn't what he felt when he looked at Amy. Well, not anymore. He used to look at her and feel amazed at having her, but she'd changed from those early days when she'd been such fun, so mischievous. Lucas had felt a small tug of jealousy, looking at his father and Elizabeth, thinking that their maturity gave them a kind of emotional freedom that his youth somehow didn't have. And expected.

"Luke," Dale said. She had rolled up a piece of mountain ham into a light sausage and was holding it in her fingers.

"Yes?"

"Suppose she has a baby?"

Lucas shut his eyes.

"Why do you do this?"

"Do what?"

"Build bridges you may never have to cross in order to terrify yourself into theoretically crossing them?"

Dale took a bite of ham.

"She's thirty-eight."

"So?"

"People have babies forever now. And she's never been married, so she may want the works, baby and all. Mayn't she?"

Lucas picked up a stuffed olive and removed its little plug of pimento with the prong of a fork.

"Does it matter?"

"Yes," Dale said. She put the ham down, wiped her fingers and picked up her wineglass. "We've been through all that, we've seen it all with Josie and Rufus, we've seen what's really ours being shared out beyond us, with them——"

"Are you talking about money?"

Dale took a sip of wine.

"A bit."

Lucas ate the olive. He said, "What's his house worth?"

"Dad's? Oh, I don't know. Two hundred thousand perhaps—"

"Will he," Lucas said, "put the house in their joint names, do you think?"

"He might."

"But she earns all right, doesn't she? And she's got her house she's never lived in, to sell."

"Maybe," Dale said, "she'll keep that separate, because of being so much younger than him. Maybe he'll tell her to. Maybe he'll"—her face twisted briefly—"want to look after her."

Lucas looked, without enthusiasm, into his mineral water.

He said, "She isn't a gold digger."

"No," Dale said.

"You don't sound very certain—"

"I am, of that. Really. I really believe she isn't after anything of his. That isn't what scares me."

"What then?"

Dale took another mouthful of ham.

"It's Dad."

"What d'you mean?"

"It's that Dad might want to give her things, share things, even if she doesn't ask for them. Things that are really ours."

Lucas waited. He had told himself, for years, that he didn't want to be given anything by Tom, that he wanted to make his own way, build his own life and money as Tom had done, but as time went on and he saw how hard he was finding it, he had begun to feel that he wouldn't mind some help, wouldn't mind having something he hadn't earned by effort, but just by birthright instead. He picked up another olive.

"You know," Dale said. "You saw."

He nodded, slowly.

"You saw how he is with her," Dale said. "You don't have to know him half as well as we do, to see how he feels. Especially now that Rufus likes her and she likes Rufus. That's what scares me."

Lucas raised his head and looked directly at her.

"That he loves her?"

Dale nodded. The wineglass in her right hand shook very slightly, and when she next spoke, her voice was thickened by sudden tears.

"Oh, Luke, he does. This time, he really, really does."

"Don't cry—"

"I can't help it," Dale said. She put her glass down and then put both hands over her face. Under the table, Lucas stretched his feet out and trapped hers between them.

"I'm still here, cupcake—"

She nodded violently, behind her hands. He watched her. In some ways, she drove him mad, as she always had, and in others aroused his pity as no one else in his life had ever done, pity at the terror of loss that had stalked her since childhood and probably always would, causing her to wreck, inadvertently, the very relationships she most needed. And it wasn't that she didn't fight, it wasn't that she didn't, in her own way, struggle to be different, to be normal. Of course she'd overdone it the other day at lunch, bossing the waiters about, fussing over Elizabeth, but that had been an attempt, however bungled, to feel as she really wanted to feel—pleased for Tom, fond of Elizabeth, relieved for Rufus. Poor Dale, Lucas thought, poor, driven Dale. He reached both hands out across the table and took her wrists.

"Drink your wine, babe," he said.

Elizabeth's London flat, she decided, was too big. It had two bed-rooms and a long reception room that she had originally visual-ized being full of people—it never had been—and a kitchen and two bathrooms. If she was going, as she now planned, to travel up from Bath on Monday mornings and then return each weekend, she only needed half the space, a quarter, merely a bedroom and a bathroom and a kettle. It wouldn't have to be home, as this flat had never quite succeeded in becoming, it would simply be a place to eat a microwaved supper in, to telephone Tom from, to bathe and sleep in. It should have a porter and a laundry service and a cupboard to hold those sober working suits in which Tom had never seen her, which represented that part of her life that had once seemed almost the whole, because it had had almost no com-petition from anything else, but which had now oddly receded. She liked it, she was good at it, but it didn't preoccupy her now as something that filled the view anymore. Not only was the view quite different, but it was much closer than it used to be, and full of color and people. It amazed her, filled her with wonder, that life, instead of being something she imagined she only saw other people having, had suddenly arrived and enveloped her. She wasn't the one looking in from outside any longer, she was the other side of the glass, she was included. She mattered. If the train to Bath from London was delayed, on a Friday, Tom rang her mobile phone incessantly, to see if she was all right. He rang her first thing in the morning, at work, in the evening. She had gone, in a few short months, from being a dot in the landscape to becoming a figure in the foreground, a figure who could afford to exchange a substantial flat for a living cupboard without a back-ward look.

Where she lived in London wasn't, after all, anyone's decision but her own. Tom might help choose the flat's replacement; but only as a loving adviser, not as someone with the future concern of actually living there himself. In all her delight and gratitude at her changed status, Elizabeth couldn't help noticing the relief she felt at the realization that, as far as her London life was concerned, nobody else need be consulted because nobody else would be affected by her decision. Nobody would say to her, as Tom had said to her at the weekend, very nicely, but very decidedly, "I'm sorry, dearest, but no."

Probably, she shouldn't have asked him. Or, if she was going to ask him, not so soon, and certainly not hot on the heels of that dreadful lunch with Lucas and Amy and Dale, when Dale had dominated the proceedings and treated Elizabeth as if she were some dear old fondly tolerated relation with senile dementia. Elizabeth had meant to say nothing. She could see that Tom saw nothing, or at least wasn't admitting to seeing anything, and she vowed to herself that she would not only endure during the meal but also bite her tongue after it. She had almost succeeded. She had been able to speak with real warmth about Lucas, and to remark upon some resemblance she had noticed between him and Rufus, and had then, startling herself, found herself asking if they could move house.

He had stared at her.

"What?"

She was standing in the hall of Tom's house, with her coat on, and her suitcase at her feet, because he was about to take her to catch the Sunday-night train back to London.

"You asked if I wanted any changes. You said we could make changes for your and my life together. Well, I've thought about it, and I do want a change. I want a change of house."

He said in a controlled voice, "I thought you liked this house."

"I do. I did."

"Perhaps it's like the house you bought. You like houses for a while and then, arbitrarily, you stop liking them."

"That was different—"

"I hope," he said, "that this changeableness of affection doesn't apply to people."

She felt a little surge of temper.

"You know it doesn't. What a ridiculous and unkind thing to say."

"Perhaps I feel that the suggestion to leave this house is also ridiculous and unkind. Why do you want to, all of a sudden?"

She took a breath.

"Memories of Pauline, Dale's locked room—"

He looked at her.

"Those have always been here. We'll overcome those. You'll see." He came closer. "I'm sorry. I'm sorry I spoke to you as I did."

"That's all right—"

"Dale was silly today. Very silly. But she likes you. She never liked Josie. She'll calm down, stop performing. You'll see. And there's another thing."

"What?"

"Rufus," Tom said.

Elizabeth put her hands in her coat pockets.

"What about Rufus?"

"This is home to him," Tom said. "This house is probably the best stability he has just now, the biggest anchor. I couldn't—" He stopped. Then he looked at her. "Could I?"

Slowly she shook her head.

"You saw how he was here," Tom said. "How he was with you. He relaxed, didn't he?"

Elizabeth let out a long sigh. At one point during Rufus's last visit, Tom had found her teaching Rufus the rudiments of chess, and she had felt herself almost drowning in a sudden wash of approval, warm and thick and loving. She glanced at Tom. He was smiling. He leaned forward and put his arm around her, pulling her toward him, both of them bulky in their coats.

"I do see," he said. "I do understand how it must sometimes feel to you. But equally, for the moment, for Rufus, it has to be no. I'm sorry, dearest, but no."

She had been quite angry on the train after that, angry and ashamed of herself for being angry because Tom's point about Rufus was not only valid, but one for which she should have felt the utmost sympathy. The trouble was, she discovered, gazing at her face reflected in the dark window glass of the railway carriage, that she couldn't help feeling that Tom was hiding behind Rufus, that Tom, for all his real love for her, for all his genuine enthusiasm for and commitment to the future, was held down still by the gossamer threads of the past, like a giant in a fairy tale, disabled by magic.

She slept badly that night but woke, to her surprise, quite pleased to see a London morning and her briefcase and the black wool business suit she had bought when notions of marriage had seemed to her as unlikely as encountering an angel in her kitchen. There was a working week ahead, a week of meetings and decisions and the peculiarly diplomatic kind of maneuvering that she had appeared unable, the previous weekend, to translate from her professional life to her private one. And at the end of that week, she would pack her suitcase again, and go down to Bath and to Tom, and discuss with him, with the reasonableness he so loved, the changes they might make to that house that was to be their married home. For Rufus's sake.

NADINE RANG EVERY day. Some days, she rang twice. She had elicited from the children a rough timetable of daily life in Barratt Road, so that she could ring just as everyone was assembling frenziedly to leave for school in the morning or ten minutes after Josie had, with varying success, assembled the six of them for supper. If she rang during supper, she would speak to each of her children in turn, for ages, and they would vanish into the sitting room when their turn came and emerge with expressions that dared anyone even to start asking what had been said. Mostly Rory looked shuttered when he returned, and Clare often seemed close to tears and would sit at her place at the kitchen table afterward staring down at her plate as if exerting every ounce of willpower not to dissolve. Only Becky flounced out of the sitting room glowing with secrets and defiance, and often refused to come back to the table at all, but slammed past them all out of the room and upstairs, or out of the house altogether. Josie would look at Becky's plate, stirred about but largely uneaten, and want Matthew to go after her and bring her back.

"No."

"But you're letting her get away with it!"

"Do you think," Matthew said, "that a stand-up row, twice a day at least, is a preferable alternative?"

"What about me?"

"What about you?"

"Matthew, I spend hours shopping and cooking for these kids, and then the phone rings and they stop eating. Or they won't eat in case the phone rings. Or they won't come to the table anyway, or if they do, they say they don't like what I've cooked and later I find there isn't a biscuit or a crisp left in the house—"

"I know," Matthew said.

"Well, *do* something!"

He looked at her.

"What do you suggest?"

"Talk to them! Stand up for me! Say you won't have me being treated like this!"

"In effect," Matthew said, "that's what I am doing. I don't rush after them. I don't react, I stay eating with you and Rufus. I make it plain I'm bored by their behavior."

"*Bored?*"

"Yes. Bored."

"Matthew," Josie said, and her fists were clenched, "there's open hostility in this house, all directed at me, and you tell me you're *bored?*"

When Josie heard she had got her job, it was better than she had expected. The teacher on maternity leave whom she had applied to replace had decided to stay at home with her babies, and her post had been offered to Josie. In celebration, Josie bought a bottle of Australian chardonnay and put it on the supper table.

"What's that for?" Rufus said.

"To celebrate."

"What?"

"My job. I've got a job."

Matthew smiled round the table.

"It's good, isn't it? First try, too. You're a clever girl."

Becky stood up. She gave her plate a nudge.

"I don't want this."

Josie, her hand still on the neck of the wine bottle, said levelly, "It's chicken casserole."

"So?"

"You like chicken casserole."

"I do not."

Clare put her fork down. She said in a whisper, "Nor me."

She looked at Matthew.

"Sit down," Matthew said to Becky.

"You can't make me."

"I wouldn't try," Matthew said, "but I would offer you a glass of wine, to toast Josie with."

Becky said scornfully, "Alcohol's a drug."

Matthew looked at Rory. Rory was still eating, head down, shoveling food in even though hardly anyone but Rufus had even started.

"Would you like some?"

Rory shook his head.

"Rufus?"

Rufus went pink. Tom and Elizabeth had given him half a glass of white wine when they took him out for supper, and he had liked it. He would have liked some now. He would have liked to say well done to Josie. He shot Matthew a glance and shook his head, too.

"All the more for you and me, then," Matthew said to Josie. He took the corkscrew from her and stood up, to take the cork out of the bottle.

"I'm not eating," Becky said. "And I'm not staying."

"Please stay," Josie said. There was no appeal in her voice.

"Why?"

"So that we can have supper together."

"I don't want supper," Becky said. "And I don't want to be together."

"Then get out," Josie said.

Matthew stopped pulling the cork.

"Josie—"

"Get out," Josie said to Becky again. "Just go."

Becky kicked her chair backward, hard, so that it screeched across the floor and crashed into the nearest set of cupboards. Then she spun round and headed for the door to the outside. It was locked. She banged it once or twice with her fist, and then, feeling all their eyes upon her like pairs of headlights, lurched round, hurtled through the door to the hall, and fled upstairs. Behind her she heard her father say angrily, "What in hell's name did you have to say that for?" and then someone banged the door shut, and she could only hear babble and confusion.

She opened her and Clare's bedroom door and fell across Clare's bed, which was nearest. She put her face into the duvet and bit a mouthful of fabric, so hard she could almost feel her teeth meet. Then she pummeled Clare's pillow and kicked clumsily against the nearest wall with her booted feet. Bloody cow, she said to herself, bloody cow with her fucking job. How dare she? How dare she wave her bloody job at us like she wanted us to pat her on the back for it? How dare she? And why should I care, anyway, why should I care what happens to her, ever, anyway? Why should I care about her and all her bloody cooking and cleaning and prancing about being Mrs. Fucking Perfect? Becky picked Clare's pillow up and flung it at the wall opposite, where it caught the edge of a picture and sent it spinning off its hook and crashing to the floor.

Becky sat up. She hadn't turned the light on when she came in, but by the remains of daylight left, she could see the shards and slices of glass from the picture lying winking on the carpet. It was a picture she had always wanted, a reproduction of a painting by Klimt of an exotic, dangerous, snakelike woman, but Josie had hung it there for her and, in so doing, had at a stroke deprived it of all its allure. It was an intrusion for Josie to give Becky something she desired, an invasion of privacy, a patronizing insult. Just as all those meals were, all those washed clothes, all the things Josie did to keep the house going, all the things she didn't—carefully—say.

Becky put her heel on the nearest piece of broken glass and crushed it. Then she pulled her knees up and put her face down on them, and encircled them with her arms.

"I'm fine," Nadine said, every day, whether Becky asked her or not. Her voice was often bright and theatrical. "Really I am. Fine."

She was going on with her pots; Tim was finding her a secondhand kiln; she had the radio for company.

"What about you?" she'd say. "That's what I really want to know. What about you? Are you getting enough to eat? Is school OK? Tell me what you're doing. Tell me everything."

Slowly, Becky raised her head. From downstairs, she could hear the sound of the television. Perhaps Rory had turned it on.

Most nights, he turned it on the moment he could and increased the volume so much that, when Josie wanted him to take his turn in cleaning up, she had to shout at him to make herself heard. Then the phone began to ring. At the sound, Becky felt her stomach tighten and then be filled, slowly and steadily, with renewed anger, an anger so strong she could feel it creeping up her throat, choking her. She stood up, unsteadily. The glass lay at her feet, gleaming and evil. She lifted her feet in turn, clumsily, and began to stamp on the broken pieces. Someone had to pay for this, someone had to suffer for all this unfairness, this pressure, this tension, this agonizing disappointment and hurt. Someone, Becky thought, stamping and stamping, has to be *punished.*

Matthew allowed Clare to do her homework in his attic study. She stayed up there for hours. Sometimes, when he came back from his school—always much later than anyone else—she had been up there since she got home. She came straight in from school, walked past Josie, usually without saying anything, and went directly up to the attic, where she sat in Matthew's chair and sometimes put on one of his jumpers. When he came in, she would run to him and try and get on his knee, and if Josie said anything, Clare would say, "You're not my real mother," and put her arms around Matthew.

Becky had told her to say it.

"She's not your real mother. She can't make you do anything. Tell her so."

If they were alone together, just Clare and Josie, Clare didn't have the courage to say it, but from Matthew's knee, she could say anything.

"She knows she's not," Matthew would say, trying to make

light of it. "Poor Josie, having a baggage like you. What a horrible thought."

"I don't want to be," Josie said. "I'm not trying to be."

"She does mother things though," Clare said. "Doesn't she?"

"Who else do you suggest does them?"

"Our real mother," Clare said. She held Matthew hard. If she held him hard enough, she didn't have to think of Nadine and the cottage and the lavatory in the shed. If she thought of them, she felt desperate, and the easiest place not to think about them, except on Matthew's knee, was in Matthew's attic, which held so many things from Clare's childhood that she could sometimes pretend up there that nothing had changed, nothing had broken. She counted the photographs. There were exactly the same number of all three of them, of her and Rory and Becky. But there weren't any of Nadine. In fact, when Clare looked closely, she thought that one or two of the photographs had funny edges, as if a piece had been cut out. When she looked at those cut photographs, she remembered some of the things Nadine had said about Matthew, about what he'd done, how he'd behaved, and those memories made Clare unable to leave the attic, even when Josie called her, unable to move until the physical presence of her father came back up the ladder and found her there, in his chair, in his jumper, and proved his recognizable ordinariness once more.

"I wish she wouldn't cling," Clare heard Josie say. "I wish you wouldn't let her."

"She's only ten—"

"It isn't age, Matt. It's attitude."

Clare didn't know what attitude meant, but it plainly wasn't a compliment. She was obviously doing something that Josie didn't want her to do, something to do with her father. Becky urged Clare

to behave as defiantly toward Josie as she could, on principle, but
although Clare listened, she didn't, as with homework, quite see
the point of what Becky was saying. She didn't sit on Matthew's
knee to defy Josie, she did it because she wanted to, she needed to.
She didn't refuse to eat Josie's suppers to get at Josie; she refused
because those meals, so competently prepared, so wholesome,
made her feel acutely guilty about Nadine, even disloyal. If Josie
couldn't see that, Clare couldn't do anything about it, just as she
couldn't do anything about her greedy relief when Matthew came
home.

She looked, from the safety of Matthew's knee, toward Josie,
who was sorting laundry on the kitchen floor.

"I don't want my tracksuit washed," Clare said.

Josie lay on her and Matthew's bed. She was fully dressed. She lay
quite still, her hands folded across her stomach, and stared out of
the window, where the fading light and the raw orange glow from
the street lamps were producing an effect that was neither lovely
nor natural. It was quiet in the bedroom, quiet enough to hear the
sounds from downstairs, the murmur of the television, the noises
from the kitchen where Matthew was, without much real trouble
apparently, making the children wash up. Except Becky. Becky was
in her bedroom with the door shut. She had been there since six
o'clock, after her mother rang.

Nadine had rung, this time, about money. She had spoken first
to Becky, and had then insisted on speaking to Matthew. Josie,
grating cheese in the kitchen, had heard him say, "But *I'm* paying
for the children now, you *must* have enough, you *must.*" The conversation had gone on for a long time, and when Matthew had put

the telephone down at last, Josie heard Becky say, with a mixture of fear and rage, "You can't let her starve!"

"She's not starving," Matthew said. "She's just spent every-thing she has this month and wants more."

"Then you should give it to her."

"I give her all I can," Matthew said. Josie could picture how tired he was looking, from his voice. "She's only got herself to look after now."

"Exactly!" Becky shouted. "Exactly! And whose fault's that?"

Josie heard Matthew's footsteps coming toward the kitchen door. She bent over the grater.

"I'm not talking to you about it," Matthew said. He opened the kitchen door. "It's none of your business."

Becky shoved past him. She stood briefly in the kitchen, glar-ing at Josie. Josie's hand slipped on the grater, and a bright bead of blood swelled out of her forefinger. She put it in her mouth.

"We're not exactly short round here," Becky said, still glaring, her voice heavy with sarcasm. "Are we?"

"Be quiet," Matthew said. He looked at Josie. "Are you all right?"

She nodded, her finger still in her mouth. Becky snorted and marched toward the door.

"I don't want any supper."

"Fine," Matthew said.

The door banged shut behind Becky. Matthew went across to Josie and put his arm round her.

"Sorry."

She turned her face into his neck.

"It's OK."

"Josie—"

"Yes?"

"I'm going to have to put her money back up again. I know I shouldn't, I know we've got the children here—"

"What?" Josie said, stiffening.

"I've just said. I'll have to put Nadine's money up again. I gave her less, because the kids were here, but I'll have to increase it again."

"Because your daughter tells you to?"

Matthew sighed.

"Partly, I suppose. If I'm honest. And with you working now—"

Josie shrank away from his embrace.

"I don't believe it."

"What—"

She gripped the edge of the sink and stared down at the blood seeping slowly out of her finger.

"You are telling me that *my* money will pay for *your* children so that *you* can give more to your ex-wife, who refuses to work?"

"I'd pay for Rufus," Matthew said. "If it was necessary."

Josie turned the cold tap on and held her finger in the stream. She was trembling.

"I don't ask you for a *penny* for Rufus."

"I know."

"*And* he is civil to you. He's sweet. You know he is. Whereas—"

"Don't," Matthew said. He put his arms around her, from behind. She pressed herself against the sink.

"Please don't touch me."

He took his arms away.

"I've got to behave decently," Matthew said. "I've got to juggle all these demands and do the best I can."

"Except for me," Josie said. She turned the tap off and wrapped her finger in a piece of absorbent kitchen paper. "I don't make any demands. So I don't get anything. I do everything for everyone, and nobody ever thinks that I have needs, I have hurts."

"I do."

"Well, you don't do anything about them. You just expect me to be sorry for you, you expect me to imagine what it's like for you while never even trying for one second to imagine what it's like for me."

The kitchen door opened. Rufus stood there, holding his maths book. He looked at them.

"Oh," he said.

Josie said, "Come in, darling."

"It's my maths," Rufus said. "I can't do—" He stopped.

Matthew moved away from Josie.

"Shall I help you?"

Rufus looked at him doubtfully. Matthew sat down at the kitchen table.

"Bring it here."

Slowly, Rufus approached the table. He put the book down in front of Matthew and stepped back.

"I won't bite you," Matthew said. "I'm useful for maths. If for nothing else."

Rufus moved a little closer. Josie watched them.

"Show me."

"There," Rufus said. He leaned forward, pointing, his shoulder almost touching Matthew's. It was a scene she had longed for, a scene that represented, perhaps, the first quiet, unremarkable step on the road to some kind of relationship between the two people who mattered most in the world to her—and it left her cold. She watched them, and felt nothing. Nothing. She was empty of all good things at the moment, empty of any capacity to feel joy, even to feel love. There was no possibility of loving feelings in the face of the rage and despair that filled her now with such intensity.

"I've got a headache," Josie said.

Neither Rufus nor Matthew reacted. Their heads were close.

"I think you've got these in the wrong order," Matthew said. "That's what's stumped you."

"I'm going up to bed," Josie said. "If you put the grated cheese on top of what's in that dish, and grill it for ten minutes, that's supper."

Rufus looked up briefly, his face abstracted.

"Right," he said.

"See you later," Josie said. She went out of the kitchen and up the stairs and past Becky's closed door, to her bedroom. Then she lay down, still with her shoes on, and let herself cry.

That must be almost two hours ago. She must have gone to sleep, briefly, because she was stiff and her mouth tasted sour, and the tears had dried on the sides of her face in faint salty crusts. Tears of self-pity, perhaps, tears of anger and impotence certainly. She licked her undamaged forefinger and rubbed away the tear traces. Then she turned her head. On the little table by Matthew's side of the bed lay the telephone. She could roll over the bed and pick up the receiver. She could telephone her mother, or her friend Beth, and she could then expect—and probably get—their time and patience while she talked, while she poured out all the thoughts and feelings that had come to obsess her since the arrival in her life—their lives—of Matthew's children.

"I didn't have any choice," she'd say. She could imagine Elaine listening. "Did I? I didn't have any choice in taking them on. It was *him* I chose. And we can't really talk about them, or about the fact that there wasn't time to prepare for them. Time for me, anyway. I'm so afraid of being unfair, but I'm unfair all the time. I love

Rufus, and I don't love them. I can't. How can you love children whose every effort is directed at ignoring you or hating you? How can you love children who persist in loving a natural mother who's such a rotten mother? Why do they persist? Why do they fling their loyalty for her at me, all day, every day? And now"—inside her head, Josie could feel her voice rising to a crescendo—"I'm supposed to help support them! I'm supposed to look after them like a mother, but not, oh God, *not* like a real mother, for no return, and pay for them as well? Because Matthew can't, Matthew won't, because they're his children and he won't see what I feel."

The tears were starting again. Josie rolled over and pressed her face into the pillows. Mustn't. Mustn't cry again. Mustn't telephone either. Mustn't expose this raw cauldron of feelings even to Elaine's compassionate gaze, let alone to Beth's much less kindly one.

"Oh," Beth would say, "I *am* sorry. How disappointing for you."

There'd be a note in her voice, an edge, that Josie wouldn't like, that Josie probably couldn't take, a little hint of triumph, of superiority. Of, "Well, you knew he had children when you married him."

Elaine would just worry. "Shall I come down, dear? Do you want to come here for a few days? Is Rufus all right? How is Rufus?"

Josie reached out for a tissue from the box on her side of the bed and blew her nose hard. Then she sat up. She didn't just feel stiff and a little cold, but grubby, too, disheveled, as if she'd been in contact with something polluting, impure. She swung her feet to the floor and kicked off her shoes. She would go into the bathroom, before the children all came upstairs, and shower and wash her hair and go downstairs in her dressing gown and make tea and try to be pleasant, ordinary. She stood up and stretched. Becky had turned some music on in her bedroom, so at least she was alive. Josie went out onto the landing. Becky's bedroom door was open, and the light was still on. Beside it, however, the bathroom door was firmly shut, and the sound of music coming from behind it was intermingled with the sound of running water. Becky was in the shower.

Under the bedclothes, Rory pressed a lit flashlight into the palm of his hand, into his bunched fingers. His flesh glowed weirdly, red and fiery. He took the torch away from his hand and shone it out from under the duvet onto a patch of wall, and then up, above his football posters, to the ceiling, where a crack ran jaggedly across the plaster.

"Rufe?" he said.

There was silence. He swung the flashlight beam off the ceiling in a swooping arc until it came to rest on Rufus's bed, Rufus's body under his duvet, Rufus's head with its thick, straight hair, which fell the same way whether Rufus brushed it or didn't. Rufus was lying, as he always did, with his back to Rory; the flashlight caught his neck and an ear and the navy blue collar of his pajamas.

"You asleep?"

Silence. Rory didn't know why, but he quite wanted Rufus to be awake. He thought he might say something. He didn't know what, he just thought he'd like it if Rufus was awake too and lying the other way, facing him. He'd always thought of Rufus as a little kid, a little wet kid, but tonight, in the kitchen, eating supper with just him and Dad and Clare, he'd been OK, he'd been normal. They all had. They'd all just eaten the stuff Josie had left and joshed about a bit, and Matthew, despite looking tired, hadn't watched anybody, hadn't ticked anyone off. It had felt different, this evening, without Becky and Josie, it felt as if you could just say things, as if whether you ate or you didn't eat wasn't a big deal. So they all ate. They ate everything Josie had left, everything. Rory and Clare had even argued about the last baked potato, and when Matthew gave it to Rufus and he said he couldn't eat it, Matthew had just grinned and cut it in halves for the others. Then they'd had a water fight, washing up. Matthew made them mop the floor, and Rory hadn't minded. He couldn't believe it, but he hadn't minded, he'd just pushed the frigging mop round and tried to get Rufus's feet wet, and Rufus had yelled and jumped about and you could see he didn't mind either, that he was liking it. It only stopped when Josie came down. She'd come down in her dressing gown with her hair on her shoulders, making her face look like paper, and she'd been nervous. You could see it, as if she was expecting something to happen, something she couldn't handle. Matthew showed her all the empty dishes, and she'd nodded. She put the kettle on and stood, with her hand on the handle, with her back to them, waiting for it to boil. The kitchen had gone quiet, all of a sudden, really quiet. And awkward.

Rory ran the flashbeam all down Rufus's length and back again. He looked relaxed, as if he really was asleep, not just faking. His wet shoes were jammed behind the radiator, and next to them was Rory's Newcastle United sweatshirt, which had got soaking. Rory switched the flash off. It had been odd, this evening, because it had been, well, normal. Not brilliant, just normal. He rolled over and punched his pillow. It had been fun.

IN THE SUPERMARKET Elizabeth bought things she thought Rufus would like—a selection of individual cereal boxes, finger biscuits covered in chocolate, raisins in a cardboard drum, doll-sized Dutch cheeses in a plastic net bag. She was tempted by all kinds of babyish things, too, strawberry-flavored toothpaste and pasta shaped like dinosaurs, not because she didn't realize that Rufus was too old for them but because it was such pure pleasure to shop for food from such an entirely different perspective than her usual lone adult one. She spent a long time in front of jars of baby food, too, and neat piles of cotton-wool balls and baby wipes and disposable diapers, all packaged in pristine white plastic printed with nursery symbols in primary colors. It was like being in another dimension, standing there imagining needing such things on an ordinary daily basis, like being in another world. She picked up a pale blue tin of baby-milk formula. "For babies up to four months," it read, and on the side, in darker blue letters, "Calcium and vitamins added."

Her trolley looked satisfyingly full as she wheeled it toward the exit. She had never, in her whole life, bought so much in a single expedition, had never had need to buy bulk packs of lavatory paper or more than six apples, or two items at once from the delicatessen. Certainly the fact that Rufus was coming for almost ten days made a difference, but somehow even shopping for herself and Tom had a richness to it because of all the things a household seemed to need to clean it and service it and to keep it living and welcoming. There were items in that trolley now—a box of ivory-colored candles, a packet of Italian espresso coffee, a patent cold remedy—that had nothing to do with her, in herself, but were bought because someone else needed them, wanted them, because shopping was now an imaginative experience on behalf of several people, not just a practical one on behalf of a mere one whose tastes were so familiar to her, she was sick of them.

She stopped her trolley by an empty checkout and began to unload the contents.

"Busy weekend?" the woman on the till said, watching.

Elizabeth nodded, head down, to conceal her smile. The woman picked up the cold remedy.

"Got a cold then?"

"No," Elizabeth said, and then, to her own amazed surprise and delight, added, "It's for my fiancé."

The woman swiped the remedy across the scanner panel of her till.

"If there's one thing I can't abide," she said cozily, "it's a sick man."

I'm new to it, Elizabeth wanted to say, so new to it that I don't mind. I don't mind Tom thinking he's getting a cold, I don't mind buying him the capsules he imagines will prevent it happening; in fact I'm so far from minding that I like it, I'm grateful to be asked to do it, to choose sausages for Rufus, to replenish the supplies of soap and furniture polish and bottled water.

"Fiancé, did you say?" the woman asked.

"Yes—"

She gave Elizabeth a kindly glance and picked up a bag of potatoes.

"You'll learn," she said.

There was a parking space right outside Tom's house, and it was, in addition, a big enough space for Elizabeth—who was not an experienced driver and had never needed to be a car owner—to maneuver into without difficulty. Tom had bought her this car, just like that, easily, amazing her.

"You'll need it."

"But I've never—"

"You do now. Anyway, I want you to have a car. I want you to have the freedom."

"I can't believe it."

He had kissed her.

"You're joining another world. Families have cars."

Already, Elizabeth liked it. She liked the unexpected status she felt it gave her, the independence, the choice. Even now, lifting the back to heave out the bulging supermarket bags, she felt a small pride she couldn't help relishing even though she was glad no one more experienced was there to see. She carried the bags up the steps to the front door in pairs and then locked the car, carefully checking to see that the central-locking system had actually done what it was supposed to do. Then she climbed the steps again and put her key in the front door. It wasn't locked. She turned the handle and pushed the door open.

"Tom?"

"Me," Dale called from the kitchen.

Elizabeth took a breath.

"Oh—"

Dale came to the kitchen doorway. She wore a scarlet apron tied over a black T-shirt and jeans.

"Been shopping?"

"Yes."

Dale moved forward.

"I'll help you carry."

"Dale," Elizabeth said. "Have you been here long?"

"About an hour."

"Why didn't you ring?"

"What?"

"To say you were coming. Why didn't you ring me?"

Dale stooped to pick up the nearest bags.

"Please leave those," Elizabeth said. "Please leave those and answer my question."

Dale straightened slowly.

"I don't have to ring."

"You do now," Elizabeth said.

"This is my home—"

Elizabeth put her hands in her jacket pockets.

"Mine, too, now. You are welcome any time, *any* time, for any reason, but not unannounced. I need to know."

Dale stared at her.

"Why?"

"Privacy," Elizabeth said. "Not secrecy, but privacy."

Dale said fiercely, "This was my home for twenty-five years before my father even met you!"

Elizabeth bent to take the two bags closest to her feet.

"We can't have this conversation on the doorstep—"

"You started it."

"No. You caused it by letting yourself into the house in our absence and without warning us."

"It's my house!" Dale yelled.

She turned her back on Elizabeth and marched into the kitchen. Elizabeth lifted the shopping bags from the front doorstep into the hall and then shut the door. She followed Dale into the kitchen. Half the cupboard doors were open, and the table was piled with packets and jars.

"What are you doing?"

"What does it look like?" Dale said rudely. She had pulled on a pair of yellow rubber gauntlets. "Spring cleaning. I always do it for Dad."

"Always?"

"Well, the last year or two—"

Elizabeth took her jacket off and hung it over the nearest chair.

"It's my job now, Dale. If it's anyone's. And these are my cupboards and my kitchen. I am, in an old-fashioned expression, to be mistress of this house."

Dale banged a yellow-rubber fist down on the table. She said furiously, "Oh that's obvious, you've made that perfectly plain, you don't have to tell *me*."

"What do you mean?"

Dale shouted, "My mother's photographs! My mother's pictures! What have you done with all the pictures of my mother?"

Elizabeth said steadily, "You've been in the drawing room—"

"Yes!"

"And where else? Where else have you been? In our bedroom?" Dale glared.

"In our bedroom?"

"Only quickly—"

"Only quickly! Not too quickly, I imagine, to notice that the photograph of your mother is where it's always been?"

Dale was breathing fast. She tore the rubber gauntlets off and slapped them down on the nearest counter.

"The drawing room was her room!"

"The pictures are perfectly safe. They are wrapped up and packed in a wine carton for you and Lucas. You'll find them in his old bedroom. The portrait of your mother is still in the drawing room, and it will stay there. I'm not obliterating anything, I'm just making my mark, alongside."

Dale said vehemently, "It was her room, she made it, she chose everything, she was Dad's wife, she was Dad's first choice, she was our mother—"

"I know all that. I know."

Dale slumped into the nearest chair and put her face in her hands. Elizabeth went round the table and stood next to her. She looked down at the gleaming dark hair so smoothly tied back into its velvet loop.

"Dale—"

Dale said nothing.

"Look," Elizabeth said, trying to speak gently. "Look, you're a grown-up, a grown woman, you must use your imagination and maturity a little. I can't negotiate with a ghost like this, Dale, I really can't. I can't compete with something idealized, and you shouldn't demand that I do, either. Anyway——" She paused.

Dale took her hands from her face.

"What?"

"Aren't you maybe too old to go on believing your mother was a saint?"

Dale stared ahead of her.

"You never knew her. You don't know what you're talking about."

"You didn't know her very well, either," Elizabeth said. "You were only a child."

Dale sprang up and shouted, "There were hundreds of people at her funeral! Hundreds and hundreds! They came from all over England, all over the world."

Elizabeth closed her eyes for a moment.

"I don't doubt it."

"You do!"

"I don't doubt that your mother was a wonderful person and much loved. That's not the point. The point is that she, tragically, is dead, and therefore, however fondly remembered, cannot influence how we, who are still living, choose to live our lives. When she lived here, this house was hers, and she arranged it as she wished to. Now, it's going to be mine and your father's, and we will want to live in it rather differently."

Dale bent her head and put the back of one hand against her eyes. She was crying.

"Oh, Dale," Elizabeth said in some despair. "Oh, Dale dear, do try and grow up a little. I'm not some intruder you have to make bargains with."

Dale whirled round and snatched sheets of kitchen paper off a roll on a nearby worktop. She blew her nose fiercely.

"You want to turn us out!"

"I don't," Elizabeth said. "It's the last thing I want. All I want is for you to respect my privacy and independence as I respect yours."

Dale blew again.

"You don't respect my past!"

"I do," Elizabeth said. She gripped a chairback and leaned on it. "All I have difficulty with is when you try and insist that the past has more importance and significance than the present or the future."

"You'll learn," Dale said bitterly. She untied the strings of the scarlet apron, ducked her head out of the neckband, and threw the apron on the table among the boxes and bottles.

"What is that supposed to mean?"

Dale was pulling on a jacket.

"You can't touch what we've got, what we've got because of what we've had—"

"I know that—"

"You don't!" Dale cried. "You don't and you never will. You think you can come in here with your tidy Civil Service mind and file us all away neatly so there's nothing messy left, nothing real and human and powerful. Well, you can't. What we had, we'll always have, and you can't touch it. You'll never understand us because you can't, because you can't feel what we've felt, you can't know what we know, you'll never belong. You can try changing Dad outwardly, nobody can stop you doing that, but you'll never change him inwardly because you don't have it in you. He's been where you'll never go."

Elizabeth took her hands off the chairback and put them over her ears.

"Stop it—"

"I'm going," Dale said. She sounded out of breath. She was rummaging in her bag for her car keys. "I'm going, and I'll be back. I'll be back whenever I want to because this is my home, this is where I belong, this is where I come from and always will."

Elizabeth said nothing. She slid her hands round her head from covering her ears to covering her eyes. She heard Dale's bag zip close.

"It would be nice," Dale said, "if you didn't tell Dad about this. But I expect you will. And if you do, then I will. I'll have to." She paused and then said with emphasis, "Won't I?"

And then she went out of the kitchen and the front doors, slamming both behind her.

"What's all this?" Tom said.

He stood in the doorway of his bedroom and peered into the half-dark. Elizabeth lay on the bed, as she had lain for several hours, with the curtains drawn. "Are you ill?"

"No."

He moved closer.

"What is it, sweetheart?"

Elizabeth said, without moving, "You saw."

"I saw a fair old muddle in the kitchen, certainly. And shopping all over the hall floor. Basil, needless to say, has found the butter. I thought perhaps you weren't feeling too good—"

"I'm not."

Tom lowered himself onto the side of the bed and put his hand on her forehead.

"Headache?"

"No."

"What—"

Elizabeth was lying on her side, still dressed, under a blanket. She said, looking straight ahead and not at Tom, "Dale came."

"Did she?"

"She was here when I got back from shopping. She was in the process of turning out the kitchen cupboards."

Tom took his hand away from Elizabeth's face.

"Oh, dear."

"We had a row," Elizabeth said. She rolled over onto her back and looked at Tom. "I told her she mustn't just let herself into the house whenever she pleased anymore, and the row began."

Tom wasn't quite meeting Elizabeth's eyes.

"And how did it end?"

"With Dale saying she would go on letting herself in whenever she wanted to because this was her home and always would be."

Tom got slowly off the bed and walked toward the window, pushing the curtains back to reveal quiet cloudy afternoon light.

"Did Pauline come into it?"

"Oh, yes," Elizabeth said. She stared up at the ceiling. "She always does."

"What did you say?"

"About Pauline? That I couldn't negotiate with a ghost. That Dale was too old to go on believing her mother was a saint."

"She wasn't," Tom said. He had his back to Elizabeth. She turned her head to look at him, outlined against the window.

"I'm relieved to hear you say it—"

"She was very like Dale, in some ways, but with better self-control." He turned toward Elizabeth. "Sweetheart. I'm so sorry."

"Yes."

"Have you been up here ever since she left?"

"Yes."

"Poor love. Poor Elizabeth."

Elizabeth struggled up into a half-sitting position, propping her shoulders against the bed's padded headboard.

"Tom."

"Yes?"

"What are you going to do?"

He came back to the bed and sat down beside Elizabeth.

"What do you want me to do?"

She closed her eyes.

"That's not the right way round."

"I don't follow you—"

"It isn't," Elizabeth said, "a question of what I want you to do, it's a question of what you want to do yourself, not just for my sake, but even more for our future sakes, jointly, for the sake of this marriage we're embarking on."

"You don't sound very enthusiastic about it—"

"It's not lack of enthusiasm I feel," Elizabeth said. "It's fear."

"Fear?"

She picked up the edge of the blanket that covered her and began to pleat it between her fingers.

"Fear of what?" Tom said.

"Dale."

Tom leaned forward and put his head in his hands.

"Oh my God."

"Can't you imagine?" Elizabeth said, fighting with sudden tears. "Can't you imagine trying to be married here with both of us straining to catch the sound of her key in the lock?"

"It wouldn't be like that—"

"It might!" Elizabeth cried, sitting up and dropping the blanket. "If she got in a state about something, or jealous, or lonely, she might come in all the time, any time, demanding your attention, insisting on her right to come home, informing me, as she did today, that I'll never belong here however hard I try, however much I love you, because I haven't got what you've all got, what you've had, I just haven't got what it takes to make you happy!"

Tom took his hands away from his face and put his arms around Elizabeth. He said, in a fierce whisper against her hair, "I'm so sorry, so *sorry*——"

Elizabeth said nothing. She turned her face so that their cheeks were touching, and then, after a few moments, she gently but firmly disengaged herself.

"Help me," Tom said. "Help me to decide what to do."

Elizabeth began to extricate herself from the blanket and to inch across the bed away from him.

"I'm afraid," she said politely, "that it isn't my decision."

"Elizabeth——"

"Yes."

"I can't change the locks of this house against my own daughter!"

Elizabeth reached the far side of the bed and stood up.

"We don't have keys to Dale's flat. We never go there. We're never asked there."

"But Dale was almost born in this house——"

"I know. That's one of the reasons why I wanted to sell it and move to another house, with no associations."

"But Rufus——"

"I know about Rufus. I accept the Rufus argument."

Tom stood up, too. He said, "I'll go downstairs and clear up. Why don't you have a bath?"

"I'd love a bath, but it won't make me feel any differently."

"You want me to tell Dale——"

"No!" Elizabeth shouted. She raised her fists and beat herself lightly on the sides of her head. "No! Not what I want! What *you* want for *us*, for you and me, because you can see what will happen if things go on like this!"

"But they won't. These are teething troubles, the shock of the new. We have so much going for us, so much, we love each other, Rufus loves you, Lucas will love you, too, any minute. We mustn't get things out of proportion. Dale's just in a state while she gets used to the idea of you. I'm so sorry she's upset you—"

"Shut up," Elizabeth said.

"What?"

"Stop talking. Stop mouthing all this stuff at me."

Tom said angrily, "I'm trying to explain—"

"No, you're not, you're trying to talk yourself out of having to face what's really the matter."

"Which is?"

Elizabeth took a few steps toward the door. Then she took a breath.

"That Dale is neurotically insecure and possessive, and that if you don't do something about it now, you'll have her for life."

Tom said sharply, "You have your children for life anyway."

Elizabeth looked at him. Against the light, it was difficult to see his expression, but his stance looked determined, even defiant, as if he was challenging her to know better than he did about an area of life she had never experienced, and he had. She opened her mouth to ask if Tom's pronouncement on children held good for third wives, too, and then felt, almost simultaneously, that pride would prevent her ever asking such a thing. So, instead, she closed her mouth again and walked, with as much dignity as she could muster, into the bathroom next door, closing the door behind her.

"It's really nice of you to see me," Amy said.

"Not at all, it's a pleasure—"

"I haven't been to London for ages, not for months, but then I got this interview and I thought that, while I was at it, if you didn't mind—"

"I don't," Elizabeth said. "I'm pleased to see you."

Amy looked round the sitting room.

"It's a lovely flat. It's huge."

"I thought I'd have parties here. But I haven't—"

"You could have your wedding reception here. Couldn't you? It'd be a lovely room for that."

Elizabeth went past Amy and into the little kitchen that led off the sitting room. She called from inside it, "White wine?"

"I don't drink much," Amy said.

"Tea then, coffee—"

"Tea, please," Amy said. "A bag in a mug. Lucas thinks it's dead common, but it's how I like it." She came and peered through the kitchen doorway. "I've never seen you in a suit before."

"It's my working mode."

"It suits you," Amy said. "You look really in command."

Elizabeth plugged the kettle in.

"That's exactly how I want to look. It hides a multitude of sins. What job were you interviewing for?"

"A film," Amy said. "Some medieval thing. We have to plaster them in mud and keep them looking sexy at the same time. I don't know if I'll get it, but it's worth a try."

"Aren't you under contract to the TV station?"

"Only for three months," Amy said. "Three months at a time. You can't plan anything, but that's how they all work now."

Elizabeth took a half-bottle of white wine out of the fridge and peeled off the foil around the neck. She saw Amy looking at it.

"I always buy half-bottles, I always have. My father teases me, he calls them Spinster's Comforters. He ought to be glad they're not gin."

"Don't you like gin?"

"Not much."

"It makes me gag," Amy said. "Lucas drinks vodka. He's trying not to drink at all at the moment." She paused, and then she said with a tiny edge of venom, "It wouldn't hurt his sister to try not to either."

Elizabeth put a tea bag in a mug and filled it with boiling water.

"How strong?"

"Very," Amy said. She moved into the kitchen and picked up a teaspoon to squash the tea bag against the side of the mug. "Real builders' tea."

"My father has it like that."

"Rufus liked your father," Amy said.

Elizabeth poured her wine.

"It was mutual."

She opened the fridge and offered Amy a carton of milk.

"Sugar?"

Amy shook her head. She poured milk into her mug and stirred vigorously. "Look at that. Perfect." She lifted out the tea bag. "Where's your wastebin?"

"There—"

"It's so tidy in here. You must be such a tidy cook."

"I don't cook much."

"Lucas cooks for us, mostly. He's a better cook than I am,

more sophisticated. Trouble is, he's almost never home at the moment, so I live on sandwiches at work and crisps at home."

Elizabeth moved past her, into the sitting room, holding her glass of wine.

"Bring your tea and come and sit down."

Amy perched on the edge of a sofa, holding her mug balanced on her knees. She was wearing a very short checked skirt and a black jacket and had subdued her hair under a band. She said, "I don't really know why I've come. Well, I do, but now I'm here, I don't know how to start—"

Elizabeth took a sip of wine.

"Is it about Dale?"

"How did you know?"

"I just guessed—"

Amy leaned forward.

"Do you like her? Do you like Dale?"

Elizabeth said, "I wouldn't have the first idea how to answer that question."

"What do you mean?"

"That she's so overwhelming, so complicated, so big a personality, that liking or disliking her doesn't really seem to come into it."

Amy stared into her tea.

"I know what I think."

Elizabeth waited. She looked at Amy's neat little legs in their smooth black tights, and her competent small hands folded round her tea mug.

"We used to have such a good time, Lucas and me," Amy said. "Such fun. We were always laughing. I could tease him, I could tease him all day and he'd come back for more, he'd always come back. And it was OK when she had that boyfriend. He was a bit stuck up, but he was clever, he could manage her. But since he went, it's been awful. She won't leave Lucas alone, and he's sorry for her; he says she's his sister and she really battles with herself and that I ought to sympathize with her instead of bitching. But how can I sympathize, how can I, when she's hogging all Lucas's attention? I've tried not saying anything, but it didn't get me anywhere because Lucas didn't notice and I nearly killed myself with the effort." She stopped abruptly, took a mouthful of tea, and then said, "Sorry. I didn't mean it all to come out like that."

"It always does," Elizabeth said. She picked her wineglass up and put it down again. "Why have you come to me?"

"Because you know," Amy said. "You're coping."

"What?"

"You've seen Dale in action. You've had her around, you've seen the score. But you can manage, you can deal with it."

"Oh—"

"Lucas told me that if you could manage, I could. He said you're just getting on with your life, Dale or no Dale, and why can't I. He said I'm letting it get to me, and I needn't let it, look at you, you're not."

"Amy," Elizabeth said. "I wish it was that straightforward."

"What do you mean?"

"I mean," Elizabeth said, carefully, "that it's complicated all round just at the moment. That feelings seem to be running very high."

Amy leaned forward over her tea.

"Have you had a row with Dale?"

Elizabeth smoothed her skirt down toward her knees.

"She has a key to Tom's house. She lets herself in."

"Did you go for her?"

"I asked her not to do it anymore."

Amy let out a breath.

"Wow."

"I don't want to seem stuffy about this, but I don't feel I can talk about it much. Tom thinks—" She stopped.

"What?"

"He thinks as I imagine Lucas thinks. He thinks Dale is still upset by her love affair ending and that this has unluckily coincided with my coming on the scene, which has brought back a rush of memories of losing her mother and we've all got to be very patient and wait until enough time has passed for Dale to feel calm again."

"Oh," Amy said. She stood up, pulling her skirt down with one hand. "Will you go along with that?"

Elizabeth hesitated. She remembered sitting at Tom's kitchen table the evening after he had found her despairing in the bedroom, eating an admirable risotto he had made, and putting all the energy she had left into trying to understand, and believe, the explaining, reconciliatory things he was saying. She had so wanted to believe him; she had told herself that she owed it to him to believe him because he was so much in earnest himself, and she had ended the evening by instructing herself severely in the bathroom mirror that the very least she could do—for Tom, for herself, for both of them—was to try. She looked at Amy now.

"Yes," she said.

When Amy had gone, to catch the National Express coach back to Bath, Elizabeth scrambled herself an egg and ate it out of the saucepan with the spoon she had used to stir it, standing up by the cooker. Then she ate an apple and a digestive biscuit and made herself a mug of instant coffee, which she carried back into the sitting room. Her wineglass, still almost full, stood beside the chair she had sat in when Amy came. Amy hadn't really wanted to go. Elizabeth had seen in her face that she felt she was just getting somewhere, that she had just glimpsed gold unexpectedly, when she had realized she had to go, that Elizabeth wasn't going to open up, tell her everything, spill the beans.

Elizabeth sat down, holding her coffee mug, propping her chin on its rim, and feeling the steam rising damply up against her skin. On the way home from work, she had called in at a set of consulting rooms off Harley Street, where she had previously been to visit a gynecologist who was married to a colleague of hers. Elizabeth had been examined and had had a blood test taken and, that evening, had been told that not only was everything normal and healthy, but also she was still ovulating.

"Of course," the gynecologist had said, "your chances of conceiving would be even better if you had chosen a strapping boy of twenty-two. But we don't choose these things, do we? They choose us. Good luck, anyway."

Elizabeth had sat in a taxi between Harley Street and her flat with one hand pressed against her stomach, as if its newly realized potential made it something worth guarding, something deserving of respect. She had felt mildly elated, as if she had been congratulated for an achievement or won a small award, and had reflected, with a gratitude directed at no one in particular, how this new knowledge managed to put the disturbing events of the previous weekend into a different, and altogether less menacing, perspective. Then she had got home and found Amy's message on her answering machine and had been diverted, by Amy's imminent arrival, from telephoning anyone with the joyful news that, given the limitations of her and Tom's ages, she was still fertile, still stood a chance, at least, of conceiving a baby.

But now, sitting with her mug of coffee, she wondered about

that earlier urge to telephone. Whom should she ring? Tom? Her father? What would she say? "You'll never believe it, but I'm not too old to have a baby!" And what would they say? Would they both, for various and separate reasons, be rather taken aback, her father because babies never occurred to him even as a concept unless one was actually thrust under his nose for admiration, and Tom because she hadn't mentioned babies to him yet, because he had already had three by two previous wives, because his mind was so full—painfully full—of Dale just now that a distraction as intimate as this might seem merely provocative? She thought of Amy. Did Amy visualize having Lucas's babies, had Dale wanted Neil's? When women wanted babies, was the man they wanted them by— if, indeed, this factor entered the equation at all—the first person they told, or the last? Elizabeth ducked her chin to take a swallow of coffee. Perhaps she should, in fact, tell nobody. Who, after all, needed to know but her? Just as no one needed to know her secret rapture in family supermarket shopping, in the possession of a car, in being able to say nonchalantly, "my fiancé," and mean Tom by it, so no one needed to know about this new and extraordinary possibility. She took another swallow and put her mug down, beside the wineglass. She had told Tom she would try, in the matter of being patient with Dale. She had meant it. She would try. She put her hands gently and firmly across her stomach and held them there. Of course she would try. She could now afford to. Couldn't she?

KAREN, MATTHEW'S SISTER, waited at the gates of the school where, Sedgebury's grapevine told her, Josie was now teaching. The same grapevine had informed her that Matthew's children were also now back in Sedgebury, living with Matthew and Josie, and the stories of how they got there ranged from Nadine's being hospitalized after trying to kill herself, to Matthew abducting them from their schools, using his authority as a deputy headmaster to do so. Peggy, Karen and Matthew's mother, was inclined to believe both stories, the last followed, as a consequence, by the first.

"Don't be daft, Mum," Karen said. "Why would Matthew do anything that made things worse for his kids than they are already?"

Peggy glowered.

"We all know whose fault *that* is."

"You haven't met her," Karen said. "You haven't even seen her."

"I don't need to."

"Too right," Karen had said with emphasis. "Too bloody right. You don't need anything but your own warped mind to turn someone into Enemy Number One."

Peggy said she was going round—straight round—to Barratt Road to demand to see her grandchildren. Karen had noticed that she talked a lot like that now, insisting on her supposed rights as a consumer, a public-transport user, a council-tax payer, a wife, a grandmother. It didn't mean much, any more than those years of verbally abusing Nadine had done, it was just, Karen thought, her mother's way of asserting herself, of trying to demonstrate that, even if life had dealt her a very poor hand, she wasn't going to lie down under it. In fact, Karen had come to see, her mother loved her grievances, felt they gave her a kind of stature. If Karen's father dropped dead, all the air would rush out of her mother's balloon in an instant, being deprived, as the ultimate unfair gesture, of the focus of everything that was wrong about her life, and had been wrong for the last forty-five years.

"I'll go," Karen said wearily.

"Where'll you go?"

"I'll go and see if the kids really are back—"

Peggy snorted.

"No use asking your brother—"

"I'm not going to."

"Who then?"

"Someone who'll know."

"Not *her?*"

"It's none of your business, Mum," Karen said, "who I ask. Those kids are my nieces and nephew just as much as they're your grandchildren." She looked at Peggy. "Don't ring Nadine."

"I'll ring who I please."

Karen hesitated. She knew Nadine had rebuffed her mother and thought that the rejection had hit hard, had taken the excitement out of a new emotional campaign.

"OK."

"OK what?"

"Ring whoever you like. Just remember when you go stirring that the people who'll suffer in the long run are the kids."

Now, standing at the school gates, with her hands in her pockets and her bag slung over her shoulder, Karen wondered what she was going to say. She'd recognize Josie all right—you couldn't mistake that hair—but she'd only exchanged about ten words with her at the wedding, and there didn't seem to be an etiquette for talking to someone who you hardly knew at all but who was now part of your family. It had crossed her mind to go and see Matthew, who was, after all, her brother, but Matthew on the defensive was a Matthew Karen had been well able to do without since small childhood. In any case, she didn't have anything much personally against Josie, whatever she'd felt about Nadine. Even if Nadine had possessed an eccentric vitality that Karen had never encountered anywhere else, you could see from the children, from poor old Matt, that living with her was like living in the domestic equivalent of a permanent air raid. The grapevine that had brought news of Josie's job and the return of Matthew's children also reported a marked improvement in domestic regularity.

Josie came out of the school almost last. She was wheeling a bicycle and talking to a pair of girls with their hair pulled up in identical drooping tails above their ears. Karen moved forward until she was almost in the center of the school gateway.

"I don't expect you remember me."

Josie stopped walking. The two girls, sensing at once that adult preoccupations would immediately obliterate them from

Josie's attention, ducked sideways round Karen and made for the street outside.

"I'm Karen," Karen said. "Matthew's sister."

Josie looked at her. She wore black trousers and a jeans jacket. At the wedding, she'd been in green, with a hat she'd seemed unhappy with and had discarded almost at once.

"Of course," Josie said.

"I didn't mean to jump on you—"

"You didn't. It's just that I wasn't expecting—"

"No, I know," Karen said. "Sorry."

"Look," Josie said, "I'm afraid I can't stop. I have to meet Rufus outside his school in ten minutes."

"Can I walk with you?"

"I might have to bike, if the time gets short—"

"Of course. Can we start together, anyway?"

Josie turned her bicycle and began to walk rapidly along the pavement outside the school.

"I thought you were all ostracizing me."

"We are. Or, at least, Mum is. But you don't know Mum. When you do, you'll see it doesn't mean much. I was just waiting, really. And then—well, we heard rumors."

"What about?"

"That the kids are back."

Josie paused on a curb edge and punched the pedestrian button on a traffic light.

She said shortly, "They are."

"For good?"

Josie didn't look at her.

"It seems so. Until—"

"Nadine changes her mind again?"

Josie gave Karen a small, fleeting smile.

"You've got it."

The lights changed, and Josie pushed the bicycle across the road with energy.

Karen said, hurrying beside her, "How are they?"

"I don't know," Josie said.

"What do you mean?"

"I mean that I can't tell. I feed them and wash their clothes, but they don't really talk to me. Certainly not about how they're feeling."

Karen put a hand on the nearest handlebar to slow Josie down a little.

"You OK?"

"Not particularly," Josie said.

"Are they difficult?"

"In a word," Josie said, "yes. They are. I'm not trying to play happy families, but they seem to need to insist that I am. They are actually—" She paused.

"What?"

"Quite cruel."

"Cruel!" Karen cried.

"Oh yes," Josie said. "Kids can be cruel. You know that. One of society's many myths is that stepmothers are cruel, but has it ever struck you that stepchildren can be quite as cruel as stepmothers are supposed to be?"

Karen said uncertainly, "They're great kids—"

"If I was teaching them," Josie said, "I might agree with you. But living with them is rather different."

"What about Matt, what does Matt do?"

"He's waiting for us to get to like each other."

"Is he standing up for you?"

Josie bit her lip. Karen glanced quickly at her. She might be walking like the wind, but it was willpower, not the energy of well-being, that was driving her. She looked tired to death, fagged out, like Karen knew she looked when she came off duty. It suddenly struck her that, if Josie was in a way rejecting Matthew's children in response to their rejection of her, she might also be haunted by a fear that, in time, if things didn't improve, Matthew might reject her, too, out of ultimate solidarity with his children. She moved her hand, for a second only, from the handlebar to Josie's nearest arm.

"I'm sorry. I didn't mean to pry—"

"You aren't. You didn't. I'm really pleased to see you, but I don't know what to tell you except the facts. Look, I'm sorry, but I'll have to bike now."

Karen said, "Can I come round—"

"To Barratt Road?"

"Yes."

"Of course. We'd like it. I—I'd like it—"

"I saw that marriage," Karen said. "I saw it all its life. Even if Nadine had her moments, I saw what Matt went through. And I can—well, I can sort of see how it must be for you."

Josie faced her across the bicycle. Then she dropped her gaze and her hair swung forward, half-hiding her face.

"I just found I'd taken on more than I'd ever envisaged. I'd been a stepmother before, for heaven's sake, and that had been bad, but this is quite different. And—well, worse."

"Why?"

Josie said slowly, "Because I want Matthew like I never really wanted Tom."

She pushed the bicycle past Karen and into the road. Then she turned, one foot on the pedal.

"Thanks."

"I'll ring you," Karen said. "I'll come round."

She watched Josie ride away, bent over the handlebars as if to help the bicycle gather speed. There was something about the look of that bent back that made Karen suddenly feel sorry for her, really sorry, as she'd felt about her nice little kid at the wedding. You could see she was fighting, really fighting to keep going, to make things work, but no one was truly on her side. Foster mothers, Karen thought, adoptive mothers, now they get pats on the back, don't they, everyone thinks they're wonderful but they've had time to make a choice, make a plan, and what's more, they aren't trying to get a new relationship going at the same time, are they? And then there was Matt. He'd always been a good father, taking his share when the kids were babies, but there'd grown up in him, inevitably, a sort of lack of objectivity about his children, as if he wanted to defend them from any criticism because he knew what they had to go through, having Nadine as a mother. And that element in Matt might make him not see how hard it was for Josie, especially as, if he was being as decent to Josie's kid as was typical of him, everyone'd be telling him what a good stepfather he was. Karen sighed. Everyone seemed to expect so much of women it nearly drove you mad and, by the same token, to expect so little of men that it drove you even madder. She hitched her bag higher on her shoulder. There were times, Karen reflected, when it didn't seem just blessed to be single, but also the only way to stay sane.

Josie sat on a low wall outside Rufus's school and leaned against the wire mesh of the playground fence behind it. Rufus's head teacher had asked her to wait inside, but she'd said no, she'd wait in the open air.

"It's serious," the head teacher said. "Or at least, I want it to be very serious for Rufus. It's the first time he has ever been rude to a teacher, and I want him to realize, by doing this little task for her after school, that his behavior is in no way acceptable."

Rufus, Josie had discovered, had called his form teacher a stupid cow. It had happened after he had been reprimanded three times in class for not paying attention and for distracting the attention of everyone else at his table in a science lesson where they were learning about electrical currents. He had taken no notice of the reprimands, and had then, when informed he would have to stay in after school as a punishment and an example to others, shouted, "You can't make me, you stupid cow!" He was being detained for thirty minutes doing something, the head teacher explained, repetitive, menial, but constructive for the teacher to whom he had been rude.

"Please come inside, Mrs. Mitchell. Please make yourself comfortable in the visitors' room."

Josie had shaken her head.

"Thank you. I'll be fine outside."

"Can I get someone to bring you a cup of tea?"

"No. No, thank you. I'll be quite all right. I'll just—wait for him."

She put her head back, against the wire fence, and closed her eyes. She felt so sad for Rufus that it would have been a relief to cry, but she couldn't seem to, as if the sadness went too deep and was too dark and heavy to be assuaged so easily. Poor Rufus. Poor little Rufus, living in a household where rows, or simmering about-to-be rows, were now almost a daily occurrence, where everybody seemed to be in the exhausted, angry habit of calling each other names, where every detail of daily life, every attempt to live as some kind of unit, had to be fought over as if the participants' very survival depended upon it. That Rufus should explode today didn't really surprise Josie. She would, she knew, have to explain to these kindly women who taught him what the atmosphere was like at Barratt Road just now and why it should affect Rufus—being used to the relatively calm and civilized world of the only child—so badly. But she couldn't say it now, she couldn't say it today, she couldn't say, until she herself felt a little better, that nothing even her biddable, amenable child could do would surprise her. She turned her head a little, to get the warmth of the sun on her face. How could she be surprised at anything, having herself, only the night before, hit Becky?

She hadn't meant to. She hadn't even, until the split second she did it, been aware she was going to. She didn't think she had ever, in her adult life, hit anyone before, but there had been a moment, a ghastly, out-of-control, incandescently enraged moment in Becky's bedroom when she had known that she was literally beside herself, that she was going to do something violent. And she had. She had stepped forward into the chaos and racket of Becky's bedroom and hit her, hard, on the side of her head.

The evening had, on reflection, never boded well. Matthew, perceiving tensions mounting, had announced that he was taking Josie down to the pub on Sedgebury's unremarkable little canal, for an hour at least, away from the house, "from you lot." There'd been a chorus of objection then and a flat refusal from Becky to stay with the younger children. Matthew had argued, Becky had shouted, and Matthew, to Josie's intense disapproval and the other children's outrage, had agreed to pay her. They had then bickered about this all the way to the pub and found, when they got there, that the good weather had brought out hordes of people, spilling out from the pub onto the towpath. Josie said she would wait outside.

"No," Matthew said. "No. I want you with me."

He'd seized her hand and dragged her into the pub and

through the crowd to the bar. He was grinning determinedly, as if to show Josie that he, at least, meant to put the baby-sitting episode behind him and enjoy himself. While they stood crushed at the bar, waiting for service, Matthew got into desultory conversation with a heavy middle-aged man, perched on a bar stool and trying to chat up a couple of girls in tiny, midriff-revealing clothes, who looked about fourteen and who were smoking with the hurried awkwardness of inexperience. The man had looked round at one point and seen Josie. He indicated her to Matthew with his beer glass.

"How old's yours then?"

"Thirty-eight," Matthew said.

"Blimey," the man said. "Blimey. Thirty-eight! You want to watch it. Forty—they've had it. You'll see. They just fall apart, bums, tits, the lot. You don't want to keep them over forty."

Josie had wrenched her hand out of Matthew's and worked her way furiously out to the towpath again. Matthew followed her at once.

"Hey, it was only a joke—"

"It was disgusting."

"Yes, but it wasn't serious, he wasn't serious—"

"You were laughing!"

"Not because I agreed with him, only to be pleasant—"

"I don't want a drink, Matthew, I don't want to stay here, I want to go home."

At home, despite the warmth of the evening, the curtains of the sitting room were drawn and Rory, Clare, and Rufus were watching a program about genital plastic surgery in Hollywood. Becky was in her room, with deafening music on. She had not, as she had been asked, either put supper in the oven or laid the table.

"I'll go," Matthew said wearily. "I'll go and find her."

"No," Josie said. She felt suddenly, dangerously energetic. "No, I will."

"Please——"

"It's no good your going," Josie said. "Is it? It's no good because you're so *passive*."

He had shrugged and turned away from her, opening the drawer in which the knives and forks were kept. Josie raced up the stairs.

"Becky!"

She banged on Becky's bedroom door.

"Shove off!" Becky shouted.

Josie opened the door. The room was strewn with clothes and shoes and bags and stank like a school cloakroom. It was also shuddering with noise.

"Turn that off!"

Becky, who was standing in the middle of the room with a forbidden cigarette in her hand, merely stared. Josie pushed past her and seized her tape player, fumbling for the volume control.

"That's mine!"

"I'm not harming it, I merely want to be able to hear myself speak——"

Becky reached over and turned a knob. The volume of music declined a little, but not entirely. Then she took the tape player out of Josie's hand.

"Thank you," Josie said. She was trembling slightly. "Becky——"

"What?"

"You didn't put supper in the oven. You didn't lay the table."

"Dad never said."

"No. But I did. I asked you to."

Becky climbed onto Clare's bed, still in her boots, and leaned against the wall. She blew out a nonchalant stream of smoke.

"You don't count."

"I live in this house. I run it. I'm married to your father—"

Becky gave a snort of contempt. She trampled down the length of Clare's bed, got off the end heavily, and stubbed her cigarette out on a plate on the floor that still bore a piece of half-eaten toast.

"That doesn't give you any rights," Becky said. "That doesn't mean anything." She shot Josie a glance. "It won't even last."

"What won't?"

"This stuff with my father."

Josie found that her fists had clenched. She unrolled them and held them flat against her skirt, against the sides of her thighs.

"Becky—"

Becky grunted.

"Becky, may I tell you something? May I tell you something very important and also very true? If you were to succeed, Becky, if you were to succeed in breaking up my marriage to your father, you wouldn't rejoice. You'd be terrified. Because it wouldn't be a victory, it'd just be a loss, another loss on top of everything you've lost already."

Becky looked at her. She looked at her for a long, hard time, as if she was really trying to see something, as if she was really trying to understand. Then she flung her head back and began to laugh, great derisive cackles of laughter, as if she had never heard anything so ludicrously, unbelievably pathetic in all her life. For a moment Josie had watched her, had looked at her tossed-back head and her big, open mouth and her wild bush of hair, and then, without saying anything because she knew her hands would say it all, she stepped forward and slapped Becky, hard, on the right-hand side of her face and head. Becky had whipped upright, her eyes ablaze.

"You—you *hit* me!"

"Yes!" Josie had yelled, not caring who heard her. "Yes, I did!"

"Sometimes," Matthew said tiredly some three hours later, "I feel I haven't got four children and a wife in this house, but five children. And you're the youngest."

Josie, staring into the half-darkness of their street-lit bedroom, said nothing. Every instinct clamored to scream at him that she often *felt* like an abandoned child herself and couldn't he see it, and make allowances for it, but, even as nerve-weary as she was, she could sense that this was no moment to say such things.

Instead she said, in a voice tight with self-control, "Is Becky back?"

"No," Matthew said. "But she will be. She'll go round to a friend's, to give me a fright, but she'll be back."

"And the others?"

"In bed."

"Matt—"

"Yes."

"I'm not imagining it, am I, I'm not imagining that they're taking it out on me because they're in a state about Nadine?"

He sighed.

"I don't think so. But—"

"But what?"

"We'll be the norm, soon."

"What norm?"

"Stepfamilies. By the year 2010, there'll be more stepfamilies than birth families."

"So what?"

"So we have to go through with it, get used to it, find a way—"

"Try telling that to your oldest daughter!" Josie shouted.

There was a pause. Then Matthew said, "Lashing out isn't the answer, all the same."

Josie felt, rather than saw, him stand up.

"Where are you going?"

"To do some work."

"Now?"

"Just an hour. I may—I may be in for promotion. The head's moving on."

"Oh," Josie said faintly. "Good." She tried to say something more, something congratulatory and pleased, but from the place of shame and helplessness where she seemed to have got herself, she found she couldn't. Instead she said shakily, "Rufus—"

"He's asleep. Rory watched him."

"Watched him?"

"Rory told him he'd stay awake until Rufus was safely asleep."

Josie tried not to hear the edge of pride in Matthew's voice.

"And—and Clare?"

"In bed. Listening, if you want to know, to *The Sound of Music*."

"I see," Josie said. She turned over carefully, so that her back was toward Matthew's shadowy shape across the room. She whispered, "I see. Everybody good, but me. Everybody behaving well, except Becky who is of course now a victim, but me."

"What did you say?"

"Nothing," Josie said.

"I'll be in the attic."

"All right."

"Try and sleep," Matthew said. His voice was kind, but the wrong kind of kind, too impersonal.

She said nothing. She bunched up the guilty hand that had slapped Becky and put it under her pillow. Then she heard the door open and close quietly again, behind Matthew.

"I'm here," Rufus said.

Josie opened her eyes. Rufus was standing two feet away, pale and subdued, his uniform very symmetrically in place as if someone had arranged him before he emerged from the school building. Josie held her arms out to him.

"Oh, darling—"

He came into them and stood against her, not fighting her off, but not yielding either.

"Don't worry about it, Rufus, don't worry, I'll explain to them—"

"No."

"Darling, they must know it wasn't your fault, they must understand what—"

"*No,*" Rufus said.

She held him harder. She wanted to tell him that she felt to blame, she felt responsible, that it was her inability to cope with the household in Barratt Road that was causing him to behave in a way that he'd never behaved in before, that wasn't even in his nature. I'm distorting you, she wanted to cry into his smooth, thick hair, I'm changing you, I'm making it impossible for you to have the childhood you ought to have, that you were having, before I met Matthew.

"Rufus—"

"It's OK," he said. "Mrs. Taylor—" He stopped.

"Yes?"

"It's OK," he said again. He made a small move to pull away.

"Was she nice to you? Was she nice about it?"

He screwed his face up.

"Was she?"

He nodded.

"Look," Josie said. She let Rufus go a little, so that she could look into his face. "I know you don't want to talk about it, but I don't want you to think that it's your fault either. Do you know what I mean?"

He looked at her. His gaze was veiled, almost opaque.

"Do you want," Josie said, as gently as she could, "to go and live in Bath again? With Daddy and Elizabeth?"

Rufus sighed. He took a step backward, out of Josie's embrace.

"No," he said. "But I like going there. I like—" He stopped again.

"You don't have to say any more. Are you hungry?"

"I don't know—"

"Shall we see? Shall we go and look at a pizza, or a burger, and see how you feel?"

"I'm too tired," Rufus said.

Josie got off the wall.

"Then we'll go home—"

"Yes."

"Put your bag in my bike basket."

"I'll wheel it," Rufus said. He put his hands on the handlebars of Josie's bike and his foot on the nearest pedal and began to scoot away from her.

She said, running after him, "Matthew said Rory stayed awake for you last night."

Rufus scooted more slowly.

"Yes. He did."

It had been weird, really, but kind of, well, nice, too. Rory had said, "I'll stay awake till you're asleep," and when Rufus had stared at him, he'd added, "If you like," and Rufus had felt embarrassed and pleased and hadn't known what to say, so he'd dived into bed quickly and lain, as he always did, with his back to Rory so that he wouldn't see this disconcerting, well-intentioned watching actually going on.

"That was kind, wasn't it?"

"Yup," Rufus said, and then he said, "I'm not allowed to play football for a week," and scooted away from Josie at speed.

When they reached Barratt Road, he slowed down and walked beside her. He had a little more color in his face than he'd had when he came out of school, and his uniform, on account of his exertion on the bicycle, had a more naturally rumpled look. There would be half an hour, Josie thought, before Rory and Clare returned, and in that half-hour she could indulge, and perhaps assuage, the intensity of her maternal anxiety by spoiling Rufus with hot buttered toast and dry-roasted peanuts and by refraining—oh, she thought, *oh* how much refraining lay ahead!—from mentioning his punishment, its reason, the previous evening, the situation that had got them there, Rory, Becky, Mrs. Taylor, Matthew, anything, *anything* that would cause Rufus pain by making him think about feelings he was already battling to come to terms with.

They had hardly turned up the concrete strips of the drive before the kitchen door opened and Matthew emerged, running.

"Matt—"

"Thank God you're back. Where've you been?"

Josie didn't glance at Rufus.

"We got held up a bit. I saw your sister, I saw Karen—"

"Becky isn't back," Matthew said.

"Not—"

"No. No one's seen her. She didn't go where I thought she'd gone, she didn't go to school—"

"Oh God," Josie said.

"Come in," Matthew said. "Come in, will you?" He took the bicycle from Rufus. "The police are here. They've been waiting to talk to you."

SINCE THE CHILDREN had gone, Nadine had discovered, to her surprise and even mild disappointment, that the cottage didn't feel so threateningly insecure. It was no more orderly—Nadine despised order—and no more comfortable, certainly, but somehow, when she wasn't seeing it as a frail craft incapable of keeping safe her crew of children, it revealed itself merely to be a damp, isolated, inconvenient place to live, and nothing more.

In the first week after the children's departure, she had been frantic. She had cried and cried, wandering from room to room and making a chart on one of the kitchen walls, to enable her to cross off each day that intervened before she would be able to have them back, for some, at least, of the school holidays. She paced round the telephone, willing them to call her, which they seldom did—prevented from doing so, no doubt—and in a fit of zeal turned out their bedrooms and took all the duvets and sleeping bags and blankets to the dry cleaner's, a great fusty multicolored mound in the back of the car, giving herself an extraordinary brief sense of happiness and achievement in the process. Then the tears and the energy were followed by gloom, days when she sat at her kitchen table staring out at the moist, milky Herefordshire light, making cups of coffee she didn't drink, and waiting, like a princess in a tower, for Tim Huntley to come down, as he often did, with a covered dish of something his mother had made, and tell her she'd got to eat it, or else.

Tim Huntley had been a lifeline. He was, as a person, almost everything Nadine found incomprehensible—politically traditional, socially conventional, ill-read, obstinate, and practical. His manner to her was not dissimilar to his manner to his cows, as if she, Nadine, was a living thing that had to be kept going with regular doses of the right diet and enough simple, foolproof instructions to keep her from swerving off the rails again, getting herself into a situation she couldn't manage, like a cow on a motorway. He didn't flirt with her in the least, although she had felt, once or twice, seeing his bulk occupying such a reassuring amount of her kitchen, that she would slightly have liked him to. Instead, he found her the secondhand kiln he had promised, would only take twenty pounds for it, and showed her the way to the commune he had promised, too, where thirty or so people, mostly women and children, lived in organic harmony in a roughly converted barn, growing their own vegetables and weaving blankets of Welsh wool. They made Nadine think not so much of her erstwhile women's protest groups as of the peace marchers of her childhood and adolescence, putting flowers in the mouths of guns and lying down outside the Ministry of Defense in white T-shirts, unarmed and unintimidating. They looked kindly at Nadine's pots and told her they would be happy to see her any time, whenever she wanted, and that she must bring her children, too, when she had them with her.

Gradually, the gloom lifted. As long, she discovered, as she didn't allow herself to think too much about the children nor— even more to the point—about the situation in which they were now living, presided over by the two architects of her own unjust and deprived circumstances, she could manage, she could get through the days, she could even begin to notice the spring coming, leaves unfurling, a clump of small, intensely frilly wild daffodils in the unkempt garden behind the cottage. She even walked up to the Huntleys' farm, to find Mrs. Huntley in her kitchen, dosing two lambs with something in a couple of baby's bottles, and thank her for all those covered dishes.

"It's nothing to me," Mrs. Huntley said. "As long as you eat them."

"I do—"

"How's that boy doing then?"

Nadine looked at the lambs. They were packed in a cardboard box together, sucking and sucking on the bottle with a fervor close to ecstasy.

"He's going to school, I think—"

"That's something."

"But they don't sound very good on the telephone, they don't like it there, they don't like their stepmother."

Mrs. Huntley pulled the emptied bottle away from one lamb with a small rubbery explosion.

"Who did? Who ever liked their stepmother?"

"This one—"

"Now, now," Mrs. Huntley said. "No tales." She took the bottle away from the second lamb. "Would you like to give these two their second halves?"

Nadine found she liked it. She hadn't much liked breast-feeding her own babies, but this was different, less intimately demanding, less emotionally complex, and the lambs were so comical and endearing in their single-minded obsession with food. Two days later, Tim brought a third lamb down to the cottage, and dumped it in a box on her kitchen floor.

"What's that?"

"Something for you to look after. She needs a week of hand-feeding."

"But—"

"You do it," Tim said. "You can."

"What if something happens?"

"Then you ring me."

Nadine sat on the kitchen floor and looked at the lamb.

"She lost her mum," Tim said. "You be good to her."

"Hello," Nadine said to the lamb. She put a hand on her hard little fleecy head. "Which of us is supposed to benefit from this?"

"Both," Tim said.

When he had gone, Nadine mixed the formula he had left and fed the lamb. For the first bottle, she fed her in the box as she had done up at the farm, but with the second one, she scooped the lamb up onto her lap and held her there, feeling her hard little hooves against her thighs and every muscle solid with concentration. Then she put her back in the box. The lamb wriggled and bleated.

"No more," Nadine said. "Not now. Later."

She put a hand out, and the lamb seized the nearest finger and began to suck, surprisingly strongly and roughly.

"No," Nadine said. She took her hand away. "I'm only your foster mother, I'm afraid."

The telephone began to ring. Nadine got up from crouching over the lamb and went to answer it.

"Nadine?" Matthew said.

She turned, holding the receiver under her chin so that she could see the lamb, peering at her bright-eyed over the edge of the box.

"I've got a lamb here—"

"What?"

"I've got a lamb," Nadine said. Her voice was proud. "Here in the kitchen. I'm looking after it."

"Oh—"

"The children would love it. It's only about the size of—"

"Nadine," Matthew said. "I rang to tell you something."

"What?"

"Well, it's OK now, we've found her, but Becky went missing—"

"What!" Nadine shrieked, spinning round to face the wall, gripping the telephone.

"She—well, she ran off. She ran away—"

"Why? Why did she? What happened, what happened to her?"

"It doesn't matter what happened—"

"What do you mean, it doesn't matter? Of course it matters! It may not matter to you, but it matters to me, what causes my daughter to run away!"

"Nadine—"

"What did you do to her?" Nadine screamed.

"If you won't let me talk and tell you what happened, I'm putting the phone down."

"No!" Nadine cried. "No!"

"Then shut up and listen."

Nadine closed her eyes. She wound her fingers into the telephone cord and pulled it tightly, until the flesh went white.

"There was a row," Matthew said, "a family row in which Becky participated—"

"I don't believe you!"

"In which Becky participated as much as anyone and which resulted in her leaving the house to go round, I thought, to see a friend—"

"Did you check? When she'd gone out, plainly distressed, did you bother to check where she might be?"

"I thought, to see a friend, but it transpired that she didn't do that, she didn't go anywhere near anyone she knew—"

"Oh my God," Nadine said. She disentangled her fingers and shook them to get the circulation going again. "Oh my God, how could you, how could you?"

"She went clubbing," Matthew said. "There's a new club in Sedgebury, and she went there. I didn't even know it existed, or I'd have gone to look. I thought she was staying away just to scare me."

"I bet you slept like a top," Nadine said bitterly.

"I didn't sleep at all," Matthew said. "I haven't slept for nights, not even after we found her. Or, at least, the police did."

"The police!"

"She hitched a lift. I think maybe she was aiming to get to Herefordshire, but she was found outside Stafford, in a lorry drivers' café. They brought her back last night. She's OK."

"Where is she now?"

"In bed."

"Get her! Get her for me! I've got to speak to her!"

"She's sedated. She was fine but very tired, so the doctor's given her something—"

"I must *talk* to her!" Nadine shouted.

"You can't, just now. She's to sleep until she wakes."

"I demand it! I'm her mother!"

"She'll ring you the moment she wakes up—"

"I'm coming. I'm getting in the car, and I'm coming."

"No, you're not."

"You can't stop me, I have every right, especially in the face of your neglect, your carelessness, your obsession with your new life that means you can't even——"

Matthew put the phone down.

"Bastard!" Nadine yelled into her receiver. Then she slammed it back onto the telephone. From its box the lamb, still fixing Nadine with her bright, insistent gaze, began to bleat.

"Shut up!" Nadine said. She was beginning to shake. She put out one unsteady hand and picked up the telephone receiver again, and then, with the other hand and with difficulty, dialed Tim's number.

"Come quickly——"

"What's up?"

"Come quickly. Come and take this lamb, I can't cope, I can't manage——"

"Stay there," Tim Huntley said.

Nadine nodded. She let the receiver slip from her grasp, and then she slid down the kitchen cupboards she had been leaning against until she was sitting on the floor.

"Becky, oh Becky, poor Becky, poor——"

She gathered her knees up in her arms and put her head down on them and, still watched intently by the lamb, began to shake and whisper to herself.

"I'm so sorry," Josie said.

She sat on the edge of Becky's bed, toward the foot, as if to sit any farther toward the head implied an intimacy she felt she had no right to. Becky lay quite straight, in exactly the position in which she had woken, after sleeping for nineteen hours, with her head turned away from Josie and her gaze fixed on the wall.

"I really am. I apologize unreservedly. Whatever either of us said, I should never, ever, have hit you and I regret it so much. I am truly sorry."

Becky didn't move. She lay as if she were wholly unaware of Josie, as if Josie simply didn't exist for her, as if she had never spoken. Josie looked at her face—very pale—and at the dark tangle of hair on the pillow, and then, diffidently, at the long line of Becky's body under the duvet. The police had said Becky had had a bit of a scuffle sometime in the two days and three nights of her absence, probably with one of the truck drivers who had given her a lift, but that it hadn't been serious, Becky hadn't been harmed. The doctor who sedated her said that she was a little bruised across the chest and shoulders, but otherwise all right. Becky said nothing. Whatever she had told the police or the doctor, she had declined to repeat to Matthew or Josie. She didn't seem relieved to be home, merely resigned, as if she'd suspected that this was how a gesture of spontaneous defiance would end anyway, as if her heart had not really been in it, because of that.

"Are you hungry?" Josie said. "Would you like something to eat?"

Becky gave the smallest shake of her head. She wasn't hungry or thirsty, she wasn't, at the moment, conscious of any of the usual appetites but only of a curious, weightless, detached calm.

"Becky," Josie said, "will you speak to me? Will you at least accept that I am really sorry for what I did?"

Becky neither moved nor uttered. Slowly, Josie got off the bed and stood up. She had told the police that she had struck Becky, and they had reacted as if smacks to the head followed by a child search were hardly out of the ordinary to them.

"It happens," the sergeant had said. "It happens all the time. First sign of an adult stepping out of line, and the kids do a bunk."

He hadn't looked at Josie while he said it, but at Matthew, and Josie had felt obscurely reprimanded, the one who couldn't cope, couldn't keep a hold on her temper, couldn't rely on her supposed maturity. When the police rang, almost thirty-six agonizing hours later, and she answered the telephone, they asked to speak to Matthew.

"Mr. Mitchell, please," they said, "the young lady's father."

"But have you——"

"Mr. Mitchell, please. Becky Mitchell's father. At once, please."

Matthew had wept when he heard Becky was safe. So did Josie, and Clare. Rufus and Rory sprawled on the stairs and kicked the banisters. Matthew had taken Clare on his knee, and then Rory had climbed over Rufus to come and stand by his father and sister, and Matthew had put an arm out and pulled him in.

I'm in disgrace, Josie thought.

She went into the kitchen and cried into the sink, holding on to the stainless-steel rim and letting her tears splash down in big drops like rain. Rufus came into the kitchen and leaned on the cupboards beside her.

"You didn't do it on purpose," he said.

"I did at the last minute. At the last minute, it was definitely on purpose——"

"You can't help the last minute," he said. "No one can."

Josie shot him a quick grateful glance.

"Thank you."

"It's true," he said.

It was a woman police officer who had escorted Becky into the house, and then a woman doctor had come from the Sedgebury practice Josie wasn't yet very familiar with. They had both been very matter-of-fact. Becky had had an escapade from which she had escaped physically unharmed at least. That was all they needed to know: anything else was Matthew's business, Becky's business, and to a much lesser extent plainly, Josie's business. Matthew and Rory had moved the mattress of Clare's bed to the space on the floor between the beds in the boys' room, and Becky had showered, in silence, and had then taken her prescribed sleeping pills and closed her own bedroom door behind her. Josie had put clean linen on her bed—a futile gesture, she knew, but what could she do just now that wasn't futile—and Becky had climbed in and slept and slept and slept. Before they went to bed, Josie found Matthew sitting on the base of Clare's bed and gazing at Becky intently, while she slept. There had seemed to be nothing to say to him, just as there seemed, now, nothing to say to Becky.

"Come down, when you want to," Josie said. "Or stay there. It doesn't matter. You do what you want to."

She looked round the room. Becky's boots lay on the floor, beside Clare's babyhood blue nylon fur teddy bear and a torn chocolate-bar wrapper.

"Sorry," Josie said again.

"Hello," Matthew said.

Becky turned her head very slowly on the pillow.

"Hi."

He came to stand beside the bed, looking down at her. All that sleep and almost nothing to eat had given her a luminous look, almost one of fragility. Beside the bed, on the floor, was a tray bearing an untouched bowl of soup and an uneaten sandwich.

"Josie brought you lunch, I see."

"I didn't want it."

"But you're eating chocolate." He glanced at the sweet wrappers scattered on the carpet.

"So?"

He sat down on the edge of the bed.

"How much longer do you intend to stay in bed?"

She shrugged.

"I dunno."

"You aren't ill, Becky."

She said nothing.

"We can't go on looking after you as if you were ill, if you aren't. Especially if you won't eat food Josie takes the trouble to prepare for you."

Becky sighed.

"Josie's taking time off work," Matthew said. "To be with you. I can't, but she has managed it. She's staying here especially to look after you."

"I didn't ask her," Becky said. "She doesn't have to."

"She feels she does."

"That's her problem."

"No. It's her sense of responsibility. She offered to do it, to help me, for my peace of mind, as well as for you."

Becky gave the food on the tray a brief, contemptuous glance.

"I'm not eating it."

"Then I'll tell her to stop bringing it up."

"Suit yourself," Becky said.

Matthew put his elbows on his knees, and leaned on them.

"I've got something to say to you."

"Jesus—"

"It's not about what happened. I'll never ask you about that. If you want to tell me, you can, but I'm not asking. All I care about is that you're safe."

Becky waited. She yawned. She scooped her hair up into a thick bunch at the back of her head and let it fall again.

"I love Josie," Matthew said.

Becky froze.

"I want you to be very certain of that. I love her. I want you to be very certain of something else, too. I love you. Whatever happens, whatever becomes of us, that is a given. You are my daughter and I love you."

Becky made a face.

"But?" she inquired sweetly.

"Not quite but."

"What then?"

"You seem to think," Matthew said, turning to look at her, "that I have to choose, that I have to choose between you and her. But I don't. I want you to be as certain of that as you are certain that I love you. I don't have to choose. I can have both relationships. You and her."

She stared at him.

"You can't," she said rudely.

"I can," he said. He stood up. He seemed, suddenly, enormously tall, standing there so close to her bed. "It's you that can't." There was a beat. Becky couldn't look at him. She stared down, instead, at her fingernails, which she had painted electric blue and then picked away at. Matthew moved away from her bed toward the door.

"If that's what you decide," he said.

The house was very quiet. Becky supposed Josie was downstairs, marking books maybe, or making one of her I'm-a-perfect-mummy cakes, or mending. Becky had never seen anyone mend clothes before. Nadine never did, had never, as far as Becky could remember, sewn on so much as a button. But Josie mended. She'd patched Rory's jeans and sewn up a long ripped seam in Clare's Disney tracksuit. Becky couldn't think how they'd let her.

She sat on the edge of her bed. She was dressed and felt rather fidgety but, at the same time, directionless. She was also hungry. Despite Matthew's instructions, Josie had offered her a sandwich at lunchtime, standing at the bottom of the stairs and calling up, and Becky'd shouted above the music she'd started playing again that she wasn't hungry, that she didn't want anything. The thought of a sandwich made her mouth water. She'd found half a packet of crisps in the boys' bedroom and two sticks of gum in the pockets of her jeans jacket and devoured them. She had no cigarettes. The last cigarette had been a week ago, when the man who'd run the café where the police had come had given her one. He'd also given her a fried breakfast that made her drool to remember.

"Stupid bloody kid," he'd said to her. "As if running away ever solved anything."

But he'd given her the fags and the breakfast, and when the police came in, he'd stood by her table to defend her, if necessary. It wasn't necessary. She'd never tell anyone until her dying day, but Becky had been so thankful to see the police come in, she'd nearly run into their uniformed arms.

Downstairs, the telephone began ringing. It rang twice, three times, and then Josie answered it. Becky could hear the sound of her voice, but not what she was saying. After a moment or two, the sitting-room door opened downstairs and Josie called, "Becky?" Her voice sounded odd.

Becky stood up.

"Yes?"

"Becky. Can you come?"

She went slowly out onto the landing. Josie was at the foot of the stairs.

"Becky, it's your mother—"

"Yes?"

"She—doesn't sound very well, she sounds a bit fraught—"

Becky clumped down the stairs, pushing past Josie. Nadine always sounded fraught, especially if she had to ring Barratt Road, had to risk speaking to Josie. She picked up the telephone receiver.

"Mum?"

Nadine was crying.

"You've got to come—"

"What? What's the matter?"

"You've got to, I'm not allowed to come to you, your father won't let me, and now this has happened—"

"What has?"

"Becky, I can't cope I can't manage, you've got to come, you've got to come quickly—"

"What's happened? Are you OK? Are you hurt?"

"I don't know," Nadine said, her voice ragged with tears. "I don't know."

"Jesus," Becky said. She swallowed. "Have you taken anything? Have you taken any pills or anything?"

"No," Nadine said. "No. But I need you. I need you here. I need you to come. I haven't seen you since all that happened, I have to see you, I *have* to."

"OK," Becky said. Her voice, she noticed, was shaky, as if she was shivering. "OK."

"Quickly," Nadine said. *"Quickly."*

"Yes."

Becky heard the telephone go down. She stood for a moment, looking at the receiver in her hand, and then she put it down, too, and walked slowly into the kitchen. Josie was sitting at the table with an open checkbook in front of her, paying bills. She looked up as Becky came in and said in a neutral voice, "All right?"

Becky hesitated. She put a hand up to her mouth and began to chew at a cuticle.

"Not really," she said.

Josie put her pen down. She said, less neutrally, "What's the matter?"

"She was crying," Becky said. "She sounded awful. She kept asking me to go—"

"To her? To Herefordshire?"

"She said I must. She said she needed me. She said something had happened."

Josie stood up.

"Is she ill?"

Becky looked at her.

"I don't know, she just sounded desperate. I—I've got to go, I've got to—"

"How will you get there?"

Becky's shoulders slumped.

"I don't know. Train maybe, then a taxi—"

"I could take you," Josie said.

"You—"

"I've got the car today. It's outside. I could drive you to your mother's. Just let me leave a note for the others and ring Matthew—"

"No," Becky said.

"No?"

"Don't tell Dad," Becky said. "Please. Just do it. Don't tell Dad."

"Won't he think," Josie said, looking straight at Becky, "that it's the second irresponsible thing I've done as far as you're concerned, in a week?"

Becky knew her face and voice were full of pleading. She couldn't seem to help it.

"I'll tell him—"

"What will you tell him?"

"That you did it—" She stopped, gulped and then said, "To help me."

Josie went over to the refrigerator.

"If we're going to Herefordshire, you have to eat something."

"No—"

"Becky," Josie said, "you've eaten nothing sensible for a week, and you don't know what lies ahead of you now. What help will it be to your mother if you faint at her feet?"

"We've got to go," Becky said.

Josie stepped back.

"Take three things out of there, to eat on the journey, while I turn the car round. And leave a note for your father."

"What'll I say?"

Josie went quickly past her and lifted the car keys from their hook by the outside door.

"I don't know," she said. "That's up to you."

16

RUFUS SAT AT the desk in his bedroom and contemplated his new curtains. They were green and cream, checked, quite a big check, with a dark green line running parallel to the edge. The line was made of something called braid, cotton braid. Rufus had chosen it when he went to choose the green-and-cream checks. He felt, surveying his first excursion into interior decor, very satisfied and rather as if he would like to go a bit further now and have a new duvet cover, since the arrival of the curtains had made the Batman print on his bed look babyish. Also a rug. Perhaps a red rug. He would ask Elizabeth. It was she, after all, who had taken him to the curtain place and just let him decide. She'd opened little fat books of pieces of material and said, "What about that?" and, "That sort of green?" and, "I think you said no patterns, only lines, didn't you?" and left him to it. When the saleslady referred to Elizabeth as Rufus's mother, Elizabeth had said, in a perfectly normal voice, "I'm not Rufus's mother, but I am soon going to be his stepmother." Afterward she never mentioned it, thereby relieving a moment of deep, inexplicable embarrassment. She was, he was beginning to see, to be relied upon in this way; she could be trusted to see things as they were and not as they might be, or could have been, or should be. She could be trusted not to make a fuss.

"Rufus," Dale said.

He glanced toward his bedroom door. Dale was leaning against the frame. She had shiny black boots on. Rufus looked at them.

"Hello."

"Very smart curtains," Dale said.

"I chose them."

"Excellent choice. Nice desk, too."

Rufus took his gaze away from Dale's feet and transferred it to his desktop. He kicked at the stretcher bar under his chair. He was never quite sure what he felt about Dale. He knew she was his half-sister, but she didn't *feel* like one, she didn't feel like someone who belonged to him. He'd known, all his life, that Dale didn't like his mother, and that had always been disconcerting. He could see why people sometimes got cross with his mother, but not liking her was something else, something that made him feel he didn't want to be around people who thought like that. In fact, he'd always liked the house better when Dale wasn't in it.

Dale moved from the doorway and went to the window.

"You've got such a nice view."

Rufus said nothing. He picked up a retractable pen from his desk and began to click the point in and out, in and out.

"It's much nicer than my view," Dale said. "I don't know why I didn't choose this room when I was little. I expect I chose mine so I could see the street, and then I could always see my mother and father coming home." She turned round from the window. "I may be coming back here to live for a bit."

Rufus stopped clicking.

"Why?"

"I've sold my flat," Dale said. "I sold it really easily, it was amazing. And I haven't bought another one yet. So I think I'll come home for a while and live up here. I could make Lucas's old room into a sitting room, couldn't I?"

"It's full of mess," Rufus said.

"I could clear that. Perhaps we could put some in here, in boxes, because you aren't here very often, are you?"

Rufus jabbed the pen into the palm of his hand.

"I am."

"What, once a month—"

"I don't want mess in here."

"It would be very tidy, all in boxes—"

"No!"

"OK," Dale said. "It was just a suggestion. I'll find somewhere else."

Rufus slid out of his desk chair. He wanted to say that he didn't want Dale there at all, he didn't want Dale up on his floor with him, where it was private, he didn't want her living there beside his room when he wasn't there himself, because he was in Matthew's house. But somehow he couldn't.

"I'm going downstairs," he said.

In the kitchen, Elizabeth was reading the newspaper. She had it spread flat on the table, and she had her glasses on and a mug of tea beside the newspaper. She didn't look up when he came in, but she said, "There's a story here about albino frogs in the West Country. They aren't green, they're orange and pink and white. I shouldn't like that at *all*."

Rufus hitched himself onto a chair opposite her.

"Sometimes there's toads in the garden here."

"Are there?"

"I took a baby one to school once, in some wet stuff." He began to fiddle with the edge of Elizabeth's newspaper, scuffling the pages about. She didn't tell him to stop. Instead she watched him for a bit, and then she said, "Is Dale upstairs?"

He nodded. Elizabeth sighed. She took her glasses off.

He said, "Where's Daddy?"

"In the office."

"Dale said she was going to live in her room again."

Elizabeth looked down at the paper.

"I know."

"She wants to put some of the junk out of Lucas's room in my room."

"She can't do that," Elizabeth said.

"Does Daddy know?"

"Yes."

"Is he cross?"

"No," Elizabeth said. She looked at him. "Don't worry. Nobody's putting anything in your room that you don't want there."

Rufus wondered whether to say it wasn't just junk he didn't want, he didn't want Dale up there either. He glanced at Elizabeth. She was still looking at him, very seriously, as if to reassure him that nobody was going to say, "Oh, Rufus is only eight and he's hardly ever here and he won't mind anyway," and get away with it.

"Shall we go out?" Elizabeth said.

"Out?"

"Yes. We could go and look at something or visit my father or go for a walk."

"Could we buy a rug?"

"A rug?"

"For my room. A red one."

"I don't see why not. Would you like to see my father, too?"

Rufus nodded. Elizabeth stood up.

"Would you like to go and tell Daddy we're going out then?"

Rufus hesitated.

"Aren't you going to?"

"No," Elizabeth said. "I'm not."

Rufus slid off his chair.

"Will we be hours?"

"We might be. We might decide to have lunch somewhere."

"What about Daddy's lunch?"

Elizabeth picked up her handbag and opened it, to put her glasses away.

"Dale can do that."

Rufus moved to the kitchen doorway and then stopped.

"Is Daddy cross?" he said again.

Elizabeth took a lipstick out of her handbag.

"No," she said. "It isn't Daddy that's cross. I'm afraid it's me that is."

Lucas lay full-length on one of the sofas in his flat, with his eyes closed. There was jazz—Stan Getz—coming softly from his disc player, but otherwise the flat was quiet, blessedly quiet, because Amy had gone to see a film with a friend and Dale had changed her mind about coming over because she was all fired up about this new plan of hers, for moving back into Tom's house, into her old bedroom, and Lucas's old bedroom, until she got another place of her own.

"Only until—" she'd said to Lucas. "Only for a few weeks."

He'd shaken his head.

"You shouldn't—"

"Why not? Why shouldn't I? Because of her? Because of her and Dad and"—her voice thickened ominously—"their *privacy?*"

"No," Lucas said. "Because of you."

"What d'you mean?"

"I mean you'll never go forward if you keep taking yourself backward."

"I'm not," Dale said. "I'm just being sensible."

"She doesn't know the meaning of the word," Amy said later. "She can't do anything unless there's some great emotional doodah hanging off it. Everything she does has to be a big deal—she can't even pick up the dry cleaning without it being a three-act drama."

Lucas said nothing. Amy had spoken out of turn, of course, and broken the rules of the uneasy truce that had existed between them since they'd had that major row about Dale. It had been late at night, late the night Amy had been to London to interview for the film job she didn't get, and he'd been almost asleep and she'd woken him to describe to him, mostly at the top of her voice, all the things she'd ever thought about Dale, all the elements in Dale's behavior she couldn't take. He'd tried to calm her, he'd tried to tell her that he well knew the difference between loving a sister and loving a future wife, but she'd shrieked that he didn't know what he was talking about, that anyone who called their sister "cupcake" and "pumpkin" like some third-rate American soap-opera character had a serious problem with arrested emotional development, let alone something worse, something *much* worse, and then she'd slammed out of their bedroom and spent the rest of the night where he was now lying, on the sofa.

There'd been a ragged reconciliation in the morning. He'd found her making tea, still in her clothes from the day before, and put his arms round her and said he was sorry, he never meant to upset her.

"You don't," she said. "It's her. And maybe your attitude to her."

"Then we won't talk about her."

"We have to!"

"No, we don't. Why do we?"

"To get it sorted—"

"There's nothing to sort," Lucas had said. "There's just the fact that she is my sister, and nothing you or I can do will make that fact any different. So I suggest we just don't talk about it. We just *stop*."

He didn't find it difficult. Dale was there, but she didn't have to be part of the whole of his life, only the part that related to her, to family. She preoccupied him when she was troublesome as anything else did, as work was preoccupying him now with all the uncertainties attendant upon the radio station being sold to another company. He knew that it was unlikely he would ever have an entirely quiet mind about Dale, but he wasn't going to let her and her problems expand to fill all the space available in his mind and heart. He loved her, certainly, but not as the number-one priority, not to the exclusion of all else. One of the easiest ways, he found, to reduce Dale and her demands to manageable proportions was not to think about her too much, and to speak of her even less. But, it seemed, Amy couldn't do this, Amy couldn't push Dale out of the foreground into the background. Amy's feelings for Dale were like lava: they seethed away underground, barely contained, and every so often, a stream of something molten, red-hot, would erupt into the air and scald both of them. There were times, in the last few months, when Lucas had felt like walking out, just abandoning the clamorous mess of emotions for a simple, physical, anonymous life on a building site, a road construction, even a factory floor. But he hadn't done it. He told himself that he hadn't done it because he knew that the burden of emotional baggage is not a matter of geography but of attitude, but in his heart of hearts he knew he hadn't gone because he hadn't yet reached a point where, to survive, he simply *had* to. Maybe he never would. Maybe—and this he feared more than anything—he would be afraid to seize such a moment when it came.

He opened his eyes and regarded the ceiling. He had painted it himself when he and Amy moved in together, and he had made the bookshelves and sanded the floors. He was good with his hands. He held them up and inspected them. He reflected on all the things they had made, all the surfaces they had touched, all the functions he required them to perform without consciously asking them. They were, his father said, the same shape as his mother's hands, just as his coloring was hers, and not his father's. He didn't often think about his mother now. There'd been a time when he thought about her, secretly, all the time and held long, angry, lonely one-sided conversations with her, but he'd come to realize that he was having these conversations with someone he imagined, rather than with someone he remembered, and the urgency of them had faded. And then, as time went on, he found he was surrendering Pauline's memory to Dale, partly because Dale wanted it so much but partly because he didn't need it. He often thought how wonderful it would have been if Pauline had lived, how different their lives would have been, but he only thought it, he didn't try and long for it. His father, after all, was a great father, and he hadn't minded his first stepmother—except for the pain she caused by leaving—and wasn't about to mind the second one either. All he minded, just now, was the doubt that hung over his job, the lack of harmony that clouded his relationship with Amy, and his apprehension that, if everything fell apart and he turned to his father for help, his father wouldn't see him because of being turned in the opposite direction, looking instead at Elizabeth.

The telephone, in ugly contrast to Stan Getz, began ringing the far side of the room. Lucas sat up slowly and stretched. Then he padded across the floorboards he had sanded and waxed and picked up the receiver.

"Hello?"

"Lucas?" Elizabeth said.

"Oh," he said. "Hi."

"I hope I'm not disturbing you—"

"No," he said, "you're not. I wasn't doing anything much."

He sat down in the chair by the telephone and balanced the ankle of one leg across the knee of the other.

"What can I do for you?"

Elizabeth said, slightly hesitantly, "I'm in a bit of a quandary—"

"Oh?"

"I expect you know, don't you, that Dale is planning to move back into her old bedroom here?"

"Yes."

"I rather wanted," Elizabeth said, "to know what you think about that."

"What I think—"

"Yes."

Lucas began to revolve his balanced foot, round and round, slowly.

"What does Dad think?"

There was a beat, and then Elizabeth said, "I very much want to do the right thing."

"I don't follow you."

"When I suggested, some months ago, offering my house to

Dale, your father thought I shouldn't, that it wouldn't be a good idea for Dale or for us to live so closely. But now she is actually proposing to move back into this house, he doesn't seem to see things the same way."

"Have you talked to him about it?"

"Yes," Elizabeth said.

"And what did he say?"

"He said that it was only for a few weeks, and that I must keep a sense of proportion."

"I see," Lucas said. He lowered his turning foot to the floor and lifted his other one, to balance it across his knee. "So why are you telephoning me?"

"To see if there is some piece of the jigsaw I'm missing, to see if there is something really obvious I haven't got—"

"You don't want Dale to move in?"

"No," Elizabeth said quietly.

Lucas closed his eyes. He thought of his father. He thought of his father's eternally complex commitment to Dale, and he thought of Amy and the possible insecurity of his future and the uncomfortable emotional intensity of his present. He opened his eyes again. He liked Elizabeth, he really did, but she'd have to find her own way out of the wood, otherwise she'd only get drawn back in again, and be ultimately lost.

"Sorry," Lucas said.

"What?"

"I'm sorry, but I can't help you. I can't do anything."

He thought he heard a faint sigh.

"No," Elizabeth said.

Lucas smiled into the receiver, to convey as much warmth as he could.

"See you soon," he said. "Bye."

———◦◉◦———

Duncan Brown made himself some soup in a mug. It really was most ingenious, the way a small foil envelope of fawn-colored powder, faintly speckled, became, with the addition of boiling water, a mug of mushroom soup, complete with little dark chunks of actual mushroom. He stirred it thoughtfully. His late wife, Elizabeth's mother, had always, meticulously, made mushroom soup in a saucepan, starting with mushrooms and flour and butter and going on with stock and milk, the whole process involving time and attention and washing-up. It would have troubled her to see Duncan's foil packets, though it mightn't have surprised her to see them. "Oh, *Duncan*," she'd have said, and her voice would have been exasperated and indulgent all at once.

"Am I like my mother much?" Elizabeth had said to him today.

"Only to look at, really. Why do you ask?"

"I don't seem to remember her as very maternal——"

"She wasn't."

"And I want a baby so much!" Elizabeth had cried suddenly, and then burst into tears.

Duncan carried his soup mug and a half-eaten packet of water biscuits into his sitting room. The air smelled faintly of cinnamon, on account of a spray Shane had taken to using that he claimed kept the dust down. Duncan made his way to his particular chair and sat down in it, holding his soup mug carefully level and putting the biscuit packet down on a nearby pile of books. It was on the small, broken-springed sofa opposite that Elizabeth had been sitting when she had said—quite violently for her—that she wanted a baby so badly.

"Why shouldn't you have one?" Duncan said gently.

Elizabeth blew her nose fiercely.

"Tom doesn't want one."

"Ah."

"He's had three. He says he's too old. He doesn't seem to see that I've never had one, but I badly want one, and that I, miraculously, don't seem to be too old at all to stand quite a good chance of having one."

Duncan got up and poured two generous quantities of sherry into a couple of rose-pink Moroccan tea glasses. He held one out to Elizabeth.

"Thank you," she said. "But I don't really like sherry—"

"I know you don't. But drink it all the same. It's so strong, it's distracting."

"It's like talking to someone who can't hear me," Elizabeth said. "First Dale, and now this. No, he says, smiling and kind and immovable, no. No baby. We don't need a baby, we have each other, we have our work, we have Rufus, whom we both adore— true—and we don't need a baby." She took a gulp of sherry and then said, more wildly, "But *I* do! I want home and hearth and a *baby!*"

Duncan turned the tea glass round in his fingers.

"Do you imagine the present difficulties with Dale—"

"Oh, don't *talk* about them," Elizabeth said, blowing her nose again. "You can't *imagine*, you can't conceive of how demanding she is, and how passive he seems to me in response! And I have to behave so beautifully, I have to be so restrained and careful and courteous and tactful, and never expose my true feelings while Dale thrusts hers in your face because she always has, no one's ever told her not to, she believes she has every right to impose her own needs and desires all over everyone else, and insist upon our sympathy, all the time, about *everything*, because, once upon a time she lost a mother whom I am beginning to detest with an intensity that amazes me."

"Goodness," Duncan said.

Elizabeth took another gulp of sherry and made a face.

"It's such a relief to *say* it."

"And the brother?"

"I rang him," Elizabeth said. "I probably shouldn't have, but I was at the end of my tether, and I had this mad idea of asking him to stand up for me in this business of Dale moving back in. But when it came to it, I couldn't ask him, I couldn't say. He——"

"What?"

"He sort of implied I'd got to sort it out for myself, and of course he's right."

"But *can* you?" Duncan said. "Can you disentangle all this if Tom can't help you?"

Elizabeth sighed. She reached out and put the tea glass, still half full of sherry, on the copy of *Chambers's Twentieth Century Dictionary* that Duncan used for newspaper crosswords.

"I love him," Elizabeth said. "I see how hard it is for him, I see how torn he is, I see how he is burdened with this sense of responsibility he's had ever since Pauline died. I just wonder—if he can see how hard it is for me, too."

"I expect he can," Duncan said. "And doesn't know what to do about it."

She looked at him.

"Did you do that? With Mother?"

He smiled.

"Why do you keep bringing her into it?"

"Because I keep wondering what she'd do in my place, what she'd tell me to do."

Duncan watched her. The glow he'd noticed at Christmas, gilding her like a nimbus, had dimmed a little.

"I said to Tom," Elizabeth said, her voice a little hoarse, as if tears were still not very far away, "I said, 'Can't you see, we are all lonely in this about-to-be family? There's a sense in which we're all excluded from something and another sense in which we're all powerless to change things. But we've got to *try*, we've got to put the past behind us and try.' "

"What did he say?"

Elizabeth picked up the pink tea glass again.

"He said you can't alter the past, but because of the past, everything that comes after *is* altered. Something happens, a deed is done, and the consequences just go rolling on. He made me feel—" She stopped, bit her lip, and then she said, "That I had lived too sheltered a life to know."

"A little patronizing, perhaps."

"But true, too. I've been a bit like a book on a shelf that no one's really wanted to take down and read avidly until now."

"Elizabeth," Duncan said.

"Yes?"

"You're in a corner, aren't you, up a cul-de-sac—"

"Yes."

"My dear. What are you going to do?"

She lifted the tea glass and drained all the sherry out of it in two swallows. Then she put the empty glass back on the dictionary.

"I'm going to ask him," she said. "Ask him to stand up for me."

THE HUNTLEYS' FARMHOUSE rose redly out of the red Herefordshire earth as if it had, over the centuries, just slowly emerged
from it. It was built on a slope, with carelessly arranged barns here
and there beside it, and a stream between it and the lane over which
Tim had laid a crude bridge made of old railway sleepers. As Becky
crossed the bridge, two sheepdogs tethered with long, clattering
lengths of chain just inside the entrance to the nearest barn raced
forward, barking and leaping. They couldn't reach her by yards,
but all the same, Becky kept to the far side of the bridge and made
at speed for the gate into the little farm garden. She didn't like
dogs.

The door to the house opened before she reached it. Mrs.
Huntley, whom she had never met, stood in the doorway and
regarded her without smiling.

"We wondered when you'd be coming."

Becky swallowed. She put a hand, with its chipped blue-painted nails, up to her hair and pushed it off her face.

"I've been looking after Mum."

Mrs. Huntley surveyed her. She looked at her unbrushed hair and her jeans jacket and her long, grubby skirt and her unpolished boots. She said, as if making a concession, "You'd better come in."

Becky followed her. The kitchen was low and small and shabby and clean. On a plastic-covered table by the window were several egg boxes holding weirdly sprouting seed potatoes, and to one side of them sat Tim Huntley, in his stockinged feet, eating something from a steaming plate. He gave Becky the merest glance and indicated the chair opposite him.

"Sit down."

Becky sat. She folded her blue nails out of sight and put her fists in her lap. Mrs. Huntley poured a cup of tea from a pot on the range and put it on the table within Becky's reach. Becky didn't drink tea, hadn't ever, really, had recently made a point of not drinking it, out of defiance.

"Thanks," she said.

"Well," Tim said. "What have you got to tell us?"

Becky looked at her tea. She would have liked something to hold, but she wasn't sure her hand was steady enough to expose to the Huntleys' gaze, lifting a cup. She said, "I—I don't know what happened."

Mrs. Huntley said, "What did your mother say?"

Becky hesitated. Nadine had been unable to tell her exactly but had done a good deal of hinting. She'd been wildly upset, she said, at hearing of Becky's running away and then outraged at Matthew's refusal to let her come . . .

"He didn't," Becky said wearily.

"He did, he did, he forbade me!"

... and then Tim had brought her a lamb and she thought she could cope and then she heard about Becky and panicked and rang Tim and he came and she was hysterical and then he slapped her and lugged her upstairs to bed and then ...

"What?" Becky said.

"I can't tell you."

"Did he try anything? Did he start mucking you about?"

"I don't know," Nadine said, "I can't remember, I just know he scared me, he was rough, I didn't know what was going to happen."

Becky looked away now from both Tim's and Mrs. Huntley's gaze.

"She—she's not very clear."

Tim snorted.

"We don't want any nonsense," Mrs. Huntley said. "We don't mind looking after her, a bit of food and that, but we don't want any trouble."

"I came," Becky said, loudly before her courage went, "to thank you for that, to thank you for getting the doctor."

Tim shrugged.

"She was hysterical."

Becky said nothing.

He put a mouthful in, chewed awhile, and then said, "She was on the floor when I got there, and when I tried to get her up, she went for me. So I slapped her. Slapped her to shut her up." He took a swallow of tea. "Then I took her upstairs. She was scream-ing all the way." He gave Becky a level look. "I put her on the bed. Then I went down and rang the doctor."

Becky looked at her cup of tea. It was thick, milky brown.

She said, "She's better now."

"Glad to hear it."

Mrs. Huntley said, "Did she ring you?"

"Yes—"

"Who brought you? We saw a car, a red car—"

Becky hesitated.

"My—stepmother."

"That was good of her," Mrs. Huntley said.

Becky nodded. It had been good of her. It had also been deeply disconcerting, not so much the journey itself with the disquieting forced intimacy of being alone in a car together, but more when they got there and Josie had offered to come into the cottage with her.

"No," she'd said. "No, it's OK."

"But—"

"I'll come out," Becky said. "I'll come out if there's anything—"

Josie had looked up at her, out of the car window.

"I'll wait here."

Becky had nodded. She'd put her hand on the cottage's lopsided, rickety garden gate, and for a moment had felt she could go no farther. She stood there, head bent, looking at her hand on the gate and fighting, with every ounce of strength she possessed, the urge to turn round and say to Josie, "Come with me, please come." She'd won. It had taken her some time, but she'd won. She'd gone up the path to the cottage's back door and in through the kitchen and up the stairs, step after step, to find Nadine lying in bed with her eyes closed. It was only then that she'd screamed, it was only then that she'd allowed herself to admit that she'd found what she dreaded to find, Nadine dead in bed because Becky hadn't got to her quickly enough, because Becky was living somewhere else instead of here in the cottage, because Nadine now knew that somewhere deep in Becky a weary disbelief was beginning to stir about all the things Nadine said had happened, all the things Nadine accused other people of doing and saying, in order to hurt and undermine her.

After that, it was awful. Nadine opened her eyes and said something but Becky couldn't stop screaming and her screaming brought Josie running in from the car and at the sight of Josie, Nadine just went ballistic and there was a horrible brawling scuffle that made Becky so sickened, so ashamed, that she'd gone from screaming to utter silence in a second. Josie had managed at last to free herself, and Becky had followed her, despite Nadine's demands and pleadings to her not to. They'd stood, shaking, by the car.

"You'd better come back with me," Josie said.

Becky shook her head. She mumbled something.

"What?"

"I can't."

"Look," Josie said. She was leaning against the car as if she couldn't quite stand up without its help. "I know any remark I make will sound to you like a criticism of your mother, but will you be safe?"

"Oh, yes," Becky said. She turned her face away. "She's—she's never done anything like that before." She put a hand up and tugged at a strand of hair.

"I can't leave you here like this, alone with her. I must get a doctor or something."

"OK," Becky said. Her shoulders slumped a little.

"It's Saturday tomorrow. Maybe Dad could come—" She stopped.

"I'll ring," Becky said. "I'll ring and tell you."

"I'll go and get you some food—"

"No."

"Why not?"

"She wouldn't eat it," Becky said. "Not if——" She paused, and then she said, "We've got good neighbors."

Josie stood upright, slowly.

"But you'll let me get a doctor?"

"Yes," Becky said.

She'd stood in the road, watching Josie drive away. She drove very slowly as if shock and anxiety made it almost impossible for her to let the car go forward. When she was at last out of sight, round a bend in the lane, Becky turned and went back into the cottage. Nadine was standing by the kitchen table, her hands folded in front of her.

She said, very clearly, as if she'd been planning it, "I'm very sorry."

Becky said nothing. She went past Nadine to the sink and leaned over it to open the window.

"About everything," Nadine said.

Becky breathed in the air coming in from outside.

"There's a doctor coming."

"I don't need one," Nadine said. "I've seen the doctor. Tim got her for me. I've got antidepressants and some sleeping pills. I'd taken some of them before you came."

"Typical——"

"What is?"

Becky turned round. "To ring me and then take sleeping pills, which are meant for the night anyway."

Nadine stared at her.

"I said I was sorry. I am. I'm very sorry."

"I don't care," Becky said.

She moved over to the refrigerator and opened the door. Inside were a few things in brown paper bags, a cracked egg on a saucer and a carton of long-life apple juice.

"What are you going to do?" Nadine said.

Becky slammed the refrigerator door shut again.

"I haven't decided."

"Will you stay?" Nadine said. Her voice had an edge of real anxiety. "Will you stay and keep me company?"

Becky glanced at her. She touched the breast pocket of her denim jacket and let her hand linger there for a moment. On the journey, Josie had stopped for petrol, and when she got back into the car, after paying, she'd handed Becky a packet of Marlboro Lights. She hadn't said anything. Nor had Becky.

"I'm going out," Becky said.

"Where?"

"I don't know. A walk maybe."

"Will you be long?"

"No," Becky said.

"I need to talk to you," Nadine said. "We need to talk all this through."

"Sorry," Becky said. She went across the kitchen to the door to the outside. "I'll stay till you're better. I said I would. But I didn't say I'd talk."

"You've been here a week," Mrs. Huntley said now.

"I know."

"What about your schooling?"

"It was the end of term today. Anyway, I'd been off school—"

Tim Huntley dropped a wedge of bread onto his cleared plate and began to push it round with the fork.

"What about your dad lending a hand with all this?"

"He can't."

"Why not?"

Becky looked straight at him.

"She wouldn't let him."

He put the wedge of bread in his mouth.

"So it's down to you?"

Becky shrugged. She stood up, holding the edge of the table.

"That's not right," Mrs. Huntley said. She looked at Becky. "You've got your schooling to think of."

"I'd better be getting back," Becky said.

Tim Huntley stood, too.

"Give us a call. Any time."

"Thanks," Becky said.

She went out of the farmhouse, while they watched her, and then, at a safe distance, past the barking dogs and over the sleeper bridge to the road. The stream was full—late-winter rains coming off the mountains, the postman had said—and was really running, and the hawthorn hedge was frosted with bright green leaves, each one neatly cut out, as if with embroidery scissors. Becky took her cigarettes out of her pocket and put one in her mouth. It was the last but one in the pack that Josie had given her a week ago. She paused, in her tramp down the lane, to light up, and then walked on heavily in her boots, blowing blue smoke into the clear air above the stream and the hawthorn hedge.

Nadine was sitting on the grass in the cottage garden, under a three-quarters-dead apple tree. She had her glasses on, and in her lap a pile of *Teach Yourself Greek* books she'd found in the local junk shop. She looked up as Becky came in through the gate.

"How was that?"

"Okay," Becky said.

"Are you going to tell me about it?"

"There's nothing to tell," Becky said. She leaned against the apple tree. "Tim was eating, and they asked how you were."

Nadine took her glasses off.

"I'm fine."

"For now," Becky said. She put her hand on her jacket pocket. One left. Save it for later. She slid down the tree and sat with her back against it, holding her knees.

"No, I really will be fine now. I will. I promise. Summer's coming—"

"You shouldn't live alone," Becky said.

"What?"

"You heard me. You shouldn't live alone. You can't cope."

Nadine turned on her a gaze full of distress.

"Oh, Becky—"

"You can't," Becky said. She looked up at the sky, through the apple tree's black, gnarled branches. "And—" She stopped.

"And what?" Nadine said, her voice sharp with apprehension.

"And," Becky said, her gaze still on the sky, "I can't live with you anymore. Not permanently. I can't cope with you either."

"I haven't got it," Matthew said.

Josie turned. He leaned in the kitchen doorway, still in his jacket and tie from work, but the tie was crooked and loosened.

"They made me a long speech," Matthew said. "One of those speeches where you know they hope you won't spot that the truth is the last thing they're going to tell you."

He came slowly forward into the room, pulled a chair out

from the table, and sat down. Josie pushed another chair next to him and slipped into it. She took his nearest hand.

"Oh, Matt."

"They said that, although I had all the required experience and qualifications, they felt that because of my family circumstances this wasn't a good moment in my life for me to take on extra responsibility. They said that kind of thing several times over in various ways until I felt so dysfunctional by implication I could hardly sit up. The injustice of it—"

"I know."

"I don't mean the injustice of not giving me the job, I mean the other injustice, the weasely insinuation that my family circumstances are too much for me now when they used to be far, *far* worse. And the cowardice of not being able to tell me I'm just not good enough."

Josie lifted the hand she held and put it against her face.

"Nobody can do that unless they're sadistic. Nobody likes that."

He looked at her.

"I can't bear it that the first thing I try and do after marrying you is a failure."

He leaned forward and kissed her.

"We needed this promotion," he said. "We needed something positive to happen, something to show us we'd turned a corner." Gently he took his hand out of hers. "Where are the children?"

"Out," Josie said. "Clare and Rory are next door, and Becky's gone to see a friend."

"Is—is it any better since Becky came back?"

"It's quieter," Josie said.

"Only that?"

She looked down at her hands. Something had arisen in her mind during that drive back from Herefordshire, something that was preoccupying her, she found, a great deal and which she was not yet ready to tell Matthew about. Something had changed, something in her perception of Matthew's children had altered; there'd been a small but powerful shift of emphasis, and while she considered it, and what to do about it, she found she wanted to keep it private. She'd thought, often and often, of Becky's face as she got out of the car, outside Nadine's cottage, of Becky's figure dwindling in the driving mirror as she drove away after that hideous scene. She had not expected Nadine to be so violent. Nor had she expected her to be beautiful. Nor—and this was the most astonishing nor of all—had she expected there to be a real, a palpable reluctance between herself and Becky to part. You could give a dozen reasons for the reluctance, explain it away in terms that in no way diminished the established antagonism between them, but still there remained, after all the explaining, a persistent sense that, in the momentary dropping of guards and attitudes, a glimmer of hope had flickered, faint but unquestionably there.

"Josie?" Matthew said.

She looked up at him.

"I'm really sorry," she said.

"I know. So am I." He stood up. "I just feel—"

"Please," Josie said, interrupting. "Please don't say any more. Please don't. This is a disappointment, but it's not something worse than that, it's not as bad as things have been."

He gave her a small smile.

"Maybe."

He went out of the room. She heard his tread going up the stairs and into their bedroom and then the sound of a drawer being opened while he looked for a sweater to wear instead of his jacket.

Then his feet went out onto the landing again, and she could hear the clatter of the extending ladder being pulled down, to give him access to the attic.

She looked down at the kitchen table. There were crumbs on it, and a pile of assessment sheets in a plastic folder left over from the previous term at her school, which she had got behindhand with, because of looking after Becky. There was also a cereal box, left by one of the children, and a postcard from Rufus to Rory showing a picture of the Roman baths in Bath. He'd got Rollerblades, he said, and it was raining a lot. His handwriting was small and cramped. Love from Rufus, he'd written at the bottom. When Clare had picked it up to read it, Rory had snatched it back from her. "Hey!" he'd said, holding the card against his chest. "Who said you could read it?" Josie looked at it now. Rufus had Rollerblades. Perhaps the nice Elizabeth had bought them for him, was teaching him to skate along those broad pale pavements at weekends, when she came down from her job in London and took over the house and Tom and Basil and Rufus, smoothly wheeling them about her, unruffled, undismayed.

The door opened. Becky, holding a small carrier bag from a music shop, came in. Josie looked up.

"Hello."

Becky nodded. She went over to the sink and ran water into a mug.

"I saw Dad come back."

"He's upstairs," Josie said.

Becky gulped the water noisily and put the mug, unrinsed, back on the draining board.

"I'll go up—"

"Becky," Josie said. "Becky, would you do something for me first?"

Becky eyed her.

"What?"

"Would you get the others from next door?"

"Why?"

"I've got a reason," Josie said. "I wouldn't ask you to do it if I hadn't."

Becky hovered uncertainly for a moment, and then she went out of the kitchen, and Josie could hear her boots clumping down the drive. She got up and looked at herself in the little mirror Matthew had put up for her beside the door—"So you can see if you've got lipstick on your teeth before you open it." She looked better, she thought, not wonderful, but better, less haunted, less bombed out, less like a moth skewered on a board. She put a hand up and took the hooped band out of her hair and shook it. When she was about Becky's age, she remembered, she'd dyed her hair black, dead, dense, coal black. Elaine had been horrified, really frightened by Josie's appearance, but Josie for a week or so at least had loved it, had loved the instant ordinariness it gave her, the sudden sweet freedom from the significant visibility of being a redhead.

The outer door opened again, with a bang. Josie stepped away from the mirror, toward the table.

"Thank you for coming back."

They all three looked at her.

"It won't take long," Josie said. "I won't keep you long."

Rory bent to tie up the trailing laces of his sneakers.

"It's two things, really," Josie said. She moved the chair that Matthew usually occupied, at the head of the table, and sat down on it. "Do you want to sit down, too?"

Becky closed the door and leaned against it, her hands behind her back. Rory stayed where he was, squatting over his laces. Clare came forward and sat at the opposite end of the table to Josie, holding her tape player.

"I don't know if this is the right moment to say what I'm going to say," Josie said. "I don't know, actually, what a right moment *is*. But it seems quite a good moment. Rufus isn't here, and although what I've got to say affects him, it doesn't seem to affect him like it affects the rest of us." She leaned on the table, putting her hands down flat in front of her. Then she said, "I'm afraid your father hasn't got his promotion."

They stared at her. She waited for Clare to cry, for Becky to say it wasn't any of her, Josie's, business anyway, for Rory to shove past her and go upstairs to find Matthew. But they didn't; they didn't move.

"I don't need to tell you how he feels," Josie said. "And what he says to you and you say to him about it is your affair anyway. But it's given me a chance, it's given me a chance to say some things I maybe couldn't say if nothing had happened."

Rory got up very slowly and slid into a chair beside Clare.

"The thing is," Josie said, and stopped. She pushed her hair behind her ears and said abruptly, "We don't have to be a disaster. Really we don't."

Rory began to push some crumbs on the tabletop about with one forefinger. His expression was set.

Josie said, rushing on, "Some homes have always got broken, haven't they? I mean somebody dies, or somebody leaves and there it is, broken. It's awful, it's always awful. Nobody's pretending it isn't awful, nobody's saying it isn't sad and hard and difficult. And—it makes you want the past back, doesn't it, however bad it was, because it was better. Or you think it was."

She stopped. Becky was still staring at her. Josie looked back.

"I don't know exactly what you've been through. Of course I

don't. Except—well, except that my dad pushed off when I was seven, and I've never seen him since."

Becky's blue gaze dropped. Rory's finger paused in making a tiny crumb mountain. Josie put her hands flat on the table again and looked at them, at the few freckles on the backs she had always hated, at Matthew's wedding band.

"Maybe," she said, "we've got a sort of chance now. Maybe we could start, well, mending things after all that breaking. If—if we stopped being afraid of being a stepfamily, that is." She folded her right hand over her wedding ring. "I know I'm not your mother. I never will be. You've got a mother. But I could be your friend, I could be your supporter, your sponsor. Couldn't I? Sometimes hard things turn out better because you've had to make an effort to overcome them." She stopped. "Sorry," she said. "I don't want to lecture you." She took her hands off the table and put them in her lap. "I really just want to say that we may be a different kind of family, but we don't have to be worse. Do we?"

Becky came away from the door. She moved only a few steps, until she was standing behind Clare.

She said, blurting the words out, "What about Mum?"

Josie took a breath.

"She'll have to find a way. Like we all have to. With each other."

She stood up slowly. They didn't watch her. Rory banged his hand down flat on the table and his crumb pile flew in all directions.

"You ought to go and see Matthew," Josie said. "He's the one in need right now."

"Okay," Rory said. "Okay, Okay."

He sprang up and darted past her and wrenched open the door to the hall. Clare followed him, and their feet stampeded up the stairs. Becky watched them. She stayed where she was, behind the chair Clare had been in, watching the empty hall where her brother and sister had been. Then she glanced at Josie. She opened her mouth to say something and closed it again.

Then she said, gesturing awkwardly toward the kettle, "Would you like a coffee?"

DALE'S POSSESSIONS ALMOST filled the landing on the top floor. They were very orderly, labeled boxes and bags and plastic carriers, stacked tidily and graded by size against the walls between the doors. Rufus's bedroom door was open, and inside, on the floor, lay Dale's television and video recorder and also, between the bed and the desk, a small mountain of the items out of Lucas's room. Lucas's room door was also open, revealing that it had been half cleared in order to make way for the sofa from Dale's flat and a low table and lamps and cushions and a stack of posters from art exhibitions in rimless frames. Dale's own bedroom door was closed and locked.

It had all happened in five days. Elizabeth had, as was her custom, gone back to London on Sunday evening, and had, as was also her custom, spoken to Tom several times a day throughout the working week. He had said nothing about Dale, nothing about Dale's possessions. Elizabeth hadn't been surprised. One of the agreements they had reached at the end of a long, difficult, and distressing conversation about Dale was that Tom would indeed do something about her, but must be left to do that thing, whatever it was, in privacy.

"I can't talk to Dale," Tom had said, "if I feel I then have to report precisely back to you."

"But it concerns me, too! Because it concerns us—"

He'd frowned. She'd watched him closely, trying to see what he was really thinking, what he really feared.

"I have to be left alone," he said. "I have to deal with Dale as I always have, alone. If she can't trust me, I won't get anywhere, and she won't trust me if she thinks I'm relaying everything to you."

On Friday night, Elizabeth had returned to Bath. Tom, as usual, came to meet her at the station. He looked tired. His manner was guarded. He said, trying to make light of it, "I'm afraid I'm not doing very well. But at least it's only temporary."

"What d'you mean?"

"You'll see," he said.

She went straight upstairs, when they reached the house, straight up, not even pausing to transfer her bag from her shoulder to the newel post at the foot of the stairs. She knew what she'd find when she reached the top, and sure enough, she found it, except that it was bigger than she had anticipated, and its orderliness was somehow more assertive than she had bargained for, more settled, more impervious. She stood, slightly out of breath, and looked, with something that encompassed both rage and despair, at the blatant, unmistakable evidence of Dale's relentless purpose.

She glanced at Rufus's room. Lucas's skis and poles and his tennis racket were piled on the bed, and Rufus's new red rug was almost obscured under a haphazard clutter of splitting bags and broken boxes. The order that prevailed among Dale's own possessions was plainly not a courtesy extended to anyone else's. Dropping her bag on the floor, Elizabeth ran into Rufus's room and somehow, despite their weight and bulk, manhandled the television and video recorder out into the small remaining space left on the landing. Then she began to seize the bags and boxes randomly, almost running in her breathless hurry to get them out of Rufus's room and dump them, anywhere, anyhow, among the symmetrical piles on the landing. She started to throw things, hurling them out of the door and letting them clatter and slither where they fell: pictures and books, plastic sacks of clothes and bedding, a shoebox of old cassette tapes, a hockey stick, folders of photographs and letters, a collapsible wine rack, a set of carpet bowls in a green cardboard box. Then she grabbed the skis and the tennis rackets in a great unwieldy armful and, staggering out of the room with them, flung them, banging and thumping, down the stairs.

"What in hell's name is going on?" Tom said.

He stood at the foot of the topmost flight of stairs and looked upward. Elizabeth chucked the final cushion.

"What do you bloody *think?*"

Tom stepped over a tennis racket and moved a ski from where it lay, jammed crosswise across the staircase.

"Dearest—"

"What about Rufus?" Elizabeth shrieked. "If you can't care about me, I'd at least have expected you to care about Rufus!"

"Sweetheart, Rufus isn't here—"

"Don't call me sweetheart!" Elizabeth yelled.

Tom stopped climbing the stairs.

"Dale isn't living here," he said. "Please don't be so melodramatic. She isn't living here. She's living with a friend. It's just that she's got nowhere to put anything until she finds a flat, so I said—"

"Oh!" Elizabeth cried in exasperation. "Oh, don't *tell* me what you said! I can imagine exactly what you said! You said all the reasonable, placatory, surrendering things you have so disastrously said to Dale for twenty years. What d'you mean, she isn't living here?"

"She isn't."

Elizabeth gestured wildly toward Lucas's bedroom door.

"She's going to!"

"No, she's living with a—"

"Then why make a sitting room of this? Why do expressly what Rufus didn't want, the minute his back is turned? Why keep *her* door locked? Why be so utterly, bloody provocative if she doesn't actually intend to move back in here and watch you and me like a hawk?"

"Elizabeth," Tom said. He closed his eyes briefly, as if summoning the patience to deal with the kind of unreasonableness that no civilized man should ever be required to deal with. "Elizabeth. Will you please listen to me? Will you please stop screaming and simply *listen?* I have spoken to Dale, as you requested—"

"As we agreed!"

"As you requested, and she asked if she might just store things here for a few weeks until she finds a flat. She is living with a friend called Ruth, with two young children, in Bristol. She has looked at three flats this week and is viewing two more on Saturday, tomorrow. I understand Rufus's wishes quite as well as you do, but the invasion of his room, as you see it, is only very temporary, and his room will be absolutely restored before he next needs it."

"Huh," Elizabeth said.

"What do you mean by that?"

"I mean huh, Tom Carver. I mean you are a fool if you believe any of that. And you're not only a fool, but you're weak." Her voice rose. "D'you hear me? Do you? Dale can do what she bloody well likes with you because you are completely, pathetically *weak!*"

He looked up at her. His expression was neither friendly nor unfriendly but empty, as if he didn't recognize her, as if her insults meant nothing to him because they were, in fact, perfect strangers to one another. Then he turned, extricating himself from the clutter round his feet, and went, with great dignity, downstairs. Elizabeth watched him go and, when he was out of sight round the curves of the staircase, waited until she heard him, with the same measured tread, cross the ground-floor hall. She looked down. Her bag lay where she had dropped it, opened by the vigor of her gesture, spilling keys and a checkbook and a small plastic bottle of mineral water. Automatically she stooped to retrieve the spilled things, to tidy up. Then she stopped and straightened up and, stepping over the bag and the trailing leads of the television and the scattered contents of various bags and boxes, crossed to Rufus's bed and lay down on it, facedown on the Batman duvet cover he so strenuously wished to exchange for something more sophisticated, and held onto it, for dear life.

"I'm sorry," Tom said.

He had laid two places, opposite one another, at the kitchen table, and lit candles. There was an opened wine bottle, too, and a warm buttery smell. He took Elizabeth in his arms.

"I really am sorry."

She laid her face against his shoulder, against the dark blue wool of his jersey. She waited to hear herself say, "Me, too." It didn't happen.

"It was unforgivable of me," Tom said. "Especially on a Friday night with you tired and me cross with myself."

Elizabeth sighed. She looked at the soft light of the candle flames and the wineglasses and the black Italian pepper grinder you could twist to grind coarsely or finely.

"How did it happen?"

"When I was out," Tom said. "On Wednesday. I was out, meeting a new client who wants to make a house out of an eighteenth-century chapel, and came back to find a note. Then she came the next day and sorted things out a bit, and told me about Ruth."

Elizabeth extricated herself from Tom's embrace. She said tiredly, "I don't believe in Ruth."

"She exists."

"Oh," Elizabeth said, "I believe *that.*"

"Sit down," Tom said.

He pulled a chair out on the side of the table where Elizabeth usually sat, and pressed her gently down into it.

"I bought skate. Skate wings. I knew you liked them."

"I do."

"Was it a good week? At work?"

"It was uneventful, thank you," Elizabeth said politely.

Tom put a bowl of salad on the table and a yellow pottery dish of new potatoes. The potatoes were freckled with parsley. Elizabeth looked at them. She wondered, with a kind of detachment, if it were normal to remember to garnish potatoes with parsley or if, and particularly this evening, it had a significance, a subtle message from the parsley chopper to the parsley consumer about the extra trouble taken and all that that implied, about love being expressed in practical details because it was sometimes so impossible to express it more straightforwardly. Did Tom, when he cooked—which he did often and excellently—always remember the parsley?

He put a plate in front of her. The skate lay on it, darkly glistening, beside a wedge of lemon.

"Eat up."

"Thank you," Elizabeth said. "It looks lovely."

He sat down opposite her.

"You look so tired."

She picked up her knife and fork.

"That's crying."

He said, with warmth, "You're wonderful about Rufus."

"It isn't hard."

"All the same—"

"Tom," she said, cutting carefully into her fish, "let's not talk about him. Let's not talk about children, any children."

He smiled.

"Of course," he said. He picked up the wine bottle and reached through the candles to fill her glass. "This chapel I saw, the one I saw this week, so fascinating. It's rather classical in design, pedimented and so forth, and it was built by a fervent but unquestionably dotty lady aristocrat to house a sect she had espoused who believed in the exclusive spirituality of women."

"Good for them."

"It was founded by a man, of course."

"Of course."

"He wouldn't let any other men in. He persuaded Lady Whatnot that she needed his physical and mental strength to keep the polluting effect of other men at bay. It's a lovely building, full of light, all gray-and-white paneling. Badly decayed, of course."

Elizabeth took two potatoes out of the yellow dish.

"Can I see it?"

"Of course. I'd love to show it to you. It's listed, so we have to make practical rooms out of the vestry and back quarters and leave the chapel itself as a living space."

"Does it need to be deconsecrated?"

"I don't think," Tom said picking up his wineglass, "that God ever came into it much. I think the founding father saw to it that no one else shared center stage. I'd love to know what actually went on."

Elizabeth looked up suddenly.

"What was that?"

"What—"

"Something," Elizabeth said. "The front door—"

Tom half got up. There were quick footsteps in the hall, and then the kitchen door opened.

"Hi!" Dale said.

She was smiling. She carried her handbag and keys in one hand and a bunch of Stargazer lilies in the other. She swirled round the table and pushed the flowers at Elizabeth.

"For you."

Elizabeth took a breath.

"Oh—"

Tom was standing straight now.

"Darling—"

"Hi, Daddy," Dale said. She spun back round the table and kissed him.

"You didn't say you were coming—"

"I didn't know," Dale said. She winked at Elizabeth. "I didn't know until I got back and found that Ruth's hot date from last night was still there, wearing nothing but a bath towel. Ruth didn't exactly say push off, but she hardly needed to. Hey, don't stop eating your supper." She bent briefly toward Elizabeth's plate and sniffed extravagantly. "Smells *wonderful*. What is it?"

"Skate," Elizabeth said.

"Dale," Tom said. "We are having supper together, Elizabeth and I—"

Dale bent forward again and lifted the lilies from Elizabeth's lap.

"I'll put those in water for you."

Elizabeth closed her eyes.

Dale ran water noisily into the sink. "I'm not going to interrupt you," she said. "Honestly. I've had some soup, I'm fine, and I've got so much to do upstairs you wouldn't believe."

"Tonight?" Tom said. "Now?"

She turned from the sink, the lilies dripping in her hands, her hair and teeth and eyes shining.

"Honestly," she said again. "*Honestly*, Daddy. Have you even *seen* it up there? I promise you it's going to take me a couple of hours just to make enough space to *sleep*."

Amy hadn't turned the lights on. She sat slumped on one of the pale sofas in the sitting room of the flat with her feet on the coffee table, nursing a mug of tea balanced on her stomach and watching the daylight fade above the roofs of the houses opposite. In a while, maybe in only a few minutes, the streetlights would come on and the sky would instantly darken in contrast, as if it were offended by being eclipsed. The mug of tea on Amy's stomach was her third. She'd drunk them slowly and savoringly, one after the other, working her way round the top of the mug until there was a completed circle of lipstick marks, like a stenciled pattern on a wall.

While she drank her tea and stared at the sky, Amy had been thinking. Or rather, she had lain there and let thoughts wash through her mind, or round and round it, while she had a look at them. It occurred to her, after a while, that the thought that persistently swirled slowly through her brain was how tired she was, not physically tired, but emotionally tired, weary with strain and frustration and the awful boredom of realizing that human beings don't change, really, and that if she was going to love one of them, she had to learn to love things in him that she'd never even countenance putting up with in someone else. It was when she was spooning sugar into the third mug of tea that it came to her—with relief rather than shock—that she couldn't really be bothered. "I'm tired of love," she told her reflection in the kettle and then, a second later, emboldened by a sweet, hot swallow of tea, "I'm tired of trying to love Lucas."

This thought had then overtaken previous thoughts of weariness. Amy went back to the sofa and replaced her feet not just on the table but on Lucas's prized book of photographs of the temples of Angkor Wat, and realized, with a slow surge of energy, that the very idea of leaving Lucas made her feel different, better, less hopeless. It made her feel sad, too, unquestionably, sad enough to bring tears to her eyes, because of all she had invested in their relationship, because of all their hopes, because—above all—of Lucas's lovableness. But despite the sadness, there was a sensation of wonder, too, a realization that a small new hope lay in a decision that would effectively give her her own life back, that would restore her to the center of things after all these months of circling unheard, she often felt, unseen, round the edges.

The streetlights outside the window went on, and the rooftop view changed abruptly from something real to something theatrical. Amy sat up and put her mug down on the table and swung her feet to the floor. A girl at work was going up to Manchester; she said there were good opportunities in the north because so many people still wanted to come south, still believed that the energy drained out of the media world anywhere north of Birmingham. Why shouldn't she do that? Why shouldn't she go north and start another kind of life with herself in charge of it? It might be lonely, of course, certainly to start with, but she was lonely now, living with Lucas, who always seemed abstracted, preoccupied with something that wasn't her. She'd said to him, over and over again, that she didn't want all his attention, but she did feel she was, as his future wife, entitled to at least some of it.

She looked down at her left hand. Her engagement ring, a square-cut citrine in a modern setting of white gold, seemed to sit on her finger as if it wasn't entirely comfortable to find itself there. Maybe it had always looked like that; maybe she had always known at an unacknowledged level, that it didn't suit her. Lucas had chosen it. The girls at work had been vociferously divided between those who thought this a truly romantic gesture and those who felt it was, in terms of a modern relationship, completely out of order. Amy herself had felt it to be a bit of both and in her confusion had allowed good manners and a desire to please Lucas to prevail. She slid the ring off now and held it in her palm. It looked, as it always had, classy and impersonal. She put it on the table, beside her mug, and then spread her naked hand out, holding it in the air. It seemed fine—too fine, perhaps, to belong to someone who had just taken a unilateral decision to break off an engagement to marry.

She stood up and stretched. Lucas would be back around midnight, weary but in the slightly wired condition he was always in after three hours of hosting a radio show. She had, perhaps, three hours until his return, three hours in which to decide what to say to him and how to say it; or three hours in which to pack her clothes and most intimate possessions and take herself off to her friend Carole, leaving the citrine ring and a letter on the coffee table, for Lucas to find.

Dale was singing. Elizabeth could hear her clearly from the kitchen three floors below. She had a good voice, light but true and sweet. She was singing along to a CD of the score of *Evita*, and the sound came spiraling down the house, rippling through open doors, flowing everywhere. As a sound it was quite different, the complete opposite, in fact, of the sound that Dale had made the night before when she discovered the havoc Elizabeth had wreaked on the top floor. That had been terrible; screams and howls of rage and outrage, thundering feet down the stairs, cascades of furious tears. Elizabeth had sat in her place at the table and refused to react, declined, mutely and stubbornly, to have anything to do with what was going on. It was Tom who had reacted, Tom who had attempted to soothe Dale, Tom who had gone back upstairs with her to help her sort out the muddle, to reassert her rights. Elizabeth wondered if Tom could hear the singing now in the basement. He had been down there for hours now, since four or five that morning, when he had given up all attempts at trying to sleep and had slid out of bed, trying not to wake Elizabeth, who was awake already and pretending not to be in order not to have to say anything.

She had taken coffee down to him about eight. He had been sitting, wrapped in a bathrobe, in front of his drawing board, looking at drawings for the chapel. He took the coffee and put his other arm around her, still looking at the drawings.

"Would you still like to see this?"

"Of course," she said.

He took a swallow of coffee.

"I'm afraid of you," he said. "I'm afraid of what you're thinking."

She moved herself gently out of his embrace.

"I'm afraid, too."

"Shall we—shall we go and look at this, this morning?"

"Yes," Elizabeth said.

He took her hand for a second.

"Good."

Half an hour later, he had come into the kitchen to leave his empty mug on his way upstairs to shave and dress. Elizabeth was sitting at the table, already dressed, reading an arts supplement from the previous weekend's newspaper. Tom bent, as he passed her, and kissed her hair.

She said, "Breakfast?"

"No thanks. I've got about another half-hour to do downstairs before we go. Can you wait?"

"Yes."

"You don't mind waiting?"

"No," Elizabeth said.

She had tidied up the kitchen, watered the parsley and the lemon verbena in their pots on the windowsill; swept the floor, and fed Basil one of his tiny gourmet tins. He had eaten it seemingly in a single swallow and had then heaved himself onto a kitchen chair so that he could gaze steadily and pointedly at the milk jug and the butter dish. It was then that the singing began. Elizabeth was just stooping to tell Basil, in a voice of profound indulgence, that he was the greediest person she had ever met, when the first wave of sound came rolling lightly down the stair-well. She straightened.

"It's Dale—"

Basil seemed entirely indifferent. He leaned his chins on the table edge and purred sonorously at the butter.

"She's singing," Elizabeth said out loud in amazement. "She's woken up and found herself to be exactly where she intended to be, and she's singing. In triumph."

Basil put a huge paw on the table, next to his face. Elizabeth knelt beside him. She put her forehead against his densely furry reverberating side.

"I can't bear it. I can't." She closed her eyes. "I think I'm going mad—"

With surprising supple agility, Basil leaped from the chair to the table. Elizabeth sprang up and seized him.

"No—"

He made no struggle. He lay upside down in her arms and regarded her with his big yellow eyes and continued to purr. She put her face down into him, into the soft spotted expanse of his stomach.

"What," she whispered into it, "am I going to do?"

"Dearest," Tom said from the doorway.

She looked up. Basil turned himself easily in her arms and slithered back onto the chair.

"Are you ready?" Tom said. "Shall we go now?"

The chapel stood in a side street in the north of the city, balanced precariously on a hill, between a short row of shops and a terrace of neglected houses, mostly divided into flats. In front of it, separated from the street by iron railings and a locked iron gate, was a rectangle of unkempt grass. Behind it and beside it, Tom said— and this was what had so attracted the purchasers—were spaces of land that the original sect had intended for their own private ceme- tery, the graves to be arranged like the spokes of a wheel around a neoclassical monument to the founding father. These plans had never come to anything. The aristocratic lady benefactress had been milked of all her money, and no other obliging source could be found to replace her. The sect had gradually disbanded and the founding father had disappeared to France, taking the two prettiest acolytes with him, and all remaining funds, and the spaces around the chapel were abandoned with the building and gradually taken over by alder and cats and willow herb.

The chapel had handsome double doors under a nobly pedi- mented porch. Tom put a key into the lock and turned it.

"There."

Elizabeth peered in. There were windows down both sides, a second tier of them running above a graceful gray-painted gallery. The nave space was empty, except for debris and a little huddle of pitch-pine pews below a magnificent paneled pulpit, waiting humbly, as it were, for the next soul-saving utterance.

Elizabeth walked forward, her feet grinding on the dust and fallen plaster.

"It's lovely."

"I thought you'd think that."

"Won't it make rather a funny house?"

He drew level with her.

"That's what they want."

She leaned on the back of one of the pitch-pine pews.

"Do you feel excited, every time you get a new commission, every time you look at something like this that you can rescue?"

He went past her and gave the paneling of the pulpit a professional pat or two.

"Not as much as I did."

"Because of still wanting to be a doctor?"

"I think that's too generous an interpretation."

Elizabeth slid her hands back and forth along the pew back. It was slippery with varnish, ugly in so elegant a place.

"Tom."

He didn't turn from the pulpit.

"Yes?"

"I can't marry you."

He leaned forward and put his forehead against the pulpit, one hand still resting against the paneling.

"You know why," Elizabeth said.

There was a long, complicated silence, and then Tom said, indistinctly, "I warned you about Dale."

Elizabeth brought her hands together on the pew back and stared down at them for a moment. Then she looked up at Tom.

"Yes," she said. "You did. You told me not to offer my house to her. You warned me that she might try to overwhelm me, to overwhelm us. But——" She paused and then she said, very softly, "You never warned me that you'd do nothing to stop her."

Very slowly, Tom took his head and his hand away from the pulpit and tuned round to face her.

"I love you," he said.

She nodded.

"I didn't know," Tom said. "I never dared to hope that I could love anyone as much again. But I have. I do. I love you, I think, more than I've ever loved any woman."

Elizabeth said sadly, "I believe you——"

"But Dale——"

"No," Elizabeth said. "No. Not Dale. There isn't anything more to say about Dale. You *know* about Dale, Tom. You *know.*"

He moved forward a little and knelt up in the pew one away but facing her.

"What about Rufus?"

Elizabeth shut her eyes.

"Don't—"

"You'll break his heart—"

"And mine."

"How *can* you?" Tom shouted suddenly. "How *can* you let this—this single aspect get to you so?"

"It isn't a single aspect," Elizabeth said steadily. "It's fundamental. It colors everything, and you know it. It colors the present, and it will color the future."

"And you blame me?"

She glanced at him.

"I think I understand something of your position, but I also think nobody can change things but you."

He leaned toward her, over the back of the pew. His face was eager.

"I *will* change things!"

"How?"

"We'll move, we'll do what you wanted, another house, another city, a baby even, we'll start again, we'll put distance, physical distance, between ourselves and the past—"

Elizabeth shook her head. She said unsteadily, "It doesn't work like that."

"What do you mean?"

"You can't—shed the past just by moving. It comes with you. You only deal with things if you face them, challenge them, reconcile yourself to them—"

"Then I will!" Tom cried. He put his arms out to her. "I will! I'll do anything!"

"Tom," Elizabeth said.

"What?"

"There's another thing."

He dropped his arms.

"Yes?"

She came slowly around the pew she had been leaning on until she was only a foot from him. He didn't try and touch her. Then she put out both hands and held his face and leaned forward and kissed him quietly on the mouth.

"It's too late," she said.

19

"JUST TALK TO me," Elizabeth said.

She was lying on the broken-springed sofa with her eyes closed. Duncan got up to move the window curtain a little, in order to shade her face from the afternoon sun.

"What about?"

"Anything," Elizabeth said. "Anything. I just need to hear you, to hear you saying things."

Duncan looked down at her.

"I don't think you slept much last night. I'm afraid that bed is hardly comfortable."

"It doesn't matter. I couldn't sleep anywhere. At the moment I couldn't sleep on twenty goosefeather mattresses." She opened her eyes. "Oh, Dad—"

"My dear one."

She put a hand up to him.

"What did I do wrong?"

He took her hand and wedged himself onto the edge of the sofa beside her.

"You didn't do anything wrong."

"I must have—"

He folded her hand in both his.

"No. Nothing *wrong*. You may have done things out of innocence or lack of experience, but not things you should blame yourself for."

Elizabeth looked away from him, out of the large-paned window—shining clean after Shane's ministrations—at the high, bright, early-summer sky.

"I certainly didn't know about Dale."

"No."

"He's afraid of her," Elizabeth said. She turned her face toward Duncan. "Can you imagine that? He's her father, and he's afraid of her. Or, at least, he's afraid of what will happen if he stands up to her. He thinks that if he confronts her with her own destructiveness, he will, in turn, destroy her. He said to me, 'I can't risk breaking her mind. She's my daughter.' So, he's trapped. Or, maybe, he believes he's trapped. Whichever," Elizabeth said with a flash of bitterness, "she's won."

Very gently, Duncan unfolded Elizabeth's hand from his own and gave it back to her.

"Do you know, I don't think it's just Dale. Or just Dale's temperament. I don't think that's the sole reason."

"Oh?"

He sighed. He took his reading spectacles out of the breast pocket of his elderly checked shirt and began to rub his thumbs thoughtfully around the curve of the lenses.

"I think it's maybe the myth of the stepmother, too. Unseen forces, driving her, affecting you, affecting Tom, everyone."

Elizabeth turned on her side, putting her hand under her cheek. "Tell me."

"There must be something behind the wicked stepmother story," Duncan said. "There must be some basic fear or need that makes the portrayal of stepmothers down the ages so universally unkind. I suppose there are the obvious factors that make whole swaths of society unwilling even to countenance them, because of the connotations of failure associated with divorce, because, maybe, second wives are seen as second best and somehow also a challenge to the myth of the happy family. But I think there's still something deeper."

Elizabeth waited. Duncan put his spectacles on, took them off again, and replaced them in his shirt pocket. He leaned forward, his elbows on his knees.

"I grew up," he said, "believing my childhood to be happy. I believed, and was encouraged to believe, that your grandmother was an excellent mother, an admirable woman, that the comforting rituals of my life that I so loved were somehow because of her, of her influence. It was only when I was much older that I saw it wasn't so, that my mother, who loved society and was bored by both children and domesticity, had left my upbringing almost entirely to Nanny Moffat. You remember Nanny Moffat? Now, Nanny Moffat was indeed excellent and admirable."

"She had a furry chin," Elizabeth said.

"Which in no way detracted from her excellence. But when I realized this, when I saw that the happy stability of my childhood was actually due to Nanny Moffat and not to your grandmother, my mother, I was terribly thrown. I remember it clearly. We were on holiday, on the Norfolk Broads. I suppose I was about fourteen, fifteen perhaps. Not a child anymore. I had accompanied my

father to Stiffkey Church—he was passionate about churches—
and I was sitting on the grass in the churchyard while he looked at
inscriptions on the tombstones, and I suddenly found myself
thinking that my mother had allowed me, even encouraged me, all
these years to believe in and rely upon maternal qualities in her that
simply didn't exist. I can feel the moment now, sitting there in the
damp grass among the tombstones, simply shattered by a sense of
the deepest betrayal."

"Oh, Dad—"

"I just wonder," Duncan said, "if stepmothers have something
to do with a feeling like that?"

Slowly, Elizabeth pulled herself up onto one elbow.

"I don't—"

"It's as if," Duncan said, turning to look directly at her. "It's as
if stepmothers have come to represent all the things we fear, most
terribly, about motherhood going wrong. We need mothers so
badly, so deeply, that the idea of an unnatural mother is, literally,
monstrous. So we make the stepmother the target for all these
fears—she can carry the can for bad motherhood. You see, if you
regard your stepmother as wicked, then you need never feel guilty
or angry about your real mother, whom you so desperately need to
see as good."

Elizabeth drew a long breath.

"Yes."

"And we exaggerate the wickedness of the stepmother to jus-
tify, in some human, distorted way, our being so unfair."

Elizabeth turned herself round and sat up, putting her arms
around her bent knees and leaning her shoulder against Duncan's.

"I find all that very convincing."

"Do you?"

"Yes," Elizabeth said. "Except that I can immediately think of an exception."

"Can you?"

"Rufus," Elizabeth said.

"Oh, my dear—"

"You know when something like this happens, something unbearably painful and sad, the way you keep saying to yourself, 'Is this the worst? Is this the darkest hour? Is this the bottom of the pit?' "

"Yes."

She moved a little.

"I did that all last night. I expect I'll do it for nights to come. And I kept having to admit to myself that, however awful it's all been already, the worst, almost the worst, is yet to come." She put her face down into the circle of her arms, and said in a whisper, "I still have to tell Rufus."

The pub was full. Half the customers had spilled out onto the pavement and were lounging about in the sunshine, leaning against parked cars, sitting on each other's laps on the few chairs there were. Tom saw Lucas almost immediately, taller than most people and with a preoccupied air, standing by the bar and holding out a twenty-pound note above the heads of the people in front of him.

"Gin and tonic?" he said to Tom, almost without turning.

"A double," Tom said.

Lucas glanced at him.

"A pub double is nothing," Tom said.

"Two double g and t's," Lucas said loudly to the barman.

"I thought you drank vodka—"

"Like you," Lucas said, "I'll drink anything just now. In any quantity."

"It's kind of you," Tom said, "to sympathize so—"

Lucas glanced at him again.

"I'm afraid it isn't all sympathy."

The barman handed up two glasses of gin and two tonic-water bottles, held by their necks.

"Ice?"

"No, thanks."

"Lemon?"

"Got it."

"I'll take them somewhere," Tom said. "While you collect your change."

He took the glasses and bottles from the barman and, holding them high above his head, threaded his way toward the darkness at the back of the pub. There was a low bench, in a corner under a mirror advertising absinthe in elaborate art deco lettering.

"Why couldn't we meet at home?" Lucas said, joining him and stuffing his change haphazardly into his jeans pocket.

Tom handed him a glass and a tonic-water bottle.

"You know why."

"Isn't she out at work?"

"She's taken this week off."

"Oh," Lucas said. He poured the whole of the tonic into his glass and put the bottle under the bench. "Staking her claim." He took a swallow of his drink. "It just means I'll have to tell her separately."

"Tell her what?"

"Amy's left me," Lucas said.

Tom stared at him.

"You don't mean it—"

He pulled a face.

"Real soap-opera stuff. The ring and a Dear John waiting on the table."

Tom put his drink down on the floor by his feet. He leaned forward and put his arms around Lucas.

"Oh, dear boy, dear Lucas, poor fellow—"

Lucas let his head lie briefly against his father's.

"It wasn't a surprise."

"Wasn't it?"

"It was a shock—I don't mean I don't feel it, I feel awful, I feel utterly bloody, but I can't pretend I didn't see it coming." He pulled himself gently out of Tom's embrace. He said, "I wasn't putting her first. Or second, really, if I'm honest."

"I'm so sorry, so *sorry*—"

"Yes," Lucas said. "Thanks." He gave Tom a quick, sidelong glance. "Same boat, then."

An expression of extreme pain crossed Tom's face. He bent to retrieve his drink.

"Maybe." He paused, and then he said, "Did Amy blame Dale?"

"She blamed my attitude to Dale."

"Yes."

"It wasn't the only thing, but it was a big thing."

Tom said, hesitantly, "Elizabeth said—" and then stopped.

"What did she say?"

"That we weren't doing Dale any favors, you and I."

Lucas gave a little mirthless bark of laughter.

"We don't have much choice."

Tom leaned forward.

He said earnestly, "But is it Dale? Is it just Dale?"

Lucas took another mouthful of his drink.

"I suppose," he said slowly, "that it is, but only because Dale's been honest enough to know that it's no good her looking anywhere else for love. We've both tried it, haven't we, and I've come to see that I don't think I'll ever find it here; I can't somehow, round Dale. That's why I'm going to Canada."

Tom's glass shook suddenly in his hand.

"Canada!"

"Yes," Lucas said. He looked down. "Sorry."

"Why Canada?"

"The new company that's bought the radio station owns stations in Canada. They said would I go because they couldn't keep me on in England and I said no, at first, and now I'm going to say yes."

"Where?"

"Edmonton," Lucas said.

Tom put his free hand across his eyes.

"Sorry," Lucas said again.

"No, no—"

"It was Amy going that finally did it. And, well, thinking that we were all going backward somehow, back to somewhere we should have moved on from."

Tom took his hand away and gave himself a little shake. He said a little unsteadily, "Good for you."

"Thanks."

"I mean it. I just wish—" He stopped.

"You can't, Dad," Lucas said. "There's Rufus."

"I know. I didn't mean it, really. There was just a moment, a wild, fleeting moment—"

"Yes."

Tom looked at Lucas.

"Where has Amy gone?"

"To Manchester. She has some idea of a new life there."

"She might be right."

"I think," Lucas said sadly, "she was right about quite a lot of things."

Tom dropped his eyes to his drink.

"And Elizabeth," he said quietly.

"What is she going to do?"

"Go back to London. Buy a house instead of a flat. Get promoted to the very top of the Civil Service."

"Has she moved out?"

Tom gave a small smile.

"There was almost nothing to move. You never met anyone less imposing of themselves on anyone else. She left her car parked outside, tank full of petrol, keys on the hook where she'd always hung them. I find——"

"What?"

"I find I'm desperately hunting for traces of her. Anything, *anything*, tissues in the wastepaper basket, magazines she bought, the mug she liked drinking out of——"

"Don't, Dad."

Tom gave himself a little shake.

"Quite right. *Most* unfair, to say such things to you."

"I don't think," Lucas said gently, "we were quite in the same league of love."

"No. Perhaps not."

"Will you see her again?"

Tom lifted his glass and drained it, as if he were drinking water.

"Next week. When Rufus is back."

"Rufus——"

"Yes," Tom said. He put his glass under the bench and stood up. "Yes. She's coming down next week, to see Rufus. She wants to tell Rufus herself."

Dale had made osso bucco. She had Elizabeth David's *Italian Food* propped up ostentatiously against the coffee percolator, and she was chopping garlic and parsley and lemon rind with a long-bladed knife as she had seen television chefs do. The smell was wonderful. She hoped, when Tom came back from this mysterious drink with Lucas, he would say how wonderful the smell was, and not, as he had done the last few days, appear not to notice the effort she was making, the way she was trying to show him that she knew he was in pain, and was sorry. She *was* sorry, she told herself, chopping and chopping, of course she was sorry. It was awful to see him hurt again, heartbreaking in fact. It was as if the air had gone out of him, the energy, the vitality. But it would come back, of course it would, when he remembered, when he was reminded. She heard his key in the lock, and began to chop faster.

The kitchen door opened.

"Hi!" she said, not looking up.

Tom came slowly over to the table and dropped his keys on it with a clatter.

"How's Luke?"

"You know perfectly well," Tom said.

Dale paused in her chopping for a second.

She said quietly, "You mean about Amy."

"Yes."

"Maybe," Dale said, "maybe in the long run, it was the right thing to do?"

Tom pulled a chair out from the table and sat down heavily in it.

"Put that knife down."

"What?"

"You heard me."

Carefully, Dale laid the knife beside her green-speckled mound on the chopping board. She looked at Tom. After a moment he raised his head and looked back at her with an expression she did not recognize.

"Satisfied?" Tom said.

She was truly startled.

"Sorry?"

"I said, are you satisfied?" Tom said.

"What d'you mean?"

He leaned forward.

He said, in a voice so raised it was almost a shout, "You've seen off Elizabeth, you've seen off Amy. Are you satisfied now?"

She gasped.

"It wasn't me!"

"Wasn't it? Wasn't it? Making it perfectly plain to a nice girl and a wonderful woman that your brother and father would never belong to anyone but you?"

Dale was horrified. She leaned on her hands over the chopping board, breathing hard.

"I didn't, I never—"

"The keys?" Tom demanded. "The invasion of this house? The little deceits and subterfuges? Your bloody possessions staking your claim louder than words could ever do? Making Elizabeth feel always and ever the outsider, the intruder, and Amy, too?"

"Don't," Dale whispered.

Tom rose to his feet, leaning on his side of the table, his face toward her.

"You're not a child," Tom said, "though God knows your behavior would disgrace most children. You're a grown woman. You're a grown bloody woman who won't accept it, who won't accept the loss of childhood, the need to make your own home, your own life—"

"Please," Dale said. "Please."

Tears were beginning to slide down her face and drip onto the chopping board.

"And because you won't accept those things, you want to make Lucas and me live out the past with you, over and over, never mind at what cost to us, never mind the suffering, never mind losing probably the best person—do you hear me, the *best person*—I have ever known, never mind, never mind, as long as you, Dale, have what you think you want."

Dale began to sink down behind the kitchen table, crumpling softly onto the floor, her arms held up around her head, wrapping it as if to hold it on.

"Please, Daddy, don't, don't, I never meant—"

"What did you mean then?"

"I didn't mean anything," Dale said unsteadily. "I only meant not to drown. I didn't mean to hurt, I didn't, I didn't—"

"But you did hurt!" Tom shouted. "You caused terrible deliberate destruction. *Look* at what you did!"

Dale unwound her arms and leaned against the nearest table leg. Her hair had escaped its velvet tieback and swung over her face, sticking here and there to the damp skin.

"I wasn't doing it for that," she said. "I wasn't doing it to hurt someone else. I did it because I couldn't help it, because I couldn't breathe otherwise." She heard Tom sigh. She said in a steadier voice, "You don't know what it's like, what it's always been like. For me. I don't want it, I've never wanted it. I've fought and fought, I've tried not to be—" She stopped, and then she said, "Sorry."

There was a silence. She glanced sideways under the table and saw her father's legs, planted slightly apart, cut off across the thigh by the tabletop.

"Daddy?"

"Yes," Tom said. His voice was tired.

"It's true. It's true what I'm saying about myself, about what I'm afraid of, what I've tried to do."

"Yes," Tom said again.

Dale swallowed.

"I'm sorry. I'm really sorry."

Tom sighed again, a huge gusty sigh, and his legs moved out of her sight, across the kitchen toward the window to the street.

"Oh, Dale—"

Slowly, she got to her knees and held the edge of the table, pulling herself up, peering over.

"I didn't want to break you and Elizabeth up, I just couldn't bear—"

"Please don't talk about it."

She watched him. His back was toward her, his hands in his pockets.

"Daddy?"

"Yes."

She held the table edge hard and whispered fiercely across it.

"Don't leave me."

Rufus sat up in bed. He had been surprised, but not very, not to find Elizabeth in the house when he arrived. Tom explained that she sometimes had to work late and thus had to get a later train, on Fridays. What had surprised him, and not very pleasantly, was to find Dale there. Dale was in the kitchen, where he had expected to find Elizabeth, in a dress he disapproved of, with almost no skirt at all, frying sausages. She said the sausages were for him. She said this in a very bright, excited voice, as if he ought to feel pleased and grateful, and then she kissed him and left the smell of her scent on him, which he could still smell now, even though he'd scrubbed at the place with a nailbrush. After he'd eaten the sausages—which were not the kind he liked, being full of herbs and stuff—Tom offered to play chess with him, which was very peculiar and rather elaborate, somehow. They'd played chess for a bit, but it hadn't felt right and then Dale had come prancing back in even more scent and announced in a meaningful voice that she was going out now until much, *much* later.

It was better when she had gone. Tom poured a glass of wine and gave Rufus a sip, and Basil managed to lumber onto the chessboard and knocked all the pieces over. Rufus kept yawning. He didn't seem able to stop, and yawns kept coming and coming like they did sometimes in assembly in school. Tom had asked, after a while, if he'd rather wait for Elizabeth in bed, and although as a general principle he liked to hold out against bed as long as possible, he'd nodded and gone upstairs and washed without being reminded, using some of Dale's toothpaste as one small act of defiance and failing to replace the cap on the tube as a second. Then he'd climbed into bed, lying back against the headboard, and wondered, with a dismalness that dismayed him, why the contemplation of his new curtains and his red rug and his desk didn't seem to fill him with any satisfaction at all.

It seemed ages until Elizabeth came. He heard the front door open and close, and then murmuring voices. He imagined Tom taking Elizabeth's luggage from her, and perhaps her jacket, and offering her a glass of wine or something. They'd probably go into the kitchen and talk for a bit, while Tom got started on their supper—he hadn't done anything about it while Rufus was downstairs—and then Elizabeth's feet would come running up the stairs, and she'd sit on his bed and he might be able to hint, at last, at some of the things that troubled him, about finding Dale there, about the feeling in the house, the oddness in his father. He picked up a Goosebumps book that he'd left lying on his duvet earlier. Tom didn't like him reading Goosebumps, he'd said they didn't stretch his mind enough, but sometimes, Rufus thought, his mind didn't in the least want to be stretched; it wanted to be treated like a little baby mind that didn't have to worry about anything.

"Hello," Elizabeth said.

She was standing in his open bedroom door, wearing a navy blue suit.

"I didn't hear you," Rufus said.

"Perhaps these are quiet shoes—"

He looked at them. They were so dull, they certainly ought to have been quiet. Elizabeth came over and sat on the edge of his bed. She didn't kiss him, they never did kiss, although Rufus thought sometimes that they might, one day.

"I'm sorry I'm so late."

"I kept yawning," Rufus said, "so I thought I was sleepy. But I'm not."

She was wearing something white under her suit and some pearls she nearly always wore, which she said her father had given her. The microscope her father had given Rufus sat on his desk in a black cloth bag. Rufus had promised to take it back to Matthew's house, to show Rory.

"How are you?" Elizabeth said.

Rufus thought. Usually he said, "Fine," to ward off any more questions, but tonight he felt that questions might almost be welcome. He jerked his head toward the wall behind him.

"Dale's living there."

"I know."

He sighed.

"Does she have to be my sister?"

"I'm afraid so. She's Daddy's daughter, just as you are his son."

"But it feels funny——"

"I know," Elizabeth said again.

Rufus began to riffle through the pages of his Goosebumps book.

"Will it be long?"

"Dale being there? I think it might be. I don't think she likes living alone."

"And I," said Rufus with some energy, "don't like living with *her*." He glanced at Elizabeth. Her face was very still, as if she was thinking more than she was saying. "What are you going to have for supper?"

"I don't know——"

"Isn't Daddy cooking it?"

"No," Elizabeth said. "He offered, but I'm going round to Duncan's."

"Why?"

"Because——because I'm not staying here."

Rufus stopped riffling.

"Why?"

Elizabeth put her hands together in her lap, and Rufus noticed that she was clenching them so hard that the skin on her knuckles were greenish white, as if the bones underneath were going to push through the surface.

"Rufus—"

He waited. He stared at Batman's hooded face, spread across his knees.

"Rufus, I don't want to say this to you, I don't want to hurt you, and I don't want to hurt myself or Daddy or anybody, but I'm afraid I can't marry Daddy after all."

Rufus swallowed. He remembered, briefly, the registry office last year and the registrar with gold earrings and the picture of the queen.

"Oh," he said.

"I would like to explain everything to you," Elizabeth said. "I'd like you to know all the reasons, but for one thing it wouldn't be fair, and for another, I expect you can guess most of them."

Rufus nodded.

He said kindly, "It doesn't matter."

"Doesn't—"

"There's people at school whose parents aren't married. It doesn't matter."

Elizabeth gave a small convulsion. For a second, Rufus wondered if she might be going to cry, but she found a tissue in her pocket and blew her nose instead.

"I'm so sorry—"

He waited.

"I'm so sorry," she said, and her voice was unsteady. "I'm so sorry, Rufus, but I'm not even staying, I'm not going to live here anymore. I'm going away. I'm not marrying Daddy, and I have to go away."

He stared at her. She seemed to him suddenly very far away, very tiny, like something seen through the wrong end of a telescope.

He heard himself say loudly, "You can't."

"Can't—"

"You can't go away," Rufus said, just as loudly. "You can't. I *know* you."

She blew her nose again.

"Yes. And I know you."

"Where are you going?" Rufus demanded. His throat felt tight and swollen, and his eyes were smarting.

"Oh, just London," she said. Her hands were shaking. "I expect I'll buy a house with a garden, and then my father can come and stay with me at weekends."

"Can I come?"

Tears were now running down Elizabeth's face, just running, in wet lines.

"I don't think so—"

"Why not?"

"Because it wouldn't be fair—to Daddy, to you even—"

"It would!" Rufus shouted. He hurled the Goosebumps book at the black shape of his microscope. "It would! It would!"

"No," Elizabeth said. She was scrabbling about in her pockets for more tissues. "No, it wouldn't. It might make you think things were going to happen, when they weren't. It's awful now. I know it is, but at least you *know,* and it's better to know."

"It isn't," he said stubbornly. He put his fists in his eyes, like little kids did. "It isn't!"

He felt her get off the bed. He thought she was looking down at him, and he couldn't bear that, not if she was going to London and wouldn't let him come, too.

"Go away!" he shouted, his fists in his eyes. "Go away!"

He waited to hear her say, "All right, then," or, "Good-bye, Rufus," but she didn't. She didn't say anything. One moment she was there by his bed and the next she had gone and he could hear her quiet shoes going quickly down the stairs and, only a few seconds later, the front door slamming, like it did when Dale went out.

Slowly and stiffly, Rufus took his fists away from his eyes and eased himself down in bed, onto his side, staring at the wall. He felt cold, even though it was summer, and rigid, as if he couldn't bend anymore. The wall was cream-colored, as it had been for ages, forever, and on it Rufus could still faintly discern where he had scribbled on it, in black wax crayon, and Josie had scrubbed at the scribble with scouring powder and been cross with him, not just for scribbling in the first place but also for not doing a proper picture, or proper writing, but just silly, meaningless scribble. The thought of Josie made the tears that had been bunching in his throat start to leak out, dripping across his nose and cheeks and into his pillow, and with them came a longing, a fierce, unbidden longing, to be back in his bedroom with Rory, in Matthew's house.

Josie came all the way down to Bath, to collect Rufus. She'd offered to, almost as if Tom were an invalid, when she heard about Elizabeth's leaving.

"I'll come," she'd said. "It's no bother. The last thing you want is that awful lay-by, just now."

He'd let her. He'd been grateful. She'd arrived with her stepson, an unfinished-looking boy of perhaps thirteen whom Rufus had been suddenly very boisterous in front of, as if he were extravagantly pleased to see him, and couldn't say so. They'd gone up to Rufus's room together, Rory holding Basil.

"He's great," Rory said to Josie. "Isn't he? Why can't we have a cat?"

"I expect we can—"

"Soon, now—"

"Maybe—"

"When we get back," Rory said. "Can't we? A kitten?"

"Two kittens," Rufus said.

"Go away," Josie said, shaking her head, but she was laughing.

Tom made her coffee. She was very nice to him, sympathetic, but her sympathy had a quality of detachment to it.

"I don't want you to be sorry for me—"

"I'm not," she said, "but I'm sorry it's happened, I'm sorry for Rufus."

Tom flinched slightly. He couldn't say how awful it had been, couldn't admit to Josie how Rufus had longed for her arrival, his bag packed for twenty-four hours previously, his microscope wrapped up in layers and layers of bubble wrap. And Josie didn't ask him anything much. He didn't know if she was being tactful, or whether she guessed so much she hardly needed to ask. She looked around the kitchen, but only cursorily, and not at all in the examining manner of someone eager to observe every change, every shred of evidence of someone else's occupation. She was pleasant, but a little guarded, and only at the end, when she was getting into the car and the boys and Rufus's possessions were already packed inside, did she say, as if in fellow feeling, "Don't be deluded. Nothing's as easy as it looks," and kissed his cheek.

He went back into the kitchen after the car had driven off and looked at their coffee mugs, and the empty Coca-Cola cans the boys had left. Rufus had said good-bye hurriedly—lovingly but hurriedly, as if the moment needed to be dispensed with as quickly as possible because of all the unhappy, uncomfortable things that had preceded it. He hadn't talked about Elizabeth's fleeting visit much; indeed, had rebuffed Tom's tentative attempts to explore his feelings about it, leaving Tom with the distinct and miserable impression that Rufus held him at least partly responsible but was avoiding overt blame by simply not mentioning the subject.

Tom sat down at the table. Dale had put a jug of cornflowers in the middle of it, cornflowers and some yellow daisy things with shiny petals. She had put lilies in the drawing room too, and poppies on the chest of drawers in Tom's bedroom. He wasn't sure he had ever had flowers in his bedroom before, and they made him uncomfortable—or perhaps it was Dale's intention in putting them there that caused the discomfort. They were also very brilliant, pink and scarlet with staring black stamens. It was a relief to see that they were shedding their papery petals already. Perhaps Dale, after this first flush of happy reassurance, would feel no need to replace them, no impulse to point out to him, yet again, what he and all he represented meant to her. Perhaps she would, unthreatened, calm down again, calm down to a point where she might again venture on a love affair and this time, oh so devoutly to be wished, with someone who could handle her, could skillfully convert her fierce retrospective needs into, at last, an appetite for the future.

"Until then," Tom had said to Elizabeth, "I'm responsible. I have to be."

She'd said nothing. She'd given him one of her quick glances, but she hadn't uttered. She had, she made it plain, no more sympathy left for his abiding sense of guilt about Dale, his conviction that, not only was the burden of Dale naturally his, as her father, but that he couldn't, in all fairness, offload it onto anyone else who didn't actively, lovingly, seek to relieve him of it.

He stood up, sighing. Basil, stretched where Rory had left him, on the window seat, reared his head slightly to see if Tom was going to do anything interesting, and let it fall again. Slowly, Tom walked down the room, past the sofa and chairs where, at one time or another, all his children had sat or sprawled, where Josie had kicked off her shoes, where Elizabeth had curled up, a mug in her hand, her spectacles on her nose, to read the newspaper. The door to the garden was open, and on the top step of the iron staircase was a terra-cotta pot, planted with trailing pelargoniums by Elizabeth, pink and white. Tom looked past them, and down into the garden.

Dale was down there. She was crouched against the statue of the stone girl with the dove on her hand, crouched down, with her arms around her knees. She was waiting, just as Pauline used to wait, for him to come and find her.

20

KAREN WALKED SLOWLY up Barratt Road. It was hot, for one thing, and for another, she had offered to collect some dry cleaning for Josie, and although it wasn't heavy, it was uncooperative to carry, slithering through her arms in its plastic bags, or sticking to her skin in unpleasant, sweaty little patches. Anyway, she hadn't bargained on her car breaking down again and needing to spend three expensive days in the garage, forcing her to take the bus to work and her feet everywhere else. It reminded her of what it was like when she and Matthew were small, and the only car her parents had was her father's works car, which he wouldn't use for family outings after she was sick on the backseat once, from a surfeit of heat, ice cream, and temper.

She hardly ever lost her temper now. Josie had remarked on it, had said how equable she was. Maybe that was true. Maybe she'd realized, living with her mother, that temper never achieved anything much for the person who lost it, beyond that first, brief swoop of excitement when you opened your mouth to begin. She'd told Josie quite a lot recently, about her and Matthew's mother, as well as about her job and the love-hate relationship she had with it, and about Rob, the Australian dentist, newly arrived in Sedgebury, who was displaying the kind of interest in her nobody had shown for ages. She found that Josie was very easy to talk to, much easier than she used to be.

She'd cut her hair off, too. Karen had been amazed. One day there'd been that heavy, coppery mane that seemed almost to be Josie's trademark, and the next day it was gone.

"How *could* you?"

"I had to," Josie said. "I just had to. I feel extremely shy about it, now I've done it, but I had to."

"What about Matt?"

"I think he likes it."

"You look about fourteen."

"That's not why I did it—"

"No, I know. What did the children say?"

"Nothing," Josie said. "They all just stared as if I'd grown a second head. Rufus asked where all the hair was, and I said in the hairdresser's dustbin. They keep sneaking looks at me. Especially Becky."

Two weeks later, Becky had done the same thing. If Karen had been amazed about Josie's hair, she was absolutely astounded at Becky's.

"Is that a compliment, or what?" she said to Josie.

"I don't know. I'm trying not to work that kind of thing out because I always get the answers wrong. But she looks good, doesn't she?"

"Yes," Karen said. She was gazing out of the kitchen window at the square of patchy grass that passed as a lawn, where Becky was playing with the new kittens and a golf-practice ball on a length of knitting wool. "Yes," she said.

"Maybe," Josie said, "like me, she felt a lot of things might go with the hair—"

"You said you weren't thinking like that."

"I know," Josie said. "But sometimes I can't help it. I can't help wondering how we're doing."

They were doing all right, Karen thought, especially if you compared it with only three months previously. Josie had certainly relaxed a bit, had stopped ironing every item of laundry and tidying up after everyone and making an ostentatious labor of cooking. The house, which was too small for all of them anyway, looked thoroughly lived in, sometimes over–lived in, but the children's friends came round now and rode skateboards up and down the sloping drive or kicked footballs against the garage wall or lay in the girls' bedroom, with the curtains closed and music on. Matthew had sunk an empty food can in the back garden, and was teaching the boys to putt with golf clubs his father had given them. Karen was watching her father with some amusement. When she had started going round to Barratt Road, he'd always cross-examine her, when he next saw her.

"How did you find them, then?"

"Who?"

"Matthew and Co. The kids. You know."

Karen would pretend to be looking for something in her bag.
"Fine."

"Working hard, are they? Going to school? Not playing truant?"

"I wouldn't know."

"And the other little boy, the little redhead. Is he getting on with them?"

"Seems to be."

"And her. Matthew's wife. How's she doing, how's she coping?"

"Dad," Karen would say, "look. If you want to see how they are, you go and see for yourself."

And in the end, he had. First, he'd sent the golf clubs round, and then, after he heard that Nadine had bought herself a large, secondhand mobile home, and parked it at some commune near the cottage, and was helping to grow vegetables for the people there, he somehow seemed to feel that he was let off the hook, that he was no longer shackled by the conventions of first loyalties. He'd gone round to Barratt Road, saying he'd be ten minutes, and he'd been over an hour. He'd given the boys a golf lesson, he said, and Josie had made him a cup of tea. When Karen's mother had begun on him for going round at all, he'd said, "Not going is your loss, Peg, and no one else's," and walked out of the room.

Now, Karen thought, you'd think he'd never had a qualm. He mended things for Josie Matthew didn't have time to mend, promised Becky a hundred pounds for Christmas if she stopped smoking, and told the boys he'd make them members of Sedgebury Football Club's junior league next season. He began to tell Karen things, as if he knew more about them than she did, about Matthew having met the newly appointed headmaster and finding him sympathetic, about Rufus's father planning to take him to Legoland, in Denmark, later in the school holidays because there were complications at home, about Becky saying she would spend a week at the commune with her mother, but refused to promise more until she'd seen what it was like.

"Nadine still rings," Derek said. "She rings all the time."

"From a caravan?"

"She's got a mobile. She rings from her mobile."

And, Karen thought, no doubt she always would. Just as you couldn't rely on the commune to occupy her for long, any more than anything else ever had, so you couldn't believe that Nadine would ever really change, ever really develop the capacity to like where she was, what she was doing, herself even. Josie said she never mentioned Nadine to the children unless they spoke of her first, but she couldn't help noticing that, when she telephoned now, there was often a palpable reluctance to go and speak to her.

"I just say," Josie said, "you've got to. She's your mother."

Karen winked at her.

"*Aren't* we behaving nicely—"

"It's easier," Josie said, "when you don't try too hard."

"But not easy—"

"No," Josie said. "Not easy. Not impossible, but not easy, either."

Karen shifted the dry-cleaning bags, peeling them off one bare arm and transferring them to the other. She sometimes wondered what part Matthew had played in all this, how much he had stuck up for Josie, or his children, how hard it might be to relinquish entirely the old habit of acquiescence to Nadine to buy even a few moments of peace. Josie didn't talk to Karen about that. She was very open about most things, about herself, about Rufus, about Matthew's children, about her first marriage, about the complex remorse she had that she'd done nothing to help the woman who'd almost become Rufus's stepmother . . .

"But what could you have done?"

"Nothing, probably. But I would like her to have known that it wasn't her fault, and that Rufus really—loved her."

. . . But she never spoke of her relationship with Matthew. Karen could understand that. She might have relished a good discussion about her brother, but she could see, very clearly, above and beyond that fairly base eagerness, that if you were going to build any kind of relationship in a small house largely lacking a general esprit de corps, you have to give it such privacy as you could, for any hope of success. Watching them, Karen thought, they weren't doing badly. They were facing in the same direction, certainly, and, even if they weren't on paths that had quite joined up yet, she felt that they would get there in the end because they wanted to, they intended to.

And these thoughts, which preoccupied Karen sometimes with interest, if not with any particular urgency, were beginning to encompass another one, one that Karen, less than a year ago, thought she might never have. Sometimes, when she went to Barratt Road, she found she had an idea. It was only a fleeting idea as yet, not much more than an instinct, a hunch almost, but it was becoming as persistent as it was embryonic. It came to her, walking into the house on an ordinary day, as she was about to do on this ordinary day, and finding the kitchen in chaos, laundry on the line, the television yattering on to nobody, and Josie in the midst of it all, that she looked less foreign than she used to, more familiar, less superimposed on someone else's background. She was beginning, Karen thought, to look almost as if she belonged there, as if she had the beginnings of a sense of belonging herself, that seeming was slowly turning into being. And it occurred to Karen, watching her, that in time, in the length of hours and days and years of time, even the children would come to feel she belonged there, too. For the last time, Karen shifted the dry-cleaning bags from one arm to the other, and turned up the drive on which an upturned skateboard lay like a beetle on its back. She glanced up at the house. Almost all the windows were open. One day, she told herself, one day.

"IT WOULD BE advisable," the court official said to the security guard, "just to keep the laddie up here for half an hour."

They both looked along the courtroom waiting area at the defendant. He was smoking rapidly. He was also head and shoulders taller than the little group of women clustered round him, like hens preening a cockerel, clucking and soothing and flattering.

The security guard rattled the bunch of keys chained to his belt.

"Trouble downstairs then?"

"Not exactly trouble," the court official said, "but there's a few of the girl's friends and family waiting. Just waiting. Like they do."

The security guard sighed.

"Wish he hadn't got bail. Wish I could just take him back to Horsfield. At least I'd know where he was, then."

The court official glanced again at the defendant. Good-looking chap, in a flashy, come-and-get-it-girls way. But not reliable-looking; not reliable, at least, where his stepdaughter had been concerned.

"He won't skip."

"I'd still rather have him behind bars."

A young woman went past, a briskly walking, black-clad young woman with reddish-brown hair tied back behind her head with a black ribbon. She was carrying a square black attaché case and she had a black coat over her arm. She nodded to the court official as she passed.

" 'Night," she said.

The security guard watched her go. He'd been watching her all day in court, Miss Merrion Palmer, counsel for the prosecution, and admiring the way the tail of her wig sat so precisely above the tail of her natural hair.

"Nice legs," he said.

The court official blew out a little breath and heaved at the slipping shoulders of his black gown.

"Oh," he said, "nice all right."

He glanced along the waiting area to right and left, then said, *sotto voce*, "Know our judge?"

"Come on," the security guard said, "I'm here half the month, aren't I? Course I know the judge."

The court official leaned closer.

"What's just gone past," he said, his eyes fixed on the glazed door at the end of the waiting area that led to the judges' corridor, "is not just an advocate, any old lady advocate. What's gone past is His Honor's babe."

Back in his room the other side of the glazed door, Judge Guy Stockdale took off his wig and hung it on its wooden stand. Both wig and stand had belonged to his father, as had the pocket watch in his waistcoat pocket, which he carried every day out of a superstitious apprehension that he might make a public fool of himself if he didn't, and the silver pencil with which he made his meticulous notes up there, alone, on the Bench.

He then took off his robe—purple, claret, and black silk—and hung it on the plastic hanger from a nationwide dry cleaning chain that seemed to have replaced the heavy, curved wooden one he had brought in especially for the purpose. Then he removed his black coat and put it over the back of a gray vinyl armchair and sat in the chair, leaning his head in his hands and putting the heels of his hands into his eye sockets.

"Would you like me to take off my wig?" he'd asked the girl-child witness over the courtroom's video link at ten-thirty that morning. "Would it be easier for you?"

She'd stared back at him, a clever little foxy face framed in a fake-fur coat collar.

"I don't mind," she'd said. She hadn't seemed daunted. She hadn't seemed daunted by anything, all that day, except, occasionally, by the miserable intensity of remembering what she had felt, what had happened to her. "You suit yourself."

Oddly, he had rather wanted to take his wig off. He didn't usually. Usually, he was so conscious of being an upholder of an office and a representative of justice, rather than Guy Stockdale, aged sixty-two, height six foot one, shoe size ten, no need yet—impressively—for spectacles or false teeth, that he was happy to have his wig and gown remove him from the particular to the impersonal. But today had been different. Today had been different because he had come, without particularly intending to, to a point when he had to implement a choice; he couldn't go on just looking at it and thinking about it and laying it carefully to one side to act upon some other day when the light was clear and courage was high. This knowledge had made him look at the girl on the video link not just as an abused child—there were thirteen charges against her stepfather, six of indecent assault, five of unlawful sexual intercourse, two of rape—but as something of a fellow traveler in a world where things you wanted and needed began to conflict badly with the things you already, acceptably, had.

There was a light knock and the door opened. Penny Moss, a young clerk who had come to work at Stanborough Crown Court as an intern, came in with a file. Guy took his hands away from his face and blinked at her. She took no notice of having found the Resident Judge with his head in his hands. She took no notice, ever, of anything except the immediate matter she had in hand at any given moment. She put the file down on the desk.

"It's Mr. Weaverbrook of the animal sanctuary, Judge."

Guy looked at the file. Mr. Weaverbrook ran a so-called animal sanctuary as inadequate cover for dealing in stolen farm machinery and horse-trailers. When required to come to court, he pleaded acute anxiety levels. His wife usually came instead and sat shaking in her seat, worn out with the effort of trying to divide her loyalty between Mr. Weaverbrook and the need for law-abiding conduct. Guy felt pity and admiration for Mrs. Weaverbrook.

"Do you want the case reserved to you, Judge?"

"Yes, Penny, I do."

"And Mrs. Mitchell and the order concerning her children?"

Guy shut his eyes again. Mrs. Mitchell was a nymphomaniac with sadomasochistic tendencies whose three children, by three different fathers, were being removed, with difficulty, from her nominal care.

"That, too, Penny. I'd like an earlier date for that case."

"Judge—"

"Penny," Guy said, "I'm not delaying. I have the future of an eight-year-old to consider."

Penny opened her mouth. She was going to say, as she always

said when asked to do something she didn't want to do, "Martin won't like it." Martin was the court manager.

Guy stood up.

"Goodnight, Penny. And thank you."

She picked up Mr. Weaverbrook's file. He noticed that she wore, on her wedding finger, a band made of two little gold hands clasping one another. It looked vaguely Celtic.

" 'Night, Judge," she said.

Outside, in the early spring dark, the narrow court car-park was bathed in a weird orange glow from the streetlights beyond its wall. The buildings that ringed the court were as modern and uncompromising as the court itself, mixtures of bloodred brick and concrete, with a lot of glass set into brushed metal frames. They managed to look, without exception, profoundly inhuman, with elements even of menace, such as the great steel doors that slid shut across the court entrance at night. Guy was all for the impressive in architecture, and especially in architecture pertaining in any way to the rule of law, but not for threat, not for anything that suggested pitilessness, inclemency.

His car was one of only three left. The other two belonged to the two regular district judges who, like him, were inclined to work on until six most evenings, even though the courts rose at four-thirty.

"I work," he said often, and meaning it, "with lovely people."

He opened one of the car's rear doors and put his work bag on the backseat. Then he climbed into the driving seat and turned the engine on. Then he turned it off again, and sat looking at the neat little red lights on the dashboard, bright, precise little lights who knew what their business was and how to do it.

I do not, Guy thought, want to go home. He took his hands off the steering wheel and put them on his knees. I do not want to go home and confront the fact that I have finally decided and must now implement that decision. What I hate, he told himself, closing his eyes, is the inevitable infliction of pain. Whatever I do, I'll cause that, to myself as well as to everyone else. In fact I am already, have been for years. It's just that they haven't all known.

Merrion had looked at him—when she did infrequently look at him—very directly that day. She had never appeared in court before him until today, and he had thought, and said, that she never should. But she had accepted this case, had indeed never considered doing otherwise, and when it became plain that they two would be in public together professionally and for the first time, she'd said he wasn't to make anything of it.

"It's no big deal," she said. "A three-day trial and I won't even be staying in Stanborough. You know my feelings about Stanborough."

He did. He knew her feelings about most things. It was one of the elements of her character that charmed him most, her directness, her candor, her capacity (and courage) to see and describe things as they were, and not as they might have been or as she wished they were.

"You're married," she'd said. "You've been married for over thirty years. You've got two sons and you've got grandchildren. I'm young enough to be your daughter. I'm not married. I'm mad about you. *Mad*. We have a big, big problem and it's going to get bigger. No question."

She'd been twenty-four when they met. That was almost seven years ago. He'd been taking an evening train up to London to have dinner with his son Simon, one of those attempt-at-bonding dinners that Simon's mother, Laura, was so keen on.

"Do go. Oh do. How will you ever cross all these gulfs between you if you won't even try to *talk?*"

There was a girl in his train compartment reading a book that was convulsing her with laughter. She was helpless, crying with it, holding the book up to her face every so often so that she could shake privately behind it. He could see that it was a battered old paperback of Lawrence Durrell's *Esprit de Corps*. He could also see that she had wonderful hair and long legs encased in narrow blue jeans. She wasn't in the least pretty, in any conventional sense, but once he had started looking at her, he found he didn't much want to look anywhere else. So he stopped trying. He watched her steadily, smilingly, until she put the book upside down on her knees and said, still laughing, "I can't *help* it."

He bought her a drink at Paddington Station. She'd been to see her mother in South Wales and was on her way back to London and work. She was a pupil in a set of barrister's chambers specializing in family law. She had a lot of theories—which he admired—about the need for more women at the Bar, especially in family law.

"People want it. The public does. They feel safer with us in this particular area."

He didn't tell her he was a judge. He didn't tell her anything much except his name, and roughly where he lived and why he was in London. Then he took her telephone number, put her in a taxi, and went to meet Simon. He ordered a bottle of champagne.

"What's this for?" Simon demanded. "What are we celebrating?"

Guy raised his glass.

"It's purely medicinal."

Almost seven years ago. Seven years of what the newspapers would call his double life—home with Laura and the house and the garden and the dogs and the familiarity, and away, with Merrion. Sometimes away was in London, sometimes in hotels, sometimes abroad when he went to conferences, once—when they were desperate—it was a ten-minute meeting in the buffet on Reading Station.

"I'm your mistress," she said.

"No," he said, flinching a little, "no, not that. My love—"

"Nope," she said, "sorry. Mistress it is. We sleep together, you pay for some things for me, I keep myself exclusively for you. That's what they do, mistresses."

Guy lifted his right hand and turned the ignition key again. He'd heard that word again today in court.

"Did your stepfather," the defending counsel asked the girl witness, "ever refer to you as his mistress?"

"No," she said. She licked her lips. "He said, 'We're lovers, we are.' That's what he said. And then—" She paused.

"And then what, Carly?"

"He'd say, 'You're better than your mum.' "

"Better? In what way were you better?"

"At sex," the girl said clearly.

Guy reversed his car out of its parking space, and drove slowly out into the one-way system of central Stanborough. There were few people about, but the roads were busy, streams of cars with their headlights on passing beneath the orange sodium lights.

He'd glanced very briefly at the jury when the girl said that. They'd started the day, as most fresh juries did, looking reasonably alert and capable and then, as the time wore on, and the alleged facts of the case were spelled out in the baldest language imaginable, they had shrunk in their seats, their gazes fixing, their minds struggling to take in precisely what they were hearing.

"He liked it in the mornings before I went to school," the girl said. "When I had my uniform on. In the living room."

"In the *living* room?"

"Yes. With the door open."

"With the door *open*? While your mother and sister slept upstairs and the foot of the staircase was immediately opposite to the living-room door, he liked to have that door *open*?"

"Oh yes," she said, "he liked the idea that Mum might catch us. That's why he liked it in the bathroom and the kitchen."

A picture was emerging, a picture of an apparently common-place three-bedroom terraced house on a housing project on the edge of Stanborough in which a family lived, an equally apparently commonplace modern family of a woman and a man and the woman's two child daughters by a previous husband, where nothing was in fact what it seemed.

"He never touched Heather," the girl said. She sounded almost proud. "She's younger than me, but he never touched her."

"Why," the defending counsel demanded, "did you let him touch you?"

She looked sulky, almost angry.

"He conned me."

"Conned you?"

"He said, 'You want periods, don't you? If you have sex, your periods will come.' And they did. I wanted—I wanted boys to like me. He said they would, if I let him. But they don't."

The defending counsel leaned forward. He had a full, fleshy face and his manner was mildly abrasive.

"But you say he conned you."

"He did."

"But if you knew you were being conned, why did you let him continue?"

There was a pause. The girl looked down. Perhaps she was twisting her hands but they were hidden below the bottom frame of the television screen.

"Carly," the barrister said, "did you hear my question?"

She nodded.

"I will repeat it. If you knew you were being conned, why did you let your stepfather continue?"

She whispered something.

"Carly, the court cannot hear you."

She took a breath and said tiredly but with a simultaneous small pride as if she was quoting something authoritative, "He was like a god to me."

A god. A forty-five-year-old man playing god to a besotted woman and her equally spellbound child. The terraced house, with its neat front garden and rather less neat back garden where the girls were allowed to keep pet rabbits in hutches, was, it seemed, less a family home than a cage for playing games in, improper, dangerous, degraded games, power games, cruel, harmful games. The jury had looked drained. Several of them looked as if, for all their worldly knowledge already gleaned from television and the press, they'd heard more than they'd bargained for, been faced with a raw reality they couldn't just switch off when they'd had enough. And this was only the first day.

But a god! That was what she had said, this fifteen-year-old child who had lived with her stepfather from the age of eight until a year ago, when she had finally told her mother what was happening. A god. You could, it seemed, go on about equality between the sexes until you were blue in the face, you could legislate, you could try to educate, but then along comes this child, this late-twentieth-century child, with her boldness and her unquestioned prospects, talking quite simply and unselfconsciously about a man being like a god to her.

Guy wondered, detachedly, if he had ever seemed like a god to Laura, even in that first glory of love when the love object is truly, literally, something quite extraordinary. They had met at university, he reading law, she reading French and Spanish. They had both worked diligently—she because she was conscientious, he because he was ambitious—and had emerged with similar degrees.

He had gone immediately to Bar School and she had applied to join the Foreign Office, failed, and taken a translating job with a firm of small manufacturers who were developing their business in Europe. It was a dull job. Guy urged Laura not to take it.

"Try the BBC," he said. "Try the World Service. Try publishing. Try teaching."

"I can't," she said. "If one of us doesn't make some money, we can't get married."

"We *can*. We don't need money to get *married*. And if we do, I'll borrow it. I don't mind borrowing until I'm earning. But you can't do something your heart's not in."

"I can," she said. "I don't mind."

But she did. He remembered, now, how much she did. She didn't say anything because she had been brought up to endure in silence, but her attitude, her moods, even her walk indicated that she felt she was drudging, that she wasn't allowing her brain to race ahead of her, as his was doing.

"Are you resentful?" he said, every so often.

And she'd look at him, with that clear hazel gaze that appeared to display such transparency of mind and heart.

"No," she said.

He used to take her shoulders, give her a little shake.

"Can I believe you?"

"Yes," she said.

So he did. Or, at least, he lived as if he did. He read as assiduously for the Bar as he had read for his law degree, and every so often, he asked Laura to change her job. She refused. Once, he went to their bank manager and secured a loan for six months, to enable Laura to leave her job and take time to find a more congenial one. A week later, she too went to the bank manager and canceled the loan.

"I hate it. I can't do it. You *know* Mum and Dad were always in debt and how much I dread it."

"But we aren't like your parents. We don't have their problem with money. And I'm going to be earning. In two years' time, all being well, I'm going to be earning reasonably and I'll go on to earn well."

"I can't believe anything," Laura said, "until it happens."

That was not, he thought now, the sort of thing you said to a god. Laura's anxious practicality was not likely, ever, to find itself swept away by the presence of superhuman possibilities. Not as a young woman; certainly not now. Now! Well, how to think about that without a clutch of dread, of panic? Impossible. Laura was sixty-one. Not a particularly young or old sixty-one, but a nice-looking, well-kept, largely unassuming woman of sixty-one with the same clear hazel eyes but set, somehow, in a different context. Indeed, the way Laura's still-young eyes looked out of her much older face was a metaphor for the way things had changed place, moved round in the last seven years: since meeting Merrion, the whole landscape in which Laura lived in relation to Guy seemed different. It was like walking very, very slowly away from something you knew very well, something you could visualize minutely when you were parted from it, and as you moved away, that something shrank against its background and lost solidity, lost significance.

Guy cleared the last of Stanborough's raw, newish suburbs and turned down a minor road toward open country. The streetlights petered out into darkness and the tires of the car began to click stickily through mud. Five miles now. Five miles, and then, across a curve in the road and before he got to the village, he would see the lights glowing along the façade of his house and the twisted bare black outlines of the apple trees in the little orchard in front of it.

They'd bought the house thirty years ago, when Simon was

eight, and Alan was five. It had been three cottages, run-down and discouraging, sitting in a muddy welter of disused sheds and pigsties. But there was the orchard, and a modest hill behind it, and a village with a church and a pub, and there were good rail connections to London from Stanborough, ten miles away. And, in any case, Laura wanted it. She had finally given up her job when she became pregnant with Simon, and presumably because Guy was now earning, she didn't mention getting another one after he was born. She became a conscientious mother just as she had been a conscientious student. From the tiny terraced house in Battersea that they could scarcely afford, Laura took him out to Battersea Park every day, and played with him. She cut out letters and taught him to read when he was four. She fed him bread she had baked herself and rationed his hours of television—he saw enough to enable him to fit in at school, but not enough to prevent him using his own imagination.

When Alan came along, three years later, he joined in this earnest and busy enterprise.

"Is this what you like?" Guy said to Laura, intending to be supportive whatever her reply. "Is motherhood enough for you?"

"For now," she said, not looking at him. She was pulling a soft tangle of colored clothes out of the drier. "There's nothing else we can do for now."

"What do you mean?"

"I mean, with you working so hard."

He crouched down on the little kitchen floor beside her. He was still in his dark suit from court, his black shoes, his sober tie.

"Laura, I have to work hard. I'm self-employed. Barristers *are*. You know that. The harder I work, the better I'll do."

She sat back on her heels, holding the plastic laundry basket of clothes on one hip.

"Will it always be like this?"

"Like what?"

"You working all the hours there are, most weekends, ring-binder files even in bed—"

"Not if I become a judge."

"A judge!"

"I can't even think about it for fifteen or twenty years. But if that's what you'd like—"

She got to her feet.

"It's not my choice."

"Laura, it is. It's as much your choice as it's mine."

She'd looked down at him, holding the laundry basket, biting slightly at her lower lip.

"I didn't quite visualize this."

He stood, too.

"What?"

"Well, when I was working and you were still a student, I didn't think we'd—well, we'd get so *uneven*."

"But we needn't be. You could go back to work. Alan's five, for heaven's sake."

She rumpled some of the clothes in the basket with her free hand.

"Could we move to the country?" she said.

"Would that help?"

She gave him her clear, open look.

"Yes," she said.

Even then, even temporarily relieved by a seeming solution, he hadn't been quite convinced. If she wanted to do it, if she was sure that a change of scene and society would, as it were, round her out once more, then they would do it. But he was haunted by feeling that it was possibly the worst thing they could do, that the hours he would have to travel would be added to the hours he would have to work, that a separateness would happen, that their priorities would cease to be united.

"Are you sure?" he said over and over.

"Yes," she said, "I want to be somewhere where I can make my own life. I'm—I'm confined here. I want the boys to have a garden."

"You won't be lonely?"

She took a little breath, as if she was about to speak but she didn't say anything. He had an uneasy feeling that she'd been about to say, "I'm lonely now," and in her self-disciplined way had decided against it. Sometimes he wished she had less discipline, less reticence, that that elusiveness that had so captivated him when they first met—coming as he did from a family of loudly outspoken, opinionated people—was less opaque. Mystery was one thing, so was understatement and obliqueness and self-containment—but quiet stubbornness was quite another.

"Look," he'd said, with some energy, "I can't give up the Bar because it's all I'm trained to do and I'm good at it, but I'll do anything else you want, anything. Move house, move to the country, have another baby, anything."

She put her arms around his neck.

"I'd like to go to the country. I'd like to be somewhere where I'm visible. To myself as well as everyone else."

"But if you wanted to work again—?"

"I won't," she said.

But she had. Two years into the restoration of Hill Cottage, and she had. Guy changed gear to negotiate the curve of the road before his drive, and saw the familiar pattern of lit house lights; sitting room and hallway, landing and main bedroom, front door and—glow only visible—back door. It was twenty years ago—

twenty years!—that he had begun to see that Laura was feeling, however much she battled against it, that she had paid too high a personal price in marrying him.

And now. Now what was he about to do? He turned the car into the drive and felt the tires crunch into the stones of the gravel.

"I feel like a slut now," the girl on the video link had said that day. "I'm not a virgin anymore. I feel dirty. I feel naive and stupid."

Guy let the car coast quietly to a halt in the graveled yard outside the back door. Inside the house, the dogs began barking, rapturously welcoming however long or short his absence. He turned off the engine. That's how I feel, he thought. Dirty. Naive and stupid and dirty. He opened the driver's door and climbed out, a little stiffly, onto the gravel.

ABOUT THE AUTHOR

Best known as the author of eagerly awaited and sparklingly read-able novels often centered around the domestic nuances and dilem-mas of life in contemporary England, Joanna Trollope is the author of *The Choir, A Village Affair, A Passionate Man, The Rector's Wife, The Men and the Girls, A Spanish Lover, The Best of Friends, Other People's Children, Marrying the Mistress,* and *Next of Kin,* and, as Caroline Har-vey, *The Brass Dolphin* and *Legacy of Love.* She lives in Gloucestershire and London, England.

From: Joanna Trollope

Dear Reader —

I am so pleased — and grateful! — that you have bought one of my novels. I do hope you enjoy it.

I'd also like to tell you that I have a new book out which is — at last — set largely in America I chose Charleston — surely one of your most beautiful cities — where I had a fascinating time, doing research.

See what you think!

Joanna Trollope